OUT OF
DARKNESS

OUT OF DARKNESS

ASHLEY HOPE PÉREZ

HOLIDAY HOUSE · NEW YORK

Text copyright © 2015 by Ashley Hope Pérez
HOLIDAY HOUSE is registered in the U.S. Patent and
Trademark Office.
Printed and bound in June 2019 at Maple Press, York, PA, USA.
www.holidayhouse.com
1 3 5 7 9 10 8 6 4 2

All editions are published by arrangement with Carolrhoda Lab, a
division of Lerner Publishing Group, Inc., 241 First Avenue North,
Minneapolis, MN 55401 U.S.A.

Library of Congress Cataloging-in-Publication Data
Pérez, Ashley Hope.
Out of darkness / by Ashley Hope Pérez.
    pages cm
Summary: Loosely based on a school explosion that took place in New
London, Texas, in 1937, this is the story of two teenagers: Naomi, who
is Mexican American, and Wash, who is black, and their dealings with
race, segregation, love, and the forces that destroy people.
    ISBN 978-1-4677-4202-3 (trade hard cover : alk. paper)
    ISBN 978-1-4677-6179-6 (EB pdf)
    [1. New London (Tex.)—History—20th century—Fiction. 2.
Explosions—Fiction. 3. Schools—Fiction. 4. Race relations—
Fiction. 5. African Americans—Fiction. 6. Mexican Americans—
Fiction.] I. Title.
PZ7.P4255Ou 2015
[Fic]—dc23 2014023837   2014023837

ISBN 978-0-8234-4503-5 (paperback)

IN MEMORY OF MY GRANDMOTHER,
VICTORIA RAY, WHO WAS ONE OF THE FIRST
TO TELL ME ABOUT THE NEW LONDON
EXPLOSION, AND TO MY PARENTS, WHO
MAKE EAST TEXAS HOME

Gather quickly
Out of darkness
All the songs you know
And throw them at the sun
Before they melt
Like snow.

—Langston Hughes, "Bouquet"

It was not darkness that fell
from the air. It was brightness.

—James Joyce, *A Portrait of the Artist as a Young Man*

PROLOGUE

NEW LONDON, TEXAS: MARCH 18, 1937

From far off, it looks like hundreds of beetles ringed around a single dome of light. Then the shiny black backs resolve into pickups and cars and ambulances. The bright globe divides into many lights. Work lamps. Spotlights. Strings of Christmas bulbs. Stadium floodlights borrowed from the football field nearby. Men and dust and tents. Thousands of spectators gather, necks craned. But it is not a circus, not a rodeo.

Within the great circle of light, men crawl over the crumpled form of a collapsed school. They cart away rubble and search for survivors. For their children. Mostly, though, they find bodies. Bits of bodies. They gather these pieces in peach baskets that they pass from hand to hand, not minding their torn gloves, torn skin. They say nothing of the stench.

A man squats and pulls away crumbled bricks. Under a blasted chunk of plaster he finds a small hand missing three fingers. He places it in a basket and heaves the debris into a wheelbarrow. Farther down in the tangle of wood and schoolbooks and concrete, he uncovers a bruised toe. Later he finds a child's leg, still sheathed in denim. Bent at the knee, it fits in the basket.

Red Cross volunteers with white armbands stand at the edge of the work site and hand out cigarettes and sandwiches. They pour scorched coffee into paper cups. As if nicotine, pimento cheese, and caffeine were any match for this horror.

Just after midnight it starts to rain, but no one runs for the tents. Some men take off their hats. Water runs down their faces, the perfect cover for tears. East Texas clay mixes with plaster dust from the school; red sludge sucks at the soles of work boots. But the floodlights and lanterns and lamps shine on, their collective light so bright that later people will say they saw it ten miles away, a beacon shooting up through the storm clouds. Across the school grounds and in the woods and in backyards and in every corner of the county, pumpjacks continue their slow rhythm, humping at the earth. Steady, steady, they draw up the oil that made this school rich.

Near dawn, every square foot of the collapsed building has been sifted and scoured for survivors and for remains. The rescue workers wander, stare, peel off their shredded gloves. They smoke and drink coffee, and then they climb into trucks and drive home. But the work continues as armies of undertakers and volunteers tend bodies in makeshift morgues. With no time for embalming, they brush the dead with formaldehyde from buckets. Eyes burn and swell shut from the fumes. Mothers and fathers walk among sheeted bodies, stop, move on. Faces are a mercy; most identifications come after scrutiny of birthmarks, scraps of clothing, scars.

There are not enough small caskets to go around. A call goes out for carpenters, and planks flow from the lumberyard into the pickups of anyone who can handle a hammer. Rough coffins come together, and a new round of digging begins; graves open up in rows.

For the next three days, alone or in numbers, families mourn their children and their neighbors' children. There are so many funerals that the pews in churches have no time to cool. Voices grow thin and hoarse from singing. Throats tighten. Consolation falters. Silence settles, and in silence they bear coffins. More than grief, more than anger, there is a need. Someone to blame. Someone to make pay.

THE
EXPLOSION

THURSDAY, MARCH 18, 1937, 3:16 P.M.

WASH Wash drove his shovel into the flower bed and turned the soil. Fast but not too fast; he had to be sure to earn out the hour. He liked working at the superintendent's place, liked being close to the school, liked how Mr. Crane always paid him fair. A quarter an hour was a decent take, and he was saving for third-class train tickets to the Mexican border, the price of a new life with his girl.

He pulled up a loose bit of clover and brushed his hands on his pants. He'd ask for more hours tomorrow. Now that the long, wet winter was over and it was warm enough for planting, Mr. Crane would want him to fill the flower beds with petunias and pansies and the little pink impatiens that his wife favored, color to tide her over until her azaleas and rose bushes bloomed. But today the weather was too fine to waste, the sky rolled out bright as a bolt of blue fabric, the warm breeze combing back the last of the chill. It was weather for being in love, and Wash was in love. He counted the minutes until Mr. Crane would be done with his meeting and could pay him and the minutes after that until his girl would be done with school and they could get to the tree and be together.

He was thinking out his first touch for her—a kiss, one hand to her long, soft hair, the other to her waist—when a thundering roar filled his ears. The ground bucked. The trees above him lashed back and forth.

4

Wash picked himself up and stumbled forward. When he rounded the corner of the house, he saw the walls and roof of the school crumple. He ran hard across the muddy schoolyard through drifting clouds of thick black and gray and white dust that choked and blinded him.

◊ ◊ ◊

He found the side door of the school and stumbled into what was left of the main hallway. His arms went white with dust. Grit caked his tongue. He could hear shouts from the schoolyard. The building groaned around him, but there was no other sound inside.

He'd been in the school to do odd jobs, but he hardly recognized it now as the dust began to settle. The walls along the hall were blasted out, and what was left of the ceiling sloped at a dangerous angle. One brass light fixture dangled, bulbs shattered. He inched forward, boots crunching on broken tile. A few yards ahead there was a dark cavern where the floor had been. Above the hole, the ceiling and the second floor were completely gone. A patch of sky showed and then disappeared behind a cloud of dust.

He was edging toward the blown-out wall of a classroom when he saw it. A black shoe with a worn strap and a red button. A shoe he knew.

BEFORE

SEPTEMBER 1936

BETO Beto jabbed an elbow at his twin. "That's no way to start our first day," he said.

Cari ignored him and turned back to their older sister Naomi. "And if we don't follow Daddy's rules? He never got to make any before." It was a challenge, not a question. Before Naomi could say anything, Cari ran farther down the path. She looked small amid the high straight pines. They stretched up fifty, maybe even a hundred feet before the first branches. Smaller trees with ordinary leaves grew between them.

Beside Beto, Naomi stayed quiet. Her fingers worked the ends of her long braid. Beto knew she would say something sooner or later. She was going on eighteen and in charge. And anyway, the new rules weren't so bad. Especially considering that they came with the new house and the new school, the new town and a new daddy. Daddy had been their daddy all along, only he hadn't been there so they hadn't known. Cari said they didn't need him; Beto thought they might.

He bit his lip and waited. The woods gave him the feeling of being inside and outside at the same time. Full of birds and animals but hushed, too, like a church the hour before Mass. Back in San Antonio, there were no woods. If you were outside, you knew it. The trees there were no match for the sun.

"Get over here, Cari," Naomi called finally. Cari stopped walking, but she didn't come back. "That's enough sass," Naomi said when they caught up to her. "Let's hear the rules."

Beto jumped at the chance to put things on track. "We keep to ourselves. We stay out of trouble. We go to church. We do good in school. And the main thing is—"

Naomi stopped him. "I want to hear it from her."

Cari scowled.

Naomi raised an eyebrow and said that seven wasn't too old for a spanking.

"Despot," Cari said. She jutted her lip.

Beto could see that Naomi didn't know what the word meant, but she just gave Cari a long hard look. With a sigh, Cari said, "The main thing is, we don't talk Spanish in the street or at school or anywhere. Which is stupid, if you ask me."

"All right, then," Naomi said. "Just remember. And what else?"

"We call Henry 'Daddy,'" Cari said. She frowned. "And what about you? Do you have to even though he's not your daddy?"

"Me, too, and you know it," Naomi said. She crossed her arms over her chest.

"There!" Beto stopped and pointed up at a leaf on a low branch. The morning sun turned it into a pane of green, brighter even than the freshest limes in Abuelito's store.

"Why that one?" Cari asked. She stretched and pulled it from the branch. That was how the good luck game worked. If one of them noticed something worth having, the other picked it up. That way, it belonged to them both. A thing shared from the start was a lucky thing.

After Cari looked over the leaf, she handed it to Beto. Shallow lobes and a jagged border and hard veins that rose up from the rubbery green flesh. He turned the thick red stem between his thumb and pointer finger, then sniffed: tea and dirt and cane syrup.

"Does not smell like tea," Cari said. She pulled the leaf out of his hand, scrunched it up, and pressed. "It smells like—"

"Careful!" He reached for the leaf.

"—an outhouse," she finished, and she let him take it back.

"I know what I smell," Beto said. He pressed the leaf against his cheek until the cool went out of it, and then he rolled it carefully. Maybe

Cari could afford to shred things before the day was even started, but he needed the luck.

He tried to think of every good thing Abuelito had said about the new school, but that only made him feel more frightened. Then the path curved to the right, and a group of buildings stood bright and yellow under red tiled roofs. Spanish style. All around the school grounds were the towers that his daddy called derricks. "That's where the money comes from, Robbie," Henry had said when they drove past some on the way from San Antonio.

Cari took off running toward the school. "Bye, Omi!" she called back. "Beto, let's go!"

Naomi reached over and squeezed his hand. "See you at the flagpole after school." She leaned close and gave him a kiss on the cheek.

Beto sucked in a breath and ran after Cari. He held on tight to the leaf.

NAOMI Belly down on a thick branch, Naomi settled into the sway and creak of the tree. She closed her eyes and let her ears fill with wings beating air and early acorns falling onto the soft pad of pine needles. She tried not to think of the kids outside the school in their neat circles. Girls and boys with their yards and yards of ease, each group knotted tight around their belonging. She listened to small things chewing through leaves and to a scurrying in the undergrowth, and it did not remind her of white smiles flashing bright in white faces, or of the girls with their trim new dresses and headbands and bobbed hair, or of the laughter rolling off the boys in letterman jackets, or of the school bell ringing, or of the circles dissolving into streams that channeled toward the entrances. She breathed in the air and the scent of sap, and it did not remind her of the quiet after the bell stopped ringing, her still standing there, watching the empty schoolyard, dumb as a rabbit in a mown field and just as obvious. She pressed her palms hard against the branch, felt all the little hurts of its years and felt how the bark had grown up tough and fierce over those hurts, and it did not remind her of her promise to Abuelito—to watch out for the twins, yes, but also to stick with school a little longer herself and so get the diploma that not one girl in their San Antonio barrio had, all of them falling away

11

to work or to watch their sisters' or brothers' kids or to marriages and babies of their own.

When she opened her eyes, the world flooded in. Light, so much light, falling down around her. Green and the shadow of green locked away in stem and bark. Green and green and green, leaves like coins pressed to the closed eyelid of the sky, and none of it reminded her of the empty space in the world where her mother should have been nor of Henry who had taken her out of it.

WASH Wash never got tired of the woods. There was the beauty of the place and also the pleasure of finding things. The woods had a way of grabbing bits out of pockets and scattering them for other people to come across. Also there were the folks who let things fall or plain dumped them when they no longer had a use for them. Mostly it was trash, but sometimes there was something worth salvaging, something he could make useful again or even sell. Things he didn't know what to do with he gathered in a small crate under his bed.

So he wasn't surprised to see a black shoe lying on its side just off the path. It looked to be a woman's shoe. He kicked through the dry pine needles and leaves, checking for its mate.

Something moved in the branches above him. For a moment, a slim brown foot dangled through the leaves. A second later he glimpsed a face. Dark eyebrows, enormous brown eyes, and a full, serious mouth. A kissable mouth.

Wash made a point of knowing every pretty black girl within walking distance from Egypt Town—knowing in whatever sense he could get away with, biblical if possible. But he'd never seen this girl. Of course, the oil field brought new people all the time. Folks looking for work and something better than where they came from. And they came from all over, what with most of the country in drought and debt and hungry to boot. Most of the oil field work was for whites only, but because of the oil there were fat cats to chauffeur, dance halls to clean, ditches to dig, pipes to lay. And there was still cotton to pick for a few nickels and a hunk of cornbread. Since most of Wash's friends were picking today, he might well be the first to meet this new girl, and he meant to make the most of it.

"Your shoe, miss?" he asked. He smiled up into the tree.

"It fell," she said from inside the green. Her voice was soft but clear.

"I'm not sure if I can reach it up. Should I chuck it?" Wash made a motion as if to throw the shoe.

"Better not."

"All right, then. I'd be happy to help you down so you can get it." Most girls lapped up the gentleman bit. When she didn't answer, Wash said, "Do you always spend your mornings in the trees?" Still no response. He took a few steps back to see if he could get a better look at her. "You still up there?" he called. The breeze rustled through the trees. A squirrel scurried past with a bulging mouthful. "Not much of a talker, huh?"

After a long moment, she said, "My grandfather says I could out-quiet a stump."

"And my ma says I could get a stone to tell its secrets," he said, still staring into the tree's dense canopy. "Listen," he tried again. "It's hard to converse like this. Why don't you come down from there? You're new to town, right? I can show you around. Be my pleasure."

"No, thank you."

He wasn't going to get her down. And anyway, he could hear the sound of children in the distance, which would be the little white kids at the New London school, hollering through their first recess of the year. The white school always started the day after Labor Day. Much as his father hated it, Wash and his classmates wouldn't be in class until after all the cotton was picked. That looked to be October, maybe later. So today his time belonged to the New London school superintendent. Mr. Crane wanted a fresh coat of paint on the trim of the house, which sat proudly on the edge of the school grounds.

Wash tossed the shoe between his hands. "If I can't get you down, I'll leave you to your thinking. I'm Wash, by the way, Wash Fuller. What'd you say your name was?"

"Naomi." He thought he could see those pretty red lips moving, but he couldn't be sure.

He poked around in the underbrush until he found a long, sturdy stick. He balanced the shoe on the end and raised it up to the branch. A hand reached down, and for a second Wash saw that sweet face again. Also smooth arms and a long dark braid hanging down over one shoulder.

"Thanks," she said.

"Nice to meet you and your shoe, Miss Naomi." He lifted his hat to the tree.

The only answer was the swishing of the leaves.

BETO   Beto stroked the top of the desk he shared with Cari. It was smooth as a church pew. Not a single scratch or initial. While the other kids finished their sums, a thought floated between the twins: what did they think of Miss Bell?

They had had prettier teachers and younger ones, too. Miss Bell looked like an untinted photograph of a teacher, all pale skin and black hair and black dress, lips gray and puffy as the worms that sometimes ended up in the big jugs of tequila that their uncles in San Antonio brought from Juárez. A birthmark on her throat peeked up over the high collar of her black dress.

Beto wondered if Miss Bell liked him or might come to like him. That was something Cari would never waste a thought on. Their last teacher in San Antonio had dipped her fingers into Cari's curls at least once a day. She was always saying things like, "You sweet thing, I could eat you right up!" But if one of the Gutierrez boys so much as sneezed, she'd pin her lips into a line, slap him with the ruler, and tell him to stay home if he was going to be nasty. Teachers weren't mean to Beto; they hardly noticed him. When they did, they seemed to be studying the gap between what he was and what he should have been: a real twin, a double of Cari.

The black sail of Miss Bell's dress appeared at Beto's side. He kept his eyes on the floor while she checked their work. She tapped a finger on each answer before setting their slates down on the desk. Then he watched her flat black shoes go up the long aisle to the front of the room. A moment later, she was back, and she set a fat red book with gold lettering in front of Beto and another one in front of Cari.

Beto's book was Volume 1 of the 1917 *World Book*. It had tidy columns with block letter headings and drawings on nearly every page. And there were hundreds and hundreds of pages. It would not run out in an hour like the ripped and soggy mystery magazines he sometimes fished out of the garbage bins behind newsstands near Abuelito's shop. It wouldn't bore to death, either, like the dull primers they were used to at school.

He started with AARDVARK. The name meant "earth pig," and the book said that a "sharp blow with a stout stick" was all it took to kill one, if that was what you wanted to do.

"We like her, don't we?" Beto whispered, his finger holding his place.

Cari nodded once, then went back to her own reading.

WASH When Wash pulled the front door closed behind him, he kept the knob turned so the lock wouldn't click too loudly. Inside, the cover was down on the piano, and the hymnbook was closed. Usually Peggy practiced until Ma needed her help for dinner. Already cooking smells were drifting from the kitchen. It was even later than he had thought. He should never have let Cal talk him into that detour to the creek, girls or no girls.

"Wash?" his mother called. "You come in here."

He strolled into the kitchen, hands in his pockets.

"What you using the front door for?" Peggy asked. She balanced her paring knife on a neat pile of turnip peels and put her hands on her hips. A lot of nerve for a fourteen-year-old with buckteeth and a weak chin.

"Free country," he said, tossing his hat onto a chair.

His mother shot Peggy a disapproving look. "*Why* are you using the front door. Wash, you use *complete* sentences, and pick up your hat."

"It is a free country," Wash mumbled. He reached for the hat and put it on a hook by the back door.

"Now you, Peggy," Rhoda prompted.

"Wash, why are you using the front door?" Peggy rolled her eyes at Wash, but she did it so that their mother couldn't see. Rhoda Fuller had been a schoolteacher until the state started making laws to free up jobs for unemployed men. One was that a woman couldn't be employed in the same school district as her husband. Wash's father was already principal of the New London Colored School, so that was the end of her teaching. Now she stayed home. Mostly, she looked for ways to make extra money and hassled him and Pegs.

Wash was sliding toward his bedroom when Rhoda said, "No, sir. Empty your pockets right here."

"Ma," Wash sighed.

"Don't 'Ma' me. You pay Booker first thing, as always."

◇ ◇ ◇

When Wash was ten and Peggy was seven, their father hung two empty frames on the wall in the living room, one to the left of his own Tuskegee diploma, one to the right of their mother's. "This is where your college diplomas will go. That's what you're working for. Don't you forget it," Jim told them.

◇ ◇ ◇

Rhoda inspected his earnings, counting out the four pennies and three nickels twice to make sure before she looked up, eyebrows raised. "Is that all?" She clucked her tongue as all but one coin clanked into the tin with the rest of that week's Booker money. "A whole day you've been out and you don't have anything more to show for it? It makes me wonder if you've been working or loafing around with Cal. That boy is lazier than a slug in summer."

"Come on, Mama. Mr. Crane is paying me tomorrow when I finish the painting. I did a little work for the Waters family out that way, but then Mrs. Bourne caught me and had me chop her firewood again. You know how she is."

"I hope she paid you."

Wash shook his head. "She tried to give me a bucket of buttermilk. First off, she knows we've got two good cows. And it was the middle of the day to boot. I couldn't be lugging that bucket all over with me. There was no time to bring it back here even if I wanted."

"So what'd you do?" asked Peggy.

"Reminded her of our cows. And when she still wouldn't take the milk back, I poured it out right there and gave her the bucket."

"Wash!" Peggy said, her mouth hanging open for a moment. "Did she light into you for sassing?"

"Oh, she fumed a little and threw her bucket down. That's all."

His mother laid a pot on the stovetop and turned to face him. "You be careful. That woman is so tight she can barely sit down, but that doesn't change a thing. What would your father say?"

"I'm not aiming to tell him," Wash said.

She gave him a hard look. "I'm as serious as sin, son."

Wash thought on it for a second, then puffed his cheeks out, lowered his eyebrows, and worked wrinkles into his forehead. He rested one hand on an imaginary belly and raised the other in the air, waggling a disapproving finger. Wash deepened his voice and gave it the gruffness and urgency that were his father's signature. "I know she's a cheat, son. But that's how it is. You can't show your anger. Never show your anger. Otherwise you give them power over you. You don't have to look for trouble for it to find you. Remember the Mississippi turkeys." Wash stifled a chuckle and pressed his face back into character. "Remember, son, when it comes to whites, 'yessir, yessum' is the only answer you know."

Peggy giggled, and a smile twitched at the corners of his mother's mouth. "All right," she said. "I'm persuaded. Those turkeys were no joke, though. Got a man lynched, understand? You steer clear of Mrs. Bourne from now on even if you have to go out of your way."

"Yes, ma'am," Wash answered, all earnest now.

"And I hope it puts you in the way of some better-paying work," his mother said. "Now go clean up. You can set the table."

He kissed his mother on the cheek before picking up the lonely nickel that was left for him to spend as he pleased.

NAOMI Naomi wiped her hands on her apron and lowered herself into a kitchen chair, wishing for Henry to be at work so she didn't have to sit through a meal with him. "Let's say grace," he said with his born-again smile. He stretched out a hand to the twins on either side of him; at least she was spared touching him. "Thank you, Lord Jesus, for this food. Bless it to our bodies. Amen."

It was over before she remembered to close her eyes. Cari hadn't closed her eyes, either, but she did it on purpose, staring up open and bold at the ceiling. Or maybe at God beyond it. If anyone could look Him straight in the eye, it was Cari. Beto kept his eyes closed tight for a full second after the prayer ended, and Naomi saw that he held on to Henry until Henry pulled his hand away and started serving his plate.

Henry forked up a slice of ham from the platter and dribbled a glob of lumpy pepper gravy onto a biscuit. Naomi watched and waited for a complaint. She'd never cooked this kind of food before, and it showed.

"So," he said, "how was the first day of school?"

Beto told him the class was small, not even forty kids. All the students had their own seats, and no one had to sit on cigar boxes like they did back in San Antonio. That put a satisfied smile on Henry's face. Cari rounded out the description with an impression of their teacher, who sounded formal but kind. She'd given them something called a world book, and then somehow Beto was talking about a pig that ate ants.

Naomi stopped listening and stared out the window over the sink, which pointed straight at the neighbor's kitchen window. A heavy-set woman was trying to wash a bottle with one hand while she balanced a red-faced baby on her hip.

When Naomi looked back, Henry was looking at her. "How about you?" he asked.

She shrugged. Who knew what would happen once she actually went to the school. The enrollment card with the name Naomi C. Smith—not her name at all—was still inside the pocket of her dress. Henry had taken away the twins' names, too, registering them as Robbie and Carrie, never mind that her mother had named them Roberto and Caridad in the days before she died. When Naomi asked him about the names on the cards, he'd waved her words away. Nobody would ask for a birth certificate here, he said; people were in and out of the school all the time because of the oil field. It would be simpler, he said, to have everybody enrolled under the same last name.

"Smith" was a slick, faceless thing, a coin worn smooth. Maybe that was why he did not understand that carrying a name was a way of caring for those who'd given it. Naomi Consuelo Corona Vargas. That was her name. She closed her mouth hard around it. Let him handle the silence. Let him decide what to do with it. She stared out the window and watched the dusk turn the white of the neighbor's house pale purple, then gray.

"Y'all got the stuff unpacked right quick," Henry said.

Naomi nodded. There hadn't been much to unpack. But she could still feel the handle of her mother's guitar case in her hand as she slid it under her bed, way at the back toward the wall. Not that she could hide it from Henry; he'd seen her put it in the back of the truck in San Antonio and then had handed it down to her again in East Texas. She guessed he recognized it, but she couldn't say for sure.

Maybe he'd been too busy gloating over the twins' delight at the neat little oil camp house with its running hot water, electric lights, and fancy appliances. They'd run from room to room, flipping light switches, turning on the taps, bouncing on the beds. It might have been brighter and more modern than the cramped space they'd shared with their grandparents in one of the San Antonio corrals, but for her, the house was too full of Henry. Every fork and spoon and glass in the place had touched his lips. His shaving things sat on the shelf in the bathroom alongside the same aftershave she remembered from years earlier. She saw an oily handprint on the kitchen wall and a wadded handkerchief on the couch in the living room.

"What's for dessert?" Henry said, cutting into her thoughts. "You kids want some dessert?"

Naomi frowned and went to the pantry. She found a can of fruit cocktail and spooned it into three dishes. She divided the sweet syrup then used her fingernail to split the cherry into two bits for the twins to share. They began eating as soon as she set the bowls down in front of them, but Henry cocked an eyebrow. A moment later, he slid his bowl across the table to her. She thought about pushing it back, but instead she got up to do the dishes. She was only here to watch out for Cari and Beto; she wasn't about to take anything from him if she could avoid it.

She ran the water hot, filling the sink and leaning into the steam. The twins were slurping the last of the syrup from their bowls when Henry's spoon began to clink against his dish.

HENRY Henry had brought the twins to East Texas because his pastor told him to. Told him in words about lost sheep and duty. Told him with a hard stare from the pulpit. Told him down by the river. Told him gentle and told him mean. Told him till his ear was full again with Jesus and promises and a calling, but still Henry held back. He tried to explain about the accidents, about his bad luck, but each time Pastor Tom cut him off, called it evil superstition.

"Jesus is calling on you to act," he shouted to Henry over the drilling equipment one day after his shift ended. "Bring 'em home." Tom steered him down one of the rutted work roads, his hand a sweating brick on Henry's shoulder. He talked and preached till Henry wore down and said, "I'll see about it."

Henry hadn't really meant it, but when the words were out, feeling rose in his gut. He felt, briefly, like a boy straining over the handlebars of a borrowed bicycle, cresting a high rise, flinging himself into the downhill.

The preacher yipped and jabbed at the sky with his fraying Bible. "You can triumph in Jesus' name!"

"In his name!" Henry answered, hands trembling. A second swell of excitement grew in his belly. Sweat slid down from his armpits and back, soaking the waistband of his pants.

"It won't be easy now," the pastor said. His eyes shone bright in the twilight, full of the challenge he was calling Henry to, full of the promise that Henry would meet it.

"No, I reckon not," Henry said. Already, though, he was picturing himself walking his bright, clean children up to Pastor Tom during an altar call, sunlight coming through the windows, the choir singing, the whole church looking on.

After Pastor Tom prayed over him, Henry drove straight to the Humble Oil work yard and went to the boss's trailer. "I need a place for my family," he told Graham Salter, the man whose good luck Henry had followed through the oil fields since he was sixteen.

Salter looked up at him with weepy gray eyes. He stubbed out his cigarette on a bit of scrap metal.

"Since when have you got a goddamn family?" Salter said. Then he held out an application for the Humble Oil Company housing.

◊ ◊ ◊

For the first time in years, Henry wrote letters to the kids' grandparents in San Antonio. He described the church and the landscape. His work. He watched for bits of news that might sway Estella's parents. He saw an article that talked about special classes in the new school that had just been built in New London with tax money from the oil companies. The kids got band instruments, sports uniforms, and new books. There was even a football stadium with electric lights. The reporter said that New London had built the most expensive rural school in the world. Henry clipped the article, folded it into thirds, and mailed it.

Henry's days were long with work and waiting and wondering if he had done enough. A house came open in the Humble camp, and he had two weeks to lease it or not. He wrote again and sent along a drawing that a little girl at church had made of her house in the Humble housing camp, which was the same as the one Henry could get, which was the same as all the others.

He took his hat off in church and rested it on his knee. He did not know if he was hoping for the kids to come or hoping for them to stay away.

A letter arrived in July. The grandfather wrote that the twins could come, but only if Henry took in the older girl as well. She was nearly grown and would help look after them.

For years Henry had worked not to think of her. When he did, he remembered a skinny brown girl with sad eyes, sharp teeth, and a mouth full of Spanish. He remembered her dark face in the rearview mirror just after he'd married Estella and moved them to Houston, a face as long as the braid down her back. Serious, suspicious, watchful. In the beginning, she'd been a bit of baggage from Estella's first marriage, a shadow at the edges of his happiness. Later, she'd been a brief, disastrous solution. When it was all done and Estella was dead, he wished he could bury her with her mother and so be free of the shame of it.

Now she would be a reminder of all the mistakes he had made. No, not him; the fallen man from before. The man who had died so that the Henry he was now could be born. The Henry that was putting a family back together. The Henry bound to make his Savior and Redeemer proud.

The week before he went to get his children, Henry mopped the floors of the house with vinegar and water and laid out the sheets and blankets he'd bought. On the drive down to San Antonio, he ate sunflower seeds until his belly ached, spitting their woody husks into an old paper cup. He tried to pray but stalled out a few words in each time.

He held a handkerchief over his nose as he drove down a dusty, crowded San Antonio street. He thought he was going the right direction, but there were no house numbers. The place was packed with lopsided row houses patched with tin sheets and scrap wood and cardboard. Boxes of garbage and piles of junk were heaped around wrecked porches. Dark faces looked out at him from dirty windows.

A skinny spotted dog ran out in front of the truck. He braked and veered, barely missing it. When he looked up, he saw her, plain as day.

Estella.

He recognized her first by her braid, then by the easy music of her walk. She was headed away from him on the plank sidewalk, a basket in one hand. Then she turned around, and he saw that it wasn't Estella. The girl was far too young and shades darker. And of course there was the obvious: it couldn't be Estella because Estella had been dead for nearly eight years.

It was the girl. She recognized him, he knew. Her dark eyes widened; her lips parted. A shadow crossed her face, and she took a step toward the truck.

NAOMI Naomi looked up from the shirt she was patching to see the twins hovering in the doorway from the hall.

"Now what?" she asked. It was raining out, and the twins had been moping around all afternoon.

Cari blew air into her bangs. Beto wandered to the stove and lifted the lid from a casserole dish. "What is this?" he asked.

"Chicken and rice," Naomi said. "Daddy brought home some nice bright green beans, too."

"But what's for dessert?" Cari asked.

Naomi frowned. "Some sweet oranges a neighbor sent over yesterday," she said. "A treat."

"Some treat," Cari grumbled.

"How about cake? Cake is nice," Beto said.

Naomi stabbed her needle deep into the pincushion and stared at the twins. A week ago they would have been grateful there was *supper*.

Their grandparents' store had the best fruit on the West Side of San Antonio. Bright limes and lemons and speckled oranges for juicing. Grapefruits you could smell across the room. Mangoes so firm and sweet they made pregnant women weep. Strawberries like fleshy hearts, mounded in little baskets. Peaches and nectarines dusted with a careful hand. But all this was reserved for customers.

"What we eat, we can't sell," Abuelita always said, and she only allowed Abuelito to bring home unsellable items. Split watermelons, ripped sacks of cornmeal, cucumbers gone soft or moldy in places.

"Come sit at the table," Naomi said to the twins. "We're going to write to everybody back home."

"Do we write in English or Spanish?" Cari asked.

Naomi shrugged. "There's no rule against writing in Spanish. It's up to you." Spanish was a talking and singing language as far as she was concerned, but when Abuelito had finished teaching the twins to write in English, they'd begged him to show them what was different in Spanish. They'd caught on right away, like they did with everything, and he showed off the flawless signs that the twins lettered in Spanish for the store.

Beto decided to write to Abuelito in English, and Cari wrote to Abuelita in Spanish. Naomi started a letter to her cousin Josefina. "Dear Fina," she began. She wrote the usual things, printing out each word carefully. When she finished, she looked over the letter and signed it. Hers was only a half dozen sentences. She glanced at the twins, who were still writing, their pencils stitching words together like bits of lace. The Mexican schools didn't teach cursive, but one of the twins' teachers had taken an interest and shown them.

Naomi left her letter on the table, got up, and went to light the stove. Henry had warned her about the raw gas. Usually it was fine, he said, but it could flare up fast since the pressure wasn't steady. She bent down with her match, lit the gas, and stepped quickly back. When she was sure of the blue line of flame, she finished her sewing and started in on the last preparations for dinner. She looked for a heavy pan to fry the green beans, but she couldn't find one. She needed to hurry; after dinner, there was still cleaning to do. First, the bathroom. She suspected that it hadn't been cleaned once since Henry moved in, and maybe not before that. Small dark hairs flecked the sink basin, and dust was gathering in the grout lines between the tiles. She had to figure out what to do about the bathtub drain, too. Greenish water lines ringed the tub from where the water sat for hours before finally going down.

She was sliding the casserole dish into the oven when the laughing started. Every time she turned around, the twins lowered their heads and acted like they were writing.

"What's funny?" she asked, walking over to the table.

"Nothing," snorted Cari. She tucked her chin into her neck and pulled the corners of her mouth down, but still the smile twitched back up. She held Naomi's letter in her hand. It trembled with her suppressed laughter. "I'm . . . *hopping* you are fine!" she said, exploding into giggles.

Beto pressed his hand over his mouth and gasped with laughter.

Naomi's heart accelerated. She felt her face go hot, but her tongue was heavy in her mouth. She put her back to them and waited. When they stopped laughing, she turned and picked up her letter from the table. "Put your letters on the counter. We'll ask Daddy to mail them tomorrow." She did not look at them.

Then she got out the green beans and began trimming them. Each *thunk* of the knife rang out loud in the silence of the kitchen.

THE GANG We knew she was a Mexican the second we saw her standing there behind Tommie in the doorway of our senior homeroom. It rolled off her in waves. Like when someone's been slopping pigs or digging around sewer lines. She wasn't the first in the school; oil field trash blew into town all year long, and a few greasers had come and gone from the lower grades, but we'd never had one in our class before.

We craned our necks. Some of us caught a glimpse of her, but most of us had trouble seeing around Tommie. Tommie Kinnebrew was also new, and we'd learned her name against our will by the sheer force of her gab on the first day of school. Her talk followed us in the halls and filled our ears like our little brother's tom-tom, which is to say, unbearable. A couple of the guys—Chigger Watson with his pimpled hands and also Josiah Pleaton—were of the private opinion that even if Tommie talked too much and had some bacon on her, she did have tits. But most of us just wished she would move out of the way, especially now since we wanted to get a better look at the Mexican girl who had missed the first two days of school.

Those of us in the back who could see reported to those in the front. Clothes and dirt and scandal for the girls. For the boys, pussy or the idea of pussy or the idea of the idea of pussy.

"This here is Naomi Smith," said Tommie, taking a step into the room and talking loud over the whispers. She waved the Mexican girl's enrollment slip like a winning bingo card and trotted to the front of the room. Mrs. Simmons took the card and motioned the girl to come to her desk. But still she stayed back. We all turned to stare. It was plain that she wanted to be invisible, but no amount of wishing was going to stop us from noticing her, not even in that faded dress and ratty cardigan. Even the girls had to admit that, Mexican or not, old clothes or not, she was prettier than any girl in school. Elliott Grovener whistled. Dot Miller hissed back, "Go on, catch yourself a disease."

Some of us could be jealous, and the greenest of all was Miranda Gibbler. None of us liked Miranda; all of us pretended to. She was ugly and had spite enough to poison the whole town. But what mattered was her daddy's money. "A Mexican is a Mexican is a Mexican," she said, plenty loud for the rest of us to hear. The girls among us followed Miranda's lead and began to tally flaws. Clothes from five years ago, a braid long out of style. Patch on the back hem of her dress. And also: how come her name is Smith when Smith isn't Mexican? Look at her, making eyes at Fred Carter, not wasting any time.

The boys among us had no trouble getting past the plain clothes and laying down plans. Take her out back, we boys figured, then: hand on the titties; put it in her coin box; put it in her cornhole; grab a hold of that braid; rub that calico. The nicer boys among us thought, buy her ice cream first; dance with her once or twice?

"Looking for the cigar factory?" Miranda said when the Mexican girl walked past on her way to the one empty seat at the front of the room. Miranda raised her eyebrows at Vanessa and Gladys and Betty Lee. They laughed. Some of us joined in.

Most of us couldn't see the Mexican girl's face from where we sat. Still we wondered, could Mexicans blush?

BETO All around Beto, sweating pink faces nodded to the rhythm of murmured and hollered amens. The preacher paced and shouted at the front of the tent, coming close to the revival crowd then veering back behind the plywood podium.

"The wages of sin is death!" he shouted with his fist raised high. Sweat rolled down his face. His dark beard and sharp cheekbones made him look like the cards with Jesus and the martyred saints that Abuelita pinned to the wall around her altar.

Beto was afraid to blink, desperate for the answer, desperate to know how to be safe. How to be saved. Terror swelled inside him, and he clutched the fan someone had given him. Beside him, Naomi held her shoulders back, swaying a little. Her fan lay abandoned in her lap. Henry's eyes were fixed on the preacher. Cari was tracking a fly, clearly bored. How did she not see that they were in danger?

"The wages of sin is death, are they not, my brothers?" This time the preacher whispered the words, closing his eyes as if in pain.

"Amen!" voices in the crowd called together.

"But the gift of the Lord—is eternal life! Mothers and fathers, brothers and sisters, young and old: we are all sinners, every one!" The words thundered out at them.

"Yes we are!" a woman shouted.

"We're born drinkers and gamblers, profaners and idolaters, liars and thieves, all hateful in the sight of the Lord, every one of us, down to the smallest." He pointed a trembling finger at a fat blonde baby sucking on her fist. "We deserve death!" The words rang out over the sweating congregation, and Beto's pulse pounded in his ears. "But if we confess our sins, we can be saved! By the blood of the lamb, we can be saved! By his death on the cross, we can be saved! Washed in his blood, we become clean!"

Cries of "Amen!" filled the tent. The preacher swabbed his red face with a handkerchief. A bread loaf of a woman wearing a small hat began to hum. Her rich alto filled the tent.

"Come forth and be cleansed," the preacher said, his voice gentle now. "Come and be saved. Now is the time! You think it's hot tonight? The fires of hell are hot, but God's grace is a soothing balm! Come now, brothers and sisters. Come and pray with me."

A few people moved slowly toward the front. More followed until almost a dozen were kneeling with the small man in his damp suit. He went to them one by one, whispering in their ears, waiting for their responses, praying over them. Then he shouted, "Who else has heard the call? Is there anyone else?"

"Me," Beto whispered, "me." He caught Cari's eye, wanting this to be the thing that they shared, but she shook her head. The preacher reached a hand out toward him, waving him forward. Beto slipped past the stout legs of the mothers on their bench and climbed over their squirming babies to get to the aisle. And then he was inside the hot circle of prayer at the front, and the preacher's hands were pressing a prayer down onto his shoulders, telling him he was a sinner, and Jesus was his Savior, and he was washed in blood, and there was the promise of forgiveness, and most of all he would be saved, saved, saved. A throng of bodies carried him out of the tent and toward the river. He was glad because the river was the outward sign and he needed the outward sign to have the Spirit, and he needed the Spirit to know he was safe.

◇ ◇ ◇

Eyes shut tight, tipped back into darkness, icy currents against his face. Then Beto was lifted up out of the water. The late-afternoon sun streamed warm and gold around him like a second baptism. Water came down his face and dripped from his chin, and the shivers were happiness and safety. He could not wait to see his daddy.

As they waded back to the shore, the preacher asked Beto where his sister was. When Beto pointed her out, the pastor began to wave and call to her. "Join your brother in the army of the Lord! Pray the redemption prayer and be freed from sin!"

Cari crossed her arms, but at least she was singing along with everyone else. Beto tried to figure how to explain to Cari and Naomi that they must go into the water, that it had to be now because later might be too late.

A lady handed him a towel, and then Naomi was there, looking sad as usual. His daddy was smiling, and Beto just knew that he was going to hug him, but then the preacher came up and started shaking Henry's hand.

"At last!" the preacher said. He reached out a hand to Naomi next. "I'm Pastor Tom. We've all been praying and waiting and hoping to meet y'all. Welcome to New London."

"You already met Robbie. Here's his sister, Carrie." The names stretched long in Henry's mouth.

"Delighted to make your acquaintance," Cari said in the sweet, singsong voice that meant she didn't like someone.

"The oldest here is Naomi," Henry said.

"Nice to meet you, sir," Naomi said.

Pastor Tom clapped a hand onto Henry's back. "Didn't I tell you, brother? You steered straight, and your Savior Jesus Christ rewarded your efforts. A family brought together, and another soldier for the Lord! Now let's get over there and have some of Mrs. Clarkson's fried chicken and pie."

Beto, suddenly starving, followed the preacher toward the picnic tables under a stand of oaks, but all along the way they had to stop and meet church ladies. "My son, Robbie," Beto heard his daddy say over and over, and he tried to think of himself that way. It was hard but not too hard. Cari stood stiff beside him through the introductions, and Beto wanted to tell her the thing that would make her happy, but he didn't know how. He scanned the ground and the trees and tried to see what might make her understand.

He did not like the women who reached out and touched him with their gloved hands or the ones that leaned down to kiss him, bumping his head with their wide hats.

Then a woman with nice gray eyes and a heart-shaped face and a baby on her hip came and rescued them from the other ladies. A little boy in cowboy boots followed her. His mouth was stained purple.

"Y'all gonna try my fried chicken and blueberry pie?" the lady asked. "J.R., you say good evening." The boy stuck out a sticky hand for them to shake, and the baby grinned and drooled some more.

"This is Mrs. Muffy Clarkson," his daddy said. "She and her husband Bud, they've been real good to me."

Muff was their neighbor, and while they ate the fried chicken and mounds of potato salad and fluffy white biscuits, she talked about people that she knew, people his daddy knew, too. People that he and Cari would know because now this was their home. She told them how Pastor Tom was the best thing that ever happened to this oil field. She talked them right to the bottom of their plates and through a round of seconds, but when a stink came up from the baby's diaper, Muff sighed and held him away from her dress.

"That's our cue," she said. "Sure was nice meeting you all. Listen, Naomi, you mind getting my blueberry pie tin when the picnic's all over? It's on a red dishcloth. Has a Clabber Girl stamp on the inside."

Naomi managed a nod, and then Muff hurried toward the cars with J.R. clomping after her. After that, Beto watched Henry walk off to talk to some men smoking at the edge of the parked cars, mostly out of sight of the ladies. It was just Beto and Naomi and Cari left at the table then. He was still looking for the chance to tell them what he needed to say, but he also didn't know what that was, and so he settled for a big piece of the blueberry pie and also some cake with pineapple on top.

After they'd cleared off all the dishes, Naomi said they could go play. Beto tried and tried to get her to come climb trees with them. Naomi could climb a tree better than anyone. But she said no, and so he trailed Cari toward a group of kids. The bright taste of blueberry and pineapple lasted for a moment, and then all that was left was the mystery of being saved.

NAOMI Naomi watched the twins play until some of the church ladies started drifting in her direction. She did not want to meet another Miss Glenda Fae Hawkins or Miss Susannah Sally Peters, had no desire to face their smiles and clucking and gloved hands. Some inquired about "eye-talians" in her mother's family. Others did not, but their faces were pinched with the strain of not asking, not saying.

She considered waiting in Henry's truck, away from the dressed-up chickens that would peck and peck at her until they found something tasty. But the men were smoking over there, so the woods seemed like a better escape. She hurried in that direction.

It was cooler under the trees. High in the branches, tree frogs sang shrill *serenatas*. The sharp, clean scent of pine was in the air. Naomi stepped off of the path, leaned against the smooth trunk of an ash tree, and slid down to sit at its base. She put her mind on the small things in the brush. If she focused on all the little lives creeping and fluttering and scurrying around her, she wouldn't have to feel what she was feeling.

Which was mostly betrayal. She was losing Beto already. He was hungry for Henry's attention. She wondered if Abuelito and Abuelita knew this would happen—and if they would care. She didn't get to have an opinion; they had sent her here without once asking what she thought.

Even when Abuelito had sensed that something was wrong, it hadn't mattered. "Don't you see it's for the best?" he had said that last night in San Antonio. He'd reached out a trembling, spotted hand and guided her over to the bed she shared with Beto and Cari. He pulled his chair close and laid his dry palm gently against her cheek. "This is for you, too, *mi corazon*. I want you to go to the big school. They must let you, you see? None of this . . . " He pulled his hand back and waved it through the air to sum up all the ways the San Antonio schools kept Mexican students apart from whites. The too-small primary schools and the split grades that meant Mexican kids were always and forever behind. The "Mexican wing" of Crockett High School, which was really five dank and crowded basement rooms that no white student ever entered. Abuelito's excitement swept him along. "You will give the twins this opportunity, *¿verdad?* And you will go to the school?"

She had closed her eyes and nodded. It wasn't really a question anyway.

Now she had seen the school. She didn't care about the science lab or the math classes or the typewriters. She didn't want any of it. She only wanted to be away from the eyes on her, the snickers, the too-loud whispers, the boys bumping against her in the halls, halls that were never crowded enough for it to be an accident.

The only thing worse than going there was staying home, where Henry might be. And so she had to go to school. For now. She practiced wiping Henry out of all the places that she had to see him. She filled his seat at the kitchen table with blankness, cleared him from the revival bench, vanished him from behind the wheel of the truck. She was about to subtract Henry from the bathroom mirror where he had stood shaving that morning when she saw him walking toward her.

"There you are," he said. He came over to where she sat and offered a hand to help her up.

She ignored it, rearranged her legs quickly, and stood up on her own. "I was just going to see the river," she said, walking fast away from him and toward the sound of the river.

His voice followed her. "I wanted to make sure you were having a good time."

"Fine, just fine." She threaded her fingers through the tail of her long braid.

To touch her braid was to remember her mother. The code was simple: when her mother had a braid, she belonged to Naomi. When Estella fixed her hair in swirls and curls and combs, she belonged to her dancing and to the men she danced with (and, later, to Henry) and she did not come home for hours and hours and the bed Naomi shared with her was wide and lonely. On this particular evening, Naomi was six; her father was dead; she and Estella still lived in the back bedroom of the nice house Abuelito and Abuelita owned before the stock market crash.

"Like this?" Estella asked, spinning to show the curls pinned in swirls over the nape of her neck. Her mother's yellow dress rode up around her slim brown legs as she moved.

Naomi shrugged and traced the pattern of the lace coverlet on the bed. Snowflake, snowflake, flower. Snowflake, snowflake, flower. She was the snowflake, pointy and awkward. Her mother was the flower.

"Well?" Estella reached out a slender finger and lifted Naomi's chin.

"I like it best in *una trenza*," Naomi mumbled.

"A braid! But why is that?" Estella studied her. "Don't you like Mami to be elegant?"

Naomi shook her head. Tears began to fall onto the lace.

"Do you want me to stay in tonight?" Estella unpinned her hair and let it fall over Naomi's face. "Here, you braid it for me."

Later, they draped the ends of their braids over their mouths like mustaches and pretended to be mariachi singers.

That was one of the good memories. The bad ones were edged with silence and blood. Estella's eyes gone glassy, her face gray. And between the good and the bad there were others, moments colored not so much by fear or danger but by tiny heartbreaks, thimblefuls of betrayal. Estella was a woman, not a saint. But at least Naomi had her braid.

◇ ◇ ◇

When she was small, Naomi would snuggle into bed beside her mother, taking in the smell of her skin, tangy like grapefruit. She held on to her mother's braid, rubbing the glossy tail between her fingers until she fell asleep. Even after her mother married Henry, sometimes Naomi slept next to her when he was away working in an oil field.

They were alone in Henry's house when the first disaster happened. Naomi had awoken to the sound of Estella moaning. When she turned over, she saw that her mother's nightgown was plastered to her thighs, dark with blood.

"Mamá—" Naomi shook her. In the moonlight she could see pain move across her mother's face, and then she saw her reach under the dark wet hem of her nightgown.

"*Mírame, mi amor*," her mother said. "Just keep looking at me."

Naomi tried to obey. But her mother's lips seemed almost white, and her eyes were wide and full of tears. Naomi looked down and saw what her mother had found between her legs. It was the size of a plum, but it had legs and arms that looked black against the white of her mother's hand.

That was the first time Henry made her mother pregnant. That was the first baby she lost.

Abuelita and Tia Cuca came to Houston for a week. They told Estella that this was something that almost every woman went through once. They fed her special soups and brushed her hair, and Estella began to look like herself again, only smaller.

And then they left and Henry came back, and Mami's smile closed down again. At night, Naomi heard their noises through the bedroom wall and her mother crying afterwards. Naomi lay alone in her bed. She held her doll in one hand and her own thin braid in the other.

◊ ◊ ◊

Naomi walked along the riverbank with Henry following behind her. At the edge of the woods, he pointed down the slope to the clearing. The picnic was winding down, and the sun was setting. Cari and Beto were small dark figures moving among other small dark figures in some kind of play.

"Kids sure are taking to the place," he said.

She shrugged. If he actually knew Cari, he'd know that she could turn anything into a game and make herself at home with anyone. That was just her way.

She turned to the breeze coming off the water. There was a whiff of honeysuckle and rot and skunk musk. The sun shifted a little lower in the sky, and all at once the brown river was tricked out with bits of glittering sun. A water moccasin swam past, a dark head trailing a V-shaped ripple. The boys hustling bait in the shallows scooted back, calling out, "Cottonmouth!"

"Prettiest place in the world," Henry said. He edged closer. "Pastor baptized me there, just like Robbie today."

"Beto," Naomi said, turning to look at him.

Henry slid a finger up under his collar and scratched. "Right there in those sweet waters."

She stared at a spot in the middle of the river and imagined the moment. Henry's eager face as he was lowered back into the murky waters. If only the preacher had had the sense to hold Henry down just a little longer . . . there might have been a small struggle, but in the end, they would have all been better off.

Henry took another step toward the river. Sweat beaded across his forehead. He searched his pockets for a handkerchief, came up with nothing. He prodded the damp ground with the toe of his good shoe. Later, he'd be tracking that mud into the house for sure.

"I thought I ought to . . . to explain a bit . . . ," he mumbled. Naomi heard only part of what he said. There was a vague mention of "that time before" and of saving grace and a promise that he had changed. When he looked up, his eyes shone.

She didn't say anything.

Henry wiped his hands down the front of his pants and smiled. "I guess that's that. Maybe you all can meet a few more folks?" He delivered the final word too brightly. She knew he did not really want another round of introducing the brown stepdaughter.

"I'll be along," she said, fixing her eyes again on the water. The light was gone from the surface now; the river was just a dark onrushing.

Henry's footsteps grew faint, and for a moment Naomi remembered also the dark blank of her mother's grave, the casket lowered in, Henry next to her, his grip tight on her arm, his mouth so close she could feel his breath on her ear. And his words, slipping in and wrapping around her heart before she could stop them: "You could have saved her." The twins, bawling in Tia Cuca's arms, were two weeks old. He did not hold them once.

Naomi squatted and trailed a hand in the shallows. Pastor Tom could dunk Henry in saving grace till he was sleek as a muskrat, but he couldn't shake those mistakes off easy as drops of water. If he'd been born again once, what was to say that he couldn't be born again a second time, back into his old ways?

◇ ◇ ◇

When it was time to go, Naomi went over to the long table that had been heaped with food earlier. Her eyes slid past empty plates, crumbled bits of cornbread, a smear of potatoes in a casserole dish. She spotted an empty pie plate on a red dish towel. A stray blueberry was stuck to the side. Naomi reached out a finger and swept it into her mouth. Then she picked up the tin and cloth and began looking for the dish she'd brought.

A moment later she found the chipped blue plate and lifted the napkin she'd draped over the top to keep flies off of the tortillas. They had not been touched. Not one.

She grabbed the plate and turned toward the trucks and cars still parked at the edge of the clearing.

There was a burst of laughter, and two girls tumbled from behind the nearest tree. They had matching freckles and strawberry blonde hair, and they wore dresses cut from the same pattern. The smaller of the two girls looked a few years younger than the twins; the other might have been a year older.

Naomi sidestepped the little one, but she darted right back into her path.

"Excuse me," Naomi said. Now the older one was blocking her way, too.

"Hold on," the older girl said. She draped her arms around her sister's shoulders, rested her chin on the little girl's head. "We had the table staked out, see? We was watching to see, wondering who brought them goofy flat pancakes."

"Okay," Naomi said.

"Don't you know how to make pancakes? And why'd you bring 'em to a picnic? Ain't picnic food no how."

They were children. There was no reason to be embarrassed, but she was. It was Henry's fault. If he'd bothered to tell her about the picnic, she could have made something else. There wasn't even an hour left when he mentioned a dinner after the revival, not even time enough to get the oven hot for biscuits.

"Told ya," said the older girl to the little one.

"What?" Curiosity unglued Naomi's tongue.

"Only somebody new would be dumb enough to bring pancakes for a supper."

Naomi took in a sharp breath. Her palms itched, and she had a brief impulse to slap the older one.

"They're not pancakes. They're tortillas," she said, pushing down her embarrassment. She shoved past them and ran toward the cars. Their voices trailed after her.

"Ain't she stuck-up, though?" said the bigger girl.

"I think she's pretty." That was the little one.

"You would, snot box."

"Ain't a snot box!"

"You was picking it just now."

"Wasn't, neither!"

Naomi slid into the truck beside Cari and shut the door. Beto stood between the dash and the gearshift holding a small black Bible. "I got it for being baptized," he said. His face was bright in the gloom.

"We already got baptized when we were babies," Cari said.

Henry ignored Cari and smiled at Naomi. "The welcome committee found you?"

"Something like that," Naomi said. She shoved the dishes down to the floorboard.

WASH Wash couldn't see the girl from where he was unloading potatoes into the cellar of Turner's General Store, but through the trapdoor opening he recognized her shoes. They were the same ones, he was sure, but he couldn't fathom what she'd be doing coming through the front door of a white grocery store.

Voices drifted down to him. Naomi said something he couldn't hear, but Mr. Turner's words rang out clear. "Where you think you are, girl?"

"Hold on, Amos." That was Mrs. Turner. "Where you from, honey? Who's your folks?"

Before Naomi answered, Mr. Turner started in again. "So there's brown ones and black ones, that don't matter. What matters is that they don't sully up my store."

Whatever came next was drowned out by the electric grinder. When the whirring stopped, Wash heard Mr. Turner again.

". . . what I said? You're greasin' up my floor just standing there."

There was a long silence, then Naomi, barely loud enough for him to hear: "I need to buy things, sir."

"Listen, now." It was Mrs. Turner. "The hours for your kind are posted at the back door."

"I'll tell you plain, girl," Mr. Turner barked. "Get out."

Wash emptied the last of the potatoes into the bin. He folded the sacks and hurried up the ladder. When he came out the back door of the store, Naomi had already reached the edge of the woods. She was moving fast, almost running, and her long braid swept back and forth across the pale blue of her dress.

"Naomi?" he called. "Wait!" He opened his canvas pack and dropped in the dented cans Mrs. Turner had given him as payment, then called her name again.

She didn't slow, but he kept after her. When he caught up, he reached a hand out and put it on her shoulder. She whirled around.

"Oh," he said. He realized his mistake as soon as he saw her up close. "Pardon, I . . ."

"What?" Her voice was sharp even with the tears in it. "Never seen a girl cry?"

"No—I mean, yes, sure. But you're—"

"A filthy Mexican? Yes, I was just told." She worried the tail of her thick braid.

"No, it's not that. . . . I didn't mean to be . . . I thought . . . well, I thought you were . . ." He gestured at his own skin. "You know, from Egypt Town."

"I don't even know what that is." She eyed him.

"It's where we stay. Colored folk, I mean."

"We just moved into the Humble Oil camp." She wiped her fingers under her eyes and glared at him. Splotches of red cropped up across her cheeks.

It was plain now that she wasn't black. Sure, her skin had the same caramel tone as the more yellow girls at his school, but her eyes were wider apart and deeper set. Her full mouth looked Spanish to him, although he couldn't say why. There was a small gap between her two front teeth.

"Dang it," she said. "Here come the twins."

"The twins?" Wash followed her gaze and saw two pale kids, about seven or eight, running up the path. Only when he looked from Naomi to the two little ones did he notice the similar shape of the eyes, a certain tilt of the upper lip.

"I win!" the boy shouted, plowing into her and hugging her around the waist.

The girl slowed to a walk as if she'd never intended to race to begin with. "What kind of candy did you buy?"

"I didn't buy anything." Naomi said. "Did you finish sweeping the porch?"

The boy stepped closer, his eyes riveted on Wash's pack and fishing rod. He looked at the girl, and she nodded.

"Is that for fishing?" she asked.

"Yep." Wash untied it so they could get a better look. "You like to fish?"

"I do. I think I do," the boy said.

"We've never done it," the girl said.

"Never? How's that?"

The boy said there wasn't much water in San Antonio, but his daddy was going to take them just as soon as he could. The girl reached forward and grabbed the rod. "Can we come with you? What's your name? Where's the river?"

He laughed. "I don't know which question to answer first. I'm Wash Fuller."

The twins told him their names. The boy was Beto, which he said like Bay-toe, and the girl was Cari—and full of questions. She started in again. "How do you know our sister?"

"Just a friend," Wash said. "And I reckon you all can come along. I've only got one rod, but we can take turns."

"Can we?" Cari asked.

"Please, Omi?" Beto added.

Naomi bent and looked at the twins hard. "If I say yes, you two have to promise to behave. And I want you home by dinnertime." She sounded calm, but there was still a thread of hurt in her voice.

"You're not coming?" Wash asked. He hoped she'd look at him.

"Laundry," she said. She was already walking away. "That porch better be swept," she called back to the twins.

"You can meet us by the river if you change your mind," Wash called. "The Sabine's just a half mile the other way on the county road." Naomi lifted a hand and kept walking. He watched her braid sway between her hips.

"Sometimes she likes to be by herself," Cari explained.

Wash worked up a smile even though what he wanted was to forget the kids and go after Naomi. "Well," he said, "Let's go catch us some bass."

NAOMI Naomi stood with her hand on the porch door. Her eyes stung from trying not to cry. The truck was gone and Henry was supposed to be on a twelve-hour shift, but she needed to make sure. She waited another minute. When she still didn't hear anything, she went in, letting the screen slam shut behind her.

Henry's clothes lay in a heap on the floor where he'd left them that morning. "I used to take my wash to a gal out by the truck yard," he had said. "I reckon you can do it now." He was out the door before she could answer.

Washing his clothes. It wasn't just one more thing to add to the work of cooking and cleaning and tending the twins and trying to buy food. It meant handling shirts and pants that he'd worn. It meant touching things that had touched his body. It meant the smell of him.

Naomi crumpled into one of the kitchen chairs and laid the side of her face on the cool tabletop. She imagined telling the twins to pack their things. She slid her hand into her pocket and pulled out the money she'd gotten from Henry for groceries. Five dollars. She'd seen five-dollar bills in Abuelito's store, but she'd never had one in her own possession before. Still, it wasn't enough to get them back to San Antonio, that much she knew.

The worst was how Wash had seen her cry. He probably thought she ought to have known. She did know; she wasn't a fool. Back home, she never would have gone into a store in the white part of town. But there was only the one grocer here as far as she knew, and the man had told her plain enough to come back during colored hours.

It wasn't just that it kicked at her pride. It might make trouble. She wasn't worried about herself; she already knew she wasn't wanted here. The woman in the school office had given her a long, hard look when she brought in her enrollment card. She'd have sent Naomi to a Mexican school in a heartbeat if they'd had one. But if Henry heard that people in his town saw her not just as Mexican but as colored, he might try to send her back and keep the twins. She couldn't risk it.

When Naomi opened her eyes, they landed on Henry's coffee cup and the stained red work rag he had wiped his mouth on at breakfast. She pulled herself upright and lifted the mug, considering the heft of it and willing herself to throw it. Instead, she carried it to the sink, washed it, and set it in the dish drain.

She needed air, but the window above the sink was painted shut. She swept three dead flies from the sill into the basin. Their bodies stood out stark against the white enamel until she turned on the faucet and sent them spiraling down the drain. She went to the refrigerator and let the cold spill out around her. The waste didn't matter; like everything else, the thing ran on free gas.

Inside there were three eggs, one piece of ham, a wedge of waxed orange cheese, and the quart of milk that came every three days. She went over to the pantry. She shifted a can of pears, a shriveled carrot, and two small potatoes to one side. In the middle of the shelf, she grouped the baking powder, a box of salt, the mostly empty sack of flour, and the tin of lard. On the right, she straightened a half-empty bag of dried beans. Three days' worth of food, maybe four if she skipped a meal or two.

She thought about distracting herself with the laundry, but she didn't feel like it, not yet. She went into the hall, and saw that the door to Henry's room was ajar. She pushed it partway open with her foot and walked in. The room was bright with light from the bare window.

There was a Bible on the nightstand, the same kind that Pastor Tom had given to Beto last week after his baptism. Black leather with gold-edged pages, each one thin as a bit of onion skin. Henry's was open to

Psalm 77. Her eyes fell on a phrase: *Thy footsteps are not known.* The bed-covers were in a tangle, and there was a greasy spot in the middle of the pillowcase. Sourness rose into her mouth. She thought about swallowing it back down, but instead she spat. Before she walked out, she looked for the small glob of saliva glistening on his pillow. Probably it would dry and he'd never know it had been there. Or else it would be something new for him to read.

BETO Beto chased Cari up from the river, racing through spots of light and shadow as the summer sun poured through the trees. At the edge of the woods, they flung themselves down in the pine needles and waited for Wash to catch up. When he came into view, Cari leaned her head against Beto's and whispered, "Our best find yet."

On the rest of the walk home, Wash told them jokes and they laughed until their happiness was the loudest thing in the woods, louder than the tree frogs or the squawking grackles in the treetops. Then they came out on the oil-top road that ran along the Humble Oil camp and turned onto the packed dirt road that led to their new house.

Naomi was on the back porch waiting for them. "*Ya llegamos,*" Cari shouted. She ran up the steps with Beto following after.

"Talk English," he called, mostly to show Naomi he remembered the rules.

By the time Wash strolled into the yard, they had pulled Naomi down the porch steps. She still held her sewing in one hand.

"Too hot for laundry?" Wash asked.

Naomi frowned. "Didn't get to it."

"Ask us something," Beto said to Naomi, yanking on her sleeve.

Naomi made a face like she was thinking hard. "Did you catch anything?"

Wash pulled his hands from behind his back to reveal the two strings of fish they'd caught. Five fish on each string. Fish fooled by bits of worm stabbed onto hooks. Cari had delighted in that job, but Beto had looked away, unsure about the whole business until they pulled in the first fish. It thrashed hard at the end of the line, its scales lit by the sun. River bass, Wash had said. River silver, Beto had thought. Even now that the fish hung still and straight, they gleamed in the late afternoon light.

"Nice little bass. Not bad for the first try," Wash said.

Naomi nodded and put a hand on Beto's elbow. "What do you say?"

Beto glanced at Cari. "Thank you," they said together.

"Y'all know how to clean fish?" Wash asked.

"Soap and water?" Beto ventured. He blushed as soon as he said it.

Wash laughed. "Not hardly. Come on, let me teach you." He looked over at Naomi. "Can you spare two dishes and a good sharp knife? We'll get these cleaned and ready for frying."

"I already made dinner," Naomi said.

"Fried sand bass go good with everything, I promise."

"All right," she said.

WASH Wash set the bowl of scraps on the edge of the back porch and handed Naomi the other bowl, now lined with neat filets. She thanked him and sent the twins inside to wash up and set the table. "I'll be checking on you soon," she called.

They hollered good night to Wash and ran up the steps. The screen door banged behind them as they went in, and their laughter grew faint.

"They had fun," Naomi said. A smile escaped her then. Wash watched it transform her face into a fuller beauty.

"What?" Naomi asked. Her smile vanished.

"You figure on a better way to get your groceries?" He lowered his voice. "Mr. Turner can be downright unkind. Old man gargles with the devil's mouthwash, you ask me."

"We're fine," she said, but the wrinkle in her forehead was back. All Wash could think was how bad he wanted to find a way to put a smile back on her face.

"Listen, there's a store in Egypt Town. Mr. Mason sells to everybody. Mostly it's us shopping there, plus backwater folks that's shy of town and only come around couple times a year. Anyway, you won't have to wait at Turner's back door for him to try to pass off his worst stock on you. I've seen him sell moldy potatoes back there and dare folks to complain about it." He hooked his thumbs through his belt loops, then pulled them free. "I can take you over to the store tomorrow if you want."

After a long pause, she nodded. "Please."

"That wasn't so hard, was it?"

"What do you mean?" she asked. She pressed the bowl to her apron and stared at the ground. He thought he saw color in her cheeks, but it might have been the light.

"Never mind," he said. "See you tomorrow in the woods by the school? I'll find you all."

"All right. Good night," she said.

"Evening, Naomi." Wash lifted his hat and waved, but Naomi was already on her way up the porch steps.

◊ ◊ ◊

Of course, Wash knew better. Knowing better came with being the son of the black school principal, who was also Egypt Town's de facto mayor. It came with singing in the AME choir and taking Sunday school attendance. It came with paying Booker, speaking proper, and polishing his father's shoes. It came with "yessir, yessum" for Mr. and Mrs. Turner and the other white folks he crossed paths with. On the side of knowing better were his mother and father, all the teachers he knew, the deacons from church, Booker T. Washington, and the diligent faculty of the Tuskegee Institute. Knowing better had its secrets too, like the tin of condoms Wash's father had given him, saying, "I don't want you messing around. But if you do, think of your future."

Better was a safe place. Better was what you were supposed to do. That's why better was *better*. Better was big enough to include Rosie Lynn Horton, who sang soprano in the choir and had slightly mismatched nipples on nutmeg-brown breasts that were otherwise perfect. (Wash knew because Rosie didn't spend all her time singing in the choir.)

But Wash wasn't thinking about Rosie Lynn anymore, and he wanted to know Naomi more than he wanted to know better.

BETO After school, Beto waited in the woods with Naomi and Cari. Most everybody who was walking to the Humble camp had already gone on. Some of the kids from the revival came toward them in matching dresses. An older girl was with them, someone from Naomi's class named Tommie. When she saw Naomi, she invited the three of them for snacks.

"My ma made some applesauce cake," Tommie said. "Might be some lemonade, too."

Beto and Cari tugged on Naomi's sleeves, but she shook her head.

"Maybe another time," she said, giving them a hard look. "Thanks for the invitation."

Nobody said anything until the girls were far down the path.

"Could've eaten cake, too, for how long it's taking," Cari said. "When is Wash coming?" She swatted at her damp curls.

"Don't know," Naomi said. "If you want, you can fix my braid."

Cari sighed and rolled her eyes. A moment later, though, she came over behind Naomi, undid her braid, and began to redo it. At home, sometimes Naomi let Beto fix her hair, too, but he couldn't ask for a turn out here.

"Want to know what we learned today?" Cari asked.

"Of course," Naomi said. She reached out to push a few sweaty strands of hair off Beto's forehead.

Cari said, "I read 'ACKERMAN, FRANCIS,' 'ACKERMANN, RUDOLPH,' and 'ACNE.' Blech, that one was nasty. I sure didn't want to, but I couldn't help finishing it." Then she named the good entries, sometimes telling whole long passages she knew by heart.

Beto was a good reader, too, but he couldn't remember things the way Cari could. For him it was bits and broad outlines, never the perfect whole.

She was mostly generous with her gift. Like today, when he had wanted to keep the entry on the albatross, she had agreed to read it. All that it took for them to have it forever was for Cari to read it once. Sometimes Cari would tell him bits at night if they were both awake. And during the day, too, if he agreed to give up something in exchange or do her some favor.

Halfway through Cari's recitation of an entry on astrology, Wash came jogging up the path from the direction of the school. "Y'all ready?" he asked. He pulled a wristwatch out of his pocket and checked it. "Sorry I'm late."

Naomi nodded, and they followed him into the woods.

After ten minutes on the main trail, Wash pointed to a smaller path to one side. "Egypt Town's this way," he said. The place sounded like magic. Beto and Cari tore down the path because if a place was worth walking to, it was surely worth a run.

"Turn right at the road," Wash called.

On the road they passed a half dozen brightly painted houses, some tidy and some not, and then they were in front of the only thing that looked like a store. MASONS was painted in big white letters straight onto the shingle siding of the building, and it had a wide front porch with a few homemade rockers. The front door was propped open with a barrel.

Inside, Wash introduced them to Mr. Mason, the owner, who had gentle eyes and shaky hands that reminded Beto of Abuelito. A few stray white hairs stuck out from his chin. He greeted Naomi with a "Good afternoon, miss," and gave Beto and Cari a broken peppermint stick apiece. Naomi went over her list, and Mr. Mason brought down the items she asked for from his shelves and cabinets. Beto and Cari squatted at the counter, eyeing the big glass jars of candy and figuring on what they could get for the dime Naomi had given them.

Once their candy was picked out and Mr. Mason had scooped it into a paper bag, Wash led them back out onto the porch so that Naomi could finish her shopping. They played a while and sucked on their candy until they were down to just one piece of red licorice. Beto wanted to be sure Naomi got some, so he darted back through the open doorway to give it to her. Mr. Mason was talking to Naomi somewhere in the back part of the store.

". . . good people here in Egypt, but maybe you should think about shopping elsewhere."

"Mr. Turner didn't want me in his store. I'd have to go clear to Overton, almost five miles," Naomi said.

"You're sort of . . . in between. You keep comin' here, that's fine. But see to it that you don't get too familiar with . . . folks." Mr. Mason walked over to the counter then, and when he saw Beto, his face seemed to change, to go stiff somehow, and he smiled. "Got one more scrap of peppermint if you want it."

"Please," Naomi said, "save some for other children. They already had plenty."

Mr. Mason nodded slowly, and then after counting and recounting, he reached across the counter and dropped some coins into Naomi's hand. "There's always someone looking to make talk." He spoke softly, but Beto still heard.

THE GANG Most of us couldn't like the Mexican girl on account of Miranda not liking her, which made it downright dangerous, socially speaking. But Tommie Kinnebrew was near evangelical on the subject and spent half her talk trying to win us over. Mary Ellis said that the Mexican girl went to Tommie's church, which was why she was obliged to like her.

We would be sitting at lunch in the cafeteria or eating under one of Mr. Crane's big trees that only the seniors were allowed to use, and Tommie would barge in and force some dull story down our throats about how the Mexican girl was such a hard worker. She let some interesting facts slip along the way, though. She told us how the girl didn't have a mama, poor thing, and also didn't know how to do her wash. She'd learned that tidbit from Muff Clarkson, also a member of the New London Baptist Church. Muff stopped by to bring the girl's family a cake and found her up to her elbows in laundry—in the bathtub of all places. How come? The true-fact answer was that she didn't know how to use a crank wash machine since she was poor as all get-out, and we reasoned that she had not even lived in a real house but had slept with horses or pigs back in some nasty corner of San Antonio, a town we knew to be full of dirty Mexicans. According to Tommie, when Muff told her that she'd never get that red clay out by slopping things around in the tub, the Mexican girl burst into tears.

Tommie's stories weren't much, but they gave us material for working up something better. The boys among us liked to think on how the Mexican girl surely got wet doing the laundry. Word was that she didn't wear a slip; just a splash of water and you'd see damn near everything. The girls among us focused on the obvious fact that a Mexican girl who didn't know how to do laundry had to be just about the most unsanitary creature on earth. That was proof that Mexicans were filthy, they said. You might get a disease just by standing near this one, and you surely did not want to share a sewing machine with her in home economics. The girls on the homecoming committee said, "See?" The boys on the football team shrugged and grinned. In the locker room during the second week of football practice, Forrest Evers said that he'd gone all the way with her out back of the cafeteria. We didn't believe him, but we liked the thought of it.

There were other questions, too, like what the relation was between her and the little white kids that she watched and also between her and her "daddy," who plain as day was not her daddy. A few of us decided that she wasn't a Mexican at all since the little kids weren't brown. The explanation was that her mama was white but there'd been a nigger in the wood stack, which was where the girl's color came from. That story was told mostly by those who thought she shouldn't be in our school but instead ought to be out learning with the coloreds, but there was pushback from folks who insisted that she was a Mexican and that it was hardly fair to make a Mexican go to the darkie school.

Besides, we didn't want to lose her. She was the only pretty thing that every boy among us believed could be his, at least ten minutes at a time. Without her, we'd have nothing to talk about but football, Miranda's new charm bracelet ordered from Dallas, Chigger Watson jacking off in the woods, and who was finishing the year out and who was going to get married or go work the rigs. Without the Mexican girl, the only stories we'd get from Tommie Kinnebrew would be about Oklahoma and the last oil field her daddy worked and how they had to share a one-room garage with another family. "Didn't have nothing to separate our smells and sounds except for a big blanket tacked up in the middle," she told us more times than we wanted, which was none.

We needed the Mexican girl, each in our own way. She gave us something to do. She kept us thinking. How to get rid of her (Miranda); how to stay clear of her (the other girls); how to get in her (the boys).

NAOMI   Naomi started when the screen door swung open. She looked down. Her hands were drifting in the gray dishwater, long gone cold. She could not say when she had finished the dishes.

"Daydreaming?" Henry said.

"Just cleaning up. I didn't hear you come in," she said. She pulled the stopper. "Kids are asleep. There's fried ham and beans. Potatoes and creamed corn. I can warm it for you." She uncovered his plate.

He tossed his hat onto the counter. "Don't bother. I'll eat it cold." He rolled up his sleeves and began to lather up with the bar of Lava soap.

"Where'd that come from?" he asked, pointing a soapy finger at a small boat Wash had made for the twins. One of them must have left it there when they washed up for dinner.

"Oh, the kids made a friend." She wiped her hands on her apron.

"Colored boy?" he asked over his shoulder.

"That's right," she answered. She laid a fork and a napkin on the table.

"Bud said something to me about seeing a Negro boy pass by." Henry ducked down and splashed a little water on his face then rubbed himself dry with a dish towel. She made a mental note to put that one in the laundry bin at the first opportunity. "Seems like they ought to be making friends with kids at their school."

"They are," she said. "Kids from church, too. I saw Cari eating lunch with Cassie and Janey Horton today, and Beto was playing football with some boys."

"That's good. Better for them to stick to their own kind. Not that I've got anything against coloreds."

She might have said "yes, sir," and left it at that. But then she thought of what Wash had given her. Not just a way to get the groceries but also relief, warmth. That afternoon on the way home from the store: light angling through the trees, cicadas clattering high in the branches, the twins racing and laughing with Wash, her not needing to say anything. She felt the worth of it, and a bit of boldness sprouted up in her.

"It's a big help to me, the time they spend with him. That boy, I mean. He's called Wash, I think. They look forward to it, get their chores done quick so they can go off."

"I don't want them working," Henry said, crossing his arms. "They should be learning their lessons and playing."

"Not work, really. Small things to help," she said. "It takes a lot to run a household."

He stretched. His joints popped as he flexed his fingers, and he rolled his head from side to side till his neck cracked. "They're just kids."

"I need the help, Daddy." She forced out the last word.

"Not too much, is all. I work so they don't have to."

"Of course," she said. She set his food down in front of him.

As she did, Henry threw his head back and laughed. "This joke I heard today on the rig . . ."

"Well?" she said finally. He seemed to want her to ask.

"Can't repeat it—not fit for a lady's ears. Not fit for Christian ears, neither. Pastor Tom would swallow his tongue if he could hear them boys talking trash on the rig."

Naomi poured him a glass of milk. "Anything else?" she asked as she set it in front of him.

Henry grew serious. "Pray with me, Naomi."

Before she could answer, he had snatched up her hand. And so she stood there, unable to hear his words so long as he was gripping her fingers. She forced out an "amen" and then jerked her hand back.

"Good night," she said. She all but ran to the bathroom, locking the door behind her. She washed and washed her hands. When she came out, she told herself she was not going to look at him, but she did anyway.

Henry was smiling. Whatever the oil field crud and filth on the rest of him, his arms and face and hands were scrubbed and clean. For a moment, she could see what the church ladies saw: young, handsome, hardworking, strong. He had the wholesome look of the redeemed. But she had not forgotten. Could not forget.

Back in the bedroom, she made sure the twins were asleep, and then she reached under the bed, found her mother's old guitar case, and carefully flipped open the snaps. She touched the things inside one by one.

◇ ◇ ◇

"Naomi? Are you awake?" Cari's voice came in a whisper.

Naomi bolted upright. Cari's side of the bed was empty. She felt a moment of panic but then saw her sitting cross-legged on the bare hardwood floor.

"¿Qué pasó?" Naomi asked.

"It's raining," Cari said. She pulled her knees up to her chin and hugged them tight. The old nightgown tented over her, bluish in the weak light.

Naomi listened. There was a faint patter on the roof, and droplets slid down the window over their bed. On the other side of the room, Beto was still asleep. His bottom was lifted in the air, a habit he'd had as a baby and that still came back sometimes when he was very tired.

"Why are you on the floor?" Naomi asked.

"It's not coming in," Cari said.

Then Naomi understood. In San Antonio, rainstorms were rare, and if one hit at night, you woke up with water dripping on your face. Then there was a mad scramble to shift furniture and get pans and bowls and buckets in all the places where the roof leaked.

"You're right," she said. "We're nice and dry. It rained before, remember? When we first got here."

"It feels different at night," Cari said. "A good thing."

"Sure, cariño. Now come to bed." Naomi lifted the blanket up for her. Cari crawled back under the covers and snuggled close.

"I like that you still call me that," Cari whispered. "*Cariño*. That's another good thing."

"Just when it's us, okay? Go to sleep now."

"And Wash," Cari said. "That makes *tres*. Three good things."

Naomi stroked Cari's hair. Even with her eyes closed, she knew the exact moment when her sister fell sleep, knew it by the little sigh that came just before her breathing turned steady.

Naomi held her sister and drifted toward sleep. She should have known it could go bad, what with the prayer and Henry's hand on hers, and inside that the dark kernel of before. At first the dreams were just numbers and words and bits from science class. Then came something about her Spanish teacher, whose black button eyes stared from under her prickly gray eyebrows. In the dream, she spoke to Naomi in accented Spanish without moving her mouth. Then she rode a bicycle ahead of her, leading her toward a door at the end of a long hall that was at the same time the door to the bathroom in the little Houston house where Naomi had lived with Henry and her mother. Then pink tile and his hand on the lock and *Just like you're making butter. That's all you have to do. You can keep your mama safe* and her heart in her throat and no words coming out.

She awoke trembling and terrified of finding him there. Naomi leaned her face against Cari. The nape of Cari's neck was warm and dry, and Naomi thought hard about staying safe, staying just this side of sleep where there would be no dreams. She lay listening to the rain slap against the roof until it began to sound like *nope nope nope nope nope*, and she took some comfort in it.

◇ ◇ ◇

Escuse, aye juan tu fin amen namad Henry. Es mi papa.

That was how Naomi's brain, still keyed to Spanish, stored the words her mother sent her with when the second disaster came just after Naomi's seventh birthday.

For the record, Estella had actually said, "*Vete a buscar a Henry en el icehouse. Di,* 'Excuse me, I want to find a man named Henry. He is my papa.'"

Under normal circumstances, Naomi would have protested that

Henry was not her father and that she didn't know the way to the icehouse. But the situation was not normal; her mother spoke to her from the floor of the bathroom, where she crouched, hand up under her dress. Already, bright red drops stood out on the pink tile. She'd called Naomi back a moment later, telling her to bring a towel. She couldn't ruin another dress, she said.

Naomi pressed a towel into her mother's hand. Then she turned and ran, out of the house, down the steps, and along the cracked sidewalk. She ran until by stupid luck she found herself staring at a wood plank sign printed with the words White Oak Icehouse.

It was not a house at all, nor was it made of ice. It was just a sloping building covered with corrugated tin panels hammered together. It had a regular door on one side and a big garage door on the other. The garage door was open, and inside Naomi could see shelves with cans of food and tin signs advertising Lucky Strikes and Chesterfields. A small shack was attached to the side of the building, and a few picnic tables and benches were scattered under the shade of two elm trees.

Three men sat together at one of the picnic tables, but Henry was not among them.

There was a heavy-breasted woman behind a bar in the garage and a lean yellow dog who lay drowsing by a pan of water, his ears twitching in sleep.

Naomi moved toward the woman. As she walked, she repeated the words her mother had given her to say. *Escuse, aye juan tu fin amen namad Henry . . . Escuse, aye juan tu fin . . . Escuse . . . Escuse . . .*

"What ya need, honey?" the woman asked. Her hair was the color of carrots and her teeth were very bad. She was wiping the metal counter with a limp rag.

Naomi knew she had been asked a question but did not know what it was. She tried to force her lips to form the words her mother had told her to speak, but they sat like lead on her tongue. She studied the milky streaks on the counter, hoping for a miracle.

The woman came from behind the counter then. She leaned down and took Naomi's hand. "You can tell me."

"Escuse, aye juan tu fin amen namad Henry, es mi papa." The words came out in a rush. Naomi trembled with the expectation of failure. But the woman gave no indication either of understanding or of confusion.

Instead, she pointed over at the group of men. "You know any of those fellas?"

Naomi shook her head.

"Then it must be Henry you're looking for."

When Naomi heard the name, she grabbed the woman's sleeve. "Es hem," she said, nodding in case the words hadn't come out right.

"You wait here. Let me see if I can raise him, darlin'." She folded her towel into a wet square and moved off behind the shed in the direction of a little white house on the next lot.

Naomi took a step toward the sleeping dog, and for a moment she thought about stroking his floppy ears, but she did not want to disturb him. He whimpered softly, then his legs began to twitch and move.

The woman came back with Henry. His hat was askew, and he was still buckling his pants.

Another man called over to him, "You give old Mona somethin' to moan about?"

The other men laughed, but Henry ignored them. He looked at Naomi. "What're you doing here?"

Naomi stared up at him. She realized her mouth was hanging open, so she pulled it shut. But she could not bring herself to speak. Her mother had given her words to ask for Henry but no words to speak to him once she found him.

She swallowed, remembering her mission. "Mami," she said, "Mami." She could tell from his eyes that he understood, and he took off running toward the house, leaving her behind.

◇ ◇ ◇

It was the second miscarriage in less than six months. Something was not right, the doctor said, and he cautioned against another pregnancy. When Estella miscarried a third time, the doctor spelled the consequences out more plainly: "Another pregnancy could kill your wife."

Naomi stood listening at the door to her room as the doctor and Henry talked in the hall. Naomi's English was getting better, but she did not know what was meant by "abstinence," "substitution," "self-care," or "prophylactics." Whatever it was made Henry very angry. "She's my wife, dammit, a man's got a right," he said.

Naomi had loved the bathtub in Henry's house. It was the first porcelain tub she'd seen outside of the movies. In those days before the crash, Abuelito and Abuelita had had a nice house, but they still took their baths in a galvanized tin tub. Henry's bathtub was big enough to float in without touching the sides if she pulled her knees up. She liked to lie there, drifting, until the bathwater turned frigid and her mother called her out.

Sometimes at night, she would sneak out of bed, creep down the hall, and curl up in the tub. She didn't dare run the water for fear of waking her mother or, if he was home, Henry. But with her cheek pressed against the cool white porcelain she could swim through imaginary waters and sometimes fall asleep.

She was there when Henry came into the bathroom and closed the door behind him. She watched as he placed both hands on the wall beneath the mirror and pressed his forehead against the glass. A moment later, one of his hands slid down into his pajamas. It was like some small creature was trying to escape from his throat. His hand moved fast. His body jiggled. He kept his forehead against the mirror and his eyes closed. Then he grunted once and seemed to shudder all over. He stood there for a moment more, a sudden slackness in his body. Then he held his hands under the water before walking back out.

That time, he never once looked at her. She would never know if he followed her into the bathroom or if he had somehow not noticed her.

◊ ◊ ◊

Even as a child, Naomi was not a heavy sleeper. The first night Henry came into her room, she heard the door open, heard the footsteps that were too heavy to be her mother's. And anyway Estella never woke up at night, not now that the doctor had put her on sleeping pills to help her rest.

Naomi lay as still as she could. She knew he was standing there, looking down at her.

Then the footsteps went back toward the door. She waited a moment, and when she thought surely he had gone back to bed, she opened her eyes and gulped in a breath.

Henry was staring right at her. He grinned. "You thought you fooled me, but I fooled you," he said. "I knew you were awake."

He closed the door behind him and locked it. He had put locks on all the bedroom doors the week before. When Estella asked him why, he said simply, "It's how a house should be." She hadn't protested.

Henry came to the side of her bed and pulled back the covers. Naomi sat up quickly and scrambled backward.

"Shh," he said. He took one of her hands in his and squeezed it. "Come on over here." He pulled her to her feet, close to him.

He shifted in his pajamas, and the part of him that made him a man stuck out, reddish purple and frightening. She had never seen one before except on a baby. This was different.

He lifted her hand to his mouth and licked it. Then he lowered her hand down and closed it around the hardness. His hand moved hers. His left hand gripped her shoulder, pressing her head tight against the hard, flat plane of his stomach. She watched her hand move back and forth like it didn't belong to her. In the distance, she heard the train pass. A moment later, the thing leaped. Henry's whole body shuddered, and a hot mess lay across her palm and between her fingers. Henry wiped himself quickly with a handkerchief. Then, never letting go of her shoulder, he urged her toward the door. "Come on," he said once it was open. He walked her to the bathroom and then guided her hand to the sink.

"There," he said, rinsing her hand and patting it dry. "All better." He walked back to his room like he had merely gone to get a glass of water.

In the morning, when her mother asked her what was wrong, Naomi smiled a bright, false smile and said that it was nothing. Henry, sitting across from her at the table, raised his eyebrows at her over the top of his coffee cup and smiled. "She's a good girl, ain't she?" he said. He winked at her as if he were promising to keep her secret rather than commanding her to keep his.

◇ ◇ ◇

The fourth pregnancy took, but it also took away what strength Estella had left. As her belly grew, she seemed to shrink. Her skin turned translucent. The twins came early in a rush of blood that slowed to a trickle but never stopped.

Naomi was in the room when her mother died. The babies lay curled on Estella's chest, their small bottoms rising and falling with her breath. Then there was no more rise and fall. The babies began to cry, but Naomi could not move. Tia Cuca came in, murmured a prayer, and scooped the twins up. "Get him," she said.

Henry was in the kitchen, his head in his hands. Naomi tugged his sleeve. When he looked up, there was a flash of something, then his face reddened. He stood up suddenly, knocking the chair over. She backed out and went to her pallet in the corner of the living room.

Naomi sat on the blankets with the tip of her braid in her mouth and her doll tucked under her arm. Henry did not look at her when he walked past.

A moment later, Tia Cuca came out of the babies' room and motioned to her. "*Mira*," she said.

Naomi crept over and looked. The twins were nestled into each other, asleep. Beto's head was tucked in under Cari's armpit.

"There are many things to arrange," Tia Cuca said, laying a hand on Naomi's shoulder. "The priest and . . . the body. Henry is not able right now. You will watch the babies, *¿sí?* Just until I come back. Then we will talk."

Naomi didn't need to be told. She felt safest in the room with the sleeping twins. She did not want to see her mother's empty face, her strange swollen body drained of color. She did not want to be out in the part of the house where Henry was.

She curled up on her old bed, wishing she had brought her doll Nana with her, but too afraid to go out of the room to get her. She slept for a while and dreamed strange sounds, tearing and something that wanted to be music but wasn't. The opposite of music. There was china falling, too, and a thudding sound. Then she opened her eyes. The sounds were coming from the living room. When they stopped, Naomi opened the door just wide enough to see out. One of her mother's dresses lay on the floor of the hallway. She eased her head out a little farther and saw a shattered bowl, the one her mother had used to serve Henry's mashed potatoes. She saw the caved-in, splintered wreckage that had been her mother's guitar.

Naomi could not keep herself back when she saw what else was broken. She ran into the living room, tears already welling up in her eyes.

Naomi did not speak. The doll's head was shattered, and the sand that had filled her body spilled onto the floor from a rip across her back. Black curls dangled from bits of broken porcelain. One blue eye stared up from a pink shard.

She had lived through Nana for two years, had imagined her life with other dolls, a life of giggles and talking and holding hands.

Tears ran down the end of her nose. She couldn't speak.

"Crying for a doll?" Henry scoffed. "For a doll when—" his voice cracked, and the twins' cries rose behind him. "Do something, dammit," he said. There was a sob in his voice.

She grabbed the guitar case and the closest bit of what had been Nana. She ran to the twins' room and shut the door.

The twins were wailing, their fists thrashing. Naomi picked up the tin of powdered formula the doctor had brought a few days before when he had said that her mother's body was too weak to produce milk for the babies.

Estella had turned her face to the wall while the doctor explained how to use the formula, but Naomi had listened. Now she mixed the powder with the water from the pitcher on the dresser, guessing at the proportions.

She picked up Cari first because her cries were sharpest. But when she tried to put the rubber nipple in Cari's mouth, the baby spat it out. Naomi put her back in the crib and tried with Beto, but his reaction was no better. She tried dribbling milk into their mouths. After a few minutes of that, Cari finally latched on to the nipple, tugging at it greedily. Naomi stopped her when the bottle was half finished and gave the rest to Beto. "There," she said, "there."

She bounced them like she'd seen Cuca do until they burped. She changed their diapers then laid them back on the bed and watched their eyelids grow heavy. They curled in toward each other like kittens, and Naomi lay down beside them. This was her family now. Mami was gone, and her doll was gone, but she still had the twins. She laid her braid across them. *Yo te tengo a ti*," she whispered in each twin's ear. "I've got you."

OCTOBER 1936

NAOMI Naomi tapped a floury fingerprint on Baby Joe's nose as he toddled past in one of his many tours around Muff's kitchen table. They were working up a batch of biscuit dough while J.R. played with his truck in the corner and Joe Joe practiced walking.

"See, these are what you need for biscuits." Muff nodded at the heavy baking trays on the counter. "Those pans of Henry's are hardly better than a garbage can lid. We'll see that he gets you something decent. That's a man for you. Spends money on his truck but won't buy a decent pan or skillet unless you press him into it."

She nodded approvingly as Naomi turned out the biscuit dough. "You don't need me to tell you what to do now," Muff said. She grinned and made to take off her apron. "Think I'll just go put my feet up."

"You could, you know. You've helped me so much. I'd like to be useful to you, too," Naomi said. Thanks to Muff, Naomi's Southern cooking had improved. Muff taught her to fry chicken legs and turn the small bits of dark meat into chicken and dumplings. They made chocolate sheet cakes, pork chops, fried squash, and the flaky, soft biscuits that were her specialty.

"You certainly know your way around my house, seeing as how it's the exact same as yours."

It was true that the layouts were mirror images of each other. Kitchen at one end, living room at the other, a hall with two bedrooms and a bathroom in between. But for Naomi, the feeling inside the two houses could not be more different. It wasn't just that Muff had a radio and better cooking gear; the house had the warmth of a place where people were happy together and would go on being happy.

Muff went on. "But you know I can't pass on the chance to gab. And anyhow," she turned her face and rubbed her nose against the side of her arm, "you already darned up J.R.'s church pants real nice. Maybe you can sew something for the new baby. The twins both said it was a girl. Real confident of it. We'll see." She wiped a doughy hand against the slight bulge under her apron. "Where are they? I'm surprised they aren't here waiting for fried biscuit scraps with honey." She raised her voice. "We all know that's why J.R.'s playing in here and not eating dirt in the yard."

"The twins? Probably off in the woods somewhere," Naomi said.

Occasionally the twins came along and played with "the babies," as they called J.R. and Joe Joe. Other times they ran with the neighborhood kids or stayed late to help Miss Bell. Today, like most days, they'd gone off with Wash. Where exactly or to do what, Naomi didn't know. Fishing, woodworking, treasure hunting, wandering.

What mattered was that she got things done. Lighting the gas stove no longer took much thought, and she knew how to handle the oil- and mud-stained laundry Henry left in heaps for her to wash. After clearing away leftovers and washing dishes at night, Naomi packed four lunches, folding wax paper around the sandwiches and laying out the thermos for Henry's coffee. She tried to stay on top of the sewing and to keep dust from gathering in the cracks between the floorboards. But there was always more to do.

Naomi dipped her glass in flour and began cutting out the biscuits. Muff did the same from the other end of the table. "I could show you how to make tortillas. Or tamales," she suggested.

Muff shrugged. "I'd like that, but Bud, he's just a country boy. We went to San Antone for our honeymoon, did you know that? I tried some of that good Mexican food, but Bud likes his chicken-fried steak and mashed potatoes."

Naomi persisted. "Isn't there something?"

"Well . . ." Muff looked to be thinking hard. "How do the twins feel about animals?"

Naomi remembered the small gray cat Cari and Beto had fed in secret until Abuelita found out and put a stop to it on account of the waste. And there was the sparrow with the damaged wing. The twins had kept it in a box and fed it nothing but bits of candy cane for over a week. It hadn't occurred to them that their favorite food might not sustain the creature. By the time they showed it to her and asked for help, it was just a beating heart inside a cage of matted feathers. She still remembered the bird's glossy dark eye, how it trembled when she lifted it out of the box.

Naomi blinked the memory away. "Fine. What do you have in mind?"

◇ ◇ ◇

That was how Naomi and the twins started feeding Muff's chickens and gathering eggs from her coop. Technically, residents weren't allowed to keep animals other than pets in the Humble camp, but plenty of folks worked around that by putting pens and makeshift henhouses on the far side of the camp's back fence. It was mostly chickens, but there were also a few goats and hogs.

Tending chickens was something Naomi knew how to do, a small way to be useful. And Muff pressed them to take half of the eggs each day, which helped stretch the groceries. For the rest, Naomi shopped at Mason's on afternoons when she could count on Henry to be working late. She felt a need, without ever exactly announcing it to herself, to conceal her solution to the grocery problem. At first, Naomi worried that Muff might question her about her ingredients when she came over to help her cook—Calumet baking powder instead of Clabber Girl, Sunshine Saltines rather than Nabisco—but if she noticed, she didn't say anything.

The strangeness of the place wore off little by little, but Naomi's hostility toward Henry did not. She dreamed of taking the twins away from him. She socked away a dollar, sometimes two, from each week's grocery money. Just in case. But by the time she thought she might have enough to get them back to San Antonio, there was another problem. The twins loved their school. They were growing. They came home flushed and laughing from the woods.

And Henry was mostly gone, often working twelve- and sixteen-hour shifts for days in a row until his team hit oil and they moved on to look for a new site. As far as Naomi was concerned, the less she saw of him, the better.

NAOMI Naomi found the tree on her way to call the kids home from fishing one day. She knew the way; she'd gone along once or twice to watch them fish with Wash when Henry had the day off and she wanted to be sure to be gone.

Her steps slowed as she neared the river. The path was soft with pine needles, and squirrels hurried up and down the trees with acorns in their mouths. In the shade, the air smelled of true autumn. The wind whipped up a froth of fallen leaves on the ground around her, and she pulled the sleeves of her sweater down over her hands. She felt a sudden need to climb. She paused in front of a stand of hardwoods and studied the trees. A ways off the path, two enormous oaks grew close together. Apart, they would have been impossible to scale because the lowest limbs were too far up. But she thought she could brace her back against one and inch her way up to the branches. She went closer, picking her way through brambles and brush. As she walked around the trees, she saw that there was a split in the larger tree that widened to almost two feet across at its base. She crouched and peered into the dark opening.

And then she was inside. The tree was hollow. Not just at the base, either, but at least halfway up the trunk. She stood up inside and stretched her arms over her head. The feeling of safety was glorious.

BETO Beto fingered the frayed edge of his shirt and looked over at Cari. She was squatting near the bank of the river with her dress pulled down over her knees against the cold. Wash was gathering small, flat stones from the edge of the water. While they'd been walking to the river, Wash had gone from telling them he'd teach them to skip stones to saying he could do it blindfolded.

"I don't think you can," Cari said. She gave her curls a shake in Wash's direction. "Beto doesn't think so either."

"I didn't say that," Beto protested.

"I'll show you," Wash said. "I just need a blindfold." When he couldn't find anything big enough, he unbuttoned his shirt, shrugged it off, and rolled it. He handed it to Cari with a grin. "Tie it tight, now. You'll see. Doubting Thomases, the both of you."

Cari knotted the shirt behind his head. "Why aren't you working in a circus, then, if you're such a talent at it?" She smirked at Beto.

Beto bit his lip and tried not to let her doubt in.

Wash smoothed the blindfold over his eyes. "Now hand me one of those nice flat ones I had picked out."

Beto slid a stone into Wash's hand and stepped back.

"Come on, y'all are going to at least have to put me at the edge of the water."

Cari and Beto grabbed his arms and led him down the steep slope to where the river washed up over a sandy bit of shore. "Thank you, lady and gent. Now, behold the mastery of the master!" Wash bent and felt for the water, dipped his stone in, and then lowered himself to one knee. He kissed the stone and then whizzed it toward the middle of the river.

Beto watched as the stone hit the water. It didn't sink but spun and leaped one, two, three times more before disappearing into the water. At the sound of the last plop, Wash stood and frowned. "Only four skips? I can do better than that."

Admiration bloomed in Beto. He handed Wash another stone.

This time there were six skips before the stone disappeared almost at the other side of the river.

"Can you make it go all the way across?" Beto asked, a little breathless.

"Blindfolded," Cari added. There was still a hint of challenge in her voice, but Beto could tell that she was impressed.

"Of course I can." Wash rubbed the last stone between his hands. "Just watch."

He took another step forward, swinging his arm harder this time. The stone sailed across the surface of the water, but the momentum of the pitch threw Wash off balance, and he tumbled into the river.

He surfaced, spluttering and tugging off the blindfold.

"Wash!" Beto and Cari shouted. They felt the same fear because they had the same knowledge: people could die in water.

Wash waved and looped the shirt over his arm. "I'm fine," he called. But instead of swimming back to where the twins crouched on the bank, he swam to the far side of the river. A moment later he was back, grinning. He held up a flat gray stone. The sun played across its wet surface.

He grinned and lobbed it to Cari.

"It's the same! It made it all the way across!" Beto cried when he saw the stone in her hand.

Cari frowned. "It looks like it." She glanced over at Beto with a cocked eyebrow, and he nodded. He took the stone from her and slid it into his pocket. Even through the fabric of his pants, the rock felt cool against his leg. A lucky find.

"Told you," Wash said. He was still treading water in the river.

"You think it still counts if you fall into the river?" Cari said.

"Sure it does," Beto said.

"I have my doubts." Cari spoke just as someone came running through the trees.

Beto spun around to see Naomi. "Wash!" she called as she scrambled down to the edge of the river. "Get out of there! It's too cold. You'll get sick for sure."

"Thanks for your concern, ma'am." Wash sidestroked a few yards downstream until he reached a spot where the bank wasn't as steep. He climbed out and shook himself like a dog. Then he put on his wet shirt and came high-stepping through the brush to where they were. His grin was wide, but his teeth were chattering.

"You need to get dry," Naomi said, crossing her arms.

"It's only a little chill, I'll be fine. You enjoyed the show?"

"We're going home," Naomi said to the twins. "Wash, go dry off and eat some soup or something. Warm up."

"Aye, aye, captain." Wash winked at Beto.

"I'm serious," she scowled, but already a bit of a smile broke through in her voice. "Who'd keep the twins busy if something happened to you?"

"I'm off, then," Wash said. "I have my orders!" He gave a salute and jogged up the path and was already almost out of sight by the time Beto made it into the woods. Before he rounded the bend, Wash turned to wave, and then kept on running.

BETO Beto and Cari waited in front of Mason's while Naomi finished shopping inside. They liked to line up their candy along the low handrail that ran along the far side of the sloping porch. After, they ate the candies one by one until they met in the middle. They finished all but the last candy—that one was for Naomi— and hopped down from the porch to play marbles on the packed dirt in front of the store. Two black girls about their sister's age walked past them and up the steps carrying books against their chests.

Beto peered up over the edge of the porch.

"I don't see why you're mad," the girl in blue said. "You know how he is."

"Sure, but it's *Wash*." The other girl plopped down in one of the rockers.

Beto turned to Cari. "Do you think they're talking about our Wash?"

Cari shrugged, but he could tell she was listening, too, even if she wasn't watching.

"He never talks to me at church anymore, never wants to go on a walk. You know I miss that." The tall girl sighed and smoothed her hair.

"Time to move on, if you ask me," her friend said, settling into the other rocker. "You know he's going to Tuskegee in the fall. It's not like

Mr. Fuller is going to let him get serious with a girl before then."

"I've got to get him before he goes or else my chances are ruined. And there's no one handsomer in Egypt Town."

"Come on," said the girl in blue. She stood up from the rocker and started toward the open door of the store. "I'll buy a Hershey bar to share with you, but only if you promise not to say his name again like some lovesick puppy."

"Deal," the girl in pink said, "and if we get married someday, you'll be my maid of honor for sure."

Beto watched them walk in, and he was going to ask Cari what she thought they meant, but then Naomi came out with the grocery sacks.

"They knew Wash," Cari said, taking a small bag of flour from Naomi.

"I thought I heard his name," Naomi said, and she started walking. "Did you save me any candy?"

"One piece," Cari said, "but first you have to tell us what was Mami's favorite candy."

HENRY   On Saturday, the sun was already up by the time Henry came into the kitchen. Naomi had fabric laid out across the table. "Morning, everybody," he said.

"Morning, Daddy," the twins called from the living room. Cari was clipping pictures from a catalog, and Beto was reading a thick book. Something like paternal pride pushed away Henry's drowsiness.

"Coffee?" Naomi asked. She folded her sewing into a neat pile.

"Thanks," Henry said and settled into his chair at the table.

Naomi crossed to the stove and lit one of the gas burners under the percolator. She wiped her hands on her apron. "Breakfast? Twins said they aren't hungry yet."

"Just coffee," he said. He fiddled with the salt and pepper shakers on the table in front of him, trying to figure out what to do with the fatherly feeling. "So what are we doing today?" he asked. He looked up at Naomi and grinned.

Naomi turned toward the sink. "The twins already got the eggs for Muff, and I thought after breakfast I'd finish the curtains for the bedrooms. Mrs. Wright down the street offered me her sewing machine for the day. The twins . . . the twins said something about going fishing."

"I can take them fishing." Henry unscrewed the top to the salt shaker, then screwed it back on more tightly.

"I'm sure they'd love that," she said, but there wasn't a hint of conviction in her voice.

After a while, Henry tried again. "Are they meeting up with that colored boy again? Don't see what business he has with them, really. Or why they're so damn fascinated with him. Ought to be with other white kids."

Naomi got a mug and poured the coffee.

"Don't like it," he continued. "Them running the woods with a nigger."

She set the cup of coffee in front of him. A bit sloshed out, but she didn't wipe it up.

Henry stared at the spill. He picked up the cup, pulled coffee through his teeth, and measured its bitterness on his tongue. "Did you hear me?" he asked.

She seemed about to say something when Beto came into the kitchen. He loitered around the edge of the table until Naomi whispered something into his ear. Then he went back down the hall.

"They would like to do things with you, you know," Naomi said. Her eyes met his for a moment.

A chastened resignation settled on Henry. He added more sugar to his coffee and nodded slowly. He remembered, but did not feel, the stirring he sometimes got at church meetings. "I reckon you're right." He pushed his chair back. "Call them in here."

She did. "It's okay. You're not in trouble," she told them.

Henry pointed the twins toward their seats at the table. He felt a flush of accomplishment at their obedience until he realized that Naomi had given them a nod.

"We're going out today," Henry said, pushing back the nagging irritation he felt when he saw how easy it was for Naomi. "Whatever you want. Something special. You name it. Fishing, hunting, a restaurant, even. Your choice."

The twins looked at each other and then said together, "The Cozy Table!"

He should have expected it; the kids had been talking about the Cozy Table's famous pancakes since the start of school. But Henry wasn't thinking about the pancakes. The "No Negroes, Mexicans, or dogs" sign hanging from the diner's door flashed in his mind.

"How about another diner?" he suggested. He didn't know what Naomi knew about the place. He hoped he wouldn't have to explain.

Naomi held up her sewing. "It's fine. The three of you go. I've got plenty to keep me busy."

"Will Wash go fishing without us?" Beto said. His eyes had a troubled look that unnerved Henry.

"Don't worry about that. You can go another time," Naomi said. "If Daddy says okay," she added.

"Okay," Beto whispered.

Henry reached for his hat, and the twins went to put on their shoes.

NAOMI Naomi sat for a while at the kitchen table. She figured Wash would be fine fishing alone, but it seemed unkind not to let him know that the twins weren't coming. She hesitated for a moment, thinking of the curtains. Then she saw her schoolbooks in their tidy stack on the counter by the kitchen door. That was where they usually stayed unless the twins wanted to read them.

She scooped up her school things and headed out the door toward the river. The half-truth was that she had homework. The whole truth was hidden in some inner pocket of her heart.

BETO   Beto and Cari sat in the booth, leg to leg. They pressed wordless messages into each other's hands under the table. Henry tugged on his ear and rubbed at his neck. The jukebox rattled out one honky-tonk tune after another.

The food came, and Henry prayed. Beto held his fork in his left hand. Cari held hers in her right. They each cut a bit of golden-fried pancake dripping in syrup. Beto looked at Cari, and she nodded. They put the food in their mouth at the same time, each chewing five times before swallowing. The pancakes were perfect. Naomi would have loved them. But he'd read the sign on the restaurant door, and that changed things.

HENRY Henry ate his eggs and bacon and grits, barely tasting the food. He watched the twins match their bites and felt again how little he knew about them. They always seemed to be conspiring, although he couldn't say what it was exactly. He did know that they didn't really want to be here, pancakes or no pancakes.

Pastor Tom would tell him to make it easy for them. But what did that mean? What was he supposed to do? He pushed his plate away and dug his hands into his pockets. "I could show you where I work. One of the drilling rigs," he ventured. He groped for the warmth he'd felt earlier.

Beto glanced at Cari, who gave the slightest shrug. "Sure," Beto said. "I mean, please, sir."

WASH Wash held the fishing rods and tackle box loose in his hand as he walked down the path to the river. There wasn't any hurry; unless the twins had taken up a vow of silence, they weren't there yet. He could always hear them half a mile off. When he got to the bank, he walked upstream toward his favorite fishing spot.

Then he saw her.

Naomi was sitting on a broad, flat rock at the edge of the river. Her knees were down, and her feet were tucked up under her dress. Her braid hung loose along the length of her back, the curled tip just touching the stone behind her. A book lay open on her lap, but her eyes were closed. Her face tilted up toward the sun. Listening.

As he stood there on the bank above her, he thought, I'd like her to listen to me like that.

Something in him jumped back from the thought like a hand pulling away from a stovetop even if it's not on. Wash felt the warning, but he didn't heed it.

"Hey," he called. "Did you go and drown the twins for all their craziness?"

Her eyes popped open and her brow furrowed. She turned and stared at him, not speaking.

"It was a joke," he said. "Ha, ha."

"Not funny." She straightened her legs out.

"Probably not." He walked a few steps closer to her. "But then, you don't have to be mean about it. Wouldn't kill you to smile," he said.

Her frown deepened. "I'm not mean."

"So what do you call it then?" He lifted his chin and grinned, a friendly challenge.

She shrugged. "I'm just . . . careful."

"Careful? I thought that was when you remembered to look both ways before crossing the street." He walked closer to where she sat by the river. "But, hey, what do I know? You're the one with all the fancy schoolbooks."

She glanced down at the book in her lap and shut it quickly. "A waste."

"Mind if I take a look?"

She pushed the book toward him like she couldn't wait to be rid of it, but he thought he saw a bit of a smile. He picked it up and sat on a fallen tree a few feet from her rock. He was thumbing through it when he realized he had forgotten to ask where the twins really were, so he did.

"Their dad took them to breakfast."

"Oh," he paused. "So he's not your dad?"

She shook her head. "My father drowned."

Wash winced. "No more drowning jokes from me. Sorry."

"You didn't know." Her fingers slid along her braid. "It happened before I was born. There was a flood. He was trying to save the house he was building for my mom and me, but he didn't know how to swim. The creek took him."

"So Henry's a stepdad?"

She nodded. "My mother married Henry when I was little, but I never really knew him. We went back to live with my grandparents when she died."

"Sorry to hear that, too," he said.

She did not look at him but smoothed the sides of her dress and tucked the fabric around her thighs. She had a sweater, but it was too chilly out for the thin dress she had on. He thought about offering her his jacket to cover her legs, but he didn't want to let on that he'd been looking.

She watched the river and then closed her eyes again. Her eyelashes stood out dark against her cheek.

After a few long moments, he thumped the book with his fist and asked, "What do you think of all this?" When she looked, he pointed to a page with the Pythagorean theorem.

Her face reddened. "I don't. I mean, I try, but it doesn't really make sense to me. The teacher doesn't expect me to get it anyway."

"How do you figure?"

She dragged a stick through the shallows of the river. "Teachers usually think Mexicans are too slow to bother with."

"Come on, anybody can learn anything."

"Maybe you. And the twins, of course. They're smart. Everyone says so, even people who think Mexicans are only good for shelling pecans and picking strawberries."

Wash whistled. "Those two are quicker than the Holy Spirit on Judgment Day."

She smiled at that. "Like you. I can tell by how you look at the books. And how you teach them things."

He fingered the edge of the book. "I like doing things more. One of my uncles was a carpenter. I think that'd be good, spending my days with a hammer and a saw and a bit of sandpaper." His hands curled a little, remembering the feel of his tools. "But that doesn't fly with my folks, especially my dad. 'Education is the key to the advancement of the Negro' and 'Be a credit to your race,'" Wash said, deepening his voice so the words came out like items from the Ten Commandments. "My ma's near as bad. Every move she makes is aimed at saving up a penny for my sister and me to go to college."

"It must be nice. To have them believe in you like that. Your teachers too."

"I guess," he said. "I hadn't thought on it."

"Our teachers in San Antonio hated teaching us, maybe hated us, too. The Mexican kids, I mean. In the high school, they gave us elementary school books, like we were stupid. Everything was either about being a good citizen or about 'learning a trade.' But nothing useful. Like, we learned to make mattresses. But there's not a single mattress factory in San Antonio, so what was the point of that? And get your English wrong once, and you're on the teacher's bad side forever."

Wash thought about that for a minute. "Mexican students, white teachers."

"What's your school like?" she asked.

"Four classrooms, an outhouse, and a patch of packed dirt out front. Not much to look at. Or learn from. But the teachers work hard. Some students, too. I do what it takes to keep my pa off my back."

"You mind?" Wash asked now, pointing to the spot on the rock beside her. She didn't say no, so he moved closer.

"We could take a look at your math together. Or just keep talking. It's nice, hearing you talk."

"Homework's good," she said.

And that was how the lessons started.

NAOMI Naomi felt her face warm as sun streamed through the leaves of the cottonwood tree above her. It was nearly noon, and the figures Wash had drawn with a stick in the damp dirt were now dry. Naomi had to admit that the angles and lines made some sense to her, at least more than when she was sitting in math class.

While Wash read aloud from her English book, she stared out at the river. At this spot, branches stretched all the way across the river to form a canopy. She remembered the green of a few weeks back, the kind of green made to announce the beauty of the sky behind it. Now the leaves were edged with brown. The breeze made them tremble, and some spiraled down and spun away in the currents of the river. She glanced over at Wash, who had stopped reading.

"It's nice here," she said. "In San Antonio, everything looks thirsty. Not like this."

"There's beauty here for sure." He smiled as he stood up and stretched. "If I don't get some paying work done, my ma will tan my hide tonight. I'm supposed to be one county over digging ditches right now."

"Of course," she said, jumping up. "I was going too. Thanks for the help."

"Bye, Naomi."

WASH Wash shot his best friend Cal a look. Cal's bellyaching was not a welcome sequel to the morning with Naomi. "Nobody asked you to come," Wash said.

"If I don't," Cal said, "I won't have a dime to my name. And a dime is what I need to get into the dance hall Tuesday."

"Colored Night," Wash sneered. "There's motivation."

For a while, Cal's wheezy breathing was the only sound between them. "Hey, see where that footpath breaks off?" Cal asked. He pointed to a narrow trail off to one side. "Scoot was saying the other day that that's the way to Tall Man's place. Think that could be?"

Wash shrugged. "From what I hear, nobody finds Tall Man; he finds them when he's got whiskey to sell. I wouldn't expect any path to go straight to his door."

"You're probably right. People that come to live out here don't want to truck with anybody else," Cal said.

Wash raised an eyebrow. "And you're an expert on the backwoods folk? You've lived on Liberty Street since you fell out of your mama."

"All I'm saying is, Tall Man went off to live in the woods for a reason," Cal said.

"I'd like to try that," Wash said. "Just light out."

"Good luck. Your daddy's done planned out your whole life. You cain't go off to no shack in the woods; you're going to the Tuskegee Institute to get learned."

Wash scowled. "Wouldn't mind a little peace."

Cal fell silent for a moment. "You want to hear what I heard about Tall Man and his brother? He did the same, did you know?"

"Made whiskey?"

Cal shook his head. "Naw, lived way out. You're saying you never heard this?"

"Just tell your story, Cal," Wash said. He wasn't going to beg for some yarn that was sure to be more gossip than truth.

Cal gave in. "My aunt SueSue said Tall Man's brother, Blue was his name—"

"Short for Blue Balls?"

"SueSue said he was real dark, kind of blue-black. Anyway, Blue went to work on a logging camp in Louisiana, but Tall Man was digging ditches for the oilmen over in Kilgore right after the Boom hit. Money was better logging, but he wanted to stay close to home and be with his honey. SueSue said she died trying to have a baby. Baby died, too."

"And so did their pet goat?" Wash rolled his eyes.

Cal ignored him. "When Blue came back, he didn't stay with his folks in Egypt Town or the Bottom but went and built himself a cabin on some backwoods scrap of land. Nobody could pin Blue down for why he wanted to be way out like that when before he was plenty sociable. Folks started noticing things, like how he bought flower seeds and carried home more food than even a big man like him could eat."

"We're five minutes from the oil yard," Wash said. "You'd better get to it if you want to finish your story."

"Well, talk started that Blue had some Louisiana gal tucked away in that little cabin of his. But the question was, why wouldn't he bring her around none?"

"Maybe she didn't want to. Maybe she was ashamed of not being married."

Cal shook his head. "You know that ain't it. Plenty of folks take up with each other. Even more back then when the logging camps hired blacks and the men went off to the camps and found new lady friends. So it came down to either Blue's gal was crazy or she was so ugly that he didn't want to claim her in public. Folks started teasing him till he'd get real mad, but he still wouldn't bring her down."

"And none of the fine ladies of Egypt Town could satisfy their curiosity with a little housewarming visit?" Wash asked.

"No one knew for sure where he was staying. At least until the day when Dusty Matthews—you know, from the icehouse, only he was just a kid then—until Dusty decided to follow ole Blue back to his hideout. And do you know what he saw?"

"Oswald the rabbit." Wash said. Before Cal could answer, Wash jogged ahead of him toward one of the creeks that fed into the Sabine. He sped up and jumped across the creek. The water was low, but the bed was deep. Jagged rocks stuck up through the red clay. These were things you worked at not noticing until you were safe on the other side.

"Show-off," Cal grumbled.

"Go on, granny." Wash nodded at the fallen tree somebody had laid over the creek. "I came this way to make sure you'd have a way."

Cal stared into the creek and hesitated.

"Come on." Wash got out his wristwatch. "Let's see if you can beat your record. I think it took you seven minutes the last time we crossed here."

Cal glared at him and eased out across the log, crouching low to keep his balance.

"Don't lose your glasses, man," Wash called.

Cal jutted his chin out to keep his glasses well back on his nose, but he kept his hands close to the tree. When he was almost to the other side he dove onto the bank and scrambled up, grabbing at the brush for balance.

"Three minutes, forty-two seconds." Wash slid the watch back into his pocket and gave a single, mocking clap.

Cal exhaled and brushed the grit off of his hands. "You fix everything else, how come you don't fix the band on that watch?"

Wash shrugged. "I meant to, but now I'm used to it. And sometimes I don't want to know the time. Now, are you gonna finish that story?"

"So Dusty saw Blue going up to a little shack in the woods. Said there was clothes hanging out on a line in the sunniest spot there was. And there was flowers, too, planted neat in old oil cans that somebody'd split in two. And then when Blue went to open the door, Dusty saw a white woman in a raggedy dress come out and give Blue a kiss."

Wash felt a sudden coldness between his shoulder blades, a tightening in his groin. He could feel the pull of the story, its inevitable downward turn.

"Thanks to Dusty's big mouth, the talk went around that Blue had him a white woman hid up in them woods, but nobody knew if it was true. They'd never seen her and couldn't really count on what Dusty said since he was just a kid. Some folks said she wasn't white, just looked it from afar. Said how in Louisiana a lot more mixing happened during the slave days."

"So they let them alone and then the two of them took off for someplace else? If that ain't the ending, I don't want to know any more," Wash said.

"Black folk didn't like it much, but the white folks . . ." Cal shook his head and paused. "You too sissy for the rest?"

"Tell the damn story, you little shit." Wash swatted Cal's arm.

Cal jumped back. "No telling how the white folks caught wind of what was happening. But one way or another, a crew of old loggers and some of the roughnecks who came with Pop Joiner, they all decided they'd ride out in their sheets and pay Blue a visit. Some say it was Tall Man that left the tracks they followed, others said Blue himself was careless. Anyway, I guess the gal looked white to the whites, and that was enough to get Blue hung by the tree in front of his house with his balls stuffed in his own mouth."

"Jesus," Wash breathed.

"Tall found Blue. SueSue said some of the folks over in Kilgore still have the photos they sold down at Longhorn Drugs. Souvenirs."

Wash felt the story lodge in his gut.

"Well," Cal said. "We almost there?"

"Just about." Wash swallowed hard, then tried to smile. "Better start pretending you're a hard worker. It's just over that rise. And hurry up. We don't get out there before every other black fool, we'll be out of luck."

NAOMI Naomi braced herself back against the seat. Henry drove fast and then faster, a grin plastered across his face.

When the truck hit a bump, Cari and Beto flew up off the bench. They stayed standing, bouncing with excitement and the rough road.

Naomi yanked them back down.

"Aw, let them have a little fun," Henry said. "Just stay out of the way of the gear shift, and it don't matter."

"Slow down a little, please," Naomi said.

Henry shook his head like a dog, then raised a mud-splattered arm and whooped, "Black gold ahead!"

"The twins didn't have dinner." Naomi had been laying food on the table when he'd burst into the kitchen calling them all out to the truck.

"Never mind that. Once the oil comes in, the place'll be crawling with folks. Somebody always sets up a stand to sell burgers. Well's gonna come in any minute now. Salter didn't believe me, but I knew that was the spot."

Naomi seethed. Almost everybody at school and church and around town had some connection to the oil field, and when there was nothing else to talk about, people would start in on stories of things that had gone wrong. Boiler explosions, well fires, men slipping into the tanks they were cleaning, sinkholes that opened up right under the happy spectators who came to celebrate a new find. All she could think of was the risk—and how willing Henry was to put Cari and Beto in the middle of it.

"Hope we make it in time," Henry was saying. "It's like nothing else you'll ever see. Loud as heck, too, when that oil comes up. Might want to plug your ears."

Henry swerved suddenly to the left, steering the truck down a rutted side road. The headlamps pierced the gathering darkness.

Some creature dropped straight down in front of the truck. Naomi gasped.

"Do you think we hit it?" Beto whispered, looking at Cari.

She shrugged.

Soon they had to slow down because trucks were parked bumper-to-bumper up and down the side of the narrow dirt road. Naomi thought Henry would park there, too, but he kept driving. "We park up front. There's one bonus from being the derrick hand who's a slave to these old rigs."

There was light at the end of the road, and they pulled into a bull-dozed clearing. Henry double-parked beside one of the company trucks and threw his door open.

The twins piled out behind him before Naomi had even opened her door. She stepped down from the truck and slammed the door.

"Carrie, Robbie!" Henry was halfway to the rig, but he stopped to call back to them. "You stay right there with Naomi, don't go no further. I tell you to drop back, you'd better listen fast. And mind your sister, you hear?"

So now they were supposed to obey her; at least there was that.

Naomi studied the scene from the outside in. Men smoked at the edges of the clearing, waiting to see how big the strike might be. Most of them wore oil field gear and had probably been tipped off by rig workers who'd gone back to the yard. But ordinary people were arriving, too. Seeing some rich man get a little richer was something, and there wasn't much else to do in East Texas on a Saturday night. Folks wandered around the clearing. It was packed red clay, scraped clean of trees and grass. Spotlights shone on the drilling machinery. Workers hurried around the base of the derrick.

The oil derricks were everywhere in East Texas. Most of the derricks were leftovers, Henry said. It wasn't worth the trouble to break them down when wood was so plentiful and cheap that you could just build new ones. So the odd towers of crisscrossed boards dotted the landscape, taller than most trees but not near as pretty.

Naomi hugged herself tight and wished she'd brought a sweater. "Are you two cold?" she called up to the twins. They were squatting right at the halfway point where Henry had told them to stop, watching the men working.

"No!" they shouted together.

Naomi could feel the hair begin to stand up on her arms with the cold.

"Here." A heavy jacket settled onto her shoulders. She turned quickly and saw Gilbert Harris from church. He was a year older than she was and had already graduated. Like just about all the men and even some of the boys from school, he worked in the oil field.

"Oh—well, thanks," Naomi managed. She thought about giving the jacket back, but the warmth was too welcome to deny.

"You were shivering so hard, looked like you might end up digging a hole to China." He toed the ground with his boot. "This one's definitely coming in soon," he said.

"Do you work on this rig?"

Gilbert shook his head. "Nah, no such luck. I do whatever needs doing. If the pumper's out sick, I hook up sucker rods to pumpjacks. On a rig, I can fill in as lead tong hand. But mostly I'm stuck being a tank cleaner. Got to work my way up."

Naomi shifted from one foot to another. Tommie Kinnebrew had introduced her to Gilbert one Sunday after church, and he'd said hello to her a few times. Other than that she'd never spoken to him.

"Too bad about the trees." She nodded at the bald expanse in front of them. She scanned it and spotted Cari and Beto talking with a few kids from their class.

Gilbert laughed. "It's not like we're going to run out. Those pines grow up like weeds, don't you worry. Hey," he touched her arm lightly, "you can smell the oil."

Naomi sniffed, but all she could smell was the tang of cologne mixed with sweat coming off of the letterman jacket.

"A little like the ocean, a little like gasoline," Gilbert said. "That's oil for sure."

The twins noticed the smell, too, lifting their noses like hunting dogs catching a scent. "It's coming from over there!" Beto shouted, pointing toward the rig.

Beto was running toward the rig before Naomi could call him back. A moment later, a black geyser exploded through the wooden frame of the derrick. It was too loud for him to hear her screams.

She started to run, but Gilbert was faster, shouting something over his shoulder as he charged after Beto. Naomi grabbed Cari. She could feel her little sister's heart pounding through her rib cage.

Gilbert scooped up Beto and ran back with him under his arm like a football. Behind them, the oil sprayed a hundred feet in the air. It splashed down in a sudden, black lake. Most of the workers had gotten back from the rig in time, but a few men were covered.

"Thank you!" Naomi shouted when Gilbert plopped Beto down in front of her. She hugged Beto tight then bent him over her knee right there and gave him a spanking to remember.

◊ ◊ ◊

For the next three hours, the crowd of spectators grew. There was a hamburger stand just like Henry had predicted, and Mr. Turner from the grocery store brought a truck with candy, pickles, and sausages on sticks. Naomi made sure to keep her distance, but when Gilbert offered Hershey bars to the twins, Naomi nodded to Cari, who took his dime and got in line.

Beto started to protest, but Naomi shook her head and tightened her grip on his shoulder.

"Little oil tycoon," Gilbert teased Beto. "Couldn't wait to get your hands on that black gold?" He nudged Naomi and pointed in the direction of a shiny maroon Packard Eight coming down the road toward them. "Speaking of tycoons, look over there. That's got to be Mr. Gibbler. Zane Gibbler's the only one in East Texas with a car like that. This is his land, so I reckon he wants to see how he's going to make out. He's got more deals with the oil companies than anybody else around."

They watched as the sleek car pulled past all the mud-splattered trucks and inched forward into the crowd, which parted quickly to make way.

"He don't like walking much," Gilbert said.

The car slowed to a stop near the rig. An older black man got out of the front seat and opened the back door. A moment later, a pair of polished cowboy boots appeared, followed by a mountain of a man dressed in a suit and ten-gallon hat. His clothes were expensive, but his enormous belly strained against the buttons of his shirt. A man in khakis ran to meet him.

Cari ran over with the chocolate bars. "Who's that?" she asked, turning her face up to Gilbert.

"That's the man who owns this land. The other guy's the tool pusher," Gilbert said. "He's in charge of the whole operation."

A second pair of legs appeared beneath the Packard's door, and a moment later, Miranda was upon them. She laid a freckled hand on Gilbert's arm. "Hey, Sneaks!" she giggled. She hugged him.

Gilbert carefully freed himself from her arms. "Didn't know you'd be here, Miranda. Usually it's just your pa."

She shrugged and twirled her blond hair around a finger. "Me and Daddy were eating at the Hilltop Restaurant over in Tyler when he got word of the strike. He didn't want to lose a minute, so that's how I ended up coming along. But, hey, what luck. I get to see you. It's been ages!" She looked up at him through curled eyelashes.

"Workin' man now," he said, slipping his hands into his pockets.

"Oh, my. Why, Naomi!" Miranda took a step back in mock surprise. "Gosh, it's so dark over here, I didn't even see you. You just blended right in with the night." She pasted on a stiff smile. "Sneaks, have you been holding out on me? I didn't know you knew our new neighbor."

"Church," he said. "We both go to—"

"By the way," Miranda interrupted, "Sneaks is Gilbert's nickname. What his friends call him."

"Actually—" he began.

"That jacket's a little big on you, isn't it?" Miranda said, taking a step closer to Naomi and plucking the sleeve of Gilbert's jacket between index finger and thumb. "But you probably don't have one of your own. Or did you leave yours down in Mex-i-co?"

Naomi opened her mouth, but nothing came out.

"Whoa, Emmie," Gilbert said. "We're all friends here." He laid an arm around Naomi. She stiffened, shrugging it off.

"I *bet* you're friendly. Say, what happened to you playing ball for Kilgore College?"

"You know what, Em." Gilbert's shoulders sagged.

Just then, Naomi saw Tommie walking up from the road with her cousins Katie and Jean. Not as good as disappearing into the dark woods, but a clear escape.

"Excuse us, please." Naomi did not look at Miranda but shrugged off the jacket and handed it back to Gilbert. "Thanks," she said.

"Keep it as long as you want," Gilbert said, pushing the jacket back toward her.

She backed away. "That's okay."

As Naomi turned and hurried the twins toward Tommie, she heard Miranda say, "Better clean that jacket good, Sneaks." Her high, false laughter filled the air.

◇ ◇ ◇

"Hey," Tommie said. She gave Naomi a quick hug. "Gilbert Harris, huh?" Tommie raised her eyebrows but waited to say more until Cari ran to join Katie, Jean, and a group of other kids.

"I saw you, but I didn't want to interrupt," said Tommie.

"You should have come over. I was dying to get away," Naomi said.

"From Gilbert? Why? He's the handsomest boy in church."

"Come on, Tommie—"

"Those blue eyes, that button in his chin just asking for somebody to kiss it . . ." Tommie gave a sigh.

"Yuck," Beto said.

"Oh," Tommie looked down, noticing him standing behind Naomi for the first time. "Didn't realize you were there. Why don't you go play with the other kids?"

"Can't," he mumbled.

Naomi swatted Beto's bottom to refresh the memory of the spanking. "You can go on and play for a while, but you'd better stay where I can see you or else you're going to be holding my hand next."

Beto nodded and ran.

"Miranda's green with it, you know," Tommie said.

"With what?"

"Jealousy, silly. I heard she liked Gilbert a lot and was after him last year when he was the star quarterback. If he liked her back, I don't know, but her dad cornered Gil and said he'd never be good enough for her, and if he ever wanted a job with any oil company in East Texas, he'd better keep his hands to himself. To show he was serious, Mr. Gibbler even got the president at Kilgore College to take away Gil's football scholarship."

"That's some kind of mean."

"At least her life isn't absolutely perfect. Otherwise she'd be even more unbearable. Hey," Tommie glanced over her shoulder, "listen, I need to get over there and help my cousin Franklin mix a little. He's visiting from Oklahoma. I told him he was lucky that a well came in tonight. Otherwise, we'd be stuck playing dominoes with my parents." She grabbed Naomi's elbow. "Come with me. We've got some blankets."

By the time the well was tapped, the twins were asleep in the bed of someone's truck, wrapped in borrowed blankets and snuggled in tight as puppies alongside Katie and Jean. When Henry gave Naomi the nod and motioned toward the road, she gave her blanket back to Tommie and tugged Cari and Beto out of the pile. She led them, still half-asleep, back to Henry's truck.

◇ ◇ ◇

Naomi perched on the toilet, feet pressed against the stall door, in the girls' room by the gym. All week, in every class she shared with Miranda, Naomi paid for being seen in Gilbert's jacket. On top of the meanness of Miranda's words and of her friends' laughter, there was the shame she felt at her heavy tongue and the embarrassment of the other students' pity. A dozen times a day, she thought about walking out of the school and never coming back. Henry would not care. But there was her promise to Abuelito, and the twins to look after, and also the unbearable notion of spending her days in Henry's house.

What she wanted now was her tree in the woods. But the bathroom was easier to explain. All she had had to say was "Lady problems," and a male teacher wouldn't ask any more questions. She'd learned that trick from Miranda and her friends.

She'd picked the gym bathroom because it was far from the classrooms and there were no P.E. classes after lunch, but it turned out to be a bad choice. Only a minute after she'd arrived in search of solitude, PTA mothers poured in after some meeting.

Naomi watched the feet of the women as they crowded around the mirror. Snatches of overlapping conversations washed around her. Fundraisers and dance classes. Choir outfits. Cigarette brands and casserole recipes and the best way to get a Jell-O salad out of a mold. Finally the last ladies walked out. Naomi was about to slip out of her stall when two more women pushed through the door.

One wore black oxfords. The other had on stylish pale blue pumps.

"Smart as can be," a husky voice, the one that went with the blue pumps, pronounced. "I heard Max's teacher say they read better than half the senior class. And them only in third grade."

The woman in the black oxfords laughed shrilly. "Nothing like my kids. You'd have to hide a quarter in a book to get them to open it. You know, the other day I went into Miss Bell's room and saw the boy reading an encyclopedia, of all things."

"And her curls, doesn't she make you think of—"

"Shirley Temple!" They spoke the words at the same time, then laughed some more.

"Adorable. But the older sister . . . Can that really be their sister?" That was Blue Pumps.

"Dark. And sneaky-like." The woman in the oxfords clucked her tongue. "Maybe a little retarded. A lot of those Mexicans are."

"She might be slow when it comes to books, but have you noticed how she walks?" asked Black Oxfords, lowering her voice. "A girl like that can be fast in other areas of life, you know."

"Runs in the blood." Blue Pumps coughed, then made a kissing sound at the mirror. "Is my lipstick on straight?" A moment later, she added, "You can just tell that she wants the boys to look. Did you see that thin little dress she was wearing the other night out at the oil strike? You could see what Gilbert Harris had on his mind."

"I had a son, I'd be watching him like a hawk around a girl like her."

"Mm-hmm." Blue Pumps began to walk toward the door. "Michael and I took a train all the way down to Brownsville once, and do you know that there were Mexicans not even thirteen years old waddling around big-bellied?"

"Can't help it, maybe." Black Oxfords followed Blue Pumps to the door. "That kind will follow their animal urges."

Blue Pumps laughed, and then they were gone.

Naomi stayed a long time in the stall, working her fingers through the tail of her braid, fighting to get free of their words.

NAOMI   On Saturday, Naomi woke up hungry for the river before the sun was even up. In the gray morning light she saw the twins snuggled together in Beto's bed. Beto was burrowed into the pillow. Cari was sleeping on her side, snoring a little. The corner of her mouth glistened with drool.

Naomi slipped on her dress and shoes and tiptoed into the bathroom. After she cleaned her teeth, she surveyed what she had on hand in the kitchen for breakfast. It was barely six; she couldn't imagine that Wash would be down by the river yet. Since Henry had started playing Daddy, Naomi had seen Wash almost every weekend.

She got out Muffy's recipe for sweet rolls and started the dough. For once she wanted to be the one to spoil the twins a little. Last week Henry had taken them to Henderson to see *Camille*, the movie everyone at school was talking about. When he brought it up, Naomi had felt torn between her desire to stay away from Henry and her interest in seeing the film that, according to Tommie, would make anybody with a heart cry. In the end, though, she didn't get to decide. "You've probably got heaps to do around here," Henry had said. "We'll stay out of your hair for a while." And then he and the twins were out the door.

While the rolls were rising, Naomi cleaned the living room and did every chore she could without causing a racket. After half an hour, she shaped the dough, pressed it into cinnamon, and slid the rolls into the hot oven. It didn't take long to wipe up the kitchen, and she found herself looking over her school things for what might interest Wash. She pulled out her last science assignment. It was marked with a B+, the best grade she'd ever gotten. Maybe she would show it to him.

As soon as the rolls were done, Naomi wrapped four in a napkin, scribbled a note about going over to Tommie's, and headed out the door with her books.

WASH Wash got to the end of the path just in time to see her smile. He pulled the collar of his jacket up and headed toward her.

"Studying?" he called.

She looked up. Her dark eyes were flecked with points of reflected light. "I thought you might come." She handed him one of the rolls. He finished it in two bites and reached for another. He'd skipped out on seconds at breakfast because he hadn't wanted to miss the chance to see her.

"Thanks. You make sweets like this for your sweethearts?" he asked.

"Sweethearts?" She squinted at him. "You see any Mexican boys around here?"

He shrugged. "Maybe back in San Antonio."

"No," she said. "What do you do for your sweethearts?"

"Don't have one at the moment, but I'm hoping that might change." He winked.

A look he couldn't read crossed her face. Or maybe it was just a change in the light. Clouds were rolling in and threatening rain.

They didn't have long to read before raindrops began to prick the surface of the water. Wash scrambled to gather up the books. "Dang it,

I don't have my bag." He yanked off his jacket and wrapped the books up inside.

She took the books back from him and shook his jacket free. "It's fine," she called over her shoulder as she ran up the bank. "Maybe I'll see you next week."

He reached down to find his pencil. When he went to follow her up the path, she was already gone. He scanned the branches of the trees along the path, thinking maybe she'd climbed a tree, but he didn't find her.

WASH Wash steered the twins toward a sunny spot just beyond the shade of the magnolia tree in front of his house. "Wait here," he told them.

As he ran up the porch steps, he could hear them whispering about the big shade trees, the cushiony grass, his mother's tidy azalea bushes. His folks kept the place looking good. None of the built-in-a-hurry houses in the oil field camps had trees or anything like a proper yard. Against all those drab company rentals, the Fuller house probably looked like an illustration for "home sweet home."

Wash closed the screen door gingerly behind him. The pie baking was only about half done, but his mother was not in the kitchen. Someone was playing the piano in the parlor. It was far too graceful for Peggy to be at the keyboard. He peeked into the living room and saw that it was their neighbor Fannie. The bathroom door was closed, which meant he had only a moment before his mother would be back in the kitchen.

He selected three pies from the cooling racks lined with newspaper. Pineapple, apple, and rum raisin. He held them in a careful stack in his right hand and then hurried back out the door.

Wash finished his pie in four bites. He cocked an eyebrow at the twins, who nibbled at the crimped edge of the pies with a look of determined caution. "Y'all are makin' me tired," Wash said. "If you don't eat 'em, I will."

"Amazing Grace" floated out to them through the screen door.

"You hear Miss Fannie playing the piano? She's the best piano player in Egypt Town, second to my mama."

"It's pretty," Beto said.

"I like the pie," Cari said. "Pineapple's better than rum raisin."

"How do you figure?" Wash asked. "I don't remember letting you try mine."

"I just know it," she said. She licked the bright gold filling from the edge of her pie.

"She's blind, you know," Wash said.

Beto's eyes widened. "Your mother's blind? And she can make pies like this?"

"Not my ma. Miss Fannie." He told them how Fannie had gone blind when she was five but his mother had taught her to play anyway.

Cari finished her pie and started in on Beto's. He didn't seem to notice; he had a troubled look.

"It's all right, Beto," Wash said. "Fannie's all right. We look out for her. Here in a minute, I'll walk her home."

When Wash went into the kitchen to see about some milk, his mother came out of the parlor with her arms crossed.

"Does Fannie need walking home?" he asked her.

His mother shook her head. "Not yet. Now you tell me something. Are your guests paying? I'm not giving pies away here."

"They're just kids, Mama."

"Don't 'Mama' me. These pies are for selling. If I wanted to give them away, I could find plenty of hungry black folks. I got enough trouble keeping you and Peggy and Cal from eating them all up, and now you want to bring even more mouths around."

"Sorry, Mama," Wash said. Sometimes the only way to get his mother out of a bad mood was to let her wind it down herself.

"What are you doing with those white children anyway, James Washington?"

Wash shrugged. "Their people asked could I take 'em fishing. And, hey, they helped me catch six nice trout earlier today. I'll clean them up for you here in a minute." He crossed to the icebox and pulled out a jar of milk.

"You put that back, young man," she said.

"The kids are thirsty."

"There's a water pump in the side yard."

Wash held on to the milk and grinned. "Nothing better than milk for growing strong bones and quenching the thirst after a famous Fuller pie. And you know old Betsy and Brenda give us more than we can drink anyhow. What about a broken pie to go with it? Maybe cherry?"

"You see any broken pies?"

"Sure." He grabbed one and split it in two. "Right there."

"You owe Booker another nickel," she said, wagging a finger at him.

"That Booker, he greedy." Wash grinned.

"Watch your English. You sound like a field hand."

"Thanks for the pies."

"You still owe Booker," she said again.

"Yes, ma'am, I do."

◇ ◇ ◇

Wash and the twins shared the last pie and the milk. Fannie was still playing when Rhoda came out onto the porch with her hands on her hips. Wash leaned over and told the twins, "She looks mean, but she isn't. Say thank you and you might see her smile."

They called out, "Thank you much, Mrs. Fuller!"

Wash studied his mother's face and saw that she couldn't resist their manners. "You're welcome," she said.

Then her expression turned sour. Wash followed her gaze to the back garden. Half a dozen crows were pecking around her potatoes and winter vegetables.

"Shoo!" she hollered, running toward the birds. "Go on!"

The crows retreated to the trees at the edge of the yard, cocking their heads silently, waiting.

She turned back and marched over to where Wash and the twins were. "Next time you all come around eating my pies up, I'm going to put you to work standing in my garden keeping the crows away, you hear? Or else build me a scarecrow, and then you can have all the pies you want!"

"Yes, ma'am!" Cari and Beto said together. They hugged Wash goodbye and tore off down the road.

NAOMI Even after the twins had gone, Naomi kept watching from the woods. She watched Wash carry the empty bottle of milk to the porch. She watched him pull a few weeds from the flower beds. And she watched him go into the house and come out a minute later with a pretty girl on his arm. Her glossy hair was bobbed and tied neatly with a pink ribbon that matched the dress she wore under a pretty white coat. On the way down the steps, Wash steadied her as if she were a fragile package he did not want to break. Her perfect white teeth showed when she laughed, which was often.

Naomi stood frozen. Her mind churned. Was this what he had meant when he spoke of sweethearts? No, she hadn't imagined everything by the river. She knew she hadn't. But there was also the fact of the girls at Mason's. One of them had said his name like it was all the explanation anyone needed. Was this the same girl? She hadn't gotten a good look before.

Wash walked the girl out of the yard and down the road away from the house. She could hear their laughter and wondered if he was telling that girl the same jokes he'd told down by the river.

Once they were gone, Naomi tore down the path into the woods, trying to outrun the sob that was caught in her throat. And without remembering the steps in between or the light in the woods or the sound of the river, Naomi found herself at the back steps of Henry's house. Dinner, that was what she was going to think about. In the kitchen, she hacked at a chunk of ham with a knife and brutalized an onion.

When Beto asked her what was wrong, she told him to hush and wash his hands. And even when his eyes went wet with hurt and worry, she could not summon any kindness. The part of her charged with feeling was too bruised to give or receive such gifts.

NOVEMBER 1936

HENRY Henry recoiled from the sweet-sick smell. On the porch, his only thought had been to get his boots off, wash up, and toss himself into bed like he always did after an all-night shift. Now he wanted to run.

But Naomi was already calling. "Back here!"

As he walked down the hall, the stench grew stronger. He gulped air and then pushed the door to the bedroom open. The twins were curled up on the double bed on towels spread over a spare sheet. From the pile on the floor, it looked as though they'd already soiled the other bedclothes.

Naomi wiped their faces down with a damp rag.

Henry stepped cautiously into the room.

"Hi, Daddy," Cari said. Then she lurched forward and vomited. Somehow, Naomi managed to catch it in a bowl. She set the bowl on top of the dresser and then began to clean Cari again. Henry felt a gag rise in his throat.

"I'll . . . I'll go get Muff . . ." he stammered, taking a step back.

Naomi shook her head. "She's pregnant—can't get her sick."

"A doctor, then."

"No need. It's just a stomach bug. It'll pass in a couple of days."

"Days?" Henry groaned.

"Set these on the back porch?" Naomi asked. "I'll start washing as soon as I get these two settled." She didn't give him time to respond, just scooped the mess of linens from the floor and shoved them into his arms.

Some of the stink was coming from there. He flinched, sure a glob of vomit had grazed his hand. The sheets dropped to the floor. He stared down at them like they were a tangle of rattlesnakes.

Naomi sighed. "Never mind. Maybe you could buy some crackers and ginger ale?"

"Crackers," he mumbled. "Ginger ale." And he stumbled down the hall and headed for his truck.

◊ ◊ ◊

At Turner's, he stood in front of a shelf of crackers, baffled by the variety. "Mr. Smith! Haven't seen you in a while," the pimply clerk called. Then he went back to totaling an order for a gaunt housewife.

"So," Mrs. Turner said, walking over. "What can I get for you? We've missed your business around here."

"Oh, you've still got it," he said absently. He studied the boxes on the shelf. Nabisco. Ritz. Richmond. "You don't happen to know what kind of crackers I should buy for stomach trouble?" He gestured at the shelf. "Kids are sick."

"Kids! You *have* been busy," Mrs. Turner said.

"I'm sure you've seen 'em here. The two younger ones are mine. The older one's a stepdaughter. Used to live . . . with some family in San Antonio." He scratched at his chin.

Mrs. Turner frowned. "The older girl, what's she look like?"

He hesitated, not sure how to put it. "Pretty. Long dark hair in a braid. Real serious."

A look of recognition passed over Mrs. Turner's face, but Henry did not notice. "Kids got the grippe?" she asked.

Henry nodded.

"Then these—" she picked up a box of plain saltines— "are probably the best bet."

"Thank you," Henry said, relieved.

"She don't shop here, you know," she said.

"Pardon?" Henry was already pulling two bottles of ginger ale from the cooler by the door.

"The girl. I think she come in once some time back, but you know . . . you know how Amos is. We didn't realize she was kin of yours. Sorry about that. I can talk to him. If she wants to come back in, I mean."

Henry nodded, paid for the food, and then drove back up the road toward the Humble houses. Later he would wonder: if Naomi wasn't shopping at Turner's, then where was she getting the groceries? But for the moment, he was busy trying to figure out how he would get away from the house.

He parked in front of Bud and Muff's place to keep Naomi from hearing him pull up in the truck. He eased open the kitchen door and set the ginger ale and crackers down on the table as noiselessly as he could manage. He could hear Naomi talking to the twins in their bedroom, but he did not call out to them.

He drove back along the highway toward the church, already laying down a bargain: if Pastor Tom's car was there, then he would stop in and talk to him.

He slowed alongside the white frame building and studied the emptiness in front of it carefully. No Pastor Tom. And as soon as the deal was struck, Henry knew that he had hoped all along that he wouldn't find him.

Rusk County was dry, so he'd have to drive over to a bar in Kilgore. He hadn't been to Big T's in months, but he knew the way well enough.

NAOMI Naomi did hear the truck pull into the driveway seven hours later, the second time Henry came home. She was sitting at the kitchen table finishing up the schoolwork Tommie had brought by for her. She stiffened at the sound of his footsteps on the back porch and glanced at the clock. Nine at night.

Henry came in. He set his hat on the table and stood waiting.

Naomi stared at the hat. It looked like something a dog had chewed on and abandoned.

"How are they?" he asked finally.

Her eyes flitted to him—he was wiping his mouth with the back of one hand—and then back to the hat.

"Fine," she said tightly, "still sleeping." She crossed her arms.

"Brought something," he said. He pulled a package out from under his arm and placed it on the table in front of her. "Go on and open it."

She loosened the string and unfolded the brown paper from a small radio.

"It's a mantle radio, see," Henry said, "but we'll just put it on the little table by the window. There's still an antenna outside from the folks before us."

She nodded but did not say anything.

He shifted from one foot to the other. "Maybe it'll keep the twins occupied while they're recovering. Make the time go faster for you, too, when you're cooking or whatnot." When she still didn't answer, he picked it up and started toward the living room. "Come on," he said over his shoulder. "Let's give it a whirl."

There was a patter of footsteps from the bedroom, and then the twins were running after Henry.

Naomi shot up from the table. "Back to bed," she ordered.

"Aw, let 'em," Henry called.

Naomi's jaw clenched, but she swallowed her words and walked down the hall.

Beto and Cari scurried into the living room, each wearing one of Henry's work shirts. Henry shot a questioning look at Naomi.

"Out of clean clothes," she said as she came into the room.

Beto stood a step from his father and ran his finger over the front panel of the radio. "Emerson Model 25A." Naomi could see he was pleased.

"Now we can all can relax and have some wholesome entertainment, see?" Henry said.

"Pastor Tom said that listening to the radio can interfere with Bible reading," Cari said primly.

"Christ, Pastor don't know everything," Henry scowled. "Don't you want to hear *Little Orphan Annie*? Or the Light Crust Doughboys? Or baseball games?"

Now that he mentioned it, they did. They sat on the floor, ready to listen.

Henry connected the antenna wire, plugged the radio in, and fiddled with the knobs. Nothing happened. "Well," Henry hesitated. "Maybe it needs some tuning up."

The twins' faces fell.

"I'll get it working, you'll see," Henry said. "How different can it be from fixing a rig? I just need my tools."

When he passed Naomi on his way to the kitchen, she thought she smelled whiskey and beer. A combination she knew he favored. She closed her eyes against the memories.

HENRY Henry came back into the living room with his tools. The guy he'd bought the radio from said he was selling it cheap on account of him moving to an oil field in Oklahoma and not wanting more stuff to haul. Henry had been too flush with goodwill at the bar to think about needing to test that it worked.

Now he took off the radio's back cover, revealing a tangle of tubes and wires. He prodded them tentatively. He wasn't going to let that sly Okie get the better of him. He worked at the radio, tested it, fiddled some more. He looked up in triumph when he got a staticky hum.

Naomi sat with a schoolbook open on her lap, a twin asleep on either side of her. The boy had a hand on her braid, and in a flash Henry remembered how Naomi had sometimes slept like that against Estella.

"Got it," he said, grinning.

Naomi held a finger against her lips and nodded at the sleeping twins. "Tomorrow," she mouthed.

Henry scowled. "I stay up late fixing this for y'all, and all you can say is 'tomorrow'? Tonight, damn it." He turned the tuning knob until he found music and then turned up the volume.

He grinned at the twins when they jolted awake. "See?" he said.

For a moment, it was just how he had dreamed it could be: Beto smiling, Cari's eyes full of wonder. Maybe Naomi was still silent and stern, but he imagined she was happy in her own way. She looked brighter and healthier here than she had when he took them from that grimy hole in San Antonio. And Henry was at the center of it all. A provider, a good father, a man that Pastor Tom would be proud of. So what if he'd had a setback earlier. He could hold it together for his family.

"How about that?" he called over the music. "Looks like your pa can fix more than busted pumpjacks and jammed rigs after all."

Naomi prodded each of them with an elbow.

"Thank you, Daddy," Beto said.

"Hooray, thanks," Cari said.

"It's lovely," Naomi added, and she even smiled a little.

Her words were hardly out—and the song had not yet finished—when there was a loud pop and a sudden silence.

"Come on!" Henry barked. He yanked at the knob. "Darn thing went and broke on me again." He tugged on his ear and glued his eyes to the radio as if assessing it. He didn't want to see disappointment on the twins' faces.

"I bet you can fix it again," Beto said.

"Maybe tomorrow," Henry said.

Cari hopped down from the couch and muttered something in Beto's direction.

"What was that?" Henry asked.

"Hush now," Naomi said.

Cari ignored her and walked over to Henry. "I said, what we really wanted was a cat." She gave him a nasty smile. "Daddy."

Henry's face went dark.

"*Derecho a la cama*," Naomi hissed at the twins, and they hurried down the hall. The bedsprings squeaked as they climbed into bed.

Henry sat in the cane-back chair with his fists knotted over his knees. He wanted to take the radio back and shove it up that smirking Okie's ass.

"I'm sorry," Naomi said. "They're only children. You can't expect—"

"I just want it to work, damn it!"

"We did fine without one before."

"Not the damn radio," Henry spat. "This—" He swept his hands around the room. "All this."

And then he was up out of the chair. He started pitching his tools back into the toolbox. Tomorrow, he would fix it right. He turned to say as much to Naomi, and then he saw it. Her pity. He couldn't stand it. The pliers flew out of his hands and cracked against the window frame a few feet from her.

Henry left the rest of his tools and stalked out of the house without another word, pausing only to jam his hat onto his head.

NAOMI Naomi kept the kids home from school the next day. Beto still had a fever, and Cari threw up once. While they slept, Naomi listened for Henry's truck, but he did not return.

She was out taking down the wash from the line when she saw Wash come ambling up the road. He had two strings of fish in his left hand. She hesitated. She could run for the house and shut the door, but she knew he'd seen her. She wouldn't give him the satisfaction. She carefully unpinned the clothes and laid them into her laundry basket.

"Missed my fishing buddies today," he called when he came into the yard.

"They're sick," she said without turning to face him. She threw her braid over her shoulder and reached down to resettle a sheet in her basket.

"Puking and such?"

"Yes," she said. She kept her back to him and went down the line, yanking the last clothespins off one by one.

"I haven't seen you down by the river in a while," he said, ducking under some shirts so that he was facing her again. "No time for school-work? Too cold?"

"I've got my hands full," she snapped.

"I didn't mean—" Wash took a small step back.

"Anyway," she interrupted, "I'm sure you have plenty of other friends to spend your time with. Excuse me." She shoved past him and pushed the laundry basket onto the porch. "I've got the twins to deal with."

"At least take some fish," he called. "Caught more than we can eat."

Her "no" was already forming when she considered the fact that Henry hadn't left behind any money for groceries. "All right," she said flatly. She reached out for the smaller of the two strings, being careful not to brush his hand with hers.

"I can clean 'em for you if you lend me a basin," he said.

"I'll manage," she said.

"Tell the twins I said hi."

"Good night," she said.

Inside, she dropped the fish into the sink and grabbed a knife. She slotted it into the side of one of the bass, but she went too deep. Thick red blood sluiced out into the sink and over her fingers. For a moment, she thought of her mother's hand, reaching out to her after the last miscarriage. She rinsed away the blood and tried again. She forced her trembling fingers to hold the slick side of the fish, and she covered its face with her arm. She kept thinking, flesh, flesh, flesh. Still, she worked on, clumsily at first, until she had fileted all four fish. She felt that she'd proven something to Wash.

As she breaded the fish, she seethed at the thought of Henry's little stunt. Under different circumstances, being rid of him for a while would be a boon, but now she'd been forced to accept Wash's charity again. She'd already had to ask Mr. Mason for credit just to fix some chicken soup for the twins. In a day or two, they'd be out of staples, and if she borrowed from Muff, she'd have to give an explanation. How long could they live on eggs and the scraps left in the pantry? She couldn't use the emergency money; they might need it more later.

If Henry didn't return by Friday, she would do something. She could ask Tommie if they could rent the spare bedroom in their house. She could keep the kids in school and sew full time, make enough to get by without Henry's help. And if Tommie's folks said no? She'd write to Abuelito and explain that they needed to come home. She'd check the price of train tickets or see if one of their uncles could drive out to get them. In time, the twins would come to understand. Before long they would forget East Texas had ever happened to the three of them.

HENRY Henry awoke to a face full of brown river water. He gagged and fought to clear his nostrils. He clawed his way up the shallows and wiped the mud from his eyes.

Near his face was a familiar pair of boots.

Pastor Tom scowled down at Henry. "You thinking on your baptism now?"

"Jesus!" Henry spluttered, already scrambling for the river's edge. The last thing he remembered was closing his eyes in his truck and pulling his hat down over his face.

"Well, you old sinner?"

"Geez, yes, I was just—I only meant to—"

"Save your excuses and answer me straight. You been here asleep on the riverbank all night?"

"Yeah." Henry looked away from the preacher and pulled off his sopping work boots. He stood with his wet socks glued to the sandy mud.

"You still working?"

"Yeah."

"You been to the bars?" Pastor Tom asked. When Henry didn't answer, the preacher snapped his fingers and repeated his question.

"Come on, you know I have." Henry studied an old loblolly pine that towered behind Pastor Tom.

"And why didn't you go home?"

Henry shrugged, less out of indifference than shame. "I've got this thing about puke, see, can't stand it. The kids were sick, and . . ."

"You left 'em? You think Jesus would've done you like that? Left you when you was sick? What else? What more'd you do, you stinking sinner?"

"I might've threw somethin'," Henry mumbled. He was shivering now. November fingered its way into his bones.

"You hit them?"

"Naw, I didn't. Just chucked some pliers at the wall. Not mad at them, more mad at myself, but . . ."

"And for that you took off like you didn't have a darn care in the world, just an old bachelor who could blow his pay on spirits over at Big T's. Am I right?"

"Reckon so."

"You gonna make it up to your kids, and to Naomi, too?" Tom gave Henry a push up the slope, toward his truck.

"I s'pose I got to."

"Come on, then. I'll get the missus to wash your clothes. You can dry out at our house and figure out how you're going to put this right, the way Jesus would. I didn't baptize you to see you go down the backslider's path, Henry Smith." Pastor Tom held out his hand. "Give me your keys."

NAOMI   Naomi was frying doughnuts when she glanced up and locked eyes with Pastor Tom's on the other side of the kitchen window. She started. Hot oil sloshed over the side of the skillet and onto the skin of her right arm. She jumped back, trembling. "*Ay, madre de Dios*," she gasped. Sweat beaded across her forehead. Tears sprang to her eyes.

Pastor Tom pushed through the screen door. "Oh, sister," he said, his voice high and strained. "Do you have any butter for that burn?"

"Cold water," Beto said. He and Cari had come running from the bedroom when they heard the door.

"What?" Pastor Tom asked.

"That's the safest thing. I read so in *Boys' Life*. Just keep running cold water over the burned part."

Cari nodded solemnly, taking Naomi's good arm and leading her to the sink. "Beto knows."

"Butter makes it feel better at first, but it can cause more problems," Beto explained. "It has to do with something called bacteria."

The cool water took the edge off, but their words had to climb over a wall of pain to reach Naomi.

After a few minutes, she managed to speak. "I'm so sorry, Pastor

Tom. I didn't expect . . ."

He shook his head and mashed his hat between his hands. "I didn't mean to startle you like that. I just wanted to make sure someone was up so I wouldn't be disturbing the household by knocking." He nodded at the twins. "Heard the kids were under the weather."

"Oh, we're better now," Beto said. "I threw up fifteen times."

"I threw up seventeen times!" Cari said with a note of triumph.

"No need for that, you two. Go get ready for school and let me and the pastor talk." Naomi's voice came out strained and strangled. God, but it hurt.

"They have the stomach flu?"

She nodded and swallowed hard. He might have heard the kids were sick from anybody, but her first thought was that he must have seen Henry. She turned the faucet off and dried her arm as lightly as she could. Her skin screamed. "My," she said, gritting her teeth, "that was exciting. Have a doughnut?"

He shook his head and smiled ruefully. "I'll take a seat, though. Sure am sorry."

"It was my fault." She lowered herself into the chair across from him and tried not to think about the heat that seemed to be inside the flesh of her arm. She glanced at the burn, then looked away. The sight of it turned her stomach. Her arm was an erratic welt of angry red with a smattering of white blisters.

Pastor Tom set his hat down in front of him. "You've had your hands full. That's what I came by to talk to you about."

Her jaw tightened a little. "Pardon me," she said. She dashed back over to the sink and wet a towel with cool water, wrung it out, and then wrapped her arm in it before sitting back down.

"Please go ahead," Naomi said from the sink. The pain made her desperate for distraction, and she looked at the preacher in the eyes for the first time. There was a patch of stray hairs between his eyebrows and an uneven mole above his lip.

Pastor Tom made his hands into a steeple and studied his fingernails. "I found Henry this morning. He knows he did wrong, and he'll be coming home this evening. I thought you might like to know."

"Thank you."

"I'll let him know he's welcome back?"

She hesitated, briefly imagining a life in East Texas without Henry. In the end, she said, "It's his house."

The pastor frowned a little. "Can I pray over it for you?" he asked, already stretching his hands out toward her burned arm.

◊ ◊ ◊

On the way to school, Naomi did not tell the twins that Henry was coming home. His word, even through Pastor Tom, did not fill her with confidence.

Naomi had put on a hand-me-down sweater from Muff, hoping the long sleeves would hide her burn. The wool was rough, and she winced every time it scratched against her damaged skin. And even with the sleeve pulled down, she could not conceal the burned and blistered part of her hand.

In homeroom, Miranda made a show of averting her eyes. "Too ugly to look at," she said loudly.

Betty Lee grinned. "That's sure to scar," she said.

School was a blur of agony. After the bell, the twins bounded up to her in the schoolyard. "We learned silhouettes in art with Miss Bell," Cari said.

Beto grabbed Naomi's arm for a hug. She cried out in pain.

"*Lo siento*, Omi," he said, backing away.

Naomi exhaled slowly. "It's just a little tender."

"If we can find Wash, can we go fishing?" Cari asked, already moving toward the superintendent's house, where a box of tools sat on the porch.

"Sure," Naomi said. Even with the cold out, all she wanted to do was take the sweater off.

Beto started after Cari, then turned back. "What's for supper?" he asked.

Naomi groaned. "Nothing hot."

WASH Late that afternoon, Wash looked up from the river to see Naomi coming toward him and the twins. "Jesus and his fishermen! What happened?" he shouted. Even from where he stood, he could tell that her arm was a map of blistered red. He handed his fishing rod to Beto and climbed the bank.

"We didn't tell him," Cari called.

"Tell me what?" Wash asked. "Let me see that."

"It's just a little burn," Naomi said. She tried to hide her arm under the sweater she was holding in the other hand.

Wash reached to pull aside the sweater just as she took a step away from him. He was left with the sweater, and her burn was out in the open. Worry clutched at him. "How did that happen?" he asked.

Color flooded her cheeks. She grabbed the sweater and covered the burn again. "Doughnuts," she said.

"An oil burn, then?" He shook his head. "You need to be more careful."

"What difference does it make to you?" she asked.

Her hard words took him by surprise. "I—well, what if the twins had been standing there? They could've gotten hurt bad."

"I know," she said, but she didn't look at him. Her fists were balled.

"Come on," she called to the twins. Beto started to take two fish from the basket in the shallows, but Naomi shook her head. "I'm not cooking tonight."

The twins climbed up the slope and said their good-byes to Wash, but Naomi turned away without saying anything. She was angry at him; that was plain.

"Are you putting something on that?" he called after her. "Let me ask my friend Cal's ma to mix up some salve—"

"I'm fine," she said. "Thanks for your concern." She started up the path with the twins. She did not look back.

NAOMI   That night, Henry walked into the kitchen like nothing had happened. Pastor Tom's wife must have washed his clothes before they sent him home because everything was clean and pressed like he was going to church instead of coming home after half a week away. At the least, she could count on a few days of good behavior from him. Back on Redemption Road.

"Pastor said you got a burn," Henry said.

"That's right," she said without looking up from her sewing.

Henry went over to the bread box. He pulled out an old biscuit and looked into the sink. "I could finish those dishes," he said with his mouth full. "Leave them if you want."

Naomi still didn't speak.

"Good biscuit," he said. He brushed the crumbs from his hands into the sink. "I guess the twins are up front?"

He walked toward the living room without waiting for her to answer. She noticed a slight bulge under his jacket, but she wasn't about to ask what it was.

She went back to patching Beto's pants. She didn't mind the sewing. But after that, there were the dishes, which Henry would not remember to do. She needed to prepare tomorrow's lunches. And she was behind on the cleaning and the laundry. She especially hated handling Henry's underthings, marked as they were with his sweat and smells. The thought of hot water made her arm burn. Even if the work had been harder back in San Antonio, she hadn't felt so alone doing it. And there was no Henry.

Happy cries came from the living room. She looked up and saw a calico streak fly past, tail straight back like an arrow. It skittered around the kitchen and then careened back toward the bedroom with the twins running after it.

"A cat?" Naomi said to Henry when he came back into the kitchen.

"Why not?" he said. His large hands patted at his pockets, as if a gift for her might appear there. She didn't want anything from him, but she expected an apology at least.

It did not come.

"Everything okay?" He tossed the words out casually, which only added fuel to the fire still smoldering in her. Her anger seemed to radiate from the burn itself. It hurt like hell.

Naomi stood a few feet away from him at the sink, dish towel in hand. She took up a plate, dried it, and placed it on the counter. "We ran out of food money," she said evenly. "I didn't know what to do."

A look of shame flashed over Henry's face, but he buried it under a grin. He picked his hat up from the counter and tossed it onto a chair. "Blew it, didn't I?" he mumbled finally.

He tugged at the skin of his neck and then fished out a damp roll of bills and peeled off several. "So you can get stocked back up on food." He paused, as if remembering something. "You should have told me about Turner's place. I would have talked to him, worked something out. Who's been getting groceries for you?"

She hesitated. "Depends. Sometimes Muff gets me things and I pay her back." That was true, if rare.

For a moment, she thought he was going to let the topic die. Then he frowned and squinted at her. "And other times?" he asked.

She exhaled slowly and considered her position. Short of lying, there was no way around it. And anyway, there would not be a better time to tell him; he could hardly get angry with her now, not after what he'd just done.

"Mason's," she mumbled.

"Where?" His voice was sharp.

"Mason's!" She said it clearly this time.

"That the store over in Egypt Town?" His jaw tightened. Disgust veined his words. "You've been feeding us nigger food? Feeding it to me? Feeding it to my kids?"

"There's nothing wrong with the food, and you know it." She wasn't going to be bullied about this, especially not after he skipped out on them with the kids still sick.

Henry cocked an eyebrow at her and tapped his chin with a finger. "That so? The way I see it, you're under my roof." He flattened a palm against the table. "This is East Texas, and there's lines. Lines you cross, lines you don't cross. That clear? Turners won't give you no more trouble, I promise you. In fact, I'll buy the groceries from now on," he said, snatching back the money. "You just make out a list. Don't you go back to that nigger store, hear me?"

"I have to pay the bill from this week," Naomi said stubbornly.

"Fine, but that's the end of it. Tell that colored boy the twins are always trailing behind to pay it for you." He tossed a handful of bills back down. "Come on, let's see about that cat." He stalked down the hall, no doubt expecting her to follow.

BETO Beto stroked the soft fur over the kitten's nose, and it nuzzled his hand. It lay curled into a ball of white and tan and gray in his lap. He turned the pages of the encyclopedia carefully so as not to disturb it.

Cari came into the kitchen and slid a finger down the length of the kitten's spine. Its ear twitched, and it opened a wary eye. Cari frowned, and Beto knew she was trying to decide what to do with the feeling of not being the favorite.

Beto nudged her. "He needs a name."

They'd gone back and forth for almost a week; it was time for the cat to be the somebody it was going to be.

"Sugar Man," Cari said.

"Cats don't even like sugar," he protested. "That's a name for a horse."

"Or a sweet cat," she said.

"Edgar," Beto said. The kitten started to purr. "See? He didn't purr for your name."

"Ugh." Cari rolled her eyes and tossed herself into one of the other kitchen chairs. She had tired almost instantly of the Poe poems they had read from Naomi's English book, but Beto adored their "gloomy splendor." That was what Miss Bell had said when he asked her what

132

she thought of "The Raven."

"Quoth the Raven, 'Nevermore,'" Beto said. He grinned.

"Lord deliver me," Cari said, but Beto knew she was planning something. She twirled a strand of hair slowly around her finger. "How bad do you want it to be 'Edgar'?"

Beto tried to seem indifferent, but he couldn't hide anything from her.

"You give me your dessert for two months, and you can name him," she said.

"That's nuts!" Beto bit his lip.

Cari shrugged. "I bet you anything that Daddy will like Sugar Man better than Edgar."

"He might like my name," Beto protested.

"If you want to risk it."

"What do you think?" Beto scratched the cat under its chin and pressed his fingers gently against the soft pad of one small foot.

A truck pulled up the driveway. Cari ran to the screen. "It's Daddy," she said. "Last chance to get your name."

"One month of treats," Beto said.

The truck door opened. Henry's boots thudded down on the gravel.

"Deal," Cari squealed. She ran over to shake Beto's hand. "Naomi and Muff are making pineapple upside-down cake," she said with an evil grin. "I get your piece and mine, too."

He ignored her. "Edgar," he whispered to the kitten softly. "That's your name now."

Cari pushed the screen door open and clattered down the porch steps to meet Henry. "Daddy, we named the cat!" She came back into the kitchen a moment later carrying Henry's hat.

"So what is it?" Henry asked as he walked into the kitchen.

"I picked the name," Beto said, smiling up at him. "It's Edgar."

Henry rubbed at his jaw, leaving a smear of grease. "That cat's a female."

"But . . ." Beto hesitated, shifting uncomfortably in his chair. Edgar jumped down from his lap and stretched. Cari raised her eyebrows at Beto.

"Trust me, it's a girl," Henry went on. "There aren't any male calico cats. What the hell kind of name is Edgar anyhow?"

"It's the name of a famous poet. Edgar Allan Poe," Cari said.

"Good grief," Henry grumbled. "I should have gotten a tom. Could use another man around here."

Beto blinked hard, suddenly deflated. It would be a disaster to cry, he knew. He glanced at Cari, but she just shrugged.

Henry picked up the percolator, sloshed around its contents, then set it back down on the stove. "Where's Naomi?" he asked.

"Next door," Cari said.

Henry began unbuttoning his shirt as he walked toward the bathroom. "One of y'all go over and get her. I want some coffee after I get cleaned up."

"Yes, sir," Beto said to Henry's back.

When Henry was in the bathroom, Cari walked over and planted a kiss on Beto's cheek. "Sorry about the bad news," she said, "but no takebacks on the deal."

Beto thought about it for a second. "Okay, but the name stays."

"But Edgar's no name for a girl. At least make it Annabelle," she pleaded, "or Lee, like the other poem."

"A deal's a deal," Beto said firmly. His eyes were fixed on the bathroom door, and he hoped Henry could hear him. "Now," he reached for his jacket, "Edgar and I are going to find Naomi."

NAOMI   Naomi tilted her glass to free up the last sweet drops of lemonade at the bottom. Tommie pushed the mason jar toward her. "You finish it," Tommie said. "We have more at home."

"Thanks," Naomi said. She cocked an eyebrow at Tommie, who was unusually quiet.

"About the dress," Tommie said after a moment longer, "maybe we could go look at some styles in person, like you said might help."

For home economics, all the senior girls had to sew themselves a proper dress. It was a big part of the class grade, and Tommie had been worrying about it since the day their teacher assigned it.

Naomi looked up from the catalog Tommie had brought with her. "Sure. When you find something you like, you look for a similar pattern. Or you can just use the dress to draw one."

"Just!" Tommie scoffed. "You saw how my kettle cozy came out. Total disaster. And Mrs. Anderson said we have to actually wear the dress that we make."

"You'll do fine," Naomi said with more confidence than she felt. Tommie had trouble concentrating long enough to sew a button on straight.

"I bet my uncle Ben would drive us over to Tyler one of these

Saturdays coming up before Thanksgiving. We could go to Montgomery Ward, look at the latest styles. Maybe you can help me pick a pattern."

"All the way to Tyler? You think he'd really take us?" Naomi's enthusiasm surprised even her.

Tommie beamed at Naomi and leaned forward. "Sure he would, so long as we don't mind Katie and Jean tagging along."

"Could the twins come, too?" Naomi asked.

"Of course. Plenty of room for everybody in the back of the truck."

"Okay, but check first," Naomi said. "I don't want to get their hopes up for nothing."

◇ ◇ ◇

Tommie had just left when the screen door squeaked open and the twins shoved through the door.

"You two are home early," Naomi said, looking up from her cutting board. There was still an hour before supper.

"We got cold," Cari said. She and Beto ran to the heater and held out their hands to warm them before leaning in to heat their faces.

Naomi sighed. She'd hoped that Henry would notice that the twins' jackets were too thin for East Texas, but two weeks had passed since the weather had turned really and truly cold. She'd have to bring it up.

"Not too close," she warned. "Watch your hair, Cari."

Beto broke away from the heater and pressed something small, light, and round into Naomi's hand. "This is for you."

She flashed a perfunctory smile. "Thanks," she said, and shoved it into her apron pocket.

"Omi! You didn't even look at it!" Cari protested.

"Sure I did. It's a . . . bird."

"Yeah, but what kind?" Cari pressed, hands on her hips.

"A wooden one." Naomi turned back to the turnips she was getting ready to boil.

Cari tugged on her elbow. "If you don't like it, just give it back. We put a lot of work into that, you know."

Naomi reached into her pocket and pulled the bird out again. It was made from a very small gourd with the pointed end of a twig sticking out from the narrow side and a fan-shaped bit of bark wedged into a slot on the opposite end. Two wings and slightly uneven black eyes had been painted on.

"You like it?" Cari asked.

"We did the painting," Beto added.

"I do like it," Naomi said. "Why don't you two put it on top of the dresser until we find a place to hang it?"

Ever since the day he saw her burn, Wash had been sending little presents with the twins. Except for the salve, which she'd smeared on daily out of desperation, she pushed the gifts to the back of her drawer. Naomi reminded herself of what she'd seen at Wash's house, how he'd made that girl laugh. She resolved anew not to be swayed by the presents; his guilty conscience was not her concern.

While the twins were in the bedroom, Naomi pressed her hand against the frosty chill of the window above the sink. There'd been so many cold nights now, more than she'd ever known in San Antonio. But it was easier here with a heater in every room and plenty of fuel thanks to the free gas from the oil companies. "We use it, or it goes to waste," Muff had told her one night not long after they'd arrived. "See those flames there? That's what they do with the rest of the bleed-off gas. They just flare it off."

From where they had stood on Muff's porch, the flares looked to be dancing in the woods, although in fact they were always fenced in a safe distance from the fall range of any of the trees. Naomi had found the gentle flicker of the flares entrancing, and Muff had smiled and squeezed her arm. "Some folks call oil country ugly, but I say it's got its own kind of pretty," she'd said. "You'll see."

From the back door, Naomi could see a flare close by in the woods. Two more flickered in the distance. She watched their bright dancing until the twins burst back into the kitchen.

"So are we having a turkey for Thanksgiving or not?" Cari asked. "Everybody at school is."

Naomi bit her lip and glanced at Henry's closed bedroom door. Tommie's family had invited them for Thanksgiving, but she hadn't asked Henry about it yet. She didn't dare talk about it to the twins until he said it was okay.

"I'll ask Daddy soon," Naomi said. She tossed turnips into a pot.

"You said that yesterday," Beto said. He settled at the table with one of Miss Bell's encyclopedias.

"Mmm, remember Thanksgiving in San Antonio?" Naomi asked. Usually her grandparents kept the store open on Thanksgiving and prepared tamales to sell alongside clay mugs of steaming *atole*.

"We need a turkey," Cari said. "That's how they do it here."

◇ ◇ ◇

Dinner was quick and mostly silent. Henry did not stop them at the beginning of the meal to pray. Beto glanced up when his father's fork started moving. He opened his mouth, but Naomi caught his eye and shook her head. Beto bowed his head briefly and then began to eat.

When Henry finished, he wiped his mouth and pushed back from the table. "I've got an early shift tomorrow," he said. He stood with his hands in his pockets and started toward the hall.

Cari and Beto looked at Naomi, widening their eyes.

"Daddy?" Naomi said abruptly when he was almost to the door of his bedroom.

He paused and turned, his face full of weariness and some emotion that Naomi couldn't read. "What is it?" Henry sounded hoarse, and Naomi noticed that he had not shaved in a day or two.

She walked into the hall. "Do you have a minute?" Before he could answer, she turned to the twins. "Bundle up best you can and go feed Muff's chickens, you hear?"

The twins scrambled into their jackets.

"Two things, real quick," Naomi said once the screen door clattered shut behind them and their footsteps rang out on the steps. There was a hint of pleading in her voice that disgusted her, but she needed him to cooperate. "First thing is coats for the kids. It's been so cold. Tommie said we could catch a ride with her uncle, maybe look over in Tyler—"

"Here," he pulled out his money clip and handed her three five-dollar bills. "Whatever you think is best."

He started to turn toward his room.

"The other thing is Thanksgiving . . ." she said to his back.

"Thanksgiving?" He sounded bewildered.

"It's coming up."

"We don't need nothing special." He reached for his doorknob. "Don't worry about it."

"How about eating with the Kinnebrews? Tommie's mother invited us."

Henry didn't look at her, but his irritation was plain. "I don't feel like dealing with church people every hour of the day. You and the kids go. I may even have to work."

He turned the doorknob and shouldered the door to his room open. It closed behind him with a click.

NAOMI Naomi rode in the back of Ben's truck with Tommie, the twins, and Tommie's cousins Katie and Jean.

"Sorry we don't get the cab," Tommie shouted as they bounced down the highway toward Tyler. "I didn't know my aunt was coming."

"It's fine," Naomi called. She snuggled closer to Tommie under the afghan Deedee had given them when they got in. Across from them, the twins shared a giant quilt with Katie and Jean.

It had rained during the night, washing away any whiff of oil field sulfur stink. The air smelled clean and earthy, and everything looked crisp and glossed with sun. The pines along the road pointed up so straight and stark against the blue of the sky that it seemed like the clouds might catch on them.

The woods gave way to the outskirts of Tyler. Warehouses and work yards littered with battered and rusting equipment were mixed in with shotgun houses. Most of the homes were white with flaking paint, but a few were painted brightly.

"Coloreds!" Jean shouted and pointed at a couple of black children on one of the porches. They were eating out of a bowl held between them.

Tommie slapped Jean's hand. "Don't point," she said loudly. "Poor folk don't need you gawking at them."

Naomi didn't say that the bright colors of the house reminded her, briefly, of San Antonio. Not of the crowded corrals, but of the pretty West Side neighborhoods where wealthier Mexican families lived, their houses painted in yellows and oranges and pinks.

As they got farther into town, the houses got bigger and sat on yards carpeted with green and full of thick bushes and enormous shade trees. The New London oil camp houses seemed naked and homely by comparison.

"See those?" Tommie pointed to the bushes. "They're called azaleas. In the spring that whole row will turn solid pink. Prettiest thing. I saw it last year when we visited Deedee and Ben before we moved over."

After he parked downtown in front of the department stores, Ben rolled down his window and called back to Tommie. "I'll be back for you all in a couple of hours. Katie, Jean, you girls mind Mama or else it'll be your hide when we get home."

"Yes, sir!" Katie and Jean called, already climbing down over the side of the truck and running for the sidewalk in front of Montgomery Ward. In the window, there were half a dozen evening gowns beaded with pearls and sequins.

Katie made a face. "Don't see how you'd walk in those."

"I sure couldn't," Tommie said. "But that don't keep 'em from being pretty."

Naomi herded the twins in front of her. "You two make sure that wherever we are, you can see me." The sternness in her voice was half-hearted. The beautiful drive and the memories of San Antonio had lightened her mood. It could be a good day.

"How's handsome Henry?" Deedee asked Naomi as they passed through the big glass doors into the store.

Naomi felt her own silence. She knew that, objectively, Henry was attractive; she'd seen women eye him during Sunday luncheons. "He's fine," she said quickly.

"Missed him at church," Deedee said.

Naomi nodded, her eyes locked on a display of pots and pans as if it were an object of fascination. "Boss has him working lots of shifts right now."

She wanted this topic to be finished, so she turned to Tommie. "Do you think we could look at the coats first? I have to get some heavier ones

for the twins, maybe for me. Then we can take all the time we want looking at the dresses."

◇ ◇ ◇

Not long after Naomi began looking through the enormous racks of children's coats, checking the prices, Cari and Beto tugged at her sleeve.

"We found the perfect ones," Cari said. "Look."

Naomi turned around. They had chosen well, she had to admit, at
least as far as style and fit went. Cari had on a plaid cape-style coat with
brown and blue nubby fabric and big pink buttons down the front. Beto
wore a soft black leather zip-up with a bit of fleece around the collar.

Naomi examined the coats more closely. "They're nice," she said,
"but I don't think they're warm enough."

"Sure they are!" Cari said. "They're twice as thick as our old jackets."

"It could get even colder," Naomi warned. "The weather's not like
back home."

"These ones are on sale," Cari pressed. "You can get a coat, too, and
we'll still have money for ice cream."

Naomi caved. "Fine, but I'm getting a real coat. You'll be sorry you
don't have one later."

They followed her into the women's coat section and helped her pick
out a simple navy peacoat. "You look very pretty," Cari said.

"Quit buttering me up," Naomi said.

"She wasn't," protested Beto.

"All right then. Let's go pay."

◇ ◇ ◇

Naomi fingered the soft fabric of a gray dress with flared sleeves, a blousy
top, and a skirt that flared out a bit from a belted waist. She glanced from
the dress to Tommie, thinking hard about how the contours would match
up with her body—and considering what she might change if she were
making it from scratch.

"What do you think are your best features?" Naomi asked as she
moved on to a deep maroon wool skirt with a matching jacket.

"My eyes and my . . . bosom," Tommie said. She had lowered her voice, but color still rushed to her cheeks.

"Somebody call the newspaper," Naomi said, squeezing Tommie's arm. "Tommie Kinnebrew just blushed for the first time!"

"You asked!" Tommie protested.

"I did. And we can pick a pattern that makes the most of both. What about a nice deep shade of purple to make those brown eyes sing? And . . . something to put Dwayne Stark's attention up here . . ." She gestured toward Tommie's chest.

"Now you're making fun of me," Tommie said, but she was smiling.

They were still looking at dresses when Deedee and the kids came to find them.

"We only have an hour before Daddy comes," Jean said, tugging on Tommie's arm. "Ma said we can have ice cream. Come on."

Tommie gave Naomi a questioning look.

"It's fine. I've got plenty of ideas," Naomi said. And she did; her mind was awash in patterns and textures, the perfect lines to the dresses. She'd even managed to keep Wash and Henry out of her thoughts for most of the morning.

"Ice cream, then!" Tommie said. "Might as well enjoy myself before you start measuring me for this dress."

◊ ◊ ◊

On their way to the ice cream parlor, Katie fell back from the tangle of kids and slipped her arm through Naomi's. Deedee and Tommie were still a little ways behind them.

"Hi," Naomi said, smiling and remembering what the twins were like at six, how they loved singling a grown-up out to get a little extra attention.

"Can I ask you something?" asked Katie.

"Okay."

Katie squinted at Naomi. "Do you know any dirty ones?"

"Dirty ones?"

"Dirty Mexicans. I heard a man at the oil festival say there were heaps of dirty Mexicans in San Antonio." She opened Naomi's hand and examined each of her fingers. "See, you're not dirty at all, but I thought maybe you knew some folks who were."

NAOMI From her tree, Naomi listened to the small winter sounds of the forest. Time spooled out slowly. Although her coat kept her body warm, her hands were cold even inside her pockets.

She was about to slip a finger up under her coat sleeve and scratch at her arm, but she thought of the warning from Tommie's mother earlier that day while she and the twins were at their house for Thanksgiving dinner. "Don't worry that or it's liable to scar worse," she'd said as she handed Naomi an enormous piece of pecan pie. Even if Mrs. Kinnebrew had smiled when she said it, Naomi felt the rebuke. First that she'd been careless enough to burn herself. Second that she didn't have the sense to minimize the ugliness.

The burn was healing, and now the layer of damaged skin was flaking away. Sometimes Naomi found herself picking at the scaly bits. The skin beneath looked raw and pink against the brown of her arm. It itched mightily. She clamped her hands between her thighs to keep from scratching.

Little by little, feeling came back into her fingers. Even if it was cold, she knew ways to warmth. She opened her legs a little, pressed back against the crumbling interior of the tree, and slid a hand under her dress.

As her fingers worked, the heat came up in her slowly. She felt it rise and rise until the joy of it overtook the quiet of the tree.

She froze when she heard them. The twins and Wash, walking along the path toward the river. She shouldn't have been surprised. After all morning playing with Tommie's cousins and then the long sit for the big dinner, the twins had been ready for a different sort of fun. With Henry suddenly tired of daddying, the twins melted back into the woods with Wash every chance they got, taking Edgar along for their adventures.

"Let's try it again," Beto was saying. "Come on, Edgar, fetch! Get the stick."

Cari burst into giggles.

Then came Wash's voice. "Cats are made to disobey," he said, laughing. "Y'all don't hold your breath for that cat to listen."

All kinds of forgetting were possible in the tree. Naomi could forget the grime she scrubbed from the sinks, the slap of wet sheets against her ankles as she flung them over the clothesline, the breakfasts and lunches and dinners waiting to be made and eaten and cleaned up. She could forget the stares at school and Miranda's icy words. Inside the tree, she could forget the girl she saw Wash with at his house and the ones at Mason's. She could forget that Wash belonged to the twins first of all.

She forgot until, for a moment, she remembered only Wash's laughter and the late-summer light through the trees by the river. The memory of his smile kindled hers, even now.

She began to touch herself again, this time with the memory for company. She missed Wash with her whole body. The missing was hers entirely.

DECEMBER 1936

WASH "Lord, Washington," Mr. Crane said. He let his glasses slip down on his nose and reached up to massage his temples. "Coldest December I can remember. This weather's got to break soon. School's heating bill was three hundred dollars last month."

Wash shook his head. "That's a lot of money." As he said it, something nagged at the back of his brain. For once it wasn't Naomi.

Mr. Crane went on. "Can you imagine what it'll be this month, what with it even colder? Maybe the holiday will save us."

They were standing at the edge of the lawn in front of Mr. Crane's house, the only grass that anybody had loved hard enough to get it to take hold. That had been Wash's doing, like most of the work around the superintendent's house. Wash frowned and surveyed the land in front of the school. The few flimsy trees were naked of leaves, and a long scar snaked across the packed dirt. A week before, he'd helped lay the pipe for a new Parade Oil bleed-off line that ran straight across the school grounds. As he studied it, an idea clicked into place.

"Three hundred dollars, you said, sir? To the gas company?" Wash asked.

Mr. Crane nodded. "I reckon we're the best customer the gas

company has. Except maybe Mrs. Quimbly. I hear she keeps that house so hot that you can fry an egg right on her hardwood floor."

"Older folks have their ways," Wash said, but his mind was already on something else.

◇ ◇ ◇

"Hi, Ma," Wash called when he got home.

"Afternoon, James Washington. Go on and pay Booker."

"Yes, ma'am." He slipped a quarter into the tin, hanging on to a dime and a few pennies for himself. "Is Pa home?"

"He's at his desk. Wash up before you bother him."

Wash turned on the kitchen faucet, lathered up his hands, and scraped the dark moons of dirt from under his nails. Then he went to find his father.

Jim Fuller greeted Wash without looking up from his paper. He got a few issues of the *Chicago Defender* every month or so from his cousin Lewis, who sometimes worked as a porter on trains from Chicago to Dallas and was something of a radical.

Wash took the paper as a good sign and launched into his plan.

When he was done explaining, his father removed his reading glasses and set them on top of his paper. "What makes you think they would want to give us the money?"

Wash pulled one of his mother's cane-back chairs over to the desk. "The way I figure it, it won't cost them anything."

Jim shook his head. "They won't see it that way."

"But there's a bleed-off line going right past the school. Today Mr. Crane was saying that they paid three hundred to the gas company this month. Why pay at all when there's free gas right there?"

"Hold on, son, not everybody thinks using green gas is a smart idea—"

"We use it here. And it works fine with the regulator they put in at our school."

"There's a lot more variation in pressure when it comes to those bleed-off lines."

"I know they've got a good regulator. Come on, Pa. Half the county heats with the raw gas. Who's going to complain?"

His father scratched his chin lightly. "It's an idea," he said. "But the last time Mr. Crane found money to help us out, the school board went and used it to put up those electric lights on their football field. Out of spite, I think."

"Here's how I figure it. I give Mr. Crane the idea about using the Parade line. Once we tap into it and he has the instant savings, we go see the school board with a plan for how we'd use three hundred dollars. All the numbers will match up, and everybody comes out looking good."

"I wouldn't expect too much, son. They'll think of something they want to do with the money themselves."

"That school is already a palace, Pa. They've got everything. You should see the chemistry lab, the uniforms they have, brand-new encyclopedias in every classroom, a whole room full of typewriters and another with electric sewing machines. They're flush. We could get some new textbooks for our kids, equipment for the shop class, maybe even a microscope. We've got to try for it, anyhow." As Wash talked, the plan began to take shape, offering the possibility of a kind of satisfaction he hadn't felt in weeks.

"I'll give it some thought, James."

Wash sucked his teeth. "I thought I could go ask Mr. Crane tomorrow about the gas line—"

"I said I'll give it some thought. Don't go sticking your neck out just yet."

"But—"

"You've got to be cautious when it comes to white folk. Especially when money's tight everywhere."

"There aren't money problems over there, Pa, I'm telling you that."

"Maybe not, but they can always talk about the economy, how we all have to make do and tighten our belts. What we've gotten hasn't changed since the crash. They didn't bump up our budget when the oil came in, not even when our enrollment went way up."

"And you're just going to go along with that?"

"For the time being, yes. What's got you so concerned—"

"Come on, Pa!" The words exploded out of Wash. "You wouldn't stand up for your own people if your pants were on fire."

"Watch it, James Washington Fuller. You think twice before you use that tone with me, do you hear?"

"Yes, sir," Wash mumbled.

"Retract your statement," Jim said. His face was shiny with sweat. The heat of the righteous, he probably believed. The heat of the god-damn coward, Wash thought. It felt good to speak out finally. Wash didn't care that much about the extra money. But he needed something to do, wanted something to *happen*. Above all, he wanted to put his mind on something besides the one girl who seemed to want nothing to do with him.

"I retract it." Wash said the words a little too loudly for sincerity.

"Good," Jim said.

◇ ◇ ◇

Wash opened his eyes and squinted. Even though it was hardly anyone's definition of morning yet, his father had switched on his light and was standing in his doorway with his arms crossed. "Wake up, son."

Wash pushed up on an elbow and wiped a bit of crud from his eye.

"Go ahead and tell Mr. Crane your idea," Jim said. "About the gas, I mean. But be smart about it. You find a way for him to feel like he thought of it, you hear?"

Wash grinned. "Kept you up all night thinking on it?"

His father sighed. "I suppose you did."

Wash yawned and pulled his blankets up over his head. "I think I should insult you more often."

◇ ◇ ◇

After his father closed the door, Wash tried to go back to sleep, but he couldn't. He was thinking about her again. Naomi. She'd been giving him the cold shoulder for more than three weeks now, and he still couldn't guess at her reasons—beyond the obvious, which was that neither of them had any business starting anything. That wasn't explanation enough, though. Not when they had shared those long mornings together. Not when he knew what it was to make her smile.

It had been a long time now since he'd been close to a girl, more than a month. When Rosie Lynn cornered him again after church last week and invited him to go on a walk with her, he'd been tempted, but only for a moment. Even if Naomi wouldn't talk to him, she was worth holding out for.

Wash spat into his palm and took his dick into his hand. He tried to imagine the feel of her braid, the soft skin by her mouth. He closed his eyes.

He couldn't get anywhere; the thought of her body came with the thought of her. And when Wash thought of Naomi, he fell into thinking about the why of her anger and the how of fixing things between them. He'd figure out what had soured the air, and he'd put it right.

He sighed and slid to the edge of the bed. He reached underneath and ran his hands along the slats until he felt the rough edge of newspaper. He pulled the packet out and carefully unwrapped the pictures inside. He had Nina Mae McKinney, Josephine Baker, and a photo of two Harlem nightclub dancers posing together.

He picked the Harlem girls, slid the rest of the photos underneath, and began again.

NAOMI Naomi checked the clock in the kitchen and then went back to dusting. She wanted to finish before supper so that the twins could help her sweep and mop. She'd already scrubbed the muddy tracks from the back door to Henry's room and rubbed away the grimy fingerprints on the edges of the kitchen sink. It was more than holding the oil field mess at bay; the more she cleaned, the less of Henry was in the house. With her sponges and scrub brushes and mop, she wiped him away daily.

She pushed the door to Henry's room open with her foot and walked in. She avoided his space as much as possible, but she didn't want to make the neglect too obvious.

On the dresser, she found a pile of soiled handkerchiefs and a scattering of dirt-crusted fingernail clippings. Forcing down her revulsion, she picked up the handkerchiefs with her cleaning rag and dropped them into the laundry basket in the hall. She used the rag to gather the parings into her dustpan and then wiped the dusty dresser top clean.

She squatted and swept under Henry's bed, being careful not to disturb his shotgun or the boxes of birdshot and buckshot he kept there.

On the nightstand, Henry's Bible was still open to Psalm 77. The drawer was partway out. Without thinking, she pulled on the handle.

The furniture was badly made and the drawer stuck on the frame, but it jerked open a few inches. Near the front, she saw a photograph of Henry and Estella. Naomi recognized the blue dress her mother had worn on their wedding day. She couldn't be sure, but Naomi thought that her mother's expression was already tinged with regret. She turned the photograph over and saw her mother's handwriting in faint pencil. *Nuestra boda, 29 enero 1925.* Beneath the photograph, there was a small tin of Romeos. She made sure not to touch it. For the first time, it occurred to Naomi that a tin like this could have saved her mother. Had the doctor suggested it? Catholics weren't supposed to, of course, but that didn't stop anyone. Even Abuelito sold them. Fina had showed her one afternoon when they were watching the store alone. The tins of Ramses and Romeos were kept behind displays of aspirin and skin lightener in a plain wooden box labeled "*para hombres.*" She could not fathom that Henry had been unaware of this possibility, but there was no way of knowing. And anyway, knowing would not bring her mother back.

Naomi laid the photograph back down and gave the drawer another tug. A fifth of Four Roses thudded to the front along with a Colt revolver. Naomi stared at the gun. Her pulse raced. This was different from the shotguns meant for deer and unlucky birds. A revolver was a gun for killing people.

She shoved the drawer closed and spun around, nearly tripping over her dustpan and broom. She scooped them up and ran to the other bedroom.

She could not think, could barely breathe. She could feel the tears threatening as she reached under the bed for the guitar case, which she opened with trembling fingers. She found the braid coiled inside her mother's old dress and slid her fingers along it, stroking the brittle fringe at the end. "*Para ti, mi amor. Cuídalos, mi amor,*" her mother had whispered, pressing the braid into her hands along with the shears and the care of the twins.

Now Naomi held on to the braid and whispered a prayer into her pillow. Keep them safe. Keep them safe.

But only she could keep them safe. There was no one else. She slammed the case closed and ran for the door.

◇ ◇ ◇

Naomi sprinted down the path toward the river. She needed to see that the twins were all right. She was going to bring them home, get them fed, put them to bed, tell them one of the stories about their mother that they were always hungry for. That gun—she had to find a way to get it out of the house. She had to make Henry change. And if she couldn't? If she couldn't, she would take the twins away. To Tommie's. To Muff's. Back to San Antonio. With Henry, there was too much danger, too much risk.

Before she broke through the trees, she heard a *plop*, then laughter. A moment later, there were three small splashes and a whistle of admiration.

"Beto, Cari," she called as soon as she could see them down by the river. "Time to go home." She did not look at Wash. Would not look at him. She thought of his other girlfriends, the false intimacy that amounted to lies. He was no better than Henry.

She had not thought to put on her coat, and the cold raised the hairs on her arms.

"Hi, stranger. Long time, no study," Wash called, grinning and waving.

Naomi ignored him and called down to the twins again. "It's late and the weather's turning bad. We're going home now."

Cari and Beto glanced up at the bright blue sky whisked with feathery clouds, but they stayed down by the river. They wore their new coats and had their hands full of small stones for skipping.

Naomi raised her voice. "I said let's go. Don't think you're too big for a spanking." She rubbed her arms hard, scraping the last bits of flaking skin from the burn in the process. She blinked back tears at the sudden pain, then locked her arms across her chest and lifted her chin.

"Y'all come on," Wash called as he scaled the bank in a few steps. "Hey, what's the matter?" he asked once he got closer.

"Cari! Beto!" she shouted again. The twins got slowly to their feet. Naomi turned to him and said in a hoarse whisper, "I don't want you hanging around with them anymore. I can't risk them being out and about with a—with a liar!" She flung the words at him, immediately feeling lighter and freer.

Wash looked as if he'd been struck. "Liar? I've told a few whoppers, but not to you. Never—"

"Never? I saw you with her . . . That girl at your house. Just before that you acted like . . . you made me think . . . And there were girls talking at Mason's . . ." It sounded silly put into words; it wasn't as if they'd made any promises to each other, unless she counted a question about sweethearts and a wink. Plus there was common sense to think of. Probably Wash had never thought to cross the lines that marked out who could be loved and by whom.

Inexplicably, Wash began to smile, and his smile frightened her. She knew how fast charm could turn cruel. She knew that men could take and take and leave the people who loved them wrecked or dead.

Naomi opened her mouth, then closed it. She thought of her mother's sad eyes and faded beauty. She thought of Henry's hand on hers in the pink bathroom.

"Come on, what's bothering you? We're friends; you can tell me," he said.

Friends. Fury flared up in her again. "Maybe I shouldn't have been there by your house, but I was, I was . . ." Naomi cast about for a plausible explanation. "I was looking for the twins, and what do I see?" She lowered her voice so that the twins would not hear her. "I see you laughing and joking on the stairs of your own house with some pretty girl in a blue dress, her holding your arm like she owned it. I saw you, Wash Fuller." The words came in an angry rush. It was more than she'd said to him in weeks, maybe ever.

Wash began laughing and didn't stop. The twins came running, not wanting to be left out of the joke. Naomi felt rage like she had never known before.

"Y'all do me a favor," he said when he had collected himself. "Go on and tell your sister a bit about Miss Fannie."

"She's the best piano player in Egypt Town, but she doesn't have a piano at home," Beto said.

Naomi shot Wash a look. It seemed to her that he was digging a deeper hole, but he just nodded. "What else is important about her? How come you think I'd help her down the stairs and walk her home?"

"She's blind!" the twins shouted together.

"See?" Wash was laughing again. "You see what you saw?" The twins laughed, too, without knowing why. Naomi just stared, checking these revelations against her own sense of things.

She eyed him skeptically and tried to recall exactly what she had seen. The girl could have been blind and his sweetheart; after all, she was pretty. But when she thought back to the hand on Wash's arm, it seemed to her that there had been a deliberateness that was not really romantic.

Relief flooded her. She uncrossed her arms slowly, trying on this new knowledge, testing it against her sense of things.

Wash fished two dimes out of his pocket and handed them to the twins. "Go buy some candy from Mr. Mason. And a soda, too. Cari, you share it all even, you hear me? I don't care what kind of devil deal y'all made when Beto named y'all's cat."

"Deal's a deal," she said, all mischief.

"Should I give him both dimes?"

"All right, all right, I'll share. Come on, Beto." She took off down the path and Beto ran after.

"Hey!" Wash called. "Save a piece of licorice for me! Keep it for tomorrow."

When the twins were out of sight, Wash turned, beaming, to Naomi. "You sure were worked up at the idea of Fannie being my girl."

She felt her face redden as the last of her anger evaporated. "I'm sorry. I shouldn't have . . . I just thought . . . And then—" She hesitated, uncertain what to say now.

She looked around. The sky was a gift of blue behind the delicate branches of the cottonwoods. The sun played across the surface of the river, and the breeze carried the scent of leaves and pine needles. Wash raised his eyebrows and smiled. Even in the cold, she felt all the warmth she'd fought for alone in her tree. Now, though, it was something she could give back to him.

Naomi closed her eyes and let happiness roll through her. Here they were, back together by the river. And the twins were safe—safer under Wash's watchful eye than they ever were in Henry's house. She felt foolish and ashamed of her panic, of wanting to tear them away from him. But that was only the beginning of what she felt.

She opened her eyes and looked at Wash. "Follow me."

 **WASH & NAOMI**

She was there, and then she wasn't.

Wash walked slowly, listening for her, trying to figure out where she'd gone. The only sounds were the rustling of the leaves and the cawing of a crow high up in one of the trees.

"Over here." It was Naomi's voice coming from near a pair of oaks, but he didn't see her.

He skirted a fallen tree and stared at the trees. At first, he didn't see anything remarkable. And then he did.

The opening in the tree wasn't small, but it was screened on one side by a mess of brambles and on the other side by the second oak. A perfect hiding place.

He squatted and pulled himself inside. His eyes fell on the smooth curves of her calves, and he wanted to reach his hands out and follow those curves up, up. Instead, he pressed himself back into the opposite side of the hollow and stood.

"So this is where you vanish to," he said.

Naomi didn't answer. She blinked. He was still there. Wash was inside the tree with her.

The inches of air between them turned electric. She lifted her hand into a shaft of light that illuminated Wash's face, then she laid it on his cheek. Only a few shades separated their skin color. It wasn't far to travel, not here.

"So, Washington Fuller?" she asked.

He could feel her warm, sweet breath. His mouth opened, but he couldn't find any words. He laughed a little, rubbed his chin. He reached up and took her hand in his, the interlacing of their fingers so right, so overdue. He tried to pretend that he wasn't thinking about falling against her, falling into what he had wanted and tried to forget that he wanted, this hunger that was different from other hungers before. He wanted the feel of her hips, her mouth, the sweet hollow of her neck. His muscles tightened with the effort of not taking her braid in his hand. Of not working his way down the row of buttons on her dress. Of not touching her everywhere.

"I want—" he managed.

"Me, too." She took a small step toward him and placed his hand on her waist. She slid her arms inside his jacket and pressed herself to him. His shirt buttons were cold against her cheek, but she could feel the fierce beating of his heart and the warmth of his skin. She moved her hands up his stomach and chest and over his shoulders. She pushed off his jacket. She took his arm and traced a vein from his wrist to his elbow and slid a finger under his rolled-up shirtsleeve.

His breath caught in his throat when she looked up at him. Her eyes were bright and more beautiful than he could bear. Full of the light that had drawn him from the start.

Naomi felt her shyness split. She climbed out of her self.

Wash witnessed this blooming. Color rose in her cheeks. Her fingers did not hesitate. Nor her lips. It was nothing like the awkward necking with girls from Egypt Town. It was something else entirely.

"Who are you?" he asked.

NAOMI For Naomi, everything had changed in the woods. At home, though, there was still the matter of the handgun. Naomi did not like it, but it turned out that even Muff's husband, Bud, had one. When Naomi asked, Muff had said that carrying a revolver was usual for the oil field, or had been. "You can't imagine how rough some of these places used to be before the women came along," she said. So Naomi put the gun in the same category that held Henry's Bible: things he owned but didn't use anymore.

During the week after she brought Wash to her tree, Naomi alternated between two worries. The first worry was that she had dreamed the whole thing. When she saw him, she wondered if his warmth to her was any different from what he offered the twins. The second worry was that the kisses had been real but that she had frightened him away. Girls weren't supposed to want any of that. And if they did, they certainly weren't supposed to show it. Maybe the PTA mothers in the bathroom had seen something in her she hadn't known was there.

She thought about Wash all the time. In class, at home, and—when she could manage it—inside the tree. She watched the twins run toward him after school. She wanted him for herself but did not want to take him away from them. She listened. And dreamed.

◇ ◇ ◇

One afternoon, she walked out of the school alone and saw him packing up his tools under one of the naked trees in front of the superintendent's house. The air was heavy with cold. The sky was gray, and Wash's smile was the brightest thing in sight.

Naomi couldn't say anything when she walked past; they didn't have the twins as a buffer or an excuse. Still, she thought that Wash started putting his things away faster when he saw her. She thought maybe he gave her a tiny nod.

She ran to the tree and listened for his footsteps on the path. They didn't come, not at first. And then, when she was chilled to the bone and about to give up, she heard him coming. A second later, he ducked into the tree. He was out of breath, and his forehead glistened.

"Came . . . fast . . . as I could," he said, breathing hard. Naomi leaned close. He smelled of wood, and sawdust clung to his neck. She reached up to wipe it away.

He wrapped his arms around her. She thought she might cry with the rightness of it.

"The twins?" he whispered. His face was pressed into her hair; his words tickled her scalp.

"Still at school, busy," she said.

"I'm glad you were here."

"I'm glad you found me."

That was the end of their talking. The rest was touch. And once Wash caught his breath, the rhythm was slow, slow, slow. That is, until Naomi changed it.

NAOMI When school let out for the winter break, Naomi asked Henry if they could go to San Antonio for a few days. He refused. He couldn't take the time from work, he said, and anyway they were a family and would have Christmas together. Here, in their home.

The thought of San Antonio stabbed at her. She'd written a letter to Abuelito and Abuelita and had sent along three of the dollars she'd saved with the idea that it was best to give practical help. But now she wished she'd sent them something special.

On Christmas Eve, Henry took them to Kilgore to see the lights. It was only late afternoon, but the day was gloomy and already the cars all had on their headlights. Naomi and the twins huddled with their hands under the dash to get closer to the heat.

"This cold!" Henry said. "And when are we going to see the sun again? How long has it been?"

"Seventeen days and six hours," Beto answered softly.

"I didn't know you were keeping count," Henry said. He chuckled and gave Beto a playful shove. "Book learnin'."

On the downtown streets of Kilgore, people milled about on the narrow sidewalks, looking at shop displays and admiring the strands of lights that decorated the businesses. There were illuminated stars on the tops of some of the oldest oil derricks, and across Main Street, spotlights shown on poinsettias placed on risers to spell "Merry Xmas!"

Cari wiped the condensation from the side window and stared out.

"Look," Beto said. He pointed to a large family, all of them with the same blond hair. Everyone wore a shirt or dress made from the same fabric, and they had matching Santa hats.

"How come we can't go see some of your family, Daddy?" Cari asked, her eyes still on the group.

Henry's hands tightened on the steering wheel. A heavy silence billowed through the car.

Naomi's heart pounded. "Cari," she whispered, gripping her sister's arm, "you know better than to pry." She tried to think of what she could say to draw off some of Henry's anger.

After a long moment, Henry exhaled. "It's okay," he said. "It's just a question." He turned his face to Cari. "You kids are all the family I've got. Everyone else is gone." He reached out and ruffled her curls.

◊ ◊ ◊

They ate Christmas dinner at Muff and Bud's. Besides their kids, some of Muff's family had driven up from the Beaumont oil field. As soon as the pie was finished, Henry cleared his throat and wiped his mouth with his napkin. "I hate to say it, but we have to get going. I need to check on a rig, and I reckon the kids'll want to open their presents before that."

"Oh, you're kidding!" Muff said. Her face was still flushed from all of the cooking. "Work today? You've got to tell Graham Salter there's a limit!"

Henry shrugged. "I drew one of the short straws," he said. He pushed back from the table. "At least I get double pay."

◊ ◊ ◊

Naomi and the twins waited in the living room while Henry changed into his work clothes. Like always, she chose the uncomfortable caneback chair to make sure Henry could not end up next to her on the couch.

The twins sat in front of the small tree they had decorated with popcorn and homemade ornaments. Underneath it were seven gifts, six of which Naomi had wrapped herself—two presents for Cari, two presents for Beto, and two presents for Henry. She figured the last one was for her from the twins.

"All right," Henry said, settling into the couch with a sigh. "Who first?"

"You, Daddy!" Beto said. He rushed a package over to Henry. The twins pressed in close as he tore away the wrapping.

"Huh," he said when he saw the small cigarette case that they had insisted on purchasing despite Naomi's protests. He studied the shiny surface and clicked the case open. "But I don't smoke."

"We think it'd be a good idea for you to start," Cari said. Maybe they thought it would improve his mood. There had been a sign behind the department store counter: "For digestion's sake, smoke daily!"

From the pocket of her dress, Cari produced a box of Camels.

"Cari!" Naomi said. "Where did you get those?"

Cari ignored her and filled Henry's cigarette case.

"I'll get you a light," Beto said. He came back with a saucer and the matches that Naomi kept by the stove. He set the saucer on the sofa beside Henry. "For the ashes," he said.

Henry lit one of the Camels and made a show of smoking for a few minutes. He exhaled with his lips tight and pulled down.

"Thank you," he said as he stubbed out the half-smoked cigarette. "Next?"

Naomi pointed out another gift and told Beto to give it to Henry.

"Who's this from?" he asked.

"Me," Naomi said. She did not wish him a merry Christmas.

"Very nice," he said after he unwrapped the heavy gray socks she'd knitted in home economics. "Good to have something warm in the boots with all this cold weather."

"Now we have a present for you," Cari said to Naomi. She gave her the one package she hadn't recognized.

Naomi pulled open the paper to reveal a small wooden box pasted over with flowers and pictures cut out from catalogs.

"It's a jewelry box," Beto said.

Naomi held it up and smiled. "It's perfect," she said, not caring that she had no jewelry to put inside it. She pulled the twins in for a hug. "Thank you."

Then Henry squatted and reached under the tree for the gifts he'd gotten for the twins and given to Naomi to wrap. He also dropped something into her lap. The thick rectangle was covered in grocer's paper and tied with string.

"Didn't seem right to ask you to wrap your own gift," he said. He tugged on his neck and waited.

"Naomi first," Cari said. "We want to save ours for last."

Naomi pulled on the string and opened the paper to find a folded length of yellow fabric with a tiny pattern of white flowers.

"There's enough to make yourself a nice dress. I checked with the lady at the fabric counter. And Mrs. Wright said you could use her machine," Henry said.

Naomi spread the cloth out and stroked it lightly. "Very thoughtful." She did not say what she was thinking, which was that they'd buried her mother in a yellow dress.

"Good," Henry said. Naomi could see he was proud of himself. "All right, kids. Open your gifts. I've got to get going." Henry clapped his hands together. Maybe he meant to show excitement, but it looked more like impatience. Hurry up and be grateful.

The twins thanked Henry after they opened their gifts, a doll and a fire truck. They still had Naomi's presents to open, but already Henry was pulling on his coat. "Boss man and all," he said. "Won't be home till y'all are asleep. Naomi, make sure to shut off the heaters before you go to bed. You can't be too careful."

◇ ◇ ◇

"What am I supposed to do with this?" Cari asked Naomi when Henry had left. She poked at the doll's platinum hair.

"Look." Naomi tilted the doll back so that it closed its eyes, then tipped it forward again. The eyelids with their stiff blond lashes bobbed up and down over the staring blue eyes. The weight of the doll in her hands brought memory rising up in Naomi.

◇ ◇ ◇

Henry had given Naomi a doll just three weeks after he started coming to Abuelito's house to take her mother dancing. She remembered how he had grinned and squatted down to watch her open it. How he had balanced his hat on his knee.

Estella had stood behind him, her fingers resting lightly on his shoulders. Even then, Naomi felt that an exchange of some kind was taking place. She could not be sure what she was giving up. But once she untied the thick ribbon holding the wrapping paper in place, she knew exactly what she was getting.

The doll had dark ringlets, milky porcelain skin, and pink lips parted over painted white teeth. She wore a plaid jumper, and Naomi loved her instantly, with all of her five-year-old heart. She named the doll Nana before she even found her way to *gracias*. And she knew that Nana would get to do the things that she—brown and tongue-tied and full of the wrong kinds of words—could not.

"Naomi, guess what?" Her mother smiled at her after she had said her thank you. "Henry's going to be your new daddy. *¿Te gustaría, verdad que sí?*"

And then Naomi knew that the trade was finished, and she could not go back.

◇ ◇ ◇

"Don't be ungrateful," Naomi said. "Lots of girls your age would love to have a doll like this."

Cari pushed it away. "I'm not lots of girls."

Naomi sighed. "Henry's trying." Without thinking, she had parroted the words that made her cringe inwardly every time she heard them from Muff or Pastor Tom.

"Henry?" Cari raised her eyebrows and frowned.

Naomi blushed. "*Daddy.* Daddy's trying."

Beto sat pushing his tin truck back and forth. "I like my present," he said.

"Yeah, you would," Cari scoffed. She imitated Beto's excitement when he'd opened the gift. "Oh golly! A truck!" She pointed a finger at him, taunting. "Daddy's boy."

"So what?" Beto said softly. He continued to roll the truck around his feet.

"Enough, you two!" Naomi said. "Are you going to open my presents, or should I look for an orphanage nearby where there are thankful children?"

The twins scrambled for the last packages.

"Store-bought, and so many colors," Cari said when she tore into her package and saw the ribbons Naomi had gotten her. "Thank you, thank you!"

Naomi smiled. "And you, Beto?"

Beto unwrapped his gift more slowly. The journal was small, but it had a sturdy binding like a real book. He stroked the red cover with a finger and then touched the pages inside. He didn't say anything right off, but he didn't need to. Naomi could see that she'd chosen well.

"Maybe you'll write your own encyclopedia one day," Naomi said.

"I like Christmas here," Cari said, laying out her ribbons in a neat row.

"You should," Naomi said. It was the first time any of them had been able to buy gifts. In San Antonio, they had made their own presents or exchanged oranges and small bags of roasted pecans dusted in cinnamon sugar. This year: two presents each. They were rich.

◇ ◇ ◇

As they waited for Wash, Naomi and the twins huddled together against the foggy chill. The twins read the encyclopedia they had borrowed for the holidays, the first *S* volume (*Saber* to *Spain*). "Because it's the biggest," Beto explained. They did not want to run out of reading material before school started back.

Naomi thought for a moment about getting the quilt she'd hidden in the tree, but there would be no way to explain it without giving up her hiding spot.

Their hiding spot. Before now, she never knew she longed for anything besides the impossible return of her mother. All suffering had seemed connected to that absence, however distantly. But with Wash, want opened onto more want. Pleasure inside of an aching for more.

"How much longer before Wash comes?" Cari whined. "It's freezing."

"We can have cocoa when we go back," Naomi said. "Get warmed up."

"Cocoa now . . ." Cari moaned. "It is sooo cold."

"Do you want to go home?" Naomi asked, not thinking for a moment that they would say yes.

Beto shivered. "We do," he whispered through chattering teeth.

Naomi stared at Beto, then Cari. They had to be really cold. "But what about your present for Wash?"

Cari pulled a small package out of the pocket of her plaid cape. "You give it to him, okay? Your coat is thicker."

"I tried to tell you," Naomi said. She made a show of disapproval to hide her delight. "I guess I can stay..."

"We'll rub your feet later," Beto volunteered. He was already up, stamping to get his circulation flowing.

"And after that, you'll tell us a story about Mami?" Cari added.

"Deal," Naomi said with a smile.

Beto started to run, and Cari turned to follow him.

"Wait!" Naomi called. They spun around. "No cocoa until I get home, okay? I don't want you lighting the stovetop. And be careful when you turn on the heaters."

"Yes, ma'am!" the twins called back, running faster.

When they were out of sight, Naomi walked up the path and slid into the tree. Their tree. Wash would know to look for her when he came. She stood up inside, wrapped herself in the blanket, and snuggled down to wait. His touch was all she wanted; everything else was extra.

NAOMI & WASH

Naomi felt Wash slip into the tree. "Hi," she said, opening her eyes. "Merry Christmas."

He leaned down to kiss her. "Mmm. Merry Christmas. What'd you do with the critters?"

She wriggled out of the blanket and wrapped it around the two of them. "They were so cold while we were waiting, they wanted to go home. I can't say that I mind having you to myself."

"Ah," he said, "I like the sound of that. I have presents for them, something that I made."

"They'll be thrilled."

"Let Beto pick first, okay?"

She nodded. "They sent you a gift, too. I don't know what it is, though." She burrowed into her coat pocket for the little package.

He unwrapped a hollow wooden ball with a loop of string attached on one side. He slid out of the blanket and squinted at it in the gray winter light. "Want to get a better look?" he asked.

They ducked out of the tree and saw that the twins had painted the Christmas ornament all over with tiny brushstrokes. The scene was of a river and lots of trees. Their woods. And standing in front were four figures, holding hands. Cari and Beto were in the middle, painted that odd peachy color that meant "white." On one side, there was a light brown girl. On the other, a darker brown boy.

Back inside the tree, Wash held Naomi tight. He felt his heart might burst. A thing bigger than desire was in him.

"Like a family." Naomi breathed the words into the hollow of his neck.

"They can't know," he said.

She pulled back so that she could see his eyes. "About us? This? No. But they know that I love them, and they know that you love them."

He brought her close again. For a moment, he let himself imagine what it might be like to be a family. He pictured framing out a little cabin with Beto working by his side. It would be deep in the woods, a lost place. So far away that no one would find them. Ever.

He pulled a nail from his pocket, reached up, and twisted it into the soft, crumbling wood of the tree. He lifted the ornament by its loop and hung it there. A few bits of tree flaked off and fell on them.

Wash brushed the debris from Naomi's hair. "It's called heart rot, did you know that? What happens to a tree when it gets hollowed out."

"I didn't know."

"Cari and Beto read about it from the encyclopedia." He rested his chin on the top of her head. "Here," he said and put something in her hand.

Now she knew why he had made a game of tying string around each of her fingers when she saw him the week before. She moved her finger slowly over the smooth inside of the ring. Then she traced the outside, which was carved with what felt like tiny hatch marks. "Another look," she said, and she squatted down to look at the ring in the brighter light from outside the tree.

"Birds," she said. She touched each of the small Vs.

He had carved each one as a wish for lightness, for freedom. Feelings he wanted to give her. Feelings that she gave him.

He took it from her and slipped it onto the ring finger of her left hand. The gesture brought her longing coupled with despair. They couldn't have that, not in this world, no matter how much they loved each other.

"Wash," she said simply, and he understood.

"I know you can't wear it when you're out. But when we're here . . . And you could carry it with you. If you wanted."

"I love it." She walked her fingers up the back of his neck.

He undid the bit of string that held her braid and slid his fingers through the silky strands until it fell down over her shoulders. "So beautiful," he whispered. She trembled, letting her hands fall to his arms. Her back arched a little as his fingers climbed the front of her dress. He touched each button carefully between thumb and forefinger, starting at her waist. "What's here?" he asked, tracing a slight bulge between her breasts.

Naomi blushed for the first time inside the tree. "Something for you," she said. "Hold on." She turned away, meaning to get it out herself. Suddenly the game she had planned seemed crude, not sweet and playful as she'd imagined it.

"Wait." He twined his fingers through hers and leaned close. His breath was warm on her neck, and she could almost feel his lips. "Did you hide something for me to find?"

"Yes, but . . ." She hid her face. "I can't . . . Now I feel . . ."

"Nope," he said, lifting her chin with a finger. "Don't even say it. If there is one thing you're not, at least inside this tree, it's shy."

"I'm fast, then?" she blurted out.

"No," he said, "you are bold, and I love it. I love it about you, Naomi. Do you hear me?" He tilted her face toward him.

"I hear you," she whispered.

He undid the buttons of her dress until he could slide a hand inside the top of her slip. There was a small roll of fabric nestled warm and tight there. He leaned over her and tugged it free with his teeth. When he had it, she could feel him smiling mischief at her. "What do you say I save this and keep looking to see what other treasures I can find?" He nuzzled her neck and kissed her behind the ear. He smelled of wood and pepper.

She exhaled slowly and buttoned her dress back up with shaky fingers. "It's not as beautiful as the ring, but I did make it for you."

It was a linen handkerchief with a scalloped edge and a line of embroidery all the way around. In the corner was a cursive capital W. She had studied the twins' penmanship notebooks to make sure she got it right.

"Thank you, Naomi," he said.

They held each other tight. The hunger between them grew fierce. But it was Christmas, and they both had to get back, so they pocketed their presents and said good-bye.

BETO Back at home, Beto and Cari sat by the heater in the bedroom and waited for Naomi to come. Beto spun the wheels on the truck, and Cari folded her ribbons. When she was done, she picked up her doll, then dropped it with a sigh by the side of the bed she shared with Naomi. Her eyes were fixed on the guitar case under the bed.

"Don't," he warned.

"I'm not doing anything," she said, but he could tell she knew what he meant.

Beto picked up the small red book Naomi had given him. "Cari," he whispered, "come here." He handed her the notebook. "Does this seem heavy to you?"

She balanced the book on her palm. "No," she said, "but maybe I'm stronger than you." She was, Beto knew, but that wasn't it.

He took the book back. There it was again, that strange weight.

Not good.

Not bad.

Powerful.

NAOMI Naomi spent the days before New Year's Eve making herself a dress. She thought about saving some of the yellow fabric to make an Easter dress for Cari, but Cari said she absolutely did not want to match. And so Naomi gave herself permission to be extravagant with the cloth. She planned a full skirt with two layers and a broad waistband. And she would sew in a pocket. She wanted to make sure that she had a place to put Wash's ring.

The more she worked on the dress, the better she felt about it. She was finishing the project on New Year's Eve when Edgar stalked in and began to paw at the skirt of the dress. Naomi looked up and saw Beto in the doorway.

"Oh," she said. "I thought you and Cari went to get firecrackers with Katie and Jean."

"Edgar didn't like the Black Cats," he said.

"I don't need her putting holes in anything with those claws," she said.

"Don't wear it," Beto blurted out.

"Pardon?"

"That dress. I've got a bad feeling about it. Just . . . throw it all away." Beto gestured at the last of the carefully pinned pieces of cloth waiting to be stitched together.

"Throw it away! Of course not. You know very well that that would be rude and ungrateful. And anyway, I have to make a dress for one of my classes. This is homework."

Beto's shoulders slumped.

"Go play," she said. "There'll be some good treats at the party tonight." The church was having a potluck dinner and bonfire to celebrate the New Year. The gathering was intended as a wholesome alternative to rowdier festivities for the night, and she hoped she could make sure that Henry attended.

Beto stalled. "Can I help make something?"

Henry came up in the hallway behind him then. "Cooking is women's work, same as sewing. Act like a man, Robbie. Go outside and get your hands dirty. You don't start toughening up, I might have to drown that cat of yours."

The blood drained from Beto's face, and he rushed to pick up Edgar. "Going fishing," he called shakily. A moment later, the screen door clattered behind him.

Naomi opened her mouth to tell Henry that he had been too harsh, then she stopped herself. For all she knew, it took more toughness than a woman could manage to help a boy grow up. She went back to work, but she could feel Henry standing there, watching her. She heard him open his cigarette case and strike a match.

"Want one?" he asked her, holding the case out in her direction.

She shook her head. "Thanks, anyway." Still, the offer made her feel strangely proud, like her adulthood had registered to him. Like he had noticed how much she did to keep things running for him and the twins. Or maybe he'd already been drinking and was in the friendly stage of intoxication.

"You're going to look real pretty in that," Henry said, nodding at the pieces of the dress. Then he went off toward the kitchen.

◇ ◇ ◇

At the bonfire, Naomi saw Tommie and Dwayne Stark holding hands, and she smiled. Tommie had told her that all she wanted for Christmas was for Dwayne to ask her out. When Dwayne rested his chin on top of Tommie's head, she looked up at him with the sweetest smile. For once,

Tommie wasn't talking.

"Hi, stranger," Gilbert said. He handed her a metal rod and then slid a marshmallow onto the end.

"Hello," she mumbled. She stared intently at her marshmallow, holding it outside the lower flames to avoid blackening it. She used her left hand to hold the rod and kept her right arm behind her. The burn was mostly healed, but echoes of the pain came back if she got too close to heat.

Gilbert stood close beside her. "Too bad you got that pretty new coat. Now you don't need my jacket," he said. "Did you see Tommie and Dwayne? They make a swell couple."

She smiled. "They sure do."

"We would, too," he said softly. He shifted his weight from one foot to the other.

There was a long pause while Naomi tried to think of some way of moving the conversation away from this notion. "You could have any girl you want," she said.

"You're the one I want, though," he said. His voice was low, and the flickering firelight played across his tan cheeks.

"Surely not," she said. She felt herself stiffen, and it was all she could do not to back away and run.

"Don't you know how pretty you are?"

"You know I'm . . . not like other girls here."

"You're good as anybody!" he said, his voice rising a little. "Sure, some people have their ideas, but where you're from don't bother me none. Nothing wrong with being Mexican. And anyway, my pa always said it's a man's job to bring his woman up a bit."

Naomi bit her tongue; she knew he meant to be kind. "I can't," she said finally.

"How come? You ain't seeing anybody else, are you?"

"What difference does it make?" Naomi asked, dodging his question to avoid an outright lie. "It's not enough for you to like me."

"Oh." His face fell. "You mean you don't like me. Sure, I understand." He nodded slowly and stepped back.

"It's not that," she said quickly. "I like you, but not that way. Let's be friends."

He laughed. "That excuse is more used than a box of Ivory flakes on wash day."

She shrugged. "I'm not like everybody else," she said again. Her left hand disappeared into the pocket of her skirt, and she ran her finger in rapid circles around the birds on her ring. Wash, Wash, Wash.

"Friends, then," Gil said, a touch of bitterness in his voice.

"Friends," she said.

◊ ◊ ◊

It was a quarter till midnight before Naomi could get away from the bonfire. She raced from the church, following the edge of the river. When the land started to rise, she cut sharply to the north. She needed to hurry if she was going to make it in time. She got to the top of the hill and scanned the area as she caught her breath. A moment later, she saw movement in the bushes, but it was only a small covey of bobwhites startled from their roost.

She had come across the huge magnolia tree while out on a walk with the twins the week before. The tree's thick limbs draped all the way to the ground, forming a kind of low-ceilinged room surrounded by the waxy evergreen leaves. The branches were strong all the way up into the crown of the tree, which stretched fifty or sixty feet into the sky. The twins had begged her to help them climb it, so she'd pointed out the footholds and handholds all the way up.

Now, her hands itched to find their way up again. She untied the yellow ribbon Cari had put in her hair and draped it on a low branch so Wash would know that she was in the tree. She wanted to share this view with him, and their regular spot was too far from the church for her to manage a meeting. He'd promised to come at midnight if he could get away.

She made her way up the tree, working carefully to avoid snagging her new dress. The view from the top was even more breathtaking at night. She could see the county laid out across the hills. There was the Baptist church, its steeple partly illuminated by the high flames of the bonfire. She could see lights on in the Humble camp and in houses scattered here and there in clearings. The moon was reflected in the Sabine for a moment, then heavy clouds darkened the sky again. In distant clearings, firecrackers went off. Across the landscape flares burned bright blue and gold as far as she could see.

She had counted forty-nine flares when she thought she heard movement at the bottom of the tree.

"Is that you?" she called down softly, but there was no answer. "Wash?" she whispered.

For a panicked moment, she imagined that someone had followed her from the church. Even the twins would cause her problems right now.

"Say something," she pleaded with the darkness.

"I love you?" came Wash's voice.

"That *is* something," she said, laughing. "Say it again, but not like a question."

"I love you."

The branches beneath her creaked. The heavy dark leaves rustled. Closer. Closer. She sucked in a breath, felt it cold in her chest.

"Again," she said.

"I love you." He was on the branch beneath hers, and his hands slid up her stockings slowly, slowly. His fingers crept over her knees, then stopped. "Well?" he said.

Naomi closed her eyes and listened and felt the age of the tree trunk under her hands. She remembered all the lights she'd seen over the countryside, only now they were compressed in the center of her chest. Her heart was a ball of light, and it was Wash who had made it so.

She tried on the words. "I. Love. You." Nothing had ever felt truer.

Wash let out a breath and slid his hands up to her thighs. He lifted her down onto his branch and held her tight, and she knew for certain that hers was not the only heart full of light.

Then fireworks exploded over the church in red and green and blue bursts.

Midnight.

Their kiss outlasted the fireworks.

JANUARY 1937

WASH Wash was so busy finding ways to be with Naomi that he all but forgot the scheme to get money to improve the colored school. But the seed of his idea had sprouted in his father's imagination, and a week into the new year, Wash found himself walking with his father toward Mr. Crane's back porch. They'd had a meeting set with the school board, but the entrance to the main hall and all the side doors of the school had been locked tight.

Wash stopped in the middle of Mr. Crane's yard, but his father continued up the porch steps and knocked softly at the door.

Mr. Crane's stern-faced housekeeper answered it. "Can I help you?"

"Good evening, Miss Cayla," Jim began. "I hope you can. I'm looking for the superintendent. We had a meeting with the school board set for this evening. I thought it would be in the administrative office, but the school is locked."

Cayla's eyes drifted toward the school before settling on Wash. "Mr. Crane isn't available tonight, sir."

"I'm sure the meeting was today." Jim said.

"Mr. Fuller, I'm telling you, the superintendent isn't available." Her words rang out sharply, and her hands were at her hips. Jim frowned and glanced back at Wash.

Wash shrugged and checked his watch. It was almost six o'clock, and the meeting was supposed to be at five thirty. When he looked up, he saw a curtain move in one of the parlor windows and a glimpse of Mr. Crane's long, sharp nose and close-cropped white hair.

"Come off it, Miss Cayla. I can see Mr. Crane up there in the parlor." Wash raised his voice. "Evenin' Mr. Crane! We're hoping to speak with you." He flashed a grin in the direction of the window, but the face was gone.

"Y'all best go on quick now. Don't wanna find no trouble or make none," Cayla said softly, urgently. This time her words were just for them.

"Thank you, Miss Cayla," Jim said. He headed down the steps.

"There's no trouble here. We can wait a spell," Wash called. His father shot him a warning look, but he stopped and waited next to Wash.

Cayla twisted a dish towel in her hand and went back into the kitchen.

A few minutes later, the screen door opened, and there was Mr. Crane.

"Sorry about this, Jim, I surely am."

"Thank you, sir," Wash's father said, turning on his humble-but-charming voice. "I'm obliged to you for setting up the meeting."

"Jim," Mr. Crane began, "it's like this, to make changes to the budget, we have to have the whole school board present."

"Of course, sir. That's why we came. Like we talked about last week."

"Yes, but as you saw . . . a number of board members have elected . . ."

"They're voting with their absence," came a gruff voice. "Cowardly. Or 'diplomatic' if you want a four-dollar word for it." The owner of the voice navigated his bulk through the doorway and jostled past Mr. Crane onto the porch, a tumbler in hand. He let the screen door slam behind him. "Me, I got no problem telling you that your pickaninny school is plenty good for what it's intended for. The rest of my esteemed colleagues, they'd rather ignore you till you give up than call you an uppity son of a bitch to your face."

Wash saw his father's shoulders tighten. "Evenin', Mr. Gibbler. I'm simply here to give a presentation, sir. To explain the needs of our community. And to show the benefit your help would have for white citizens as well. Of course, I know there are limits, but surely—" He gestured at the pumpjacks pulling oil out of the ground—"with the oil money . . .

with the taxes . . . and," he nodded at Wash, "the savings from switching to the raw gas—"

"We got plenty to spend our money on right over here. Your school's better than half the white schools in Texas. What in the hell is it you want now?" Gibbler asked.

"A few books for the children, sir." Jim spread his hands apologetically.

Gibbler frowned and leaned a beefy thigh against the porch railing. "Let's see, if I recall correctly, we gave you all a truckload of primers at the end of last school year. Plus books for your library. Even some supplies. Desks and chairs, I do believe." He ticked the items off on his fingers. They were as large as sausages and just as fat.

Wash swallowed a laugh. He'd spent half his summer repairing the battered furniture the whites had tossed out. And the primers—the only one that wasn't missing sections had an obscene drawing inked on every page.

"You're right, sir," Jim said, "and we're most grateful for your generosity. Most grateful, sir." Wash could hardly stand the bootlicking tone. He stared into the woods so that he wouldn't have to see the smile he knew was still plastered on his father's face.

The thought of the woods made him bold, and Wash took a step forward, then another. "They're missing pages," he said. "Sir."

"What was that, Washington?" Mr. Crane asked. "Speak up, son."

"I said, those books we got from y'all, they were all missing pages. I can fix busted furniture, but I can't make pages appear for the little ones to learn their lessons."

His father turned and gave Wash a hard stare, his lips tight. "What my son means to say is that we're keen on improving the level of education at New London Colored School. Sure want to be a credit to the county."

"Secondhand doesn't have to mean ruined," Wash said. He knew he was getting careless, but he didn't give a damn anymore. He couldn't simper around these fools and still be what he was becoming for Naomi. If he had to burn bridges to be that man, he would. The next words flew out of Wash's mouth. "How about passing down some supplies before they're worn plum out? How about that, sir?" His sense caught up with him in time for him to tack on the "sir."

"You are mighty brazen, boy," Gibbler said. He jerked his head left and then right and grinned at the cracking sound his neck made. "You want to be a high-tone colored, huh?"

Wash shook his head. "No, sir. I'd be pleased to be a simple carpenter." He didn't look at his father, but he could hear his sharp intake of breath. That was another bridge he was setting fire to, although it might not burn so fast.

Mr. Crane patted Gibbler on the back. "One thing's for sure, give him tools, and this young man can fix up anything you can find and build anything you can think of. I can vouch for that."

"Thank you, sir," Wash said.

"Shit, Dan." Gibbler rattled the ice in his tumbler, then held it up in Mr. Crane's direction. "That's something else we need to talk about. I heard from a couple of roustabouts that you got a habit of giving good work away to coloreds, work that plenty of whites would be glad for."

Mr. Crane took the glass from Gibbler. "There's work to go around."

Jim Fuller's shoulders sagged, and he lifted his hat to his head with trembling hands. "Looks like we ought to be going. Gentlemen, I sure would be glad to try for another meeting. I'll wait to hear from you, of course."

"Sure thing, Jim. That's it," said Mr. Crane.

"Yeah," Gibbler laughed. The long jowls of his face jiggled. "You just wait on us. You come back when we send for you."

"Good night, gentlemen," Jim said. Even without seeing his father's face, Wash could feel him urging him to play this right and salvage things as best he could.

"Good night, Mr. Crane, Mr. Gibbler," Wash said. And thanks for nothing, he wanted to add.

When they were a good thirty yards away, Wash's father grabbed his arm. "What in Jesus' name were you thinking, talking like that? How do you think we're going to turn them to our cause now?"

Wash gave a dry laugh. "Come on, Pa," he said, "you were right. We're dealing with some cold, cold hearts here. Heck, it'd take an explosion to wake them up." The last words rang out through the thin January air.

Wash and his father glanced back. They didn't see anyone on the porch, and Wash felt a wave of relief and then instant shame. He didn't want to be like his father, chained to "yessirs" forever, but maybe it was harder to burn bridges and break habits than he thought.

THE GANG We had all heard Miranda harping for months about how Naomi was greasing up the school. A greaser's a greaser, maybe, but the real itch in Miranda's panties was about Gilbert asking Naomi out, even if she said no. We all knew that Miranda wanted him for herself. She tried to get him last year, but old Gibbler had bigger and better plans for his one and only daughter. These days, he wasn't letting her out of his sight.

Miranda whined to the girls about how Gibbler dragged her around in the back of his Packard whenever he went to check out a strike or stare down an unproductive tool pusher. Nights after school board meetings, she was condemned to sip iced tea alone on Mr. Crane's porch while her father browbeat the old superintendent inside and drank up his bourbon. There was nothing Miranda liked less than sitting around without an audience. We had good reason to believe that, in those moments, she'd have gladly traded her diamond leash for Naomi's wetback freedom. And that only made Miranda hate Naomi more.

Maybe that's why she started whispering about Naomi and Mr. Crane's colored boy.

NAOMI   Naomi should have known that Wash and the twins were up to something when she didn't hear from the three of them for over an hour. She'd been sweeping the porch after school when Wash walked by the yard, and she wanted to run to him and soak up his smile. But that would have to wait.

She called to him. "Twins are on the side of the house, by the shed." Then she turned back to her work. After the sweeping, she had laundry to hang. She worked fast; the sooner she finished, the closer she'd be to a chance at meeting Wash in the woods.

He passed by again a few minutes later.

"Going?" she asked. "I just have to hang out this last bit of laundry." Maybe she could get away now, if only for a few minutes.

"I'll be back. I'm going to pick up my toolbox. Did you know about that little radio out there?"

She groaned. "There's a story behind it. Not a good one."

"Well, Beto's set on fixing it. I told him he could use my tools. He can't make it any more broke, right?"

"I guess not," she said, holding back her disappointment. "Sounds like a slow job."

"I reckon we'll just play at fixing it."

Naomi pulled her coat tighter around her and settled a kitchen chair onto the porch. If anyone asked why she was sewing out in the cold, she'd say she just wanted some fresh air. The house was stuffy from being closed up all winter.

Wash and Beto sat on the back steps with the radio between them. They peered inside it and fiddled with the tubes and wires. After an adjustment, Beto carried the radio into the house to see if it would turn on. Cari paced back and forth in front of the porch until Wash told her to sit down so he could teach her the names of his tools. When he finished, he gave her a wink. "Think you can tell 'em apart with your eyes closed?"

Naomi sighed. She loved the sweetness of the three of them together; she just wished it didn't mean losing her time with Wash. But he was good, too good, to deny the twins their share.

She worked on a little smock for Muff's baby and imagined that Wash was teaching her the tools. His hands, large and strong and gentle, guiding hers. Now, he was holding a hammer out to Cari.

"*Martillo*," Naomi whispered.

Maybe in Spanish she could tell him what she meant. All of it. Maybe in Spanish she would find the right words.

BETO Beto fixed the radio. He got the antenna wire to reach to the kitchen window, and he plugged the set in there so they could hear the music in the yard. Then he hopped down the steps working an imaginary fiddle under his chin to match the country tune that was playing.

"You've got a way with those tools, buddy." Wash grinned at Beto and winked.

Cari scowled. "I helped, too."

"Yes, ma'am, you did," Wash said.

Beto waited for the compliment to be repeated, for Cari to take part of the praise that had started out being just for him. But Wash left it at that. Beto stored up the words. Words he didn't have to share. *You've got a way with those tools. Buddy.*

Wash packed up his tools and left a little before sunset. Naomi appeared on the porch, hugging her bare arms. "Just a few more minutes. Then we put it away. Back out in the shed, okay?" She kept her voice bright, but Beto knew she was thinking about the first time the radio had played. He didn't want that memory, didn't want Naomi to have it either. He ran up the porch steps and hugged her tight. Because.

After a minute, Cari came up the steps. "Daddy's got the late shift," she said, twirling a finger around one of her curls. "He won't be home for hours. Can't we make a party?"

"You could wear Mami's dress!" Beto added. Naomi had shown it to them on Christmas Day when she'd told them the story of how it'd been a prize for a dance-off that their mother had won on her birthday. Estella had even written the date of the contest on the dress's label. March 18, 1923.

"Please, Omi?" They said it together, and before she had answered, Cari took her hand and led her into the kitchen.

"Just for a little while," Cari said solemnly.

"You can have the radio for a few more minutes," Naomi said. Inside, she hummed along with "Jesse Polka" and began getting out the things for supper.

"Make tortillas? Wear her dress?" Cari said.

"And dance?" Beto pressed. "Please?"

Cari looped her arms around Naomi's waist. "And dance!"

Naomi shook her free. "I can't dance like she could, you know that. And we already have biscuits." Naomi pointed to the pan cooling on the counter.

"They'll still be good for breakfast tomorrow," Beto said.

"We won't complain, promise!" Cari said. "And you don't have to dance—just tell us what it was like."

NAOMI And that was how Naomi ended up wearing her mother's frilly red dress. She'd agreed on the condition that Beto and Cari renew their promise to stay out of her guitar case. "Everybody should get to have one bit of privacy," she said. She did not say, I can't give her to you. She did not say, I need her for myself.

Naomi raised a hand to her hair, which the twins had twisted and pinned up. It looked to her like a dark tangle of rope, but she couldn't resist their excitement. "When Mami did her hair," Naomi said, "it was perfect. Not a strand out of place."

"And the dancing?" Cari asked.

"She could dance all night long, dozens of dances. Gringo dances and Mexican dances. Everything."

She retold the story of how Estella won the dress by dancing until four in the morning. And then turned to other, even more familiar stories. Stories she'd repeated so many times that all three of them knew what she was going to say before she said it. Stories that didn't require her to sacrifice some part of her heart she hadn't already given up. She had to save what she could; she dreaded the day when she'd have to tell them, "That's it. You've heard it all." Then she would have handed over everything that had been hers alone.

Even Wash belonged equally, if differently, to the twins.

While she told them the stories, Naomi began the tortillas. Once she'd worked the dough into a fine, smooth mass, she let the twins roll out their own tortillas. Cari had had some practice in San Antonio, but still hers came out ruffled around the edges like the collar of a dress. Abuelita would be appalled, but Naomi just smiled.

Beto's first try looked a little like a sunflower. The next looked like a cat, Cari said.

"Edgar!" Beto grinned. "We'll save that one for her."

Just like the first time she'd made them for the potluck, the tortillas cooked too fast in Henry's cheap pans. She needed a proper *comal* or at least a cast-iron skillet, but the tortillas were still delicious rolled up warm with sugar and a bit of cinnamon and salt. The twins sat at the table, covered in sugar but happy. For now, what she had given them was enough.

Naomi was cooking the last tortilla when she heard Henry's truck pulling onto the patch of gravel by the back porch. She froze, taking in the scene through his eyes. Her nose twitched, and she looked down to find the tortilla blackened and smoking in the pan. She flipped it into the sink and turned the gas off. She heard his boots on the steps and the double *thunk* of him kicking them off onto the porch. There was no time to hide anything, but she reached over to the radio and clicked it off. The Light Crust Doughboys faded into silence.

"Somethin' burnin'?" Henry asked as he walked in.

"Tortillas," she mumbled. "Twins wanted them."

The twins sat stone still at the table, staring down at the sugar scattered over the table.

Henry hummed a little and walked over to the stove. He picked up one of the still-warm tortillas, swiped it through the open tin of lard, and sprinkled it with a spoonful of sugar from the sugar bowl. He crossed to the kitchen table and kicked a chair out, dropping himself into it as he folded the tortilla into his mouth. "Umm," he said, winking at the twins.

They smiled back, relieved, and began chewing again. Edgar jumped down from Beto's lap and twined around Henry's ankles.

Henry put his feet up on the chair beside him. Naomi felt his eyes follow her as she tossed out the burned tortilla and washed the pan.

"Something's different here," he said slowly. When she glanced back, he was smiling. "Hey, ho!" he said. He wasn't angry, not yet. "That dress—"

"I'll go change," Naomi said quickly, already crossing to the hallway.

"Why? Don't she look pretty?" Henry said to the twins. His eyes were a million miles away.

HENRY Henry hadn't had much luck with Estella at first, but once she saw how he could dance, she couldn't keep away. He kept pace with her better even than the best Mexican dancers.

He could still remember the first night she danced only with him.

It was December, and there'd been a huge Christmas tree in the middle of the dance hall, bright with white bulbs and an illuminated star on top. When they spun past the tree, flecks of light caught on the shimmering red of her dress. Her hand was hot in his. He felt her breasts against his chest when he pulled her close, missed them when she moved away.

Other dancers watched their every move, murmuring appreciation, whispering envy.

"Where'd you learn to dance our dances?" she asked, breathless.

"How'd you learn to dance *my* dance?" he shot back, twirling her under his arm. He brought her waist close and pressed against her. Her hips were firm and inviting under his hands. She did not pull away from him, and as he tipped her back and back and back, he watched the hollow above her collarbone and the lovely slope down to the neckline of her dress. Her chest rose and fell under the bright red fabric.

And those lips.

God, how he had wanted her.

NAOMI Naomi shifted her weight from one foot to the other. She studied the floor, waiting to see what Henry would say.

"Leave it on," he said finally. "I didn't know you kept it."

"Abuelita saved it for me. From before . . . before Houston." She was careful. Once he had married her, Henry hadn't allowed Estella to dance, and his jealousy dictated what clothes she wore.

"I heard music . . ." Henry said slowly, yawning.

"Beto fixed the radio," Naomi said, omitting Wash's involvement.

"I'll be damned, Robbie," Henry said. He slapped the table and punched Beto on the shoulder. There was a certain looseness to his movements. And the cursing. Naomi began to tally the signs.

"Time for bed," Naomi said to the twins. They were about to protest, but she shot them a warning look. "Now. I'll be by to tuck you in."

"Let me do it," Henry said, grinning a little too widely.

◇ ◇ ◇

Naomi had swept up the sugar and cleaned the counters by the time Henry came out of the twins' room a few minutes later. "They're good kids," he said. "So damn smart, though. Sometimes it makes me feel dumb. You ever feel that way?"

Naomi laid her dish towel on the counter. "All the time," she said.

He pitched himself back into a chair at the table. "Ugly day. I ought to wash, but I think I'll eat first."

Naomi hadn't expected that. "Do you want . . . ?" she trailed off. He'd already seen what was on the stove. Tortillas, beans, and rice cooked with tomatoes. She glanced at the fridge. She had some leftover ham and a bit of broccoli. There were biscuits in the bread box.

One evening when Henry had come home from two weeks in the oil field, her mother had made beautiful *enchiladas rojas* for him, each corn tortilla lovingly rolled around the stewed chicken and onions and tomatoes and then spread with the sauce she made herself. Henry must have been angry about something else, no doubt, but he'd swept the food onto the floor, yelled that it was sombrero slop. He had ordered Naomi to stay at the table, too, but forbade her to touch the food her mother had served. He sat there with his arms crossed until Estella made him boiled carrots and fried potatoes with bacon. Only then did he let her clear away the shattered dishes. Estella had cut herself on a plate and hidden the bleeding finger in a dishrag.

"I—I wasn't sure if . . . " Naomi tried again.

Henry raised an eyebrow. "Havin' trouble following you, darlin'," he drawled. He was drunker than she'd realized.

She gestured at the stovetop.

Henry shrugged. "As long as it's not still moving."

"Oh." She crossed to the cupboard and pulled out a plate. The frilly hem of the dress scratched her calves. It felt wrong to be wearing the dress, wrong for him to see her in it.

"What's worrying you?" Henry asked. He had his chin propped up on one fist.

Naomi mumbled her words as she served his plate. "Once, in Houston, you said . . . you . . . " That was as close as she could get to talking about before. Her mother. What happened in the house they'd all lived in.

"Come on, now." Henry's voice was so liquor-blurred it was almost gentle. "All that was a long, long time ago. I've changed, see?"

"Mmm," she said. She did not look at him when she handed him his plate.

"Would you sit with me?"

Naomi lowered herself into a chair. She held her shoulders back to keep the dress's neckline from dipping.

Henry shoved a fork into the beans, raised it almost to his mouth, then set it down without taking the bite. Naomi winced and waited.

Nothing else happened.

"Sometimes I get the itch to go away. Start again fresh somewhere else, different place, different work. Not that I know anything else. I just like thinking that we could go away, if we wanted."

We, he had said. Did he mean the twins? Take the twins from her? She wouldn't let that happen, but she didn't want to go anywhere. Naomi held her terror in, balling it up inside a fist in her lap. When they'd first gotten here, all she had wanted was to go home to San Antonio. Now she had a home. Not here, not in Henry's house, but in the woods with Wash, with the twins. It had never occurred to her that Henry might want to move—or that he could make them.

"The twins are so happy here," she said.

Henry took a bite, chewed. "I saw a man on fire today," he said. He spoke low, but Naomi heard the catch in his voice. "Fire is the worst thing about the oil field; a well fire's just hell. This fella, he ran out of the flames toward us. Didn't have the sense to drop and roll even when we were shouting for him to. Must have been scared. His eyes were a spot of white in the flames. He was covered in oil. Burned like a torch. By the time we got to him, he was black from the burning."

Naomi shuddered.

Henry went on. "Every time I see something like that . . . a man falls from a rig, there's a well fire, guy drowns in a tank, I imagine it's me." He looked up at her. "But it's never me. I'm just there, close by. It's a risky business, but . . . seems like I seen a lot of that."

Naomi opened her mouth, but nothing came out. She closed it again.

"You think a person can be bad luck?" he asked.

"I—I—" Naomi scrambled for something safe. "I thought finding religion meant a body quit worrying about luck."

Henry sighed and twisted his napkin. "Pastor Tom's told me as much, but he doesn't know . . . he doesn't know everything."

Naomi swallowed. So many things Pastor Tom would never know.

She was casting about for something to say when Henry excused himself to use the bathroom.

HENRY Destruction dogged Henry. He was the only one in his immediate family to survive a tornado on the Kansas plains. Ever since, the sound of a train up close filled him with dread and called back the day of the tornado. Afterwards he'd been sent to live with relatives in Topeka. That ended with a fire in the barn that spread to the house. He spent a year with foster parents in Archer City, but when three-quarters of the family's cattle died off, they sent him back to the boys' home.

The oil field was his escape. It was a transitory life, so nobody knew him. The commonness of his name was a consolation, too; there were three Henry Smiths in any given oil field of reasonable size. He took solace in the fact that others, if they ever heard of the wretched accidents, might well assume that it was some other Henry Smith standing by when disaster struck.

But Henry knew.

NAOMI Naomi glanced back at the clock on the wall. Half past ten. Henry's plate was only half-eaten. She hoped he didn't expect her to sit with him much longer. She thought about going to bed before he came out of the bathroom. One night without cleaning her teeth wouldn't be the end of the world. But with the dress and the radio, she didn't want to risk angering him. Not tonight.

While she washed the other dishes in the sink, she looked out the window. There was nothing to see but wintery darkness. The lights were off at Muff and Bud's, and low clouds covered the strip of sky between the houses.

She stared at her own reflection, at the ridiculous pile of hair on top of her head. With a little sense she could have avoided this whole evening, kept their life in Henry's house as predictable and safe as her simple braid. She yanked the pins out of her hair as fast as she could and was pulling the last ones out when she heard the bathroom door open.

She slipped the pins into the pocket of her apron and started to smooth her hair so she could put it back into a braid.

She wasn't quick enough. Henry was back in the kitchen, and so she released her hair and shoved her hands back into the dishwater. She did not turn to look at him but waited for the sound of him sitting back down to his dinner.

A moment later he was behind her. Naomi's whole body stiffened. A rough hand gathered her hair and pushed it to one side. His face nuzzled her neck. He smelled of grease and dirt, liquor and cigarettes. She caught a whiff of cheap perfume. She tried to wriggle free, but his arms circled her waist and tightened like an iron band around her rib cage.

"Stell, baby," he whispered. "Let's dance." A thumb slid up the side of her breast.

"Stop it!" Naomi hissed. She was afraid to raise her voice for fear of waking the twins.

"Christ, I've missed this," Henry murmured. "It's been so long." He slotted one of his legs between hers and pressed himself in closer. She closed her eyes tight and thought of her tree, thought of Wash, thought of the river. She prayed that when she opened her eyes, she would be there.

It didn't work.

"Stell—"

"I'm Naomi!" she said, wrenching herself around to face him. She was still locked in his arms, and now his face was inches from hers. She felt the hardness of him against her hip, and the sour-sweet smell of whiskey filled her nostrils as he breathed onto her face.

"Stop it!" she said, leaning back as far as she could. She felt her hair fall into the dishwater, but she did not care, only wanted to be away from him.

"Come on, now," he said, pressing his hips against her.

She worked an elbow up and jabbed it into his chest.

Henry laughed. "Oh, honey, go on and be mad, that makes you look even more like your ma. She liked to pretend to fight, too."

"So you know who I am, then. Behave yourself for heaven's sake!"

"You like playin' mama, don't you? I can help you play all night if you want." He grinned at her as if none of her resistance had registered. "God, I'd like to give it to you just like this—" He lowered his hands to her bottom and rubbed himself against her.

"That's enough, Henry!" Naomi gave him a shove, but he didn't budge.

His smile widened. "Say it again."

"What?" she snapped.

"Call me Henry."

"Let me go!"

"All right, just say it again and I'll let you go."

"Henry," she spat.

He closed his eyes and released her. She moved away from him fast, shuddering, but he seemed not to notice or maybe was too drunk to notice.

"Don't do that again," she whispered. "Promise you won't."

"All right," he said, "okay." But already his chin had slipped toward his neck, and she was not sure how aware he was of anything.

"Baby," he murmured, sliding down to the floor. "I've missed you." He rested his head against the kitchen cabinet.

Naomi refused to feel sorry for him. She backed out of the room and rushed into the bedroom she shared with the twins.

NAOMI Naomi lay tense and wakeful beside a sleeping Cari. If she turned her head to the left, she could still smell Henry's sweat on her shoulder. She wanted to wash but didn't dare go to the bathroom for fear he'd follow her in.

Sometime during the night, she heard Henry stumble from the kitchen into the hall. She got up and sat with her back against the bedroom door, Abuelito's old rusted letter opener clenched in her hand. A threat was better than nothing.

After a while, she heard Henry snoring. She crept to the bathroom, locked the door, and undressed. She scrubbed everywhere he had touched her. She wet her comb and pulled it through her hair again and again before braiding it tightly.

She could only think: not again. Not again. She was not her mother. She was not the child she had been when Henry had first tried to use her in that way. She was herself and grown, and yet this was no protection. It meant only that the hurt he intended for her would be different from the other hurts. Her stomach churned. No matter what Henry said tomorrow, there was no making it right.

She went out onto the porch. Despite the cold, there was a familiar heat in her armpits and between her thighs. Maybe fear and desire ran along the same tracks in her body, but she refused to confuse Wash's giving with Henry's taking. She pressed her face into her knees. She wanted to run to the river to be inside the tree. To be where Wash had been. To return to the safety of their belonging to each other. But she could not leave the twins alone with Henry.

She worked her fingers against her temples. She ought to be figuring on a way for the three of them to get away. She went back into the house and checked the sock where she hid the money she saved from what Henry gave her. She'd spent too much at Christmas, she knew, especially now that he did not let her buy the groceries. She had eleven dollars left, not enough for train tickets to San Antonio. Anyway, leaving New London would mean leaving Wash. The thought of that punched through her every idea of happiness. She could not think of it being otherwise.

Around five it occurred to her to do something, so she sewed. She sat at the kitchen table and stitched her hurt into tiny perfect seams that bound a bit of lace edging to the smock and bloomers for Muff's coming baby. The blue cloth Muff had chosen was so pale it looked white.

From the edge of the camp, a rooster gave a few halfhearted crows. Naomi checked the clock. It was half past six, but the winter morning was still dark.

Naomi started a moment later when there was a knock at the back door. She opened it a crack to see Pastor Tom standing on the porch, his Bible pressed against the front of his coat.

"Hello, Naomi. Sorry for the early visit. I need to see Henry," he said. His expression was grave, and it seemed to her that he was searching her face for information.

She wondered what he saw, what secrets he was able to peel away from her. She imagined the wood planks of the kitchen floor splitting open so she could escape that stare.

"He's asleep, Pastor." She still held her sewing and fingered the seams she'd just sewn.

At least Henry was no longer on the kitchen floor. That would be harder to explain. But she wasn't going to explain anything to Pastor Tom or anyone. To talk about the night before was impossible.

"It's important," Pastor Tom said.

"It's just . . . I'd have to wake him . . ." Naomi shrugged, hoping Pastor Tom would let it alone.

Pastor Tom tugged at his beard and shook his head. "I'll wake him. If I may come in."

She stepped back to let him pass. "Coffee?"

"Please," he answered. He handed her his hat and coat. "From what I heard from Bud, Henry's going to need it."

A few minutes later, Pastor Tom marched a groggy, squinting Henry out onto the porch. Snatches of the sermon drifted in to her.

"You're part of my flock, Henry. You think word doesn't get around? That bar is a den of drinkers and fornicators!"

"It was only a little dancing, Pastor—"

"Dancing! An invitation to the devil. The Lord sees all, brother. He sees all."

"There was a well fire yesterday. Did you know that? A man roasted to death. Another one burned bad. Hell with the lid off, that's what it was. I had to get that out of my head."

"Prayer, Henry, prayer! Have you forgotten the power housed in the dwelling place of the Lord? Have you forgotten the darkness the Lord brought you out of? Have some faith, man. You're not the first one to see hurt and loss."

"Sure, but—"

"That dead man is a reminder! We cannot delay in putting things right with our Savior. We have to choose a path of righteousness. Do you hear, Henry? You're a new man in the Lord!"

Naomi wished she could run out to the porch and tell Pastor Tom the truth: there was nothing new in Henry. Just the same man rotted through and through. Instead, she snipped the loose threads from the bloomers and folded them with the other clothes she had made for Muff's baby.

HENRY "I hear," Henry said, but he didn't feel like a new man. Not like he had at first, during those early days and weeks when the church seemed to lift him right off the ground, when a new and holy life had felt possible. Now the Bible verses were riddles. The prayers and the meetings felt like work, and he already had sixty hours of that a week. He didn't want another prayer meeting or sermon; he wanted something to take the edge off of his hangover. He did his best to look like he was listening, but he was thinking about an iced-down beer.

Tom clapped Henry on the shoulder. "Flee temptation, brother," he was saying now. "And drink some coffee."

Henry nodded. "Thank you, Pastor Tom. I'm glad you're here to holler me back."

"Repent and seek sanctification. Pursue the path where you can make things right." Pastor Tom thumped a hairy hand against his Bible. "Remember."

As the pastor strode away, Henry slid down to the porch steps and rested his elbows on his knees. A tinge of pink and purple colored the sky above the woods, and he felt suddenly sobered by the cold. He could hear Naomi moving around in the kitchen, and he realized that he was afraid to go back into the house. What could he say? He longed to feel clean and strong and redeemed, like he had at first in the church. She could give him that, he knew, if she would just forgive him. Henry was hungry for the relief of it. He needed it now more than ever.

He held his hands open, then closed them into fists. Open, closed. There was a way to fix things. The solution came to him whole. When the time was right, he'd make Naomi see it, too.

NAOMI Naomi managed the day with no worse casualty than a few stern looks from her teachers when she stifled a yawn in class. After school, she left the twins helping Miss Bell and made a beeline for the tree. She curled up inside the blanket and slept until Wash kissed her awake.

But when she collected the twins and they went back to the house, Henry was there. The sight of him made something lurch in her. He left shortly after she arrived, mumbling something she didn't hear.

It was like those first days in East Texas, only worse. Even when he was gone, everything seemed marked by his presence. The dishes in the sink. The chair where he'd sat, the napkin left crumpled on the table. When Naomi went to use the toilet, she could smell his aftershave and, worse, him. She backed out of the bathroom.

After she sent the twins to bed, she waited for Henry to arrive, trying to think of what she would do, what she would say. She gave up when he still hadn't come home at midnight, but she lay awake listening for him. The sky had already shifted from pitch to a lightening gray when he finally came home. She stayed in bed this time, but she held the letter opener against her thigh. She watched the doorknob for any signs of turning. Sleep was an unreachable territory.

"You look terrible," Tommie told Naomi outside their homeroom the next morning.

Naomi shrugged. Her eyeballs were sticky with fatigue. Her head ached, and her hands trembled. The thought of the day ahead staggered and exhausted her. Before she'd left the house, Naomi had gulped down a bitter cupful of coffee. Now her stomach gurgled and clenched. She felt even worse than when she'd climbed stiff and aching out of bed.

She sleepwalked through the morning, unable to think of anything but closing her eyes. Mr. Pittluck, the math teacher, saw her head droop and called her to the front of the class. "Do what it takes to stay alert in my class," he snarled.

She mumbled, "Yes, sir," and made a move to sit back down, but he stuck out his ruler to stop her.

"You stand until the end of the hour. Here." He made her face the chalkboard.

She could hear laughing. "God, but she's stupid," someone hissed between giggles. Miranda whispered loudly, "Nobody but a dummy would dare sleep on Pittluck's watch."

"I ain't complaining," Sam Jackson said. "I'd say the scenery just improved considerably."

On any other occasion, Mr. Pittluck would have silenced these remarks, but he seemed to view them as part of her punishment.

Naomi's face burned and her eyes itched. She looked up at the pressed tin on the ceiling to keep from crying. She slipped a hand into her pocket and traced the circle of birds on the ring from Wash until the hour was over.

"Sorry about Pittluck's class," Tommie said when they met outside for lunch. "Deanna told me what happened."

Naomi let out a long breath. "I wanted to die. It's over now, though."

Tommie fingered the edge of her coat and gave Naomi a sympathetic look. "You're tired. Lay your head in my lap and doze if you want."

Naomi gave Tommie a grateful smile. "Here, finish my apple. I'm too tired to eat."

"Wish I had that problem," Tommie said a little glumly, before biting into it.

"No," Naomi yawned. "Trust me, you don't." She was asleep the minute her head touched the thick wool of Tommie's skirt.

◇ ◇ ◇

"It's nothing," Naomi insisted when Wash asked what was bothering her. She did not want to tell him, did not want to let Henry into their tree. And anyway, there was nothing he could do about it. She turned her face into the soft fabric of his shirt.

"What was your day like?" she asked, wanting to turn their talk elsewhere.

He shrugged. "School is school. But don't change the subject. Something must have happened." He rubbed her ears gently and then moved his fingers in slow circles against her scalp.

She sighed and closed her eyes. "I just haven't slept well. That's all."

"All right. In that case, here's what you do. This is a very old, very secret method, from my people."

"Your people?"

Her skepticism didn't make a dent. "This knowledge was passed down from distant ancestors, from their days as kings and queens and healers in the heart of Africa. So listen carefully and—shhh—don't tell anyone."

She smiled into the semi-darkness. "I can't wait to hear this."

"Start by putting a good sized lump of sugar on your tongue. Brown sugar's best. Right on the center of your tongue."

"They had brown sugar in the heart of Africa?"

Wash ignored her. "Then you say your lover's name a hundred times."

"Mmm-hm?"

"And then . . . if you're still awake after all that, you slip your hand under the covers . . . you slide it back and forth, up your legs and down until . . ."

"Enough," she said, swatting him lightly. "I get the idea."

"What?" He laughed. "Until you fall asleep. That's it. That's the remedy. Give it a try."

"We'll see." She curled her body closer to him. "Or I could just come here to sleep."

"Why don't you rest now," he said. He slid back to give her room and stroked her hair. She let his gentleness and the quiet familiarity of the tree lull her to sleep.

◇ ◇ ◇

Naomi propped herself up on the sofa after dinner and watched Beto try to get Edgar to fetch a bit of pencil as they all listened to a soap opera. Henry was still making himself scarce. Maybe it had nothing to do with her. He was probably working to bring in a new well.

Naomi fiddled with the fabric in her lap. For the last little shirt she was making for Muff's baby, she'd cut a bit of muslin out in the traditional Mexican style. In the end, it would have embroidery around the neck and a simple tie-close opening. But now, as she went over what she'd sewn since dinner, she saw that the stitches were wide and uneven. She tossed the shirt aside. It would all have to be redone.

Naomi rubbed her face. "We're going to bed after this program," she said.

"Come on, Omi, it's not even nine o'clock," Cari protested. "Will you at least tell us a story about Mami at bedtime? A new one?"

Beto frowned. "And what about Daddy's supper?"

"Can it, you two!" Naomi snapped. "Daddy knows how to work the stove. As for stories, I'm not a record player. Keep it up, and it'll be straight to bed."

◇ ◇ ◇

When the program ended, the twins brushed their teeth and tucked themselves in. Beto was extra helpful and affectionate, but Cari was withdrawn, still fuming over Naomi's refusal to tell a story. Naomi thought she'd seen her eyeing the guitar case, but she wasn't sure.

She knew she shouldn't have pushed the request away; it wouldn't be long before the twins would be too old to want her stories or songs. They were growing up, and it worried her. Once they no longer needed her, what reason would she have to stay in East Texas?

She stood in the bathroom and combed her hair, then she padded to the kitchen pantry and pulled out a dime-sized lump of brown sugar from the sack on the shelf. Wash's remedy was charming nonsense, but she was willing to try anything.

She slid into bed alongside Cari and tried to remember what sleep felt like. Sleep belonged to the same category as swimming; both activities were necessary and dangerous in equal parts. She and the twins had only learned how to swim at Abuelito's insistence, which had been prompted by her father's drowning. Sleep was a more complex matter, but most of the time she skimmed along, face barely submerged, coming up for frequent breaths. That kept her safe from dreams. Dreams might take her anywhere. Down into pink-tiled bathrooms and among translucent, unformed babies with unseeing black spots for eyes, and dark braids that moved of their own accord, working their way along the sandy bottom of sleep like inchworms.

But as Naomi said Wash's name over and over in the silence of her exhausted brain, her grip on the letter opener began to slip, and she descended into the blue depths of proper sleep. Naomi's body took over, and she dreamed.

Naomi was her present self, but in the dream she was shrunken to the size of a young child. She watched from beneath Henry's kitchen table as her mother and Wash sat drinking Ovaltine. As if it were normal for a dead Mexican woman and a black boy to sit laughing and talking in a white man's kitchen. Her mother's slender bare feet were within Naomi's reach, and she longed to touch them, massage them as she had on the mornings after her mother had danced late into the night. A pulsing fear displaced that simple longing. Naomi could not see the window over the sink from her position, but by dream magic she knew that Henry was there, watching. She wanted to warn them, but she could not move from under the table. She searched her pockets but could not find Wash's ring.

No disaster came in this dream, but it opened into another, and another. In whatever dream she faced, the fear of Henry was there and Wash's ring was not.

◇ ◇ ◇

Cold water soaked Naomi's chest. Her eyes flew open, and she jolted upright.

"Breakfast," Henry said. He stalked out of the room, empty glass in hand.

Less than a minute later she was in the kitchen. She filled the percolator with water and coffee grounds, lit the oven with trembling fingers, and cut lard into flour for biscuits. The wet front of her nightgown clung to her under the robe Muff had given her, but she did not dare take the time to change. She glanced at the clock—6:02, half an hour late.

Ten minutes later, she placed a cup of coffee in front of Henry. When the biscuits were done, she slit two open and arranged them on a plate. She slathered them in peanut butter and drizzled dark Karo syrup on top. His favorite.

"Looks good," he said when she put the plate on the table. She didn't look at him, but there was a note of apology in his voice.

She turned back to the stove. "I've never overslept like that. It's just that I couldn't, I haven't . . ." She trailed off. She couldn't explain. And anyway, she didn't owe him an apology.

Henry sat with his back to her. She could tell nothing from the movements of his fork. "Listen," he mumbled through a mouthful of biscuit, "I shouldn't have thrown water on you. Long shift last night. And also . . . you know."

"It's okay," she said.

She regretted her words instantly. Just like that, she'd forgiven more than she meant to. Far more.

She looked straight ahead when she hurried into the hall to call the twins to breakfast, but Henry caught her eye as she came back. He grinned at her like nothing had happened. No, not like nothing had happened, like something had happened. Something good. Something shared between them.

"The biscuits are great," he said. He forked another bite into his mouth and glanced up at the clock. "Remember those first ones you made?"

"Like rocks," she said.

"You've come a long way."

Cari and Beto tumbled into the kitchen. She served them biscuits and milk and then licked the last of the peanut butter from the knife before washing it. She had never tasted peanut butter before coming here. She loved the thick creaminess of it and the salty shadow it left on her tongue. It was a food that beat hunger, and she thought again how she would take as many jars as she could whenever Henry allowed them to visit San Antonio.

Now, Henry headed to his room with a tired wave. "See y'all at suppertime."

She surprised herself by telling him to sleep well. Part of her wanted to be angry, but the ease and gratitude that came with having slept were too great for her to hold on to any sourness.

And there was Wash.

No matter what happened here, no matter what happened at school, the afternoon would still come, and she would see him, and she would not allow even the shadow of a thought of Henry into their tree.

FEBRUARY 1937

HENRY Once Henry was sure Naomi and the twins were gone, he came out of his bedroom and locked himself into the bathroom. He braced himself against the sink and held Naomi's slip up to his nostrils. He breathed in the smell of her and set to work on himself. It wouldn't be like this for much longer, but he had to manage until everything fell into place.

Sometimes he began by thinking of Estella or the plump redhead he'd frequented out at the Chicken Ranch before he got saved. But it was the same as every time since Naomi had come to live in his house: he needed to imagine her to finish. The sooner he finished, the sooner he could pretend he hadn't done it.

He closed his eyes, bunched the thin fabric in his hand, and pressed it back up to his nose.

After he washed his hands, he shoved the slip back into her drawer and closed himself into his room to sleep.

NAOMI Naomi let her English book fall into her lap. The sun made an orange screen of her closed eyelids. The day had started out as winter but had warmed to spring. She felt the warmth of the stone she was sitting on creep through the fabric of her dress.

Arms slid around her waist from behind. She whipped her head around, terrified of finding Henry.

"Hey! Easy! It's me." Wash held up his hands and took a step back.

Naomi jumped up onto the bank and rushed past him, throwing her words behind her. "Don't surprise me like that. Ever."

"Sure, but—"

"Just don't." She took a careful breath and worked at draining the distress from her face.

"Could you tell me—"

She shook her head. She could see he was hurt. His hands wandered, looking for something to do.

"All right, then." He shrugged and shoved his hands into his pockets. "You want to keep studying?"

She climbed back down to the river and sat on a log across from him. She nudged his foot with her shoe. "Sorry," she said. "How about a Spanish lesson?"

He grinned. "That'd be good, seeing as how I keep telling the twins that you're teaching me some."

"What time is it anyway?" she asked.

Wash pulled out his watch. "Almost four."

"Okay, fifteen minutes for Spanish, and then we'll study in the tree."

"I like the sound of that."

"*Me gusta ésa idea.*"

He repeated her words. "What did I say?"

"I like that idea."

"*¿Me gusta Naomi?*" he said, testing it out.

She smiled. "That works. Now, I'm going to ask you how you are. *¿Cómo estás?*"

"And I say . . ."

WASH   Wash learned fast and liked it. He took that learn-ing with them into the tree, where he put *Me gusta besarte* into action. Gentle but bold. He could tell Naomi was enjoying herself, but all of a sudden she pulled back, frowning.

"You've done this before." It wasn't a question, but he could tell she expected a response.

He hesitated a moment too long. "A few times."

She was not pleased. "If I loved a liar, I'd hug you right now."

"Okay, more than a few times," he admitted. He tapped the wrinkle between her brows with his thumb. "But that was A.N. And I never liked it half as much as I like it with you."

"A.N.?"

"*Antes Naomi.* Is that right?" he asked. "If I want to say 'before Naomi'?"

"I'm not sure I'm talking to you right now."

"Correct me at least." He tried to play it off. Still, he could feel sweat pricking up on his forehead. She was beautiful when she was mad, but he didn't want her mad at him.

"*Antes DE Naomi,*" she corrected.

"*Gracias, señorita, mil gracias.*" He lifted her hand to his lips. Even in the dim light he could see that her frown was gone.

"You could charm the skin off a snake, you scoundrel," she growled. She was smiling.

He pulled her close and kissed her. "You've ruined other girls for me, you know that?"

"*Así debe ser*," she said softly. "That's how it should be."

NAOMI   Naomi and Tommie sat at the kitchen table in Henry's house, studying their empty glasses of milk as if the answers to the problem of Tommie's project might be there. Tommie's first attempt at a dress for home economics lay before them on the table, a malformed monstrosity.

"Mrs. Anderson took one look and told me not to even bother putting it on," Tommie said glumly. "I have until Monday to redo it. She said I could get some help but that I still have to do all the sewing."

"Well, we could try to remake this . . ." Naomi hesitated.

"Lord, no," said Tommie. "We'd better start over. Mama said I could use some of the fabric she bought for Easter dresses."

"Okay, then there's the question of a machine. You could sew by hand, but that takes more time." She slipped the last bite of her oatmeal cookie into her mouth. "Maybe ask Mrs. Wright down the street?"

Tommie shook her head. "She just took in a heap of sewing that she has to finish quick. Marla Kay from church has a sewing machine, but she said hers is jammed up bad."

Henry came into the kitchen then. He was fresh from the shower and smelled of soap and aftershave.

"Hi, Mr. Smith," Tommie said, blushing.

He nodded and reached for one of the cookies Tommie had brought. "Compliments to your mama. Listen, I might have a fix for your problem," he said. There was a sly smile on his lips. "Follow me." He shrugged on his jacket and headed out onto the porch.

"You know about this?" Tommie whispered. Naomi shook her head.

They followed him out onto the porch and then crossed with him to Muff and Bud's house. Naomi couldn't imagine what solution Henry planned to offer. She knew for a fact that Muff did not sew.

When Muff came to the door with Joe Joe on her hip, Henry leaned close and whispered.

"Of course. Come on." Muff grinned and winked at Naomi. She hefted Joe Joe a little higher and stepped back to let them in.

"I'll take him for a bit," Naomi said, reaching for Joe Joe. He waved a sticky hand and came to her happily.

"Thanks." Muff smoothed her hair behind her ears and slid a hand to her round belly. "He's going to have to give up that spot pretty soon."

They headed back to Muff and Bud's bedroom. In the corner there was something the size of a desk covered with an old quilt.

"Go ahead," Henry said. "Look."

Naomi tugged back the quilt to reveal an old push-pedal Singer machine. She'd used one like it back in San Antonio when she went with Tia Cuca to wash and sew for one of the wealthier Mexican families. It'd be easy to show Tommie how to use it. Then she remembered the radio, and her heart sank. There was no telling if the thing ran.

"It works," Henry said. "See this?" He tapped his foot against a metal case about the size of a bread box. "I got it fixed up so that it runs off of electricity instead of you having to pump the foot pedal. Pretty slick, huh?"

"Wonderful. But why?" Naomi stammered.

"Muff was holding it for me for a special occasion." He shrugged. "It just seemed like you needed it more now, ain't that so?"

"Thank you," Naomi said. For the first time, she meant it.

◇ ◇ ◇

Later that evening, a few hours into working on the dress, Tommie put down her scissors suddenly. "When's your birthday again?"

"Seventh of August. Why?" Naomi said.

"And Christmas is nearly a year away..."

"Enough riddles."

"Well," Tommie said, "I was just trying to figure out what occasion, exactly, Henry had in mind." She raised her eyebrows and tapped her chin. "My, but he's handsome. And thoughtful, too."

Naomi frowned and went back to sewing. She didn't want to know what Tommie was talking about.

◇ ◇ ◇

On Sunday, Naomi walked with the rest of the congregation to the river for all the baptisms that had been put off during the winter. It was only mid-February, but the weather had turned suddenly warm and humid. The newly saved did not want to wait any longer.

Naomi stayed behind to carry Joe Joe for Muff. As they neared the river, she felt a hand on her shoulder.

"Glorious day, ain't it?" Pastor Tom said, falling into step with them.

"Heaven be praised," Muff said. They'd only been walking for a few minutes, but she was already out of breath.

"Amen!" shouted J.R., who was running circles around them.

"There's gratitude, little brother." Pastor Tom smiled. "Could I borrow this lovely young lady for a moment?" he asked Muff, nodding at Naomi.

She glanced at Joe Joe in Naomi's arms with a look of dread. With the extra weight of her pregnancy, Muff was struggling to make the walk as it was.

"He can stay with me," Naomi said quickly. "I'll find you down by the river. That okay with you, Joe Joe?" Naomi asked. She flicked his nose lightly with her finger.

"No-mee!" He gave her a drooly grin and reached for her nose. "No-mee!"

"Thanks, sweetie," Muff said to Naomi. She winked at Pastor Tom and then hurried J.R. down the path toward the river.

Pastor Tom walked slowly, letting the last of the churchgoers pass them.

Naomi matched his pace reluctantly. As far as she could tell, nothing good ever came of these little talks.

A blue jay swooped in front of them and started Joe Joe jabbering. Naomi smoothed the sweat-dampened hair from the baby's forehead and hummed a song about bluebirds and windows that the twins had learned at school.

Finally, the preacher spoke. "You sure have a way with kids."

"Thank you," Naomi answered.

"How are things at home?"

For a moment, Naomi thought he was asking about San Antonio. Then she realized that he must mean Henry's house.

"We're getting along," she said. Best to keep her answers vague until she knew what he was getting at.

"It ain't always easy, is it?" Pastor Tom asked.

"No, sir."

"Anything change lately?"

"Don't know how you mean."

"Things a little different with Henry, maybe?" Pastor Tom probed.

Naomi shrugged. "He mentioned he might take Beto hunting some-time soon."

"Spending time with Robbie, huh. That sounds fine."

Naomi nodded.

"He's trying. He wants to do right, I can tell you that," Pastor Tom said. "Ever since he told me he had a family, I've been watching him change, grow into the man who could do the Lord's will."

Naomi let a silence build between them. She studied the tree branches above them.

Finally she said, "You told him to bring us here, didn't you?"

"The Spirit led him. Henry's got to work out his salvation like all of us. You and the twins are part of his."

"He's not my father, you know," Naomi said.

"And thank goodness!" The pastor mopped his forehead and squinted at the noonday sun beating down through the trees.

"Pardon?" Naomi said.

"I thought surely by now you'd considered . . ." he trailed off. They rounded a bend in the path. The river lay before them in a bright brown sweep. The choir was already lined up and singing sinners down to the water.

Pastor Tom gave a wave to the folks lined up to be saved and the many more there to watch and celebrate. "Guess we can talk more later. Just remember . . . the school, the church . . . it's a good place for the kids," the pastor said.

She could not argue with that.

 Naomi and Tommie finished the dress late on Sunday afternoon. Naomi was exhausted and all but cross-eyed from concentrating for so long. Helping somebody else sew was twice as hard as making something herself. They'd done it, though, and Tommie's mother had invited her to share their Sunday supper by way of thanks. She also promised to bake a fancy layer cake for the twins' birthday in July.

Naomi walked slowly on her way home from Tommie's. It was getting late, but time seemed to stretch like taffy. The pines stood out dark against the pinks and oranges creeping across the sky, and a breeze stirred around her. She found herself walking to their spot at the river. It was not a usual meeting time for them, but she couldn't help hoping.

Wash was skipping stones at the water's edge, his sleeves rolled up to the elbows. He turned and grinned. "You."

She laughed and ran for the tree.

They did not waste time; there was never enough. She leaned hard against him, liking the shape of his body against hers. He kissed her and started working his hand under her slip, sliding her dress up to her thighs.

"Wash, you know we can't—"

"Shh," he said, "I know."

She bit his lip, then kissed him hard and deep.

"Now, just, just let me kiss you," he said. The possibility formed in his mind, something he'd never imagined. Now that he had the idea, though, he could not bear not to try. A gift he wanted to give her, his beautiful, bold Naomi. He moved his lips away from her mouth, kissed his way down her neck, and worked his way lower, lower.

Before he touched her, before he slipped his hand back up under her dress, before he tugged her drawers and stockings down gently, so gently, before he knelt in front of her, before any of this, Naomi knew that she wanted it. Because it as Wash. Because this was their tree. Because they were making it all u as they went along.

His hands opened her thighs, and then he was touching her with his mouth, kissing warmth, wetness. She might have been ashamed, but she wasn't. She was alive, tremblingly alive. In the dead heart of their tree she was herself and more than herself. She let the moment lift her up.

"Please," she said, pressing her back against the inside of the tree and holding tight to his shoulders. "Please, please, please, oh." Then she was laughing and sighing and amazed at him and amazed at herself.

A moment later, she felt her usual size again, and the feeling of easy improvisation was gone. She moved her hand tentatively toward his belt. "Do you want me to . . . ?"

He took her hand and squeezed it. "It makes me feel good to make you feel good."

"But . . ." She bit her lip. She did not want him to be outside all the pleasure.

"There's always tomorrow," he said.

"I certainly hope so," she said. "Tomorrow, then." She kissed him and tucked herself against him and felt how much he wanted her. She felt also how what he had given her was part of that wanting but also something more and different.

"I love you," she whispered. "Thank you."

They stayed like that, confident for the moment that this piece of the world was theirs, and that it was enough.

NAOMI After Naomi served him breakfast, Henry asked, "What time does school let out?"

"Three thirty," Naomi answered.

"All right. It's settled." He pointed his fork at Beto. "Robbie, you wait outside your school for me and Vince. You're coming with us for some target practice. Maybe a little hunting. About time you learned to fire a gun."

"I bet I could shoot one," Cari said.

Henry chuckled. "Tell the truth, it's not you I'm worried about."

"So I can go?" she asked.

"Just the men," Henry said.

Beto sat taller in his chair.

"Not that I wanted to," Cari said quickly. "I'm going to help Miss Bell with something important."

"Everybody be home for dinner, though," Naomi said. "We're having roast, and I think Muff's baking today."

◇ ◇ ◇

"Thirty minutes," Naomi called softly when she found Wash by the river. "Check the time, okay?"

He climbed the bank to meet her. "You turn into a pumpkin at 4:36," Wash said, showing her the face of his watch.

"Tree?" Naomi asked. She hadn't forgotten her promise.

"Let's go watch the clouds," Wash said.

Naomi rolled her eyes. "Nobody actually does that. It's for people in stories."

"Well, if it's good enough for them . . ." He took off running, stopping every few feet and calling to her until she followed him down one of the paths that led away from the river. About a quarter of a mile down it, Wash pointed out a field that had been wheat until somebody'd struck oil there and made the owner so rich he didn't care to push the plow anymore. Now it had turned wild, mostly tall weeds with just a bit of grain mixed in. Naomi ran into the field behind him, hands held out into the high grasses. Grasshoppers winged up from the ground around her, thumping her forearms and fingers in a whirl of legs and hard bodies.

A moment later, she threw herself down onto the grass, flattening a patch with her back. She could see why bunnies and bobwhites loved fallow fields. She felt safe from everything here.

She stared up at the clouds and pointed. "That's a tadpole swimming out from under a lily pad."

"And that's somebody blowing out birthday candles."

"That's a person winking . . . see, with that shadow as the eyelashes?"

"And that's a field mouse . . ."

"Hey!" Naomi sat up. "When is your birthday?"

Wash exhaled deeply. "Not for another three years, unfortunately."

She slapped his arm. "Oh, stop. Really, when is it?"

He pointed out a few more shapes in the clouds before he explained that this year he didn't actually have a birthday. Because he'd been born on February 29, 1920, he had a true birthday exactly once every four years.

"The crummiest date a guy could ask for," he grumbled. "Anybody wants an excuse to forget your birthday, you can't get much better than the fact that it's not actually on the calendar."

"We won't forget it," Naomi said.

"Nobody plans to."

"You'll see." She rolled toward him. "The time, sir?"

Wash pretended not to hear her, so she slipped a hand into his pocket to find the watch.

"Be my guest," he said with a grin. "Now I'm never going to fix that wristband."

She walked her fingers past the watch and felt him through the soft fabric of the pocket. "Next time, it's your turn," she whispered, then she pulled the watch out. It was already a quarter to five.

Naomi stood up with a reluctant sigh and dusted herself off. "I have to go. Muff started a roast for me, and Henry will expect dinner when he gets done making a man out of poor Beto."

◊ ◊ ◊

"It's nothing to be ashamed of, Naomi," Muff said slyly. They were sitting on Muff and Bud's back porch so they could enjoy the fine weather while the roast was cooking inside.

"What are you talking about?" Naomi wiped her cheek on her shoulder. As soon as she got started peeling potatoes, she always had an itch that she couldn't scratch without getting starch all over.

"You tell me," Muff said. She shot Naomi a meaningful look.

"There's nothing to tell. We're sitting here, and I'm thinking about peeling potatoes." In fact, she had been thinking of Wash. That quick smile. His laughter. The fact of them together. What she intended for him the next time they were alone.

"You shouldn't lie with me sitting so close," Muff said. "When you get struck by lightning, you'll get me fried, too."

"What makes you so sure I'm thinking some big thought?" Naomi asked.

"For one thing, you've been peeling that same potato for a whole minute." Muff jutted her chin toward Naomi's hand. Without thinking, Naomi had whittled a good-sized potato down to the size of a plum. Her cheeks flushed, and she began to gather the shreds of good potato from on top of the pile of peelings.

"I guess, I guess I wasn't thinking after all," she stammered.

"Not the first time you've gotten all starry-eyed. I'm not so old that I've forgotten what it's like." Muff tossed another potato into the bowl between them. "And there's really nothing to stop you two from marrying."

Naomi froze, the paring knife trembling between her fingers. "I don't know what you mean." She had never let a single word about Wash slip. Muff was her friend, but she'd soaked up the rules of being white like a sponge in a bowl of vinegar. Without malice, but deeply all the same. Naomi didn't know what surprised her more: that Muff could know about Wash, or that she could think that marriage was an option for them.

"I have my sources, you know," Muff said. "Tommie told me you don't have a thing to do with the boys at school. I asked her on account of how I seen you go off places in your head when you're washing up or doing chores. Didn't do that so much when y'all first came, see. But of course, some loves take time to blossom. I've been figuring on it for a while. Now I get why you ignore Gilbert Harris at church even when it's plain he'd like you for his girl." She picked a few stray peelings off of her apron and began quartering the potatoes. "You know, he's a good man. Just a little confused sometimes."

"Gilbert?" Naomi said cautiously, feeling her way along, trying to get a hold of this conversation.

"Don't be silly," Muff said. "Not Gilbert. *Him*. Maybe you're all sly and shy 'cause you think he don't feel the same. Or maybe you worry that folks would disapprove, but I don't think they would, not if you two was married. Sooner might be better, considering. That's what Pastor thinks, and you know that his opinion holds some weight."

Naomi heard each word without understanding. It was like those first few years in school when everything came too fast and she could not always gather the English words into sense.

"I don't know who you mean," she said.

"Henry, of course." Muff nudged her with an elbow. "Who else would we be talking about?"

"You think, you think I'm in love with my stepfather?" Naomi had to force the words out.

"No blood relation, and y'all hardly knew each other before now. Don't be shamed. I was young once, too, you know. You live near a handsome man, you have certain thoughts. Pretty much any unmarried gal in New London would think she was lucky to be in your shoes."

"He was married to my mother. He's the twins' father!"

Muff was unfazed. "I know what I know when I look at you mooning around and shaving taters down to nubs. Who else could you be thinking of?"

A cold bead of sweat worked its way down Naomi's belly. If she persuaded Muff that she wasn't—and never would be—interested in Henry, then Muff would want to know who she was so keen on, and that was a question she couldn't answer, not safely. She forced a smile. "I guess you found me out," she said weakly.

Muff chucked her under the chin. "I don't see nothing strange about it. An older fella's not a bad idea, especially these days. Economy the way it is. And you could do more than just mama the twins. Nothing like a bun in the oven to fill your heart and your days." She slid a hand over her stomach. "Our kids would be shirttail cousins."

"Pastor Tom . . . was he the one who gave you this idea?" Naomi fought the urge to run for the woods.

Muff swatted at her impatiently. "I told you I know what I see when I see it. But the Pastor agrees. Thinks marrying would be good for Henry. Keep him steady."

"So you've been talking to him about it? And Henry?"

"Henry is Henry. Still waters and all that. But I've seen him planning. That sewing machine?" She winked at Naomi. "I think he had that in mind for an engagement present, only you needed it in a hurry, so . . . Listen, you want me to talk to him? Try to move him along faster?"

"No!" Naomi's voice cracked. "No," she said more levelly. "Please don't."

BETO Beto trembled and shook his head again.

"Fire the gun, Robbie." Henry said, louder this time. "Aim and press the trigger. A man knows how to fire a weapon."

It was only a tin can propped up on a log, Beto told himself. But he couldn't move the trigger. Henry grabbed the gun from him, took aim, and fired. The tin can spun to the side and fell from the log, but Beto saw something else: an explosion of red. Crimson blooming against yellow. He heard a cry.

"Christ Almighty, what you hollerin' for?" Henry growled. He did not look at Beto. "Men fire guns, men eat meat. That's how it is."

"Come on, Henry, lay off the boy. Hardly big enough to shoulder the recoil anyhow." Vince Harris stood back a little from Henry and Beto, his foot propped up on a stump. He drained his beer and then tossed the can down into the brush.

Henry took aim again and fired into the trees. Beto saw a shadow drop heavily from the tree onto the dried pine needles that covered the forest floor.

"See what I mean?" Henry said. He slung the gun across his back and went to examine his prey. He lifted the bloodied mass of gray by one wing.

It was a dove. Had been. A sob caught in Beto's throat, and when it couldn't find a way out, something else turned loose.

Beto's face grew hot. He prayed that his father would stay where he was, would not look at him. He fixed his eyes on the cottony bits of cloud stuck in the gaps between the pines above him.

A moment later, Vince sniffed. "Uh, Henry, I think . . . it looks like your boy . . ."

Henry looked up, squinting. His grin twisted with disgust. "Tell me you didn't just piss yourself."

"I didn't . . ." Beto stared down to see urine running down his leg and pooling in his shoes.

"Then why are your goddamn britches wet?" he roared. "You're some boy, sissier than your sister. Too much time around women, it's turnin' you queer."

"Whoa, now," Vince said. "Go easy, Henry. It was an accident, that's all."

Henry shook his head. "Come here, you little shit." He tossed the dove against a tree and stared at his son.

Beto ignored his father and ran toward the bird, though he knew it was too late. He stooped down to see the dove, but Henry grabbed him by the collar. "Hold on, there, partner," he snarled. He shoved the shotgun back into Beto's hands. "Fire on that," he said, jutting his chin toward the bird. "Do it now. It can't get away from you, so you'd better hit it."

"Kid's upset, Henry, don't you think—"

"Fired my first gun when I was five, reckon you did, too. Don't be makin' excuses for him. We're six beers in and we're still shootin' straight and keepin' our pants dry." Henry's hand tightened on Beto's wrist.

"Do it like this, Robbie," he steadied the shotgun against Beto's shoulder, forced his finger onto the trigger, and took aim over his shoulder. Henry pressed down on his finger, and the gun fired.

For an instant, the bird came back to life. It leaped with the shot and then landed, bloodier than before, on the forest floor.

Tears flooded Beto. Snot poured down his face. He tore off through the woods toward the truck. He imagined his own body ripped by bullets like the bird's, and he sobbed harder. By the time Henry and Vince returned, the crying had passed and there was only fear and, in spite of everything, a desperate wish to please Henry. On the way back to New London, Beto lay still in the bed of the truck, the certainty of his father's disappointment holding him down like stones.

NAOMI It was late by the time Henry and Beto came back. Cari was already in bed, but Naomi had waited up. The radio hummed with the faint warble of the gospel hour program. When they came into the living room, she looked up from the pile of pale blue fabric in her lap and smiled. She was putting the new machine to good use and getting a head start on an Easter dress for Cari. They'd spent the evening looking at a catalog until Naomi knew just what her sister wanted. It had kept Cari busy, and Naomi had managed to deflect her increasingly insistent questions about their mother. No, she could not tell a new story while Beto was away; that wouldn't be fair. But she knew Cari wasn't satisfied.

"How was it?" she asked when they came into the living room. "You missed the roast."

"Fine," Henry said tightly. "Robbie fired a gun."

Beto looked away.

"Did you eat? I can warm you up a plate," Naomi said. "There's buttermilk pie, too."

"No need," Henry said.

Naomi's eyes flicked from Henry to Beto, who did not meet her gaze. She thought about telling him that, along with the roast, there'd

227

been mashed potatoes and creamed corn, his new favorite. But he looked too tired to be interested. She stood up and walked over to him and lifted his chin.

"You're not hungry?"

He shook his head.

"Say good night to Daddy," she prompted, "and thank him for taking you."

She might have imagined it, but she thought she saw Beto flinch when she spoke. He mumbled the words without looking up from the floor.

When Beto had gone into the bathroom, Naomi turned around and found Henry standing uncomfortably close to her. He didn't meet her eyes but snaked an arm around her waist. "You look pretty," he murmured.

She slapped his hand away. "You promised," she said. Her whisper came out like a hiss. She took another step back from him.

"You don't have to be cold," he started in toward her again.

She did not let him continue. "I can take them back." She let the threat hang in the air between them.

Henry crossed his arms. "Look at what they've got. A real decent place to stay. A good school. You'd take that away from them?"

"I can take them back," she said. "You promised. No more."

Henry's shoulders sagged a little. "Promise," he said. It came out like a question. He gave her a final, pleading look before trudging down the hall and into his bedroom.

Suddenly, Muff's idea about Henry didn't seem so fanciful. What had the hunting been about? Making a man of Beto. And if Henry couldn't make Beto into a proper son, maybe he was thinking he'd try his luck at making one inside of her. She sank down into her chair and pressed her forehead against the cool body of the sewing machine he'd given her. There were always strings attached to his gifts. Always.

BETO   When Beto came into the bedroom after changing his clothes, he could feel that Cari was hurting with him. She climbed into his bed and wrapped her arms tight around him.

"*Lo siento*," she said, "I'm real, real sorry."

Beto swallowed and shut his eyes tight against the new tears. They burned behind his eyelids.

"Read to you from the Cs?" she offered.

He nodded.

They lay snug in his bed like matched spoons. Cari scratched his back and recited the encyclopedia entry on China from memory until he fell asleep. Then she lay awake for a while longer, thinking of a gray bird dancing in its blood. Beto had shared the sight of it with her, but it was not a good luck thing.

HENRY Later that week, Henry came home covered in mud and oil but happy as hell. He was also bone-tired and ready to get out of his mud-caked boots and overalls. He turned onto the gravel drive and pulled the truck in alongside the house. He was surprised to see light coming from the side window of the living room. He looked down to check his watch, but it was as mucked up as the rest of him. Thanks to him, they'd brought in a well in less than a week. Graham Salter said there'd be fat bonuses all around.

He thought about calling to Naomi for a towel as he stripped off his boots on the porch, but he didn't want to wake the kids. He peeled off his shirt and socks and rolled up the bottoms of his work denims. Muff had told him after church that he should be grateful that Naomi kept the house neat as a pin and ought not make extra work for her.

The kitchen was dark and still. Henry felt like turning on the lights and making some noise. Most of the other men had gone off to Big T's to celebrate. He'd begged off, but he wanted at least to tell someone about the strike and the extra fat check he had coming.

He went and wiped down and pulled on a clean undershirt and pants before walking the rest of the way down the hall to the living room to tell Naomi.

She was curled on the edge of the sofa, her shoes still on like maybe she had only meant to take a little nap. That was it; the lamp by her sewing machine was on, too. She'd been working on something. Henry went over to see what it was. He studied the small heap of light blue cloth still held in place by the machine's presser foot.

He'd seen her working on a dress for Cari, but this was something else. He could tell from the collar and the size of the sleeves that this was a man's shirt. It was far too big for Beto; that meant that the shirt was for him. Blue was his favorite color. Easter wasn't that far off, or maybe it was a gift to thank him for the sewing machine. He pictured himself walking into church with the shirt on. "My shirt?" he'd say. "No, it's not store-bought. The missus made it." He'd turn and wink at Naomi. She might blush a little and look away, but she'd be warmed at the thought of his pride in her work.

He tiptoed out of the room. He wouldn't let on that he'd seen the shirt.

Things were looking up more quickly than he'd expected.

◇ ◇ ◇

The next day when he got home from work, Henry sat on the porch steps, elbows on his knees, boots unlaced but still on. Naomi was walking out with her laundry basket when he'd driven up, and when he asked, she told him that the twins were off running in the woods.

Now Henry watched Naomi as she took the laundry down from the line, admiring how her body moved under the thin yellow dress, the dress she'd made from his Christmas gift. He could watch her all day, that stretch and bend, stretch and bend. The movements made her dress love on the parts of her that he, too, wanted to touch.

"Naomi, come over here," Henry said. His voice cracked a little.

She glanced up, and a clothespin slipped out of her fingers. She bent quickly to retrieve it. Her braid swung down over her shoulder as she knelt.

That sweetness, he thought to himself. Yes, that.

"I've been meaning to talk to you about something." *Honey*, he thought, but decided not to say.

"Oh," Naomi said.

Henry swallowed hard and smiled at her. "Have you ever thought maybe . . ." he trailed off, losing his nerve.

Naomi blinked at him. Her fingers were on the end of her braid.

"What would you say if . . ." Henry tried again. He could feel his nerves stretching a ridiculous smile across his face.

Naomi said nothing.

"How are the two wildcats?" he asked.

"Like I said, playing in the woods."

"But," he faltered. "School? That okay?" He clasped his hands together.

She released a small breath, then nodded. "Miss Bell's been talking of skipping them to the next grade, you know. I heard about it from my Spanish teacher."

"They've got you taking Spanish?" he asked.

Naomi reddened. "Everybody takes it, so . . ." she trailed off.

"I've been thinking," Henry tried again, "that maybe you and me ought to . . ." Henry wasn't looking at Naomi, but if he had been, he'd have seen her eyes widened in alarm. "How about you and me—" And then he sensed her dread. That was the only word for it. He looked up and saw the twins on the far side of the Humble Camp fence, coming their way.

"—take the kids for some ice cream?" Henry shouted the last words loud enough for the twins to hear. Then he laughed a little. Delaying the question freed up something in him that usually stayed knotted.

"Ice cream!" Cari shouted. "Beto, ice cream!"

◊ ◊ ◊

Henry took a sip of his malt, swallowed. "Some weather, huh? Everybody wants a bit of cool."

"It is hot out," Naomi said. Her spoon dipped dutifully into her dish of ice cream. Plain vanilla; she hadn't even let him talk her into a sundae.

It was the first time Naomi had sat next to him, he realized. He wanted to take it for encouragement, but it was only because Beto hadn't wanted the seat. The boy was still sore about the hunting trip. Henry knew he'd been hard on him, ugly even, but they were out eating ice cream; there was no call for sullenness.

He attempted a smile at the twins. "You like it?"

Cari nodded. "We do. Thanks, Daddy." She licked the butterscotch from her spoon, then dipped it into Beto's dish. He didn't protest.

"Robbie," Henry pressed, "How's the fudge?"

"Good," Beto mumbled. "Thank you."

The boy wouldn't look at him, just sat there like a lump. Henry sighed and looked around. The ice cream parlor was packed with men in shirtsleeves and women who had gotten out their summer dresses early. Children darted between the crowded tables. Everyone else was sweating but happy.

He drained his glass without tasting it. "Let's finish on up. I reckon somebody else might want the table."

NAOMI Naomi had an idea of what was coming from Henry. Still, she hoped against it, did everything she could not to think of it. She pressed Wash into the tree every chance she got.

"You're hungry for kisses," he teased, but she would not be dissuaded.

She would have preferred an intimate celebration for Wash's birthday, too, but the twins had been getting ready for it for weeks. Together, they planned a little party for him on the last Saturday in February. Cari and Beto brought along a gift they'd prepared on their own, something bulky in a burlap sack, and they had made a cake.

Naomi's first thought was to make their picnic on the riverbank. There'd been too much rain, though, and the gnats and mosquitoes were worse by the water. Naomi pointed out a sunny patch just off the path in the woods, and they spread an old sheet over the pine needles. Once the cake and gifts were laid out, the twins ran off to wait for Wash to finish working for Mr. Crane.

They came back with him half an hour later. Wash began laughing the minute he saw the spread on the picnic blanket. "Y'all," he said, "did I really make myself out so pitiful that you had to go to this much trouble for my birthday?"

"Yes," the three of them said in unison.

"Open your presents! Open your presents!" Cari chanted.

"What's in there?" he asked, pointing at the burlap bag.

"Not telling!" Cari said.

"Open it and find out," Beto said.

Wash reached a hand into the bag and groped around for a second. He made a face, then pulled his hand out, still empty. "You sure you didn't mix something up? This is my present?"

"Go on." Cari pushed his hand back into the bag.

Wash peered inside and grabbed something. "Just what I've always wanted! A spare foot! Now I'll never worry about sprained ankles again. Light, too." He weighed the object in his hand. It was a club-like, crudely sculptured foot painted a muddy brown with pale pink toenails. "Please thank the artist for noticing that my nails are not as dark as my skin," he said, nodding appreciatively.

"We've seen your toenails before," Beto said, barely able to contain himself.

"There's more," Cari said. "Go on."

Wash extracted three additional feet, four hands and two heads painted with garish grins. They were all a little blockier than the human parts they were meant to correspond to, but they were recognizable.

"That's unusual," Naomi managed. She tried to imagine some use Wash might have for papier-mâché body parts, but nothing came to mind.

"There are some parts of the whole missing," Cari said, "but can you figure out what they're for?"

"Think hard!" Beto pressed.

Naomi hoped he had more of a clue than she did. The only thing worse than when the twins disappointed her was when she disappointed them. She was sure that Wash would feel the same way.

He appeared to be deep in thought, but she could see a smile twitching at the corner of his mouth, fighting to break out. "How many guesses do I get?" he asked.

"Three!" Cari and Beto said together.

Wash scratched his chin. "Leftover parts from the lesser-known black Frankenstein's monster?"

"Not even close!" Cari giggled.

"A puppet I can build and take with me when I join the circus?"

Beto and Cari shook their heads.

"Hmmm . . ." Wash closed his eyes tight as if racking his brain. His eyes popped open again. "Oh, I know, it's a—"

"Wrong!" the twins shouted before he even finished.

"No fair, you don't know what I was going to say."

"There's no way you could be right," Cari said.

"Are you sure about that? I might be smarter than you think," Wash said. He was now cradling the body parts in his arms. "I might think, for example, that this is what I need to build my very own scarecrow!"

Cari and Beto clapped.

"When we finish it," Cari said, "the birds won't bother your mama's garden. And she'll give you all the rum raisin pies you want."

Beto grew serious. "One of these should be good enough to do the job, but we made two so that the first one won't get lonely."

Wash nodded as if this made perfect sense.

"What do you think?" Cari asked.

Wash smiled. "I'm going to hide these parts in the cowshed until we can get the whole setup in order. Then we'll surprise my ma." He lifted the other package. "Is this for me, too?"

Naomi threw a napkin at him. "You know it is."

"Golly," Wash said. He fondled the drawstring bag. "A bag, a magnificent bag, a bag almost as wonderful as my fine burlap sack—"

"Cut the bull, you!" Naomi said.

He winked at the twins and then pulled out the shirt. "It looks like something that came straight from France . . . all this fine stitching." He ran his hands over the shirt. The jest disappeared from his voice. He studied the monogram near the waist of the breast panel. "Look." He held it up for the twins to see. "It's got my initials."

She'd snuck an "N" in there, too, stretched out like a flourish under his initials. You had to know it was there to see it. It was like their love: invisible to anyone but them.

"You think it'll fit you?" she asked.

"Try it on, try it on!" the twins chanted.

Wash bowed and then ducked behind a tree, pulling off his shirt and buttoning himself into the new one.

When he came back out, the twins clapped.

"It fits," Naomi managed. She did not think she could stand to just sit there with him looking so handsome. Desire turned her crafty. She slapped her forehead. "Sodas! We forgot to get sodas to go with the cake!"

"We can get them!" Beto and Cari said. They were up before Naomi fished the coins out of her pocket.

When she could no longer hear the twins' footsteps on the path, she ran for the tree.

Inside, he pulled her close. "Thank you, baby."

She smiled. "Do you feel special? The cake is going to be delicious."

"Spoiled rotten," he said. "But there's one present I'd still like to open . . ." He ran a finger up from her leg and gave her thigh a good stroke before she slapped his hand away with a laugh.

"Can't blame a guy for trying."

"Sure I can," she said, biting his finger lightly.

THE GANG We were pretty sure that a year ago Miranda wouldn't have gone anywhere with Chigger Watson. For one thing, Chigger was the scrawniest boy ever to ride the bench of the football team. For another, he reminded Miranda of her dirt-poor past. Back before her daddy made his money, Miranda and Chigger were playmates. Back when the Gibblers lived in a lopsided farmhouse without electricity. Back when Miranda wore hand-me-downs. Back when people thought of her as a mangy, motherless girl.

But Chigger got lucky because Miranda was on a losing streak and was starting to get a little desperate. There was the failed business with Gil, of course, and her father's short leash. There was the blow-up in home economics when Mrs. Anderson called her out for turning in a store-bought dress as her sewing project. There was Tommie; the chubby chatterbox stayed chipper no matter what Miranda tried to bring her down. And then there was Naomi.

All of us could see there was something new, something good in the Mexican girl's life. Some folks were betting it was her handsome stepfather. Others of us thought one of the boys on the football team was putting the wood to her on the sly, and Forrest Evers wasn't the only one trying to take credit for it. Some of us had other theories, but only Miranda seemed to take Naomi's happiness as a personal affront.

Miranda was scrambling. And so none of us were really surprised that she allowed Chigger to take her on a Saturday canoe ride. She didn't give many details, but we knew how to fill in a story.

◇ ◇ ◇

We rarely felt sorry for Miranda, but the thought of being stuck in a boat with Chigger brought us close. Like we expected, Miranda didn't much care for the river. The mosquitoes weren't too bad yet, but every once in a while, a whiff of something foul would roll out of the woods.

"What is that?" Miranda asked. "Gosh but it stinks."

Chigger shrugged. "Could be you're smelling some sour crude from a rig. Or a fox carcass left by a bobcat. Even a deer that lazy hunters didn't track down."

"Charming," Miranda said.

"Down that way is the old pulpwood and paper factory. Remember how that stank?"

Miranda was not interested in traveling down Memory Lane, so Chigger dropped the subject and opened up a jar of worms. He split one in two with his fingernail and baited their fishing lines.

"Ugh," Miranda said. She didn't take the rod he offered her. "So this is what boys do for fun when they're not playing football?" Miranda said.

"Ain't it great?" Chigger grinned.

Miranda was not impressed. There were a bunch of trees, one bank full of scraggly bushes where bits of trash had caught, and another bank with a more gradual sandy slope.

But then she saw something. There was another sort of trash in the woods, apparently. She knew, like all of us, that the woods were where you went to do things you didn't want other folks to know about. Through the trees, Miranda saw an unlikely foursome being happy and alive and not at all careful. And that was the part of the story she told and retold, proof of her intuition that Naomi was a nigger-loving hussy.

MARCH 1937

NAOMI Naomi was serving Henry a late supper when it happened. In the end, he didn't even ask her. He announced what was supposed to happen: "Naomi, we ought to marry."

He spoke to her around a mouthful of fried chicken while she had her head inside the fridge. She stood up and pressed the door closed with her back. She held eggs in both hands.

"Did you hear me?" Henry asked. He was holding his fork and knife extra tight. A drop of gravy clung to the corner of his mouth.

Naomi placed the eggs on the counter and pulled a napkin out of a drawer. Time turned to syrup as she tried to take the four steps that separated her from where he sat at the table. His eyes on her were not a father's eyes. They never had been, but she still could not get over the wrongness of it.

She handed him the napkin. He took it from her. Instead of wiping his mouth, though, he dropped it to the table and grabbed her hand.

"Just think about it," he said. He flashed her a wolf's smile. It was worse than lust; it was desperation. Henry was a drowning man casting about for something to save him. For someone. He'd tried first with Pastor Tom, who gave him Jesus, and then with the twins, who still admired him at least a little. But that wasn't enough. Now he wanted her. That was how it would be: him pulling her down . . . Slow or fast, did it really matter? He would keep at it until he'd drowned them both.

He still held her left hand between his. She curled her fingers and tried to pull away, but he held on. The callouses on his fingers pressed into her hand.

"Sit down," he ordered.

Naomi lowered herself into the chair next to his. The veins in his arms pulsed as he clasped her hand still more tightly. His Adam's apple stood out stark against the flesh of his neck. He looked to have swallowed a peach pit. On his jaw, there was an island of stubble. Lately he had become careless in his shaving. The gravy was still on his lip.

She waited for a long moment and then looked him in the eye. His eyes glinted with an indiscernible emotion. "No," she said firmly, "there's nothing to think about."

To her amazement, a smile spread across his face, making his single dimple appear. He lifted her hand to his mouth and pressed it against his dry lips. "Thank you," he said. A bit of the gravy grazed her knuckles.

She snatched her hand away from his and hid it in her lap. She wiped her fingers on her dress.

"I mean the answer is no. I can't do what you're asking. It's not . . . it's not right."

His grin widened. "Of course it is. It's exactly right. It's sanctified. I've—I've prayed about this." He leaned forward and opened his hands, palm-up, on the table. "God has a plan for us. And when I say 'us,' I mean you and me. Together. That's the path he's been leading us toward since you came here." He stood and began to pace back and forth on the far side of the table. "The twins, they're like, like a rope that binds us together. You're a mother to them already. It all fits. Don't you see, Naomi?"

He went on in the same vein, filling her ears with lines cribbed straight from Pastor Tom. He didn't seem to require any response. Meanwhile, she studied the cheap, nubbed fabric of the tablecloth. There was a loose thread; she longed to pluck it out. Instead, she slid her fingers back and forth across the rough grain of the table's underside, letting her skin drag over the unfinished wood, working out a kind of counterpoint to Henry's rambling.

Only when a splinter caught under her fingernail, biting deep into the tender flesh, did Naomi react. She gasped and pulled her hand back, bringing the finger up instinctively to her mouth. She worked the splinter loose with her tongue and teeth and began to reckon up the too-few options left to her.

HENRY Pastor Tom pulled Henry aside as he came out of the church building on Sunday. The twins ran ahead to play leapfrog with the other kids while Naomi helped Muff with her boys.

"Did you talk to her, brother?" Pastor Tom asked in a low voice. He waved good-bye to some ladies as he spoke.

"Yeah, I did, but . . ." Henry shrugged, a little defeated.

"Well?"

Henry shook his head. "I reckon I botched it."

"You tell her what we talked about? Sharing a path? God's plan? The conviction you've been feeling in your heart?"

"Sure, but it don't come out so clean for me."

"What'd she say?"

"She said no," Henry admitted, "but then I explained it to her again like you told me, about God's plan, about the twins and all. She listened to that, but she sure didn't say yes."

Pastor Tom stroked his beard. "Let her think it over a bit. And pray. If there's something she's put between you, the Lord'll work it out. You just wait on Him. In the meantime, you flee temptation, you hear?" He clapped his left hand against Henry's shoulder and reached his right one out to shake. "I'll be around, and I'll be praying."

Henry weighed up Pastor Tom's words. He was a man of God; his confidence counted for something. But Henry didn't want to wait on the Lord. For one thing, he knew a little more than Pastor Tom about Naomi's reservations. For another, he wanted what he wanted.

That night, he wrote a letter.

NAOMI Naomi knew she needed to tell Wash about Henry's proposal, but after nearly a week she still hadn't caught him alone. His every spare minute was spent with Beto and Cari assembling the scarecrows. She got a report on the progress from the twins every night. Wash brought them the things they needed, worn-out clothes from his mother's scrap bin, heavy wire to connect the limbs, armfuls of straw they could pack into the sleeves and pant legs. Each day, though, their plans seemed to grow more elaborate.

She had to make her own opportunity, then. In the hours before the Wednesday night prayer meeting at the church, she made several long visits to the bathroom. Ten minutes before it was time to go, she complained of an upset stomach and women's problems. Henry gave her a look, but he didn't try to change her mind.

"Feel better!" Cari shouted as she and Beto walked to the truck with Henry.

Naomi nodded and waved from the porch. She stroked Edgar behind the ears.

As soon as the pickup was out of sight, she put the cat back in the house and made a beeline for the woods.

"I'm here," she whispered when she heard his feet on the dry leaves just outside the opening to the tree.

"Well, hello," he said. "Finally."

It wasn't quite dark yet. She could still just see the bright white of his smile.

She kissed him.

"How are you?" he asked.

"Better now."

He pulled her in tight and kissed her again. They went on like that for a while until Wash stopped and touched a hand to her forehead.

"What?" she asked.

"Do you feel all right? Your face is hot."

"You don't want to take credit?"

"Sure," he said. "But I doubt I could heat you up that much." He ran a hand over the sleeve of her sweater. The freak bit of summer that had broken in during February was gone now, and the weather had turned chilly again.

"Try," she said. "I bet you can."

"Challenge accepted."

She leaned her head back against him and slid a hand up along his smooth jaw. "I missed you," she said. She was stalling and knew it, but she could not bear the thought of spoiling the moment. "*Una historia, por favor.* Tell me a story."

She felt him swallow and stiffen, like he was pushing away a bad memory.

"How about a joke?" he asked.

"*Perfecto.*"

He laced his fingers through hers and started in. "So this old farmer went to a town two counties over to hunt for a gal. He found one with crossed eyes and gap teeth, married her, and loaded her up in his wagon to take her home. Once they crossed into his county where she didn't know the area anymore, he pointed out a nice farm and said, 'See that house there and that big ole barn and field?' She said, 'Yes, I do.' And then he stroked his whiskers and said, 'All these are mine.'"

Wash kept talking, but the rhythm of his voice lulled her. The words melted into sounds. She traced the veins that corded down his arms and the lines that crisscrossed the palms of his hand. She loved every inch of him. She let her eyes close, and it wasn't until Wash flicked the end of her nose that she realized she'd drifted off.

"That was the end, baby. Ha, ha," Wash said. He leaned in and nibbled her right ear. "Now, don't you tell me you weren't even listening."

"Sorry. You can tell me again if you want." She offered him a smile, but she kept her eyes closed.

When she opened her eyes and twisted to face him, he asked, "What you thinking on so hard, then, if you're not listening to my excellent joke-telling?"

Naomi laid her forehead against his chest and then turned to press her ear against the steady beating of his heart. She opened her mouth to tell him, but her tongue refused to cooperate.

The silence settled back in around them, comfortable but palpable. He was waiting on her.

"It's Henry...you know...he doesn't see me like a daughter." There. She'd said it.

"More like a slave, I'd say. And I should know." Wash raised his eyebrows. "It's in my blood, that knowledge. I know about taking-for-granted, about folks feeling they've got a right to their meanness."

"It's not that. I mean, it's not just what he wants me to do. He wants—he thinks...he thinks he can solve everything if...he told me he..." She couldn't say the words.

"Is he talking about moving again?" Wash asked.

Naomi shook her head.

"Just say it, baby." He studied her, waiting. It looked like patience, but Naomi felt that a distance had opened up between them.

"Wash?" Naomi tilted her head up so she could see the outlines of his face in the dark. She brushed her fingertips from his forehead down over his nose and, briefly, across his lips.

"¿Sí, señorita?" He nipped playfully at her fingers.

"Now *you* went away for a minute there."

He sighed. "It's hard for me when you can't talk to me."

"I know," she said. "Let me find my words. Tomorrow."

"I could help you."

"Let's practice not saying anything at all," she whispered. And she began to kiss him slowly, sliding her hands down to his waistband.

He wrapped his arms around her and shook her hair free from its braid. "I can get behind that," he murmured, burying his fingers in the curtain of her hair. "Yes, ma'am, I can."

BETO Beto and Cari chose Thursday, pie day, for the unveiling. They brought two sheets from the linen closet in Henry's house and draped them over the scarecrows before moving them out into the garden.

"Wait to get her until she's done with the pies," Cari suggested.

Beto tasted pineapple but focused on adjusting the scarecrow's arms under the sheet. He tied strips of fabric and foil along the lengths of them; the encyclopedia said that crows didn't like movement or shiny things.

"I bet she's mostly done now," Wash said. "I'm going to go see." He came back with Rhoda a few minutes later. She was frowning and wiping her hands on her apron, but by the time she and Wash made it to the edge of the garden, Beto thought he saw the beginning of a smile.

"On the count of three," Cari called. "One . . . two . . . three!"

Beto's sheet caught on the scarecrow's pointing finger, and he blushed as he tugged it carefully off.

"My goodness," she said. "I defy those crows to come out here this year!" She came closer to examine their handiwork. "What are these for?" she asked, pointing to the wheeled platforms under the scarecrows' posts.

"That way," Beto explained, "you can move them around. It's supposed to make them more effective."

She smiled. "You two thought of everything."

"Now can we eat a pineapple pie?" Beto blurted out.

"Pardon?"

Cari recited the exact words Mrs. Fuller had spoken to them months earlier, the first time Wash had brought them for pies: "Build me a scarecrow, and then you can have all the pies you want!"

"I guess I did say that," she said. "You all had better come on up to the porch for your prize."

A few minutes later, she held out a tray of pies to them. Beto picked pineapple, still warm from the fryer. Cari chose cherry, and Wash took rum raisin.

From inside the house came the sounds of Wash's sister Peggy practicing the piano.

"Just ignore the noise," Wash said with a grin.

"James Washington, your sister is learning," Mrs. Fuller said.

Peggy hit a sour note then, and they all burst out laughing. "I can hear you, you know," Peggy called from the living room, but that only made them laugh harder.

The tangy sweet pineapple fused with this easy happiness. Beto looked over at Cari. She felt it, too, the goodness of being here. "This," Beto mouthed to her, and she nodded. This moment was the good-luck thing they shared for the day.

Wash pretended to cover his ears when Peggy hit another wrong note, and then said loudly, "I think I'll go do some chores till this is over."

"Hush now," Rhoda said, but she gave him another pie and offered seconds to the twins, too.

NAOMI Naomi dropped Henry's work clothes into the tub on the back porch. March meant rain, which meant mud, which meant it took twice as long to get Henry's work clothes clean. She learned from Muff to pour a bottle of Coca-Cola into the soak tub to help loosen the mud, but it still took extra scrubbing before she even put the clothes through Muff's washer. At least it was Thursday; the twins would be eating pies at Wash's house and so would come home happy. Maybe Beto would save her a bit of flaky crust with a smear of fruit filling like he sometimes did.

She was on the porch wringing out Henry's work clothes when she heard a truck turn off of the main road and onto the dirt road that led only to the Humble houses. Bud gave her a wave and then pulled in next door. After he got out, he held up a handful of mail. "I was at the post office. Thought I'd save y'all the trip."

She glanced at the envelopes as she carried them inside. The top envelope was a bill for Henry, but the second one was addressed to her. It had her cousin Josefina's handwriting. She felt a pang of guilt as she counted the weeks that had passed since she last wrote home.

Naomi dropped into a kitchen chair and ripped the corner of the envelope. Then she remembered Abuelito's letter opener. She found it under her mattress and used it to slice through the rest of the envelope. She expected Fina's usual updates and gossip, but when she scanned the letter, she saw that the tone was all wrong. She flipped the page over. It was signed "Abuelita" in her grandmother's unschooled print. There was a P.S.: "Naomi, I wrote this down, but they are Abuelita's words, told to me in Spanish of course. You are probably wondering why Abuelito didn't write it for her. He has changed so much since you left. Especially since he fell last month. Part of his face is pulled down now, and when he talks, it is mostly nonsense. We have to remind him to eat and keep him from the fire. I'm sorry that you are finding out this way, but you know it is hard to phone and the telegrams are too expensive. Love, Fina."

With trembling fingers, Naomi turned the letter back over, smoothed it against her lap, and began to read again.

Dearest Granddaughter,

By the time these words reach you, Henry will have talked to you about the future. Perhaps you have already made the proper choice. If so, this will only help you to know that you have our blessing. But if you are waiting, or if you have doubts, please read my words with care as Josefina is writing them down for me.

You should accept Henry as your husband. I know that your mother had her challenges. We know also of his weaknesses. No man is perfect. Most important is that he is the father of Cari and Beto, and it is right for them to be with their father. You have seen that it is very good for them there with the school, and I know that you eat well. Your correct choice is something you can have pride in for always.

I tell you, first, that you must think of the twins. But maybe you have a woman's concerns about this. You may think of love and adventure, or maybe you remember some young man here in San Antonio and think that you might like to return to him. Forget this idea. It is better to marry an older man, Naomi. When they have aged, you know better what you get. There is no mystery, no ugly surprise down the road. Your grandfather was 28 when I met him. I was only 14. There is less difference between you and Henry. It may seem very big now, but in time it will become a small thing, like the difference in the size of his hands and your hands.

Things are hard here. Your grandfather is no longer himself, and the store sells less and less. We have taken in another family to help us pay the rent.

There is no place here, understand? Be practical, my dove. Think of the twins. Do not be foolish at this time.

Con cariño,
Abuelita

Naomi dropped the letter, but she couldn't escape its threat. Nowhere to sleep. No money. No school. No food. No future. Naomi began to feel the room close in on her. A future she did not want was closing in on her. She reached under the bed for the guitar case. She found her mother's braid and curled up on the bed, crumpled around her hurt.

Abuelita had said, "We know of his weaknesses," but she didn't know, couldn't know. Abuelito must be gone or very close to gone; he would never have forced her like this, cutting off her return.

The braid wasn't enough. She shoved the letter into her pocket, closed up the guitar case, and ran.

WASH Wash was splitting wood behind his house when he saw a flash of yellow in the woods. He held up a finger, buried the axe in the stump, and ran around to the front of the house to make sure that the twins were still busy eating his mother's pies. Then he hurried to the tree line.

"Hey," he said. "You okay?" He could see that she'd been crying. It was all he could do not to reach for her right here.

"Sorry to come here, but I couldn't wait," she said. "I need to show you something."

He nodded. "I'll make an excuse and get out of here quick. Meet you at the tree in twenty minutes?"

"I'll be waiting," she said.

**WASH & NAOMI** Wash looked up from the letter and shook his head. "He wants to *make* you marry him?"

Naomi pressed back against the inside of the tree. For once it felt more cramped than intimate. She wished the day weren't so bright; even in here, there was too much light.

"That's not the worst part of it. The worst is . . ." She pushed the words out. "Well, you read the letter. We can't go back now. Even my grandmother is trying to push me into this. But there are things that have happened . . . things I could never talk about to anyone."

Wash flinched. "Not even me?"

"There are some things . . ." she hesitated.

A picture began forming in Wash's mind of what might have been going on in that house. There was nothing to do but ask. "He hasn't tried anything, has he?"

"Not really," she said.

"Hold on. Yes or no?" He lifted her chin toward him. He wanted to see her eyes.

She looked away. "Nothing too bad. Not in a long time."

He exhaled slowly, willing himself to be patient. "Y'all have only lived with him since September. How long ago could it be?"

She felt him watching her. He'd see a lie for sure. And if she started lying to Wash, she wouldn't have anything left.

"Since we came, it was only bad once." A little at a time, she told him about the night after Beto fixed the radio. Her mother's dress. Henry taking hold of her and calling her Estella.

"That's why you didn't want me to hug you from behind?"

She gave a quick nod.

"But why didn't you say anything? The bastard, the—" Wash stopped himself. "You said 'since we came.' Why did you say that?"

His words hung in the air between them. Naomi thought maybe if she kissed him long enough he wouldn't ask again. She tried, but Wash twined his fingers through hers and brought her hands chastely back to her knees. "Not now. What did you mean when you said that it was just once since you came here?" He held her gaze, and she could feel some of his steadiness pass into her.

"Before my mother died . . ." Naomi began. She remembered Henry's face, twisted. Him in her bedroom, the bathroom. His hand gripping hers tightly, guiding it.

"He made me touch him." She gestured at Wash's belt. "He couldn't— my mom was sick and she couldn't, wasn't supposed to, you know, and so he started coming to find me." She swallowed hard. "It took me a while, but one day I bit him."

"On his . . . ?"

She laughed and shook her head. "On his arm. Hard. And that was it, he didn't do it again. But that only made things worse."

"How do you mean?"

"If I had done what he wanted, he might have stayed away from my mom, see? I don't know if he did it to punish me or because he couldn't stop himself, but he got her pregnant again. Before that she lost a lot of babies, three in just a couple of years. She got sicker every time. But the last time it took."

"The twins?"

"She had them, but it took everything out of her. She only lasted a week."

Wash pulled her close.

"I can't believe I said it," she whispered.

"Nobody should be alone with that kind of burden."

"I could have saved her."

"No!" Wash took her face in his hands. "Listen to me. It was wrong, what he did. You had to stop him. A man who would do that to a child, he wouldn't stop at anything. Not with you, not with your mother."

"He said—"

"It wasn't your fault," Wash said. He planted each word like a man laying down bricks.

Naomi closed her eyes tight and laid her cheek on his shoulder. Now he knew. She had no idea what the knowing would mean for them.

"We've got to think," Wash said slowly. "In the letter, your grandmother talks like this is something that's going to happen soon. Him asking you, I mean."

"He already did," Naomi mumbled.

"And that's what you were trying to tell me about yesterday?"

"You know how I am. Sometimes the words just don't come."

"And you already told him no?"

Naomi stiffened and began to protest, "What else would I—"

"Of course. But maybe we could . . ." Now Wash felt the frustration of not having the right words.

"It doesn't matter what I said. He hasn't accepted my answer." She gestured at the letter. "He gets started with the church stuff, and suddenly everything he wants is 'God's will' for me. But anyway, what good is time? I don't see what choices I have now." She felt a tightness rising in her throat as her future unrolled before her. It would be her unhappy face in the wedding photo. Then laundry. Dusting. Biscuits. Cooking ham hocks and beans. Mending. The twins would grow up and move out like children do. And then there would only be the ceaseless housework. And Henry. No, it was even worse than that. Him forcing his leg between hers, him pushing her down onto his bed, taking her in the bathroom, in the closet. "A bun in the oven." Henry's child. She shuddered and remembered the sound of her mother's crying overlaid with the squeaking of the bedsprings. All those miscarriages. So many wrong things that could never be made right.

"What am I going to do?" she said again.

"We," he said firmly. "What are *we* going to do." The words were another line of bricks in their defense against the world.

NAOMI "Can I tell you something, Tommie?" Naomi whispered across the study hall table.

"Hang on," Tommie mouthed and went up to one of the study hall monitors. Naomi couldn't hear what Tommie was saying, but before long the monitor was writing out a pass.

When Tommie got back, she smirked and said, "We're going to go work on our sewing project."

"What project? We already finished."

"Hush now. We're just going to head to the home ec cottage and then look for somewhere you can talk to me easy."

The home economics cottage was on the edge of the school grounds. On the front was a model house with a wide porch, living room, bathroom, kitchen, and two bedrooms. The idea was to give them a space exactly like what they'd manage as wives and mothers. Across the back of the building were the cooking and sewing labs with their banks of stoves and Singers.

Instead of going into the cottage, Tommie led Naomi to a bench in a sunny spot on the far side of the cottage, out of sight of the study hall window.

"So?" she asked. She unwrapped a Hershey bar and offered Naomi a piece.

Naomi set the chocolate on her knee. "Henry said he wants to get married."

Tommie grinned and hugged Naomi.

"Tommie!" Naomi pulled back.

"Oh, stop!" Tommie slapped her lightly on the shoulder. "Everybody knows you're in love."

"When'd I give you that idea?"

"The way you always acted, like you didn't like none of the boys at school or church . . . not even Gilbert Harris! I always thought it was because you had a secret crush."

Naomi stiffened a little at that. "But I never said anything good about Henry to you, did I?"

"No, but I thought that was on account of you liking him, see? Some folks pretend not to like the person they most love." Tommie went on, "Muff was saying the other day that you two could make a pretty sharp couple."

Naomi drew in a breath and released it slowly. It was just like talking to Muffy. There was no safe way to set the record straight; whatever she said would only confuse Tommie, who sometimes told her cousins that they'd have to go live with the colored people if they kept acting up.

She tried to think. Even if she couldn't mention Wash, there were other reasons for not wanting to marry Henry, things she could bring up to buy some time, at least, while she and Wash figured out a plan.

"He doesn't seem a little old to you?" Naomi asked.

Tommie shrugged. "Not really. And second to Gilbert, I'd say he's one of the handsomest men around."

Naomi tried again. "Thing is, I'm not ready to get married. I'm too young."

"Now that I can understand," Tommie said. "You know, Dwayne's been talking about getting married since we started dating. He can hardly stand it, but I'm fixin' on graduating first. I don't want to miss a thing. I want him and me to graduate together, and then there's the whole summer for weddings."

"Sure," Naomi said. She tried on the argument. "So you told Dwayne to hold on?"

"Well," Tommie said a little slyly, "I try to keep him satisfied with other things." She looked down and crossed her ankles.

"Oh." Naomi's cheeks colored.

"Not, you know, not that. Just a little snuggling and petting. You don't think I'm bad, do you?" Tommie looked up.

"Course not. If you're bad, everybody else is in a lot bigger trouble." She smiled and squeezed Tommie's hand. "How did you get Dwayne to agree? To hold off on marrying, I mean?"

"What choice has he got? He can't exactly do it without me. Same with Henry. If he wants to get hitched, he'll have to do it on your time. Only problem is with folks talking, on account of y'all living there together."

"But if we don't tell anybody . . ."

"And you behave," Tommie said with a wink.

The thought of Henry not behaving made Naomi feel ill. She jumped up quickly and reached out to help Tommie up. "Come on, we'd better at least stop by the cottage. Did you get your grade on your dress yet?"

WASH Wash was doing his own research. He started with the old issues of the *Chicago Defender* boxed up at the back of the cowshed. He wanted to see if there was anything about a safe place for him and Naomi. He laughed at himself a little for that. What did he expect to find, an advice column on practical miscegenation? He didn't need perfect, just somewhere he could take Naomi without getting himself strung up for being with her. And not just her. He had to figure out how to make it with the twins, too. That would be harder. With him, Naomi might pass for colored, but the four of them together didn't make any sense. They couldn't leave the twins behind with Henry, though, and that letter had made it plain that there was nothing left for them in San Antonio.

As he skimmed the pages, one article caught his eye. It was an opinion piece in favor of a black colony in Mexico. "Where we may be treated as men and not as pawns," the editorial said. Baja California.

That was something, but the paper had been printed years earlier; maybe nothing came of the plan. He checked the other papers from that year but found no other mention of the colony. Still, it was the closest thing he had to a lead.

He decided to start with his father's cousin Lewis. His work as a

260

porter had taken him to dozens of cities, and Wash remembered him talking about a train route that went all the way down to Mexico City. He would know if there was a place where a mixed couple could live with something approaching safety, and maybe he could tell Wash something about Baja California.

Lewis usually came to East Texas about once a month, and he'd been by just last week on his way to stay for a spell with his woman in Tyler.

"For heaven's sake, marry her!" Wash's mother had said while they were eating supper. "You and Skyla are near old enough to be grandparents, and there you are, shacking up like a couple of teenaged field hands." Wash's father didn't weigh in one way or another, but on more than one occasion Wash saw him slip Lewis a fresh tin of condoms by way of thanks for the newspapers.

Lewis hadn't said how long he was visiting, but with any luck, he'd still be with Skyla now. While his mother was out delivering pies, Wash copied the address from her desk drawer and headed out along the highway toward Tyler. He walked a few miles before a man driving an ice truck stopped and offered him a ride.

When they got into Tyler, it turned out that the man lived at a boarding house just down the street from Lewis's lady friend. The driver dropped off the truck at the ice plant and then pointed him toward the right street.

Skyla lived on the opposite side of town from Wash's Aunt Jennie, his mother's sister, who was just as deliberately respectable as his parents. Skyla's was a typical shotgun house—long and narrow with each room opening into the next. It leaned a bit on its foundations and was sorely in need of paint. A few skinny chickens pecked around the concrete blocks the house sat on. In one of the porch's three rockers, Lewis sat smoking his pipe and nursing a bottle of Pearl.

Wash gave him a wave.

If Lewis was surprised to see Wash, he didn't let on. He waved him over and called into the house.

A moment later, a tall woman with her hair wrapped in a scarf came out onto the porch.

"Son," Lewis said when Wash came up the steps, "this fine woman is Skyla Pines." Lewis nodded at her. "Skyla, this is Jim's boy Wash, the scholar who's going to be a doctor or something."

"How do you do, ma'am," Wash said. He worked his hat around in his hands.

"You want some sweet tea, hon?" Skyla asked. She smiled but didn't show her teeth.

"Yes, ma'am. That'd be very fine."

While she was gone, Lewis cocked an eyebrow at him. "Everything all right?" he asked.

"Yes, sir," Wash said, feeling a bit of heat come into his face.

"You've got the look of a runaway. Tell me you ain't run off or nothing stupid."

"No, sir, I ain't."

"But?"

"I'm thinking about making a change. In the future. Wanted some advice on locations and thought of you."

Lewis pulled on the pipe and nodded at the rocker on his left. "Your pa know?"

"There's nothing to know yet. Just thinking."

"This about a girl?"

Wash hesitated.

"Don't bother answering," Lewis said, pointing the bowl of his pipe at Wash. "There's always a girl."

Wash brought out the newspaper clipping from his pocket and handed it to Lewis. "You know anything about this? It's from an old copy of the *Defender*. Six years ago."

Lewis held the paper at arm's length, squinting. "Eyes gone to hell these last few years." He studied the column for a few minutes before handing it back.

Skyla came with the glass of tea then. Wash drank half of it in grateful gulps, feeling the cool and the sugar slide down his throat.

"I'm fixing to see about supper. You want to join us, young man?" Skyla asked.

"No, ma'am. I'm set with this, thank you much. I got to be heading back to New London here in a minute. Just a quick visit."

When she went back inside, Lewis rocked back hard in his chair, frowning. "Baja California . . . It's been a while since I worked the route down to Mexico City. The way I reckon, anything called California would be pretty far from that track, and I don't even know I've heard of it. Truth be told, I can't remember seeing more than a handful of black folks down far south, not counting us porters, of course."

"Guess what I'm asking is, you think it'd be any better for us there?"

"Folks are poor. Some of them mean poor."

"But will they let you be?"

Lewis studied him. "What kind of girl are you running with?"

Wash dodged the question. "Don't know that there's going to be any running. Just thinking for now."

Lewis sighed and leaned toward Wash. The runners of the old rocker groaned a little. "What do you expect your folks are going to say?"

"Got bigger worries."

Lewis made a round motion with his hand in front of his belly. "This big?"

Wash gave a short laugh. "Not that kind of trouble."

"I'm not giving you any advice, all right, son?"

"Yes, sir."

"Just happen to be chewing the bone about Mexico." Lewis turned a careful eye on Wash.

"Yes, sir."

"Let's be clear on one thing. There's no Promised Land, not like the paper makes you think. Not going up to Chicago or Detroit or even Canada. I've been all them places and worked with black folk who've gone to more. And there's nothing to be found going down to Mexico."

Wash started to protest, but Lewis held up a hand. "Hear me out, son." He drew hard on his pipe and then released the smoke slowly. "Now, I don't know a thing about these colonies in Mexico. Who knows if they even got a start. Chances are, the Mexican government shut them out. I've heard of that other places. Problem always comes when folks try to go in a big group. Drew too much attention. Tried to do everything legal. Big mistake. You can't count on anybody to give you permission, see?"

"So it won't work." Wash's shoulders slumped a little.

"You're not *hearing* me, boy. What I'm saying is that you don't make it official, you just slip in. Lots of nooks and crannies down there, little spots nobody'd find unless they knew what they were looking for. It's not a bad place for someone looking to disappear."

"Anything else?"

"They don't like Negroes, particularly, but they don't take too much time to care one way or another what anybody is doing. That's my impression, at least, from where I usually stand."

"All right, that's something," Wash said, nodding.

"How's your Spanish?" Lewis asked.

Wash grinned. "I'm learning some."

"This girl, she white?"

Wash didn't hesitate. "No, sir, not white."

"Black?" Lewis asked.

"Kind of cream-and-coffee colored."

"She Mexican?"

Wash shrugged.

"Lord help you," Lewis said, shaking his head. "Why didn't you just find you a nice yella girl and leave it at that? Never knew you to have trouble picking up the ladies."

Wash set down his glass and picked at a mosquito bite on his arm. "She found me."

Lewis frowned.

"Can you help us get there?" Wash asked.

"How can I, boy, when I don't know nothing about this?" his uncle said sharply. "All I'll say is that they hire black folk for porter positions. They like strong boys that can dress sharp and talk right. Something for you to keep in mind," Lewis said. "Not that you heard it from me."

Wash stood and held out his hand. "Thank you, Uncle Lewis. I'll be sure to forget where I heard everything you just said. Give my best to Miss Skyla."

◇ ◇ ◇

The next morning, Wash made a detour on his way to school and left Naomi a note in case she beat him to the tree later: "How about Mexico?" He pierced the paper onto the nail that held the ornament Beto and Cari had made him. It was the best future he could come up with for their strange little family.

He muddled through the day. Already his teacher was getting testy as more pupils vanished out of the classroom to go to work in the fields now that the weather had really and truly turned toward warm. She took it out on those of them who were still in school, threatening to load them down with extra lessons if they didn't get their minds on their studies.

When his classes let out at two, Wash ran to the grounds of the New London school. Today he only wanted enough work to keep him busy until he could catch Naomi's eye. But as he was crossing toward Mr. Crane's house, the janitor waved to him from the portico that connected the main school building and the cafeteria.

"I could use your help this afternoon, son," Mr. Stine said once Wash reached him. "Already cleared it with Mr. Crane. Twenty cents an hour like usual."

"Yes, sir," Wash said. "What needs doing?"

The janitor gave him a rueful grin. "Nothing but checking over every heater in every room." He paused. "That's about a hundred of 'em."

"Surely y'all aren't running the heat today!" Wash said. "It's near about eighty, I reckon."

"No, but some kids've been complaining of headaches, saying their eyes burn when they're at school. Mr. Crane thought maybe there's gas leaking at one of the connections to the heaters. No way to find it but to check every one. We'll start in the outbuildings and then move on into the classrooms after school lets out here in a bit."

Wash's shoulders sagged a little. It was a job that might not be done till suppertime—or later. He opened his mouth to say that he could only stay until four, but then he closed it. The train tickets wouldn't be cheap; they needed the money.

He rolled up his sleeves, picked up Mr. Stine's toolbox, and followed him into the cafeteria.

Mr. Stine showed him the collars that formed the connections between the heaters and the gas pipes. "Check around here on each one, make sure it's good and snug. If it ain't, just tighten it up."

They worked together through the cafeteria and then the gymnasium. After the bell ending the school day sounded, they headed into the massive main building. The halls were mostly empty, but a few students were still straggling out. Wash was careful to keep his eyes on the floor and mumble his good afternoons when someone passed him. Whites-only buildings always brought back his father's lessons.

After a while, Mr. Stine wiped his red, sweating face with a rag. "You've got the idea, Wash. We split up, we can get this job done a lot faster. You go on up to the third floor and work your way down. I'll work my way up and we'll meet in the middle. My wife's cooking meatloaf tonight, and I'd sure like to be there to eat it."

"Yes, sir," Wash said. He grabbed a couple of wrenches out of the toolbox and headed for the stairs. "I'll let you know if I find anything," he called.

Wash was done checking the heaters on the third floor and the east wing of the second floor when Mr. Stine came lumbering toward him down the main hall. "I'm done with the west wing. How's it going?" he asked, his breath uneven.

"It's going, sir," Wash answered. "Just finishing up—"

He had been about to say "with the east wing" when Mr. Stine whistled and exhaled hard. "Swell. Means we can head on home. You ask me," he said, leaning closer to Wash, "those kids will imagine a headache any day of the week to get out of their classes. I didn't find a single heater that was amiss."

Neither had Wash; chances were, he figured, that the classroom heaters in the second floor main hall were also fine. He thought about asking Mr. Stine if he'd gone down to the basement to check the heaters in the wood shop, but then he snuck a look at his watch. It was half past five; if he hurried, he might still be able to see Naomi.

NAOMI Down at the river, Naomi sat on her rock and tried to ignore the twins. They were oddly sullen today, Cari especially.

They'd all hoped to see Wash, but they'd been in the woods for over an hour, and there was still no sign of him.

"Where do you think he is?" Beto asked.

"Not sure, love," Naomi said without looking up from her book, though she'd been reading the same few lines of *Macbeth* for the past ten minutes. "Probably working." She tried to sound indifferent, but she was just as eager to hear his footfalls on the path. That was why she was here and not back at the house doing the Friday chores; she wanted to tell him what Tommie had said and try to figure out what might be next. All week, Henry had been mercifully preoccupied with drilling a well out in Smith County, which kept him away for long hours. Soon enough, though, she'd have to talk to him.

She twisted her braid around her fingers. Breathe and read, breathe and read. She pushed her eyes across the lines in front of her. "To-morrow, and to-morrow, and to-morrow, creeps in this petty pace from day to day to the last syllable of recorded time . . ."

She gave up on that bit but kept reading. Anything was better than talking to the twins right now. Since the moment school let out, they had been wheedling and prodding for stories about their mother. She was used to it from Cari, but now even Beto had started in. No doubt following his sister's lead.

Cari paced the bit of path at the top of the bank while Beto squatted down by the water skipping stones.

"It's not fair," Cari said, her voice shrill. "We have a right to know about our own mother."

Naomi leaned closer to the book. "I pull in resolution, and begin to doubt the equivocation of the fiend . . ." She tracked the line back to the speaker. Macbeth. She wished the old king would go ahead and die.

"Are you even listening?" Cari demanded. "Do you ever listen?"

Naomi snapped the book shut and pressed her face into her hands. Patience, patience, she commanded herself. "You know my stories, Cari," she said, working hard to keep her voice level. "You two can tell them better than I can, even."

"There's heaps you haven't told us!" Cari cried, stamping her foot. "There must be."

"It's not my fault that I don't have more, *cariño*. I was just a little girl when . . ." Her voice faltered. "When you were born."

Cari narrowed her eyes. "What about when she died? You've never told us about that."

Naomi heard Beto gasp as if the wind had been knocked out of him. She felt robbed of air, too.

"Oh, Cari," Naomi said. "Please, stop."

"I like the good stories," Beto began. "I think—"

"You hush," Cari snapped. "You want to know just as much as I do." She pressed on. "You tell us stories about hairstyles and pickles and dance contests, things that don't matter, but you leave out everything we need to know. Like how come she died and why did Daddy go and what did she want us to know about her."

Naomi did not turn. She did not call Cari to her. She did not reprimand her. She did not cry. She sat feeling her sister's words burrow into her.

Cari was cruelest when she was right.

But the past was Naomi's pain, something she carried and kept to herself. For herself. Somehow, Cari had caught on to that. And what she was asking for was not the kind of story that would lend anybody strength. Naomi didn't want to feed Cari's anger.

That was when he came. The steady tread that they knew so well. Beto dropped his stones, scaled the bank, and headed up the path. Cari hesitated a moment longer, waiting in case Naomi might respond to her challenge. Then she ran, too.

WASH Wash heard the twins on the path before he saw them. Cari ran fast enough to overtake Beto, and she threw her arms around his legs.

"Thank goodness you're here," she cried.

"Why? What's the matter?"

"Nothing," Beto said.

At the same time, Cari said, "Everything!" She tugged Wash toward the river. "Naomi's being a pill!"

"Your sister's here today?" Wash tried not to let his voice betray too much interest or excitement. Maybe he could convince the twins to run some small errand. He had to be careful; if they got the sense that he wanted them gone, they'd be stuck to him tight as ticks. It was one of those laws of children, like their tendency to be least grateful when you were trying your hardest to please them.

"Y'all have any extra bars of soap at home?" Wash asked as they walked the last dozen or so steps to the bank of the river. "I was thinking I could show you how to carve a sculpture."

"Do we?" Beto called down to Naomi.

She cleared her throat but didn't turn around. "Bottom shelf of the kitchen pantry. In the back."

"I'll go," Beto volunteered.

"Go on, Cari," Naomi said. "You, too."

Cari crossed her arms, gearing up to protest. Then Wash saw the briefest glint of mischief flash through her eyes. "Sure thing, sis!" she said.

◇ ◇ ◇

Wash tugged on Naomi's skirt with a grin as soon as the twins were gone.

"I know," she said. "But we don't have much time."

"You been to the tree?" he asked, settling down on a log near her.

She shook her head. "Not since yesterday."

"So you haven't seen my note. I've got an idea. Not a plan yet, but an idea." He told her about the letter in the *Chicago Defender* and what Lewis had told him.

"Wash, I've never even been to Mexico."

"At least you know the language. We don't have heaps of options right now. I might've said we could melt into some faraway backwoods spot. Even know of a few places like that. But I can't see Henry letting that go now, and there's the twins to think of, too."

"Before the letter, I thought maybe I could take them back to San Antonio, just for a while. Maybe the summer. But that won't work anymore."

"We'll bring them with us," he said firmly. "Now what do we do about him?"

"Henry?"

"No, the Easter Bunny." Wash rolled his eyes.

She shoved him. "Don't you start being a brat, too. I've got my hands full with Cari."

"What happened? She had fire in her eyes."

Naomi shrugged. "Sometimes she wants things I can't give her."

Wash assumed that she meant something like a dress or hair ribbons. "Girls can be like that," he said. He cracked his knuckles one by one.

"That's an evil sound."

"Geez, Naomi, come on. We may not have much longer to talk. Has Henry said anything else?"

She shook her head. "He's been out drilling in Smith County. Filling in for a tool pusher who got hurt, I think. I've been steering clear as much as I can."

"Good."

"So." Naomi ran her fingers along the hem of her skirt. "Tommie gave me an idea."

"Okay?"

"She said Dwayne Stark—that's her boyfriend—wants to get married, but she's making him hold off until after graduation. I was thinking I could try the same thing."

"Tell him 'Yes, but a little later'?"

She nodded. "Something like that. To buy time, like you said. I can pretend I just want to make it to the end of the school year. And I'll say we can't tell anyone yet, have to keep up appearances."

He frowned, taking it in. That horny bastard living in the same house as Naomi, and him thinking they were engaged. It stank of risk.

"I know," she said. "I don't like it, either. But how else?"

Wash stared out at the river. A beaver was swimming downstream with a long, thin branch grasped between its sharp teeth. He sighed and rolled his elbows onto his knee.

"I don't like it, but I don't see a better way until we've got enough money," he said finally. "As soon as I can scrape the funds together, we're gone. Just be careful till then."

"Gone how?"

"By the time school lets out maybe we'll have enough for the train. Third class."

"But four train tickets?" Naomi sounded doubtful. "All the way to Mexico?"

"We only need three tickets once we get to San Antonio. I'm going to sign on as a porter. You and the twins will ride together in a passenger car. Once we're in Mexico, we'll figure out our next move." It sounded far-fetched even to Wash. He tried to smile. "We'll make this work. Just save whatever you can, okay?"

"I have a little saved. I used to skim from what Henry gave me for groceries, but then there was Christmas. There's maybe eight dollars left."

"That's still *dinero*, right? And start talking Spanish to me."

"*Claro que sí.*"

"Of course?"

She smiled a little. "*Sí. Tienes razón, guapo.*"

"*Guapo?*"

"Handsome. Don't let it go to your head."

They sat for a while, listening to the sounds of spring in the woods. The sharp cries of jays and mockingbirds filled the silence between them. Somewhere a woodpecker was hammering his dinner out of a tree.

"Doesn't it seem like they've been gone a long time?" Naomi asked after a while.

"Are you complaining?" he asked. "Is it that awful to just sit and talk to me?"

She nudged him a little with her elbow. "Hush, you."

"There's the tree. We don't have to talk . . . "

She shook her head. "They should be back soon. Although . . . " she hesitated.

"What?"

"I don't know. Just how Cari's been acting. So angry." She shook off the worry. "Come on, let's walk a little. We'll meet them halfway."

BETO "Got it," Beto called. When Cari didn't respond, he walked to their bedroom and stood in the doorway. He waved the bar of Ivory at her.

Cari didn't look at Beto. She was sitting on his bed, staring straight ahead. Edgar twined around her, purring loudly, but she didn't seem to notice.

"I'm going to do it," she said finally.

"What are you talking about?"

Her expression was all impatience when she turned to face him. "You know what. There might be answers."

Beto stared at the floor. Of course he knew what. "We promised. And anyway, there are some boxes you aren't supposed to open," he said. "Remember?" They had both read the encyclopedia entry on Greek mythology.

"We've waited long enough," Cari said. "She's never going to show us."

Beto sighed, but he knew from the set of Cari's jaw that, this time, she was going to do it with or without him.

"Just a quick look," he said.

She was already reaching under the bed and pulling the guitar case out.

"What do you think she'd do if she knew?" Cari asked.

Beto swallowed. "I don't know."

"It doesn't matter." Cari grabbed the handle of the case and yanked it closer. "She was our mother, too," she said fiercely. She snapped the latches open.

They sat on opposite ends of the bed, and spread the contents of the case between them.

One red dress;

Two red high-heeled shoes;

Faded holy cards for Saint Cecilia, patron of music; Saint Francis of Assisi, patron of the animals; and Saint Benedict the Moor, patron of dark peoples;

Four bits of a broken doll: one blue eye and half an eyebrow, a bit with a curl of black hair attached, an ear, and a hand with perfect tiny fingernails;

A dented Saint Christopher medal on a copper chain;

A cracked rubber nipple from a baby bottle.

They had seen the dress back when Beto fixed the radio, but the rest was new. It wouldn't have seemed like much to anybody else, but after seven years of only having their mother secondhand, the fact of actual objects that their mother might have touched seemed to them like a small miracle.

Still, disappointment lay leaden in Beto's belly. He had expected something more. Maybe a message from their mother, something along the lines of "My dear twins . . ." Maybe a photograph that Abuelita and Abuelito hadn't shown them. Something.

"What do you think happened to the guitar?" he asked.

Cari shrugged. "Maybe Abuelita made Abuelito sell it."

Beto weighed the idea, but it didn't feel right. He picked up the medal and swung it back and forth, a tiny pendulum.

"Sleepy," he said. "You're getting very sleepy. Your eyes are heavy." He smiled. He had thought of it before Cari.

She waved a dismissive hand at him. "Please."

"Shhh," Beto said. "Follow this medal with your eyes. Your eyes are getting very, very heavy. Soon you will be in a deep, deep sleep . . ."

"You're no hypnotist," Cari insisted, her voice sharp with irritation. "But—" She tugged on one of her curls and narrowed her eyes. Beto could see that she had an idea brewing.

She fingered the hem of the red dress, then lifted a shoe in either hand. "These were hers for sure. She had Cinderella feet." Cari slipped the shoes on.

"Cari, don't!" Beto hissed.

"Why not?" she said, and she raised an eyebrow. "Look, they fit me." She pulled the dress over to the edge of the bed and shook out the wrinkles. When she did, something fell from inside the frilly skirt.

They both jumped, then stared.

"It has to be hers," Cari said. She picked up the long braid. It had been carefully banded at the top and bottom so that it wouldn't come undone. She traced a strand from top to tip. It was almost identical to Naomi's. Cari thought back to all the times she had seen Naomi holding her own braid, eyes closed.

They held the braid between them.

"This will be perfect," Cari said, stroking the tail end.

"What for?" Beto asked. He wasn't sure he wanted to know.

"You'll see," she said.

He began to protest, but he already knew that he was going to go along with her idea.

Cari studied their mother's things. "How well do you remember what you read from the S's?" she asked.

Beto shrugged. "Never as good as you do."

She went to the kitchen and came back with the Community House Coffee calendar under her arm. She tapped a date: March 18.

"That's our day," she said. "Three days away."

Beto knew only one important thing about that date: it was their mother's birthday.

NAOMI Naomi made her move the next night when Henry came home in high spirits. This had been his first job as the top man on a rig, and he'd hit oil in the first week of drilling.

"Congratulations on the strike," she said. "It's something to celebrate." She served him a plate of pork chops, butter-drenched green beans with bacon, and mashed potatoes with brown gravy, and she got out the piece of lemon cake she'd tucked up in the cupboard.

"Your favorites." She laid the plate in front of him.

He forked up a bite and then looked over at her. "You already eat?"

"With the twins." She forced a smile and pressed her trembling hands flat against the front of her apron. She wanted to turn back to the safety of the dishes she'd left in the sink, but she had to stay the course. There wouldn't be a better time.

"This is good," he said with his mouth full.

"Want to bless it?" she asked. She slid into the chair beside him and offered him her hand before he had time to answer. She bowed her head so she wouldn't have to look at him.

He swallowed. "Bless this food, Lord. We're grateful for all the riches you provide. Amen."

"Amen," she said softly. She pulled her hand back and slipped it into her lap.

"Riches, indeed," he grinned. "Tool pusher job pays real good, you know that? Graham sounded like maybe he was thinking to put me in charge on another drilling project. Said he'd call me up soon as we all have a chance to sleep off the excitement from the strike."

"That's good," she said. She smiled at the salt and pepper shakers.

"Good for us," Henry said, thumping the table. "Not a gusher, but a solid strike. It'll be a steady producer, that well."

"I'm glad," she said. The words she needed to say dried up on her tongue, and she sat by him numbly until he asked for another helping.

She refilled his plate with deliberate movements. While she was turned away from him, she said, "I've been meaning to talk to you." The words came out in a rush, but he was smiling when she turned to him.

Naomi laid the plate in front of him and sat down again. This time she chose the chair across the table. Out of reach. She could see the calendar over his shoulder; it was March 15. She wondered if he remembered that Estella's birthday was in three days, wondered if it gave him any pause.

She slipped her hand into her pocket and wrapped her fingers tightly around Wash's ring. Then she tested the waters. "Did you keep any photographs of my mother?"

Henry's eyes shifted briefly toward his bedroom. Then he rubbed his ear and looked her straight in the eye. "No, I didn't."

She should have been angry, having seen the wedding portrait in his drawer, but his lie made it easier for her to go forward with her own. "That's too bad. I thought maybe I could make a dress like hers." She forced a smile.

"Are you saying . . . ?"

"You know what I said before. I still have my doubts, but . . ."

"Your granny talked some sense into you?" He smiled and then wiped a bit of grease from his lips and ran a finger under his collar.

When she didn't say anything, he slapped the table. Her eyes widened, and he laughed. "I was kidding; that was a joke. I know you had to make up your own mind. Of course you did."

Naomi forced Abuelita out of her mind, but the image of Abuelito, bedridden and drooling, remained. If she ran with Wash, she'd be running away from them, too. She'd have to work that out, somehow. Try to send money. She pressed her eyes closed and gripped Wash's ring more tightly.

"After graduation," she said. "I want to finish school first." There were less than three months before the end of the school year. They'd have to be gone by then. Three months. She could live this lie for three months.

"So that's a yes?"

She could feel his smile even with her eyes closed, and it sickened her, but she propped up the corners of her mouth and forced herself to look at him. "It's a 'yes, but give me a little time.'" She spoke the words to a point directly above his head.

"That's swell," he said, beaming. And he was up out of his chair coming toward her with his arms out.

"No!" she said quickly. "That's another thing. Not a touch. Like I still am . . . your daughter. As long as we're not married, we need to be pure." She swallowed. "Like how Pastor Tom says, 'Thy body is the Lord's temple.'"

"I've never been so ready to get in the temple." He laughed at his own joke.

"There'd be talk if people knew . . . our plans." She swallowed. "So we wait till after graduation to tell anyone, even Muff and Bud."

"Whatever you want," he said. "Can we celebrate?"

"Have another pork chop?" she suggested.

"Nah, come on, let's take a drive." He pulled on his hat and had the door open before she could protest about leaving the twins behind.

He drove fast and talked the whole way, spinning out all manner of foolish ideas. She chose not to listen. He was talking for himself anyway. She kept her arms folded across her chest with the burn scar on top. It was faded now, but she wanted to display any bit of ugliness she had. She buried her fists in her armpits out of fear he might try to hold her hand.

When they stopped, she saw that they were at the lookout point above Happy Hollow. One rise over, she could see the magnolia where she had met Wash on New Year's Eve.

She didn't cry. Instead, she pasted a false smile on her face and made a choice. As Henry talked on, she traveled in her mind to the tree in the woods. She folded her true self up and put it away like a dress she hoped to wear again without being sure when. The Naomi of the woods, the Naomi on the twins' wooden Christmas ball, Wash's Naomi, she would stay in the tree. For safekeeping. For after they got away. For when the plan worked.

But something had to stay behind. For the next two days, Naomi's body moved through her daily routine. Whole hours disappeared uncounted, unlived. School. Washing and hanging and folding. Serving meals and clearing them away. Sweeping, mopping, dusting. The house was cleaned but not lived in, not by Naomi.

It was a way of surviving, and it was a preview of what her life would be if their plan failed.

NAOMI Naomi pulled open the door to the cafeteria cleaning supply closet with no more thought than she'd given to any other task over the last two days. She was vaguely aware that she was here to get a box of baking soda for the home economics teacher. She did not expect to find children sitting in a circle on the floor, holding hands. She did not expect to see a ring of candles with her mother's braid and red dancing shoes at the center.

Her eyes adjusted, and she recognized faces. Cari, Beto, and Tommie's cousin Katie. Their eyes were wide and surprised.

"Cari! Beto! What is this?" Naomi pulled the light chain, and the bulb blinked on, revealing two more children crowded into the back of the closet.

Cari jumped up.

"When did you take these things?" Naomi pointed at the floor. "You had no right."

"She was our mami, too." Cari's chin jutted out. "Right, Beto?"

Beto kept his eyes on the floorboards.

"Hey, am I gonna get my nickel back?" A freckled boy standing in the back crossed his arms. "This ain't no say-dance."

"Séance. And it's gonna be, just hang on." Cari flashed a salesman's

281

quick smile, but Naomi wasn't buying. She blew out the candles and grabbed her mother's shoes and tucked them under her arm. She cradled the braid.

"They're too small for you," Cari said, "and anyhow, my shoes are back in Miss Bell's room."

Naomi pushed off her own worn black shoes and kicked them toward Cari.

"You promised us voodoo," a girl by the brooms whined, fingers twined in her stringy bob.

"It's called spiritualism," Beto whispered.

"Back to class, now." As she said it, Naomi looked at each child. They shifted to their feet but didn't meet her gaze. Except Cari.

"It's not fair," Cari said. "Why should everything be yours? Why didn't she leave us something?"

Naomi stiffened. "She did. She left me."

"Well, we want her."

"Yeah? I do, too. But I lost her when you were born, so let's not talk about fair." As soon as the words were out, Naomi wished she could snatch them back. Cari's face turned to stone. Tears slid down Beto's nose.

"Go back to class," Naomi said again. She could hear the coldness in her own voice. Later, she'd explain. Later, she'd make the twins understand.

"Yes, ma'am," the girl with the bobbed hair said.

"Hey, I still want my nickel back." The freckled boy reached for Cari's sleeve.

She shook him off and stared at Naomi. "I hate you," she whispered. She shoved her feet into Naomi's shoes, pushed out of the closet, and clomped across the cafeteria. Beto and the others hurried after her.

Naomi followed them partway, seeing them out the cafeteria door. Only Beto looked back, his face a plea she could not answer, not now. She watched from the window as they trudged along the long sidewalk back into the main school building. Once she'd seen them go inside, she gripped the braid tight and stumbled back to the closet.

The mindless, mechanical ease she'd managed was now gone. Reality settled on her shoulders, and she felt the cruel weight of it. It was her mother's birthday. She was engaged to her stepfather. The twins hated her.

BETO Beto got back to Miss Bell's classroom half a minute before Cari, who refused to hurry.

He slid into his seat in the desk he usually shared with Cari. Not today he wouldn't, though.

"Deenie." Beto leaned across the aisle to whisper to the pale girl with red hair. "Come sit next to me."

Deenie hesitated for a moment and then slid over into Cari's seat.

Cari arrived just in time to see her place being taken. She glared at Beto but spoke to Deenie. "That's my spot."

"No, that's just as well," Miss Bell said from the front of the room. "You and Robbie should be separated after your misbehavior. Ida Mae's absent; come take her seat up here, Carrie. I'll be by with your punishment."

Cari shot Beto an angry look and then marched to the empty seat at the front of the room. Even the back of Cari's neck looked mad. That was fine with him; her anger was proof he'd been on Naomi's side. This time, Cari had gone too far.

Miss Bell handed him a scrap of paper. "A hundred times," she said sternly. "I expect exemplary penmanship."

He had not yet opened his notebook, but he could already hear the explosive scratch of Cari's pencil across her page. She could blast through a punishment in half the time it took him. He knew exactly how she was writing her hundred lines:

> I will not play truant when I should be learning my lessons.
> I will not play truant when I should be learning
> I will not play truant when I
> I will not play truant
> I will not play
> I will not
> I will
> I
> I
> I

NAOMI Naomi winced with each step back to the home economics cottage. Her heels hung off the back of her mother's shoes; she could not even buckle the straps. She averted her eyes as she limped past the wall of the gymnasium where a few mothers had ducked out of the afternoon PTA meeting to smoke. The school buses were lined up in the side parking lot of the school, waiting to be filled with kids who lived too far out in the county to walk home. The final bell would ring soon. She had to think. She had to figure out what she was going to do with Beto and Cari. She had to make them understand.

She would do better. She would find some way to give them a part of the truth about Estella's last days. And when the time came, maybe that would help them understand why they had to leave East Texas—and Henry—behind.

Naomi bit her lip, exhausted all over again by the complicated dance she was going to have to do during the coming weeks and months. She wished things could just go on as they had been, the four of them in the woods, laughing and playing without a plan. Carefree. Careless.

There was no point in dwelling on it. Instead, she forced herself to envision the dress she would make for Cari. An apology dress. Layers of bright red sandwiched with a pink floral pattern. She would let Cari wear their mother's red shoes with it. A double peace offering.

As she climbed the front steps of the cottage, she thought about what she might give to Beto. Then she realized that she had forgotten the baking soda. She was turning back to the cafeteria when the blast knocked her off her feet. She hit the edge of the porch and rolled onto her side. The earth rippled under her. From the ground, she watched the roof of the school rise up and rip open in a fountain of debris. Then it all came down. She held her arms over her face against bits of falling brick and wood and concrete. Something smacked wet against the porch steps. Naomi felt a splatter against her arms.

There was screaming from inside the cottage. Naomi pulled her arms away from her face and rolled onto her stomach. Chunks of brick littered the grass in front of her. A lunch pail. A splintered slate. She reached out and touched a bit of denim. Her hand came back wet with blood. She pushed herself up on her elbows and managed to sit. There were bodies across the lawn. People, lying there.

She needed to get up. She needed to help. She needed to find the twins. But instead, she sat in the dirt, arms at her side. It was a leg inside the denim, she realized now. Her brain was catching up. Go, go, she thought, but her body refused to obey. She stared through the clouds of dust at the cafeteria, which was still standing. Then she looked again at the shattered school building into which she had just sent Cari, Beto, and the others.

THURSDAY, MARCH 18, 1937, 3:25 P.M.

BETO Screams and shouts filtered into Beto's brain. He thought of flour. He thought of chalk.

His eyelids were sealed shut. Vaguely he remembered being punched in the stomach. Then a roar and a long whiteness. But now—now he was floating.

Beto forced one eye open, then the other. He saw blue sky. Wash's face. Wash was carrying him. Beto closed his eyes and tried not to know what he knew.

◊ ◊ ◊

The second time Beto woke up, it was to the sound of Naomi's voice. She was talking to Wash, and Beto saw the look that passed between them before they knew he was watching. And he knew a second thing that he did not know how to live with: neither of them belonged to him. They belonged to each other.

Naomi said something again, but Beto didn't hear. He didn't blink. He didn't ask her about the look. He could only think: Cari, Cari, Cari.

NAOMI Naomi rocked Beto in her arms and stared, numb. Teachers and students stumbled around them. Mothers from the PTA meeting called the names of their children and clutched at each other. Men from the oil field arrived in truckloads. They ran into the school and came out carrying injured children. Also bodies. The dead were laid out in rows on the sparse grass. She watched and watched, but Wash did not come out.

"Wash is going to get her," she whispered into Beto's hair. "He'll be back soon."

WASH Wash was pushing aside a desk when he saw it: Naomi's other shoe. This time, the shoe wasn't empty. He recognized the gray and blue stripes of Cari's sock sticking out from under a fallen bookcase. He sucked in a deep breath and began emptying the shelves. When the books were mostly out, he flipped the bookcase over.

His pulse pounded in his ears. His mouth went dry. There was no right way to do what had to be done. He took off his jacket and wrapped Cari's leg in it.

Then he looked for the rest of her.

He told himself that he needed to hurry, that she was losing a lot of blood. He told himself that because it made it easier to search.

He heard a shout of "Everybody out!" just as he saw the plaid of Cari's good dress showing under a block of concrete. The walls groaned around him. Plaster began to fall in chunks. He ran to the spot and fought and fought to shift the block. He could not move it, could not move it, and then he could and he did and he found her. Her face was flattened. A trickle of blood marked her temple. More was matted in her pale hair.

He lifted Cari onto his shoulder, scooped up his jacket, and ran.

BETO Beto lay still and silent with his head in Naomi's lap. His eyes were glued to the bottom level of the building's east wing, which was where the third grade classroom had been, which was where Wash was looking for Cari. Now two men were helping Deenie Edwards through the doorway of the school. He wanted it to be Cari instead. He wanted it with all of himself. He wanted it even if that meant wishing for it not to be Deenie. Deenie with freckles and carrot-colored hair. Deenie who liked him. Deenie who had been sitting in Cari's seat.

The east wing began to move.

It shifted to the right. Farther and farther until it looked like a crooked drawing. And then it fell. Beto stared at the roof of the building, now on the ground. Naomi's cry was a live thing in the air.

WASH Wash carried Cari's body around the back of the building, shaking with the closeness of the call. A man in overalls ran past him, muttering, "Damn lucky, damn lucky."

Wash couldn't call it luck, not with Cari like this. He tried not to think of all the ways she was broken.

Naomi and Beto would have to see her, he knew, but he would tell them first. Try to prepare them. He laid Cari beside a flimsy crepe myrtle sapling he'd planted the spring before. He placed the leg under the hem of her plaid dress and spread his jacket over her.

NAOMI Naomi stood by Beto as a man with round glasses and shaky hands examined him. She stared numbly at the school building.

She almost laughed with relief when she saw Wash walking toward them. Then she saw his face. "You didn't find her."

Wash swallowed and wiped his hands down his pant legs. He eyed the doctor cautiously. "I did," he said finally. He did not look at her.

"Well, where is she? Is she hurt?" Naomi asked. She did not let herself think.

"I was too late. I—I think it happened at the moment of the blast."

"She's dead?" The blunt words surprised even Naomi. She felt the finality of it. A dark curtain falling. No more. No more.

She looked at Beto. His face was frozen and gray, but tears rivered down his cheeks.

"We need to see her," Naomi said. She turned to the young doctor. "Can we go now?"

He frowned. "He might have a broken rib or two, but there's not much to do about that. Just keep a close eye on him." He nodded at the three of them and walked on to the next injured child.

Naomi held out a hand to Beto, but he did not take it.

BETO Beto lay down beside Cari on the ground. He picked up her hand. Her fingers were cramped together as if to hold a pencil. *I will not play truant . . . I will not play . . . I will not . . . I will. . . I . . . I . . .*

The lines they had written, apart. The lines they should have written side by side. The lines she had died writing.

Two men came with a sheet. One was very tall and the other was very short. Their dark suits were gray with dust and smeared with stains. They took off their hats and talked to Naomi. And then she was kneeling beside Beto, trying to pry his fingers free of Cari's hand. He held on tighter, shaking his head. Trembling.

He did not let go. He didn't because he couldn't. He couldn't because he knew they would never let him hold her hand again. He wanted to check Cari's pocket just in case he had forgotten, but he knew. He hadn't given her anything for luck today. Everything would have been different if he had.

"Look," the tall one said to Naomi. "You can carry her home for now. The funeral parlors are already full. It's gonna be a while before we get to everybody." His face loomed over Beto. "Don't worry, we'll take good care of your sister when it's her turn."

Beto held on to Cari's cold fingers.

NAOMI Naomi could not make Beto let go of Cari, so Wash carried them both to the back of a truck on a blanket. She limped after them in her mother's tiny shoes. Everywhere children were laid out on the ground and covered with shirts and jackets and pieces of notebook paper stained red in places.

Naomi tried to put her thoughts in order. Go to the house. Put Beto to bed. Call for Henry. Clean Cari. Do not think, Cari is dead. Do not think, it's my fault.

She was skimming the surface of the world again, but now that surface was shattered, littered with debris. A dark undertow threatened to pull her under, down to the horrible truth.

She heard a high voice call her name. She looked up. There, in a second story window of the school, Tommie's bloody face was framed by broken glass.

◇ ◇ ◇

By the time the men got Tommie down, she had begun to wail. Wash stayed with Beto while Naomi ran to her and held her hand. The men on ladders passed Dwayne's body through the jagged remains of the windowpanes. It was too late to worry about cuts.

Tommie sobbed into Naomi's shoulder, her chest heaving. "He was right there across the table from me, and then he was on the other side of the room." Tommie pulled back, suddenly silent. Her mouth hung open. Snot trailed through the dust on her face. She moved her mouth again. "He wanted to skip this afternoon, did you know that? Wanted to go down to the river, but I wouldn't—I was mad—if I'd listened—if I'd only listened—"

"Hush now," Naomi said. She coaxed as much gentleness into her voice as she could manage. "Come on, let's get you seen to."

HENRY Henry was squatting elbow to elbow with a couple of oil hands at a new drilling site when a Diamond T company truck barreled into the clearing. It stopped just a foot from them, kicking up dust all around.

The window of the truck rolled down, and Ken Martin stuck his head out. His face was red and beaded with sweat. "Boss said to send everyone to New London."

Henry felt something clench in him. He lifted his hat and wiped the sweat from his forehead with a handkerchief. "A well fire? Can't he get somebody who's closer? It's a good forty-minute drive from here."

Ken was already shaking his head. "It's not a well, it's the school. The school, man. They're talking dynamite, maybe a bomb. Nobody knows for sure."

◇ ◇ ◇

Henry pushed the truck as fast as it could go down the dusty back roads. A couple of miles from the school, the traffic slowed. And then it wasn't moving at all.

He slammed on the brakes and got out. "You drive it, Gary," he said to the worker beside him in the cab. "My kids are there."

He ran hard along the gravel shoulder of the oil-top road, racing against the knowledge that if anything had happened to his kids or to Naomi, he'd be to blame.

Once he reached the school grounds, he had to navigate the rings of vehicles parked on the lawn. He saw reporters and gawkers pointing at what was left of the school.

And he saw the dead. Rows and rows of them.

Parents filed between them with handkerchiefs pressed to their mouths. Looking for their children.

He pushed into the chaos. "Carrie and Robbie Smith! Carrie and Robbie Smith!" he meant to bellow it, but it came out a breathless wheeze. His next words, "And Naomi," were sucked back into his own mouth as he gasped for air.

Two men he did not recognize jogged over to him. "Easy, friend, easy," one of them said. "Catch your breath."

"Shit, shit, shit." Henry was trembling. He shook the men off. "I got to find my kids."

He scanned the bodies for clothing he recognized, for children the right size.

He saw a mangled form inside a dress like one of Cari's, but it was not her. The girl's face looked like a rubber doll someone had left in the sun. Twisted. Melted. Not the twins, Henry prayed. Tell me you spared mine.

"Henry!" Bud called to him from across the crowd. His overalls were soiled; his hands were cut and bruised.

"Bud," Henry shouted, jogging toward him. "Have you seen the kids? Naomi?"

"Naomi wasn't in the building. Beto was, but somebody got him out before the collapse."

"Carrie's still in there, then? I've got to get to her."

Bud shook his head. "They found her, too."

"Found her?" Henry's heart lifted. Then he saw Bud's face.

"I'm sorry." Bud braced Henry's shoulders with both hands and pulled him close. "I'm so sorry."

Henry felt an inexplicable desire to laugh. He twisted out of his friend's embrace. "You're wrong, Bud. I checked." He gestured at the patchwork of broken children across the grounds. "She's not there. She'd be there, if she was dead. She'd be there, wouldn't she?"

Henry turned away from Bud. He grabbed the sleeve of a man nearby. "Are there others? Where are they?"

Someone else answered him. "All over—Kilgore, Tyler, Henderson, Overton, even Marshall." The voice came from behind him. "Anywhere there's doctors and . . ."

"And what?" Henry demanded, turning wild eyes on the man who'd spoken. He was a short, stooped man with an underbite.

"Undertakers." The man intoned the words softly.

For a moment, Henry and Bud were swept along with a group of parents pressing toward a telephone pole. Some reporter had rigged up a connection to the line.

"Can't you call Tyler and ask who they've got over there? How do we find our kids when we don't know where they got took?" someone asked.

The man pressed the receiver to his chest. "It'll take time, folks."

"I don't have time!" a woman shouted, her voice shrill. "I've got to find my Johnny."

"Telephone circuits are jammed up. Everybody's doing their best. Lists of the dead and the living and the missing are going out on the radio. Give your messages to him." He jerked his chin toward a pale man with watery blue eyes who crouched over a radio microphone. "The best would be to head home and listen so you know where to go."

"You want us to wait? Would you sit on your hands if it were your child?" shouted a man with a patchy blond beard.

One woman was muttering, "Eddy, Eddy, Eddy. . . . Please, sweet Jesus, please." So Henry wasn't the only one trying to make a deal with God. He wanted to slap her. The more prayers, the worse his odds.

Then Dalton Tatum was in front of them. Henry knew him from his drinking days at Big T's. Dalton had a mole that looked like a horsefly on his cheek. His hair was slicked back, the comb marks still visible. "I sure wouldn't a let no nigger touch my daughter's body."

"Take it easy, Dalt," Bud said. "You can't be picky when folks are rescuing your kids, now." He steered Henry toward the path that cut through the woods to the Humble camp. When they were at the tree line, Bud hugged Henry. "Go see about your kids. And then, if you want, come back. Work'll hold off the hurt for a while."

HENRY Henry took a long time to walk to the house. When he got there, he couldn't go in. He pulled off his work boots. They were crusted with mud.

He thought, when did they get so bad?

He thought, I could clean them now.

He thought, if I don't go in, it can't be true.

But he knew. And not just by what Bud had told him. He felt it in his own hesitation. He felt it in the stillness of the house.

The screen door opened. Naomi came out, barefoot. Her blue dress was filthy with dust and dried blood. She had not washed the dirt and tears from her face.

"Henry," she said.

There was no warmth in it, only a truth as hard as anything he'd ever faced. He thought back to Estella and the phone call after she lost the second baby. The long silence. The miles of distance in her voice.

Here was another disaster laid before him.

He shook his head, pulled off his hat, and crumpled it in his hands. "Jesus Christ." His shoulders began to shake. "Please don't say it. Just don't say it—"

"You already heard." It wasn't a question.

He stood up and stared through the screen door. A sheet was draped over the kitchen table. Under it, Henry knew, was the daughter he had not loved enough. And so she had been taken from him.

"I only just got Beto to sleep. He wouldn't leave her."

Only then did Henry see the boy curled under the kitchen table, a quilt laid over him.

He could feel the grief rising again and he wanted her body against his, any bit of comfort. "Oh God, Naomi," he whispered and pulled her to him.

She didn't scold him, but she stood stiffly in the circle of his arms until he let go.

"Who brought you home?" he asked.

"Mr. Wright from down the street."

"Did he . . . was he the one to get her out of the school?"

Naomi hesitated. "Wash brought her out. Got Beto, too."

It was like a slap. Henry's jaw tightened.

"It should've been me," he said. "That damn boy, he's always where I ought to be. How the hell is that?" He stared at the line of pines across the oil-top road. Between the trees, a pumpjack humped the oil up out of the ground. Like nothing had changed.

A long silence lay between them.

Her voice was gentle when she spoke again. "He got Beto out. Then he went back for Cari. Brought her out just before the roof fell in."

"But what was that nigger doing at your school in the first place?" he asked. So much horror hung in the air, everything scattered by the explosion. He could choose which shattered fragment he would claim as his own. He still had that.

"He risked his life. We should be grateful."

"Don't make me angry, now," he said. "You hear me?" Henry felt a tightening in his throat. He punched the shape back into his hat. "I'm going back," he said without looking at her.

"What about Beto?"

"Robbie?" Henry shrugged, swallowed. He forced words past the lump in his throat. "He'll be here when I get back, won't he?" He put on his hat and pulled on his boots. He didn't bother to tie them before he walked away.

WASH On the kitchen table. That was where Wash had laid Cari. When he put her down, he tried to keep the jacket over her, but she was broken in so many places.

Hurt bloomed and faded, bloomed and faded on Naomi's face.

And Beto. Lost without his twin.

Wash wanted to hold them both close. Tuck Beto safe between him and Naomi. Wrap Naomi in his arms and lay her head on his shoulder. Join what could be joined. But the white man was with them. Wash could not even show his friendship.

Then he was in the back of the truck headed again to the school. But his heart was in the tree with Naomi. He would go. When the work was done, he would find a way to her. Give her what wholeness he could. No telling if it would be enough.

At the school, someone gave him a basket, and he worked. The collapsed school looked like a shattered skeleton rising up out of the earth. A lake of loss. He picked his way across the surface along with the other men. He put whole children onto stretchers. Bricks into wheelbarrows. Body parts into baskets. He sorted without thinking. Move it, boy. Find the live ones. When he looked up, he recognized the same sun above him as before. But then there would be a small hand. A toe. So many pieces.

He was pushing a wheelbarrow when he saw Mr. Crane. Glasses cracked. Suit sleeves ripped and dangling. Elbows scraped and flecked with concrete. Bloody hands.

"Kids in there," Mr. Crane said, stumbling forward. "Beau!" he called. "Garrett!" He clawed at the rubble. His glasses fell.

Wash found the glasses and pressed them into Mr. Crane's hand. When the older man stumbled, Wash took his elbow.

Mr. Crane fitted the glasses back onto his face. His gray hair hung limp over his forehead. "They wanted to go early, all but begged me. I said, how would it look, the superintendent's boy playing hooky?" Mr. Crane walked on, studying the ground. "Have to find them. Have to find them all. They're in there."

"You need to rest, sir," Wash said. "Why don't we get you some water? We'll keep looking."

Mr. Crane turned an unfocused gaze on him. "Water," he repeated.

The path through the wreckage to the Red Cross tents was narrow, and then it was gone. Blocked by a wheelbarrow. Boots. Denim.

Wash looked up. The man had a wrestler's neck and the shoulders of a chainman. His jaw worked a wad of tobacco. He stared hard at Wash.

"Excuse us, sir," Wash said. The words tasted oily. Sharecropper, bootlicker, shoeshine boy. His father's voice in him. The voice of his own fear.

The man did not move. One massive hand held a brick. Another pair of boots joined the first. Then another.

Wash took a step back.

"Whoa, boy." The gravelly voice was in Wash's ear, and when he looked back he saw more men. His stomach tightened. His hand on Mr. Crane's elbow grew hot and itchy.

"Excuse us, gentlemen," Wash tried again. He heard his father's voice again. Stay low. Don't look them in the eyes. "Just need to get the superintendent a little water."

"Who asked you to help?" the first man asked, chewing his words and then shooting a spray of black tobacco juice into the dirt at Wash's feet.

"I was just here, sir . . ." Wash stammered.

"Look at me when I talk to you, boy," the first man said.

Wash did. He stared at the man's dark hairline and tried not to look at the mole on his face.

The man turned to the others. "He's the one I seen here just after it happened. Hardly a minute after. Handling white children, for fuck's sake. Touching our kids."

Next to Wash, Mr. Crane trembled. "Listen, now just listen . . ."

A man with a crooked nose shoved forward. "I know that boy. He's that uppity nigger teacher's son. How come he was here 'fore anyone else? What the hell business did he have dickin' around a white school?" He pointed at Wash with a nub of a middle finger. His index finger was missing.

Wash glanced at Mr. Crane, but his attention had wandered. "They're in there. My kids are in there," he murmured to himself. He was crying.

"Say something, Sambo," someone called. "You'd better talk fast."

Silence would get him nowhere. "I was working, see, just over there." He nodded in the direction of the superintendent's house. "I heard the blast, and I came to help." Wash felt a trickle of sweat begin between his shoulder blades.

"You glad to see a white school blow up?" the first man asked, his dark eyes narrowed to slits.

"Nobody could want this, sir. It's a horrible accident—"

"You know an awful lot about what happened, don't you? Tell the truth now," the man continued. "You come over here now to help or to gloat and scavenge books?"

Sweat slid down Wash's back.

Mr. Crane moaned softly beside him. Then he said something everyone heard: "The gas, the gas, why did we do it?"

"What the hell is he talking about?" asked the man missing a finger.

A different voice sounded from behind him. "Y'all think a minute. Anybody could tell a gas leak sparked here. We all seen it dozens of times. Lay off the kid and let's get back to work."

"Not till we get this settled," the man with the mole growled. "What about Crane? He's got to answer for it."

"His son's in there, too." The words were shouted from the back of the crowd.

Just then, a hollow-cheeked woman in a stained housedress pushed past the men. Her hands did not leave her sides. "My baby girl is missing," she said. "Are you gonna let me go on searching alone?"

The men looked down, shuffled their feet. Someone coughed, and then one by one the men went back to work. Wash went back to being invisible. Almost.

The first man held his ground. "This ain't over," he said to Wash, showing him a mouthful of yellow teeth. Then he pushed the wheelbarrow to the side and turned away.

Wash felt a hand shove his back, and he spun around. Mr. Gibbler, the school board member who'd laughed in his father's face, stared at him. He pointed to the hand Wash had on Mr. Crane's elbow.

"Let go." Gibbler's voice was level and cold. "I'll take it from here." He settled an arm around the superintendent. "Come on, now, Dan."

"You've done enough, son." Mr. Crane said. His eyes did not focus.

"You heard him," Gibbler said. "Get out of here. We know where to find you."

HENRY Henry walked into the kitchen with his boots still on. The clock said eight, just fourteen hours since he'd left Naomi on the porch the afternoon before. But time, too, had shattered. Everything was in pieces.

"It's done," Henry said finally. He kept his eyes on Naomi. She had washed and put on clean clothes, but her face was swollen from crying. He did not look at Cari. He did not look at Beto.

Without speaking, Naomi set a chair by the heater for him. The gesture reminded him that he was cold and tired and filthy. He turned the chair away from the table.

Even over the stink of his labor, of the mud and the plaster and the rain that had wet him and then dried, he could smell Cari's body. It smelled like all the other bodies he'd handled.

They had found the last survivors just before midnight. After that, it was eight hours of digging and sifting and hauling to find what was left of the children. When he closed his eyes, he saw images from the school. Broken children gathered piece by piece. A whole school taken apart by hand.

They moved two thousand tons of debris, someone had said. Henry felt as if he were trapped under the weight of it all.

Naomi touched his shoulder, and he looked up.

"Eat something," she said.

He took the plate from her and began to eat. It was too late to wash his hands.

BETO Beto watched the square of light from the window above the sink. It shifted slowly across the floor with the sun's progress. He knew that this meant time would not stop. No Joshua moments for him, no sun stilled in the sky. Minutes and hours and days without Cari.

Her absence would always be with him. Along with the knowledge of why she was gone.

Beto felt Naomi on the floor beside him. She tried to put her arms around him, but he pulled away. He still had not spoken to her. He couldn't bear to tell her what he'd done.

NAOMI Naomi opened the door to Pastor Tom. He stood on the porch with his hat in his hand. Scratches crisscrossed his arms, and his knuckles were scraped raw.

"Naomi," he said, "I'm so sorry for your loss." He picked at the clay and grime streaked across his shirt and tie. "I was walking through, thought I should check in on you all."

Naomi gestured at the table. At Cari's body, still draped in the sheet, waiting for the undertakers. She had washed the body, but there was still a smell. She saw that Beto had taken Cari's hand again.

"That's all right. Let's talk out here," the pastor said. He shifted his feet and thumbed his belt loops.

"Get you a glass of water? Washcloth?" she asked. Time only seemed to move when she could assign herself a task. And she needed time to move.

"Thank you, sister." Pastor Tom sat down on the porch stool.

BETO Beto watched the square of light and measured the darkness around it. Cari's hand was cold, but it was no longer stiff. He could fit his fingers inside hers. He could pretend.

He let go when he heard Naomi walk by. She knocked on Henry's door. "Pastor's here. On the porch," she said.

Then came heavy footsteps.

Beto pulled his eyes away from the square of light and looked at his father.

Henry's eyes were red from crying or maybe from drink. He looked everywhere but at Cari on the table and Beto beneath it. Dead daughter. Son, as good as.

Naomi filled a glass with water.

Henry shoved open the screen door.

Cari remained dead.

Beto returned to his square of light.

HENRY Henry opened the porch door, and Pastor Tom stood up from the stool. "Brother," he said. He held out his arms.

Henry ignored him and slumped against the side of the house.

The pastor tried again. "Should we talk about arrangements?"

A bark of a laugh slid from Henry's mouth. He spat over the edge of the porch. "I don't know. Can you arrange away that dead little girl off of my kitchen table, Pastor? Work out a Lazarus number?"

"Whoa, now, Henry—"

Henry turned away from the pastor. He kicked the screen door. It hammered against the frame and then sprang back, trembling on its hinges. He swiveled back to the preacher. "Where was he, Tom? You tell me, where the hell was he when this happened?"

 Next to Deenie. That's where Beto had been when Cari went to sit in the empty desk at the front of the room.

HENRY Of course, Henry meant the "He" of the twenty-third psalm and of the gospels and of all the pastor's sermons. The God that Pastor Tom had promised would be with him now and always but who had been elsewhere when the school was exploding with the children inside.

"You told me to bring them here." A sob crept into Henry's voice. "You said it was his will."

"Let me pray with you, brother," Pastor Tom said. Hairy hands settled on Henry's shoulders.

The preacher's voice rose and fell with the same rhythms that had first drawn Henry to the altar. But even now, inside the prayer, Henry knew that it was over. The baptism waters of the Sabine were drying up inside him. Pastor Tom had nothing for him. There was no new life, just the end of false beginnings.

Henry snapped his eyes open and stepped back, leaving the preacher laying hands on air. "And where is she?" he demanded. "Tell me my girl's in heaven. That she ain't suffering now."

Pastor Tom lowered his hands slowly. "Only the Lord knows her heart, only..." he trailed off.

"You go on and tell me that God let somebody blow up that school, and then he sent them babies to hell? Say it. I want to hear you."

"Past the age of reason, each is accountable to the Lord. That's all we know."

"She never answered the altar call, did she now?" Henry pressed him.

"There are many altars...we can hope that...in her heart of hearts..." the pastor stammered. And then he was silent.

But the pause was no surrender, and the preacher began to preach. "Any day can be our last; and the fires of hell are real, realer than we can imagine, there to make sorrow for the mother or the child, the young or the old, for all who fail to repent and acknowledge Jesus Christ as Savior and Lord. The confession of sins, the cleansing blood of Jesus, only that can save. There is a Redeemer, but we must each call to Him, ask Him into our heart. Before that moment we are already committed to the burning torment of hell, a suffering that has no end, a heat that burns to the very core!"

NAOMI The screen door slammed open again, and Naomi flew out. "Stop it!" she cried. Heat flooded her face, and she dropped the glass of water she'd brought for the pastor. It rolled on its side, and the water ran down between the planks of the porch.

She wanted to push Pastor Tom. A mighty shove off the porch and a magic that would make the drop tremendous. She imagined him down below, a crumpled sack of bones in a rat's skin.

"How dare you?" she demanded, taking a step toward him. "My sister was baptized as a baby. I was there."

"Baptism is only an outward sign, empty without a decision. Did she know Jesus Christ as her personal Savior? Only that can save, hear me now, only that can—"

"Enough!" Henry took a menacing step toward the preacher. "You're done here, damn it. Don't come back." He towered over the smaller man, moving forward into his space, forcing him to retreat.

Pastor Tom held tight to his hat as he backed down the steps, still preaching. "It's a hard lesson but a powerful one. Any day can be our last. We must get right with the Lord."

Naomi covered her ears and turned away. When she turned back, the pastor was in the yard. He raised his hat and placed it on his head carefully. He brushed the loose dirt from his shirt and walked up the side road until he got to the oil-top road that led to the church. His steps were slow and heavy as if he did not carry his message lightly.

Henry pulled Naomi's hands away from her ears. "It's all right now," he said. "He won't darken this doorway again."

She freed her hands from his. She was frightened by this rare moment of shared emotion, uneasy with the lack of tension between them. It felt like a betrayal, and for a moment her need for Wash was bigger even than her grief. She crossed her arms and tucked her hands in under her armpits to hide her trembling.

Henry smiled at her sadly. "She used to do that when she was upset."

Naomi stiffened. He knew so little; Cari never trembled and rarely showed her sadness as anything but anger. But then she realized who he meant. Her mother. Estella. Yes, she had done that with her hands, wedged them away under her arms when she was afraid or sad.

"Please," Naomi choked out. "Not now. We have . . . the funeral to think of." Then she turned and ran into the house, unable to bear his gaze.

"It matters now more than ever, don't you see?" he called after her.

 Beto watched the square of light move half the width of a floorboard. He felt the fact of Naomi's silent crying beside him. He couldn't move.

NAOMI Naomi could not leave Beto or Cari. She could not put on the shoes Cari had died in. She could not run to the woods. She could not fold herself into the hiding place and wish and wish and wish for Wash to come.

She couldn't do these things, but she did them anyway.

Even inside the tree, there was a heaviness in her chest. It was Cari on the table. It was Beto's silence. It was what she had said and what she hadn't. It was Cari's anger. It was Henry, the hunger in him, the fraying boundaries. It was the want of a mother. It was being in the tree without Wash.

Then he was there.

 They held each other. Wash's shoulder went wet with Naomi's tears. Her skin was hot under his fingertips. For her, he was coolness and touch and not needing to speak. She could open his mouth and he could open hers. A kiss. For a moment, desire and relief were greater than grief.

But it could not hold.

◇ ◇ ◇

He did not say: I know why it happened. She did not say: Cari died hating me. He did not say: somewhere, there was a heater I did not check. She did not say: I sent them into that building.

She reckoned up what a braid and a pair of shoes had cost her.

He tried to recall the embrace he'd bought with his unfinished work.

◇ ◇ ◇

Naomi pulled back and leaned against the tree's crumbly insides. "Beto," she said.

Wash pulled her back to him. "How is he?" He took her hand, held it. She was wearing the ring he'd made her.

"I can't wake him up," she whispered. "He won't look at me. Won't talk. He stays under the table where she is. Just lies there."

He swallowed. He had no solutions. "Time," he said. "Give it time. Imagine. They were always together."

Her silence filled the tree, swelling the hurt that hung there.

He lifted a hand to her damp cheek. "And Henry?" He slid his thumb to her lips, down to her chin, along the smooth expanse of her throat. He found her heart and felt its steadiness.

"Naomi," he said softly. "Talk to me." He could feel her holding back.

"A little worse than usual," she said. "Impatient."

In a flash, Wash could see their situation clearly. The explosion had shattered their timeline. School was over now; Henry might not be persuaded to wait any longer. He would want to secure his hold on what was his. What he wanted to make his.

"Be careful," he said. A lump formed in his throat. The size of his helplessness. It wasn't just Henry. He thought of the roughnecks blocking his way at the school. The truck that came to Egypt Town and demanded volunteers to dig graves. Even at the cemetery, he'd heard murmurings. People were restless. They wanted answers, any answers. Anything could happen. Anywhere. Nowhere here was safe enough.

"How soon can you be ready to leave?" he asked her.

"Cari . . ." she said.

"After the funeral. Listen." He gripped her shoulders. "You know something's different with Henry. He's not going to wait around. We can't risk it anymore."

She let out a ragged breath. "Where will we get the money?" she asked. "I counted ten dollars with the coins the twins have squirreled away."

"I have some," he said. "I'll borrow the rest." He could almost feel the Booker money box in his hand. A solution.

"And Beto?" she said.

"We'll find a way to help him. But first we have to go. To San Antonio and then to Mexico. I'll get tickets."

"It's so hard to think about—it's hard to think," she said. The work of making the plan real exhausted her. She tucked her head up under his chin. Fell into the rhythm of his heart.

"Just take care of Cari and try to help Beto. I'll meet you here whenever I can, leave you a note if I don't find you here. We could be in Mexico by the end of next week. Maybe sooner."

She tried on that thought for the first time since after the explosion. It did not feel the same. But then, nothing felt the same.

"Okay," she said.

THE GANG We were lucky, that's what they said to those of us who were left. Half of our class was dead. Elliott Grovener lost a leg. Dot Miller lost an eye. Others of us took a beating. But the smaller forms of damage—bruises, cuts, scrapes—did not seem worth mentioning. Some of us came out of the school painted with our classmates' insides.

Still, in town they said we were lucky. We were lucky we were cutting class down by Propp's pond. Lucky we chose the seat we did. Lucky we were carrying out Miss Carson's wastebin. Lucky to be sewing crooked lines in home economics. Lucky not to have lost more. Lucky to be alive.

It was a new kind of luck for us. Heavy. Balanced by loss. All the missing faces. We did not know what it would mean, this luck. We avoided the mothers of our dead classmates, their hungry eyes.

BETO At around ten o'clock each day, the square of light disappeared. And then Beto felt alone until it came back, but at least he was near Cari. Sometime after the light was gone one day, Henry lifted her off of the table. Even though Beto knew it wasn't really her, knew that she was gone from the body, it being there had helped him to pretend. It had been better than nothing. It had made it possible, moment by moment, to pretend that *she* was pretending. But that was over now. A new silence took hold of him.

NAOMI Naomi flinched when Henry came crashing into the kitchen. "It's a sham and a shame is what it is," he said. He was shaking. The green of his eyes was brighter than ever. The muscles along his jaw popped.

She didn't dare hush him. "Beto," she began, gesturing to where he lay, open-eyed, under the kitchen table where Cari had been.

Henry ignored her. "We're not doing it, not if that's the way it's going to be. I won't rush her in and out like that." He hurled a wadded piece of paper against the wall. He paced the rooms with his arms crossed, bits of mud shaking off of his boots with each furious footfall. She edged over to the wall and picked up the paper, loosening the wad carefully.

He wheeled around. "See? Like a goddamn train schedule!"

She stared at the page and understood. It was a list of funerals he'd gotten from the undertakers. At the three New London churches, there was a funeral every fifteen or thirty minutes from nine o'clock in the morning until after eight.

Naomi swallowed. "We don't need a service," she said after a long while. Cari wouldn't have cared for extra time in a church anyway.

Henry turned to her with such a look of gratitude that she worried he might have misunderstood her again.

BETO "Did you hear me, Robbie?" Henry said, crouching down and giving him a hard look. "Get out from under there."

Beto was silent.

"You think I can't make a coffin for my girl? I can. I know my way around a saw and a hammer. Now get up or I'm gonna throw that cat down a well."

Beto moved. He handed Edgar to Naomi and then followed his father out to the dirt patch in back of the house. The lumber and tools lay in a careless heap. A bad sign.

NAOMI Naomi's hands were red and scalded from scrubbing pots. Pots that were already clean. There was no need to cook; Muff had filled their refrigerator with casseroles and fried chicken and potato salad and molded fruit gelatin. So Naomi dusted and straightened dishes in the cabinets. She swept the living room and the hall and the bedrooms and the bathroom and the porch. She washed the table again and felt the absence of Beto, the greater absence of Cari.

From the porch, she watched Henry and Beto. Lengths of wood were spread out in the yard. Something like a box lay under Henry's hands.

She knew about bringing parts together to form a whole; it took patience to feel how things fit together. But that was not Henry's way. Even when something wasn't right, he forced it.

Beto slumped by the pile of tools. When his eyes drifted toward the kitchen, she smiled, but his expression did not change.

She went inside then and got the guitar case out. She closed her hand around one of the dance shoes. Bits of dried clay clung to the heel. Naomi remembered walking away from the cafeteria. Fingers clutching the braid she would not share.

She felt for the braid now and coiled it carefully around her hand.

She laid it under Cari's pillow. An experiment. Nothing changed inside her except the size of her sadness. Beto, then. She would give it to Beto.

◊ ◊ ◊

Henry came into the house cursing. He passed her in the hall, smelling of sawdust and sweat and fury.

Beto was still sitting in the yard. He looked ill. The box was much too small, and the boards gapped in places. Every joint betrayed signs of force and compromise. Naomi was not going to let her sister be buried in that.

"Come on, *cariño*," she said, tugging Beto to his feet by his sleeve.

She tried to get him to his bed, but he ducked back under the kitchen table. Naomi set a plate of cold fried chicken and potato salad on the floor. She poured him a glass of milk.

She carried a second plate to Henry's room. When he didn't answer her knock, she turned the knob and nudged the door open with her foot.

He was sitting by the bed with his back against the wall. When she came in, he shoved something behind the nightstand. Naomi thought of the picture of her mother. The revolver. His hidden bottle.

She handed him the plate. "We can call the Humble Oil people back. Tell them we want a casket after all," she said.

"Charity." He spat the word out and knocked his head slowly against the wall behind him. His face was still damp with sweat. He gave a dry swallow, and his Adam's apple rolled against the skin of his throat. She lowered her eyes to the floor, tracing the red clay that he had tracked into the bedroom.

"I'll get you some water," she said.

She came back with a glass and a damp washcloth. "Here," she said. She set them beside him.

He still didn't say anything. She went for the broom and swept the clay up. After that, she passed a damp mop over the floor. Then she stood in the doorway and waited.

"I couldn't do it," Henry said hoarsely. "Not any of it. Couldn't save her, couldn't get there to bring her out, couldn't build a casket." He took a long swallow from the glass of water and then looked up at her. He was pleading, although she did not know what for.

She tried again. "We'll get back on the waiting list, accept whatever they can get for us. They say by Monday, even . . . "

He shook his head. "I want an honest coffin for her. Guess that's why I couldn't do it. My hands . . . " He looked down at them. "They're no good. Not steady, neither." He held them up. His face was awash with self-pity.

"It's just that you're tired." She crossed back over to him, picked up the damp cloth, and pressed it into his hands. She needed him to hold it together long enough to get Cari in the ground.

Henry wiped off his face and rubbed his chin. "We'll need more lumber."

"We still have time," she said. They did, but only a little. They had to collect Cari's body from Overton by seven, and it was almost two. She had to get him moving. "You get the wood. I'll find a carpenter."

Naomi made the declaration before she weighed its risks. Because she only knew of one carpenter who would put Cari's coffin before the dozens of others.

Henry reached behind the nightstand and held out a half-empty bottle of Four Roses whiskey to her. "Get rid of it," he said. "See, I don't need Pastor Tom to straighten me out. You and me, we make a good team, huh?"

Naomi swallowed and nodded. Just barely.

It seemed it was enough; Henry hauled himself up from the floor, grabbed a chicken leg to take with him, and veered down the hall toward the back door. Naomi followed and watched him cross the yard to his truck. He did not look at the monstrous thing he'd made.

 Beto went outside when Wash called because it was Wash, and Wash couldn't come in.

"You know how to handle these tools," Wash said. "Can you help me?" He handed Beto a hammer.

"Okay," Beto whispered.

It was the first time he'd spoken since the school exploded.

HENRY Henry saw him as soon as he turned onto the stretch of road lined with Humble houses. The Negro boy squatting in the yard next to Beto. There was a bit of paper, a pencil, and an open toolbox before them. The sight caused a clenching low in his gut, and his hands tightened on the steering wheel. "Damn it to hell," he muttered under his breath. He should have known.

He let the truck idle for a moment before he killed the engine and got out. Naomi had come out onto the porch. She said something to him, but he didn't hear.

Wash pulled off his cap and took a few steps toward the truck. A shuffle, really. Henry relaxed slightly.

"Awful sorry, sir. About Cari."

Henry stiffened. He eyed Wash. He knew he should thank the boy for bringing Beto out, for going back for Cari's body, but he said only, "Can you fix this?" He jabbed a finger in the direction of the box he'd built.

"I can try, sir, but . . ." Wash hesitated. "Seeing as how time is . . . of the essence . . . it might be faster to start fresh."

Of the essence. The boy turned Henry's stomach. "Let's get the lumber from the truck, then," he spat.

When the planks were unloaded, Henry turned his back on his son and the Negro and climbed the porch steps. Naomi was sitting there snapping the ends off of green beans. She stood up and offered him the stool. "Your boots?" she said.

He shook his head. "I'm going to Bud and Muff's for a while, and then I'll be back for the box. You can come with me to get her. It won't take that boy no time if he's half as fuckin' handy as he seems. Give him my . . . thanks." Henry wiped his mouth with the back of his hand. "But don't you let him in my house. And you clean that box inside and out. Clean it down good before we put our girl in there."

BETO Beto stood in the darkened kitchen and traced the edge of the real casket, the one that was right and tight and smooth from sanding. There was only a sliver of moon to see by. He slid the lid open a few inches and found the hand that was not really Cari's hand anymore. He slipped the braid into it. It had been his first, and now it would be hers.

He did not know what luck could mean to the dead, just as it was impossible to know if one baptism was enough. Either she was saved because of him, or he didn't want to be saved. Both or none.

He closed the casket lid and felt Naomi's arms around him.

"Hi, Omi," he said.

"You're awake," she whispered.

◇ ◇ ◇

Morning. Blue sky. Velvety soft clouds. Small coffin. Hymns. Dirt clods tossed into graves. Cari's body, in the ground. Their mother's birthday on the wooden marker that would turn into a gravestone for Cari. Everything else, packed inside him. Beto wanted to cry but couldn't.

WASH Wash heard Naomi coming. When she climbed into the tree, he folded her into his arms.

"We buried her," Naomi said.

"I know. If I could've . . ." He'd watched from a grave four rows over as Cari went into the ground in the casket he'd made. He'd seen Beto's face tilted up toward the sky, not blank, but strange. Naomi stood behind him. And there was Henry's hand on Naomi's elbow. Wash had seen that. He could only imagine what it had cost her.

He held her close and felt the sob rise in her. Her body stiffened against it.

"Shh," he said, "I'm here."

She pressed her face against his chest. "How soon?" she whispered.

Now, he wanted to say. But there had been no way to get away from the digging, no chance for a trip to Tyler to get the train tickets. "I'll go for the tickets first thing tomorrow," he said. "We'll leave Tuesday morning. Catch the train in Tyler where nobody will know us."

She began to cry then.

"It's okay," he said, "I know." He did not, though. And still he had to try to take the hurt from her.

He began to touch her, and he could feel the change coming over

Naomi, the wildness climbing up out of her. He breathed in the warmth from her neck.

And then she was gone, pushing her way out of the tree.

She was fast, but he was faster and caught up to her before she could get out of the woods, where it would be too dangerous for him to follow her.

"Please, Naomi," he whispered as loud as he dared. His breath came fast.

She shook her head. "I can't."

"It's okay," he said. "Let's go down to the river."

NAOMI Naomi could feel the space between them as they stood at the edge of the bank and watched the river. The water was so dark and smooth it looked like oil. Cottonwood seeds drifted down on their pale cushions, disappeared into the blackness. She thought of her desire that way, a thing floating away from her and vanishing safely into the water.

"*Mañana*," Wash said. He took her hand, squeezed it, released it.

"Tomorrow," she said.

THE GANG We filled the days after the explosion however we could. The boys helped build the coffins and dig the graves. So many graves. Blisters that ached and burst. The girls laid out meals and put them away. Washed up. So many meals, so many dishes crusted with casserole. Knuckles and fingertips raw from hot water and steel wool. We avoided mirrors and went to funerals. Some of us sat in church after church after church. Sat through eulogies and prayer meetings. Learned to turn to the Lord again. Learned to lean not on our own understanding. Trust His wisdom. Others of us followed our fathers out into the woods, carried guns and rods. Hunted and fished and trapped with them. Opened beers for them and also drank them ourselves.

Six of us, the last of the football team, followed our fathers to Big T's. We slipped into the crowd.

"Backsliding," someone said to the beer in his hand. But we were not. Backsliding. We were sliding for the first time. Only Fred Carter had the guts to belly up to the bar. The rest of us just listened.

We learned things.

We learned where they buried the body parts that could not be identified.

We learned that Tad Schmitt found a bright blue vein of gas still burning when he was clearing rubble from what used to be the school's crawl space.

Somebody asked why nobody called the gas company to get it switched off.

Tad shrugged. "I did. But they told me the school quit buying their gas three months ago. Said the school probably switched to bleed-off gas."

We learned how news moves through a crowd of men. We felt them weigh the possibility. We tried it, too. Was it green gas that did our school in?

We were still at Big T's on Monday night when the evening newspaper came with word of the investigator's report. Graham Salter stood on a chair and read it out. The men watched, listened. So did we.

"According to the investigators of this tremendous tragedy, no one individual was solely responsible for the New London school explosion. It was the collective failure of ordinary people caught up in the common practices of their community and ignorant or indifferent to the need for precautionary measures. The report concluded that even criminal negligence does not apply because lack of knowledge prevented school officials from anticipating the hazard caused by their actions. 'What we should take from these terrible events,' the lead investigator suggested, 'is the urgent need to impose strict and enforceable safety standards on each and every building in which children spend their days.'"

"What in your Aunt Pussy's name does 'criminal negligence does not apply' mean?" one man shouted.

"Nobody's to blame, that's what it means," came a second voice.

This news did not go over well. Because without blame, how would there be punishment? Who would pay? The men began to murmur.

We could feel it. An idea beginning to form.

◇ ◇ ◇

We knew a thing or two about how an idea spreads, having spread a few in our time. Before the gas filled the halls of our ruined school, we regularly filled that space with another kind of combustible, invisible poison. Gossip that could travel slow or fast, nearly silent at first. And we knew that when an idea was quietly everywhere, had been whispered far and wide, all that was needed was the right person to blow it sky-high.

We felt the idea spreading at Big T's. At first, it carried Superintendent Crane's name to everyone's lips. But he had lost his son. And a nephew. Then someone asked, "What about Gibbler and them other school board cronies? They had to know, too, the greedy bastards."

Dalton Tatum slammed his palm down on the bar. "Gibbler! That's the one to talk to. Didn't lose nobody in the blast. Cain't nobody say we tried to break a broken man."

Another twenty minutes of debate followed, and then the men headed to their trucks. We were among the last out, so we saw the bartender— the only sober man in the place—pick up a phone and make a call.

◇ ◇ ◇

By the time the caravan of mud-splattered pickups turned up the long winding drive to Zane Gibbler's house, there were four mounted Texas Rangers posted in front of his porch.

"You boys go on home," one of the Rangers told our fathers and their friends. "You're not makin' any trouble here. Turn around and go back."

We watched as Dalton climbed out of his truck. "We want to talk to Gibbler," he called. "We got a right to some answers."

A roughneck in coveralls stepped out of the crowd and faced the house. "Come out of there, Mr. Gibbler! You can't hide forever in your big house, not answering us. I buried my baby girl yesterday. Nine years old, dammit! I got—" Before he finished speaking, Mr. Gibbler came out, banging the screen door and scowling.

One of the Rangers trotted closer to the porch. "Best to stay inside, sir."

Mr. Gibbler ignored the warning. "What y'all want?" he growled. His voice carried easily in the still twilight. He crossed his arms over his chest and looked straight at Dalton. "Suppertime's over. It's late to come calling."

Dalton cut to the chase. "Did you know about the school switchin' to raw gas?"

The idea was heading in a certain direction.

"Cut the bullshit. Don't be getting high and mighty about the school tapping into a bleed-off line. Y'all use the same gas to heat your houses. You think of yourself as a criminal for that? One look at that heating bill from December, and you would've done the same thing. You hear me?" Gibbler pointed a finger and swept it across the line of trucks. "Y'all would've done the same damn thing in Crane's place, every one of you."

We looked around, saw the men knowing the truth of it. There was a faltering. The idea was in danger of fizzling before it could explode.

"We want answers!" Dalton hollered.

"I know something more." The voice was high and thin and nearly swallowed up by the night, but it took us only a moment to place it.

Miranda stepped out on the porch in a nightgown and wrapper. Her forehead was still bandaged, and her face was bruised and scratched. But knowing her, we figured that what had pained her most was being alone. No one to echo her every petty remark, round out her laughter. Her followers were mostly buried now. Miranda was not one to bear the pain of going unheard.

"You ought to be in bed, Emmie," Mr. Gibbler said, turning to her.

"I know something," Miranda repeated, this time more loudly, sensing the size of her audience. "He was there when they did it, when they tapped the line."

"Who?" Dalton called.

"That black boy. The one Mr. Crane always has working at the school."

"So what?" Tad asked.

"And he was there when it happened. He didn't like us having such a nice school. Daddy, you heard what he said that one time. When he came to see Mr. Crane with his father. About some books."

Something like gratitude crossed Mr. Gibbler's face. "That boy . . ."

"An explosion," Miranda whispered hoarsely. Then she spoke more loudly. "When he walked away after sassing Mr. Crane and my daddy, he said it'd take an explosion to make us see."

Boom.

◇ ◇ ◇

We looked back from the beds of the pickups and watched Miranda sit on the porch swing next to her father. They swayed gently in the silence. Maybe she knew what her words would do. Maybe not.

The Rangers' horses pawed at the ground. There would be no one to stop our daddies in Egypt Town. We were sure about that.

NAOMI Naomi came into the kitchen at the sound of arguing next door. A screen door slammed, and a voice shouted, "I'll remember this, Bud. You watch your job, you coward!"

There was a hard knock at the back door. Through the screen Naomi saw Mr. Turner and four men behind him. She tried to think of him as a father who'd buried a child, but she couldn't forget how he'd shamed her in his store. She did not move.

Henry came into the kitchen. "I'll get it," he said and opened the door.

"Listen, Henry," Turner said, "we've got business to see to."

Out on the porch, the men talked in urgent, hushed tones. She couldn't make out their words. When Henry came back in, he reached for his hat.

"Bring your boy," someone called after him. "Wally's with me and keen on the fixing."

Beto hovered in the hall. Naomi thought she saw his eyes brighten a bit. Out of the house, maybe he would stop thinking of Cari for five minutes. Maybe.

"Robbie, get your coat," Henry said. "You can come help."

Beto nodded and hurried to get his jacket from its hook.

"Don't wait up," Henry said. He didn't look at Naomi.

She kissed Beto on the forehead. "Be careful and listen to Daddy," she said. Already her mind was on to what she needed to do while they were gone. Pack. See what money she could find in Henry's things. Check the tree for instructions.

She did not consider what kind of fixing the men were fixed on. She pictured some broken piece of machinery. Beto perched on the hood of the Ford, drinking a Coca-Cola someone had brought along in a cooler.

She should have wondered at the toolbox Henry had left sitting in the corner of the kitchen. She should have questioned his sudden renewed interest in father-son bonding. She should have kept Beto home.

But she had other plans on her mind. Tasks to complete. Work, like always, was a certain kind of relief.

She emptied the guitar case and got out a drawstring bag. She rolled their clothes into tight bundles and packed them in. She took her mother's dress and the small treasures, but she left the shoes behind. If only she'd thought to bury them with Cari. She gathered a bar of soap, their toothbrushes, and two washcloths. She scoured the house for money, sweeping her hand to the backs of drawers and under cushions and into the pockets of Henry's pants and overalls and shirts. She said a prayer of gratitude for his carelessness and added four wadded dollars and a handful of change to her sock; it was something. She found Beto's notebook under his pillow and slid it into the bag. She brought Cari's ribbons. After that, there was only the food to pack. She wrapped cheese and biscuits in wax paper and took the last of the oranges.

Everything went back under the bed. Naomi shrugged on a sweater, rebraided her hair, and walked out into the moonless night.

WASH Wash spent the day pulling off his plan to buy the train tickets in Tyler. No room for sadness, only scheming. He slipped into the living room early in the morning to get what he needed from the tin of Booker money. When he went out after breakfast, he wore his work boots and said he was going to help pack down graves. He headed toward Pleasant Hill Cemetery, then cut through the woods toward the road to Tyler. He walked far off the shoulder, only hitching a ride when he saw a truck he was sure was from out of town and so would not have any stories to carry back to his folks.

Now he had three train tickets to San Antonio and a world of details he needed to explain to Naomi about how they'd get to Tyler in the morning, early, early.

But she wasn't at the tree. She wasn't by the river. And for all his planning, he'd left his notepad and pencil inside yesterday's pants. He could not leave her a message.

He had to, though, which meant he needed to go back to the house.

On his way home, he made sure his boots and hands were caked with a day's worth of cemetery dirt.

He shouldn't have bothered. His mother and father were blazing at each other when he came into the house. A pile of suitcases sat by the back door.

"We're not going," his father said. He sat in his favorite chair, a rocker by the lamp. He made a show of reading an old copy of the *Chicago Defender*. "It's just gossip. And anyway, let's say a couple of rednecks do come looking to ransack my property. Would you like to come back and find your piano smashed to bits?"

Peggy looked ill. She was folding linens, which their mother jammed into a sack.

"Have you lost your mind, Jim?" Rhoda asked. "Can you hear yourself? The house, the piano? We're talking about our lives."

"Crane will talk sense into them. He knows we had nothing to do with what happened." Jim turned deliberately back to his newspaper.

Rhoda crossed the room and pulled the paper out of his hands. "Mr. Crane is too busy mourning his dead to protect us. And they're blaming him, too. The talk going around about the school switching to green gas—and Wash out there when the explosion happened—it doesn't look good."

His father frowned. "You must be exaggerating."

"Look at me." Rhoda leaned close and turned his face toward hers. "Have you ever known me to be the panicky type?"

"No, but—"

"I talked to Whit Mason. His wife works for the Crims, and she's heard things. He said it's serious. These men have lost their children. They want blood. They're not going to let this go."

"We're not running. If anything, that'll make them more likely to think we were involved."

"Jim!" Rhoda cried. Wash shivered. Desperation was breaking through her anger. "This is no time to be proud. We can come back. Or we can start again. We have the money."

"That money is for the children's college." Now Jim was the one to raise his voice.

Wash's heart pounded as his mother crossed the room to the cabinet where they kept the Booker money. She opened the door and pulled out the family Bible. She reached for the tin of money they kept behind it.

He wiped his hands on his pants. "Mama," he began. "Mama—"

"Go clean up, Washington," she said. "Change those clothes. We're going to Aunt Jennie's in Tyler."

Wash swallowed and nodded.

"We're not going anywhere," Jim called as Wash hurried into his bedroom for a change of clothes.

In the bathroom he scrubbed the mud from his hands, washed his face, and put on the blue shirt Naomi had made for him. He tried to think. If his mother was right, then his family needed to be gone an hour ago. He could go along and still meet Naomi and Beto at the station in the morning. But he had to give the tickets to Naomi and tell her where to go and how to get there. He double-checked that he had the tickets and pencil and paper, then he went back into the living room to face his parents.

Rhoda stood with her arms crossed, her lips set in a tight line. His father sat with the box of Booker money on the desk in front of him, the bills laid out and counted. His face was livid.

"How dare you remove money from this household!"

"This is not the time, Jim," Wash's mother interrupted with a nervous smile. "Now, Wash, where did you put it? Just show me so we can finish packing."

"I can explain," Wash said. He did not meet her eyes. There was only one reason he could give for why he needed to leave the house now.

"James Washington?" his mother asked. Her voice trembled.

Wash didn't answer.

"Spent . . . ?" His mother's eyes were begging him to tell her it wasn't true.

"I was going to repay it. I can get it back now," Wash said. "I can explain—"

"Don't explain. Just listen." Jim's voice was deadly calm. "You go get the money. Be fast but not careless, and then—"

Rhoda cut in, pulling at Jim's arm. "Listen to me. There's no time. Forget the rest of the money. Get these bags out to the car. And then we'll go."

Wash glanced over at his father, who raised his eyebrows at him. "Did I stutter, son?"

"Oh, Lord," Peggy moaned softly from the sofa.

Wash pulled his boots back on and laced them with trembling fingers. He ran out on his mother's entreaties, calling over his shoulder, "Ten minutes, Ma!" as he pushed open the screen door.

As he ran through the yard, he could hear her shouting, "What are you thinking, Jim? It'll take too long!"

He jogged up the road. He thought about heading straight into the trees, but the night was so dark, it would be faster to take the road and then cut into the woods farther down. Naomi might be there now, just maybe. If not, he would leave the tickets and a message. He pumped his arms harder.

He was about to turn off into the woods when the first truck sped toward him, tossing up a cloud of red dust and catching him in its headlights. There was no time to hide.

A deep voice drawled at him from a face he could not see. "Don't think about runnin' no more, boy. You're caught. They's three shotguns pointed at you right now. So turn on around and start walking back to your house so's we can sort this out nice and civilized, see. Stay there right in front of our truck where we can see you."

As Wash walked slowly back up the road, his heart pounding, the pickup inched along behind him. The men didn't bother lowering their voices as they talked. From the different voices he heard, he guessed that there were six or seven men in the truck, although he couldn't be sure.

"You sure that's the right one? Niggers all look the same to me."

"You know they're guilty if they're tryin' to run, see?"

"It's him all right. I seen him skulkin' around the school the day of the explosion. Didn't have no business there, disrespectin' the dead."

"A lesson's coming for him, ain't it now?"

"Where the hell are the rest of the coons in this coon town?" one of the men asked. His words slipped over one another, slurred by booze.

Someone laughed. "They're like animals. They smell trouble and hide. After we get done with this boy, we can go nigger knockin'. Stir 'em up."

All the houses along the street were dark now, their curtains closed. Wash thought he saw a hand disappear behind a window shade when they passed Fannie's place. Only his family's house at the end of the road still had lights on. Wash prayed, though, that his family had gone out the back door. That they were crossing through yards in the opposite direction at this very moment. He moved slowly. He wanted to give them as much time as possible.

BETO Beto pressed his fingers into his armpits and bit his lip. Hard. Harder. His guts knotted as the truck swung around a curve and then flew down another country road. He wanted to be in the cab with his daddy, but instead he was in the back with five men he did not know and Wally, who was in the grade above him and mean. The men stared into the dark woods and passed a bottle between them. Their faces were shadowed, their mouths silent. From other trucks, though, he heard wild sounds. Whoops and laughter. The black of night had never seemed blacker. He did not want to be here.

They turned onto an oil-top road and passed Mason's general store. When they got to the end of it, Beto knew where they were going.

The yard was crisscrossed with tire ruts. Headlights knifed through the darkness, all turned toward the Fullers' porch.

Henry pulled into a narrow space between two trucks and got out. "Black as a nigger's nipple!" someone shouted, laughing. "Y'all leave the lights on."

"Let's make this quick," Henry said as the other men climbed out of the back.

Beto sat rooted, his face pressed to the truck's back window. Through the windshield, he followed the path of the headlights. He took in the smashed birdbath, the toppled stones around the edge of the flower bed, the flattened heads of jonquils and pansies.

And then he saw Wash's work boots. And Wash in them.

Beto wanted to be invisible. He wanted Wash. Cari. Naomi. He wanted the bright sun shining through the magnolia tree. Those days eating fried pies. He closed his eyes tight.

WASH Wash blinked into the blinding light of the headlamps. Run, run, run, he willed his family. He hoped that was what they were already doing.

There was a real crowd now. The men at the front were getting warmed up.

"Where'd you get them nice boots, boy?" came a voice thick with tobacco juice.

"Mr. Crane gave them to me, sir. When they didn't fit his son anymore."

"Tell the truth, now, you stole 'em, didn't you? Stole them from the school? Stole 'em off one of our boys' feet, didn't you?"

"No, sir, I didn't."

"You calling me a liar?" the man asked.

"No, sir. I just think you're mistaken." Wash tried to keep his voice calm, but he felt his fear creeping in. The stories he'd heard from his father's growing-up days in the country. All the ways a black man could die.

"He's calling you a liar, Gary!" one of the other men at the front shouted. He stepped forward and sluiced a spray of black tobacco juice out of the side of his mouth. It landed hot and thick and wet on the side of Wash's neck. He started to wipe it away, but the man shook his head. "Leave it be, nigger."

A man with bright red hair and freckled arms unzipped his pants, shuffled closer, and grinned. Wash did not look down, but he felt the hot liquid soaking his pant legs and socks. "There!" the man said when he finished. "Now your shoes are real special, ain't they?"

"Call your old man out," someone called.

"Make him holler for the whole stinking family," said another.

"They're not home," Wash said softly.

"You think we're stupid? Every light in the whole damn house is burning, you smart-alecky bastard."

"I'm telling you, sir, I believe that they are out."

"Call them out here," a big man growled. It was the same one who'd blocked his way when he'd tried to help Mr. Crane after the explosion. He radiated malice. "I told you we'd pay you a visit, didn't I? Call them."

"You tell him, Dalton!" someone yelled.

"Ma, Pa," Wash called, his voice cracking. "Peggy. If you're home, come out." He started to turn toward the house, but one of the men jabbed his side with a shotgun.

"You just keep facin' forward, pal. We'll take care of the other Sambos."

And then there were footsteps on the porch. The men sent Peggy and Rhoda to the side of the yard, but they made Jim stand with Wash.

"Let's get down to business," Dalton said. He stepped forward and tucked the barrel of his shotgun under Wash's chin. "You blew up that school."

"It was a gas leak that did it, sir," Wash said.

"There you go contradicting me again." He forced Wash's chin up another inch. Pain shot down the back of Wash's neck.

"We can stretch that liar's neck of yours," someone called.

"I'm just telling you what I know, sir. That's all." Wash had to talk around the pain.

"And you, what do you have to say for yourself, boy?" Dalton turned to Jim.

"There's been a misunderstanding, is all I can say, Mr. Tatum." Jim's voice sounded small and afraid.

"Zane Gibbler got firsthand knowledge that you two was complaining about your nigger school 'fore it happened. Acting real jealous. Jealousy can make a body do crazy things."

"Sir, we would never—"

"We know what your boy said that day. 'It'd take an explosion to get their attention.' Don't deny it."

A murmur ran through the crowd.

"Sir," Wash stammered, "I never meant—you can't think that—"

"It's a marvel what you can think after you've picked up pieces of children and sorted them into piles." Dalton edged even closer. "There's a lot stranger things I could believe than that you and your nigger pa had a hand in this." He turned to the rest of the men and asked, "Who here lost a child?"

More than half the men called out or raised a hand.

"Who wants justice?"

A shout went up.

Somebody hefted two heavy coils of rope into the space between the mob and Wash and his father.

"All right, let's do this," Dalton said.

BETO Beto lay in the bed of the truck, trembling. He could not move.

"Henry, where's your boy?" he heard someone say.

Beto wished to be with Cari. Even in the ground. Anywhere but here. And then his father grabbed the back of his shirt and hauled him over the side of the truck.

"You wanted to come," he said. "Now get out here."

Henry pushed Beto to the front and thrust him between Wally and another older boy from his school.

They held stones pulled up from the edge of Mrs. Fuller's flower bed. "Here, pal," Wally said with a false smile. "This one's for you. You go first."

Beto ignored the rock and looked down. His right hand was jammed deep into his pocket, his thumb flattened against his leg. His left arm hung limply. Sweat pricked his upper lip.

Then Henry grabbed his son's chin and wrenched it upwards. "This," Henry nodded at the crowd of pale men, "is our side." He grabbed the rock from Wally and pushed it into Beto's left hand.

Beto dropped it.

His father cursed and grabbed Beto's arm. He hunched low and spoke into Beto's ear. "Pick up the goddamn rock and throw it through a window. This ain't a game, boy. Unless you want to be the one they're pissing on next. Unless you want to be eating that goddamn cat for dinner tomorrow."

Henry's hand was heavy on his back, pushing him down to the ground. Beto felt his fingers close around the rock. And then he was standing again. Henry smiled a little and nodded. "Throw it."

Beto could feel tears beginning to sting his eyes. His mouth formed the word "no," but nothing came out.

He could not speak, could not even look at Wash. All those eyes.

Beto hurled the rock. Glass shattered, and the keys of the old upright piano jangled. He could hear Peggy crying. A rush of shame flooded him, and he ran.

◊ ◊ ◊

Beto knocked at the back door of the church. Then he knocked harder. At last Pastor Tom came to the door.

The preacher looked bewildered for a moment and then asked, "What is it?"

"Help," Beto whispered.

THE GANG We knew the colored boy, sure. Some of us had exchanged greetings with him around the school grounds. All of us had seen him working for Mr. Crane.

It didn't take long for the house to blaze. All that pretty trim burned bright and clean. A real torch. Some of us helped. Some of us didn't. All of us who were there wondered what would be next.

When the windows were shattered and the fire was good and kindled and the boy and his father were black and blue on top of their blackness, Dalton scooped up the rope and looped a coil of it over each arm. He pointed up at the tall magnolia. In the light of the fire, the waxy leaves and thick branches stood out black.

"Nice tree you've got," he said to the boy. "Can you see the future in that tree? Can you see it becoming real useful, real soon?"

Most of us had seen souvenir postcards in our daddies' and grand-daddies' things. The mementos of lynchings. Trees hung with strangled fruit, smiling men standing to the side, proud of their work. Sometimes there were kids in the pictures, like it was a picnic.

None of us had seen the real thing. We did not feel prepared.

Then tires skidded to a halt behind the line of trucks and a car door slammed.

"What is this?" a voice called. A few of us recognized it immediately as a Sunday morning voice.

Pastor Tom elbowed his way to the front. "Burning a house? Beating these men?" He shook his head. "Will that bring our children back? Will it, brothers?" He stared at the men in front. He caught the eyes of those of us in the back.

"Maybe you've got a different line, pal," Dalton Tatum said, "but I heard from my preacher that God meant blackness as a curse for the Tribe of Ham. Which I took to say, God don't like niggers, neither." He resettled the rope on his shoulders and cracked his knuckles.

"The Tribe of Ham has already been punished," Pastor Tom started in. Then he was preaching, leaping from one Bible verse to the next.

We did not have much hope that scripture would stop this. Some of us didn't know if we wanted it to, wanted to see how the idea might bloom.

The preacher kept trying. "Consider your actions! The hands that spill blood unjustly can never come clean." He paused. "Henry!" he called. "Tell them. You know this boy! This isn't right, brother. Didn't he bring your kids out?"

Henry glowered at the pastor but remained silent.

"Listen." Pastor Tom swept his eyes over the rest of the men. "This family is not responsible. The boy, neither. He helped at that school, he—"

"Don't you make him out to be innocent," a narrow-shouldered red-headed man shouted. "He made a threat!"

"Shit, this ain't a Sunday school," Dalton called. "Men, what do you say? We came here with a purpose!"

The preacher's shoulders sagged. We could feel the worst coming.

WASH As the men pushed Wash into the dark garden, the coarse weave of the rope made his neck itch. His body ached. There was a pulsing pain above his right eye. He felt teeth loose in his mouth, an ache in his jaw. He tried to think of Naomi. Mexico. Splitting wood for her, hauling water, planting a garden. He felt he had not fought hard enough for it, for that life.

Most of all, though, he felt that he had not held her long enough. Not nearly enough.

He lifted his face. Clouds covered the sky. There wasn't a single star to wish on.

NAOMI Naomi sat on a fallen log by their tree, listening. The creaking of branches, the steady flow of the river, the quiet scramble of small animals foraging in the undergrowth. There was a faint rustle in a high pine nearby. A desperate squeak. Silence.

Some tiny creature caught in the talons of an owl. Maybe there was a moment of exhilaration before the terror set in. She thought of Cari and the children who had died. Launched in the air. Shattered and shredded.

The same thought came to her whole again and again: *Cari is dead. I will never see Cari again.* It seemed stupid and impossible and, at the same time, true.

Where was Wash? She plucked up patience. Wash would come. He always did.

She tried to think of what it would be like to ride the train to San Antonio. While they were there, maybe she could take Beto to see Abuelito and Abuelita and spend a few minutes with Fina. No, it would be better to write to them once they were settled in Mexico. They would find rooms in some village where no one would ask questions. She would sew and clean houses. Wash would build things and sell them in a market. On Saturdays, they would walk through the plaza with Beto, buy him paper cones of mango and papaya sprinkled with chili powder. And they would find a school for him, one with lots of books. In time, maybe Wash would build them a place to live. He could do so many things.

Wash did not come.

Naomi waited. Her fingers stroked the short, dense fringe of moss that grew across the top of the log. Just a few more minutes, she told herself. She had been so sure that he would be there. And then there were footsteps on the path and she drew in a breath.

It wasn't Wash.

◇ ◇ ◇

Naomi crept down the bank, feeling for the familiar footholds and steadying herself with the thin branches of young trees. The air hummed with insects, and a cool breeze swept up from the river. She could not remember a darker night.

"Beto?" she called. Softly at first, then louder. "Beto?"

A sniffle was the only response. She followed the sounds to where he lay. She reached out a hand and found that his clothes were already caked with the sandy clay of the riverbed.

"What happened? Where's Henry?"

When he did not reply, Naomi's first impulse was to find the quickest way to send Beto back to the house. In case Wash did come. In case they could still have a few minutes alone. But Beto was shaking.

She extended her hands past him and found that they were close to the broad, flat stone where the twins often fished. Where, in fine weather, she and Wash sat studying. It was cold now, and the river seemed different, not a warm brown thing but a liquid darkness gliding past. The hair stood up on her neck.

Naomi climbed onto the stone and pulled Beto up beside her. She stroked his hair with her fingertips. When he sniffled again, she wiped his nose with the hem of her dress. Then she took his face into her hands. "*¿Qué pasó?*" she asked. "*Puedes decirme.* Go on."

A long time passed, and still she could not get him to speak. She could not see his lips moving silently, forming the same word again and again.

"We have to go back to the house, Beto," she said.

She felt him shake his head no, no, no. He curled himself into a tight knot on the rock. He moaned.

Suddenly she had an idea. She had never wanted to share the tree with the twins, but they wouldn't be here much longer now. It made her feel safe; maybe it would work for him.

"Look, if I show you a secret, will you tell me what's wrong?"

Beto did not reply, but he let her pull him up. She led him up the bank and walked him back along the path and into the woods.

"Hold on to my hand," she said and she led him to the tree. She stepped inside and then guided him through the opening. "See? A secret place." She reached up and lifted the Christmas ornament from its nail and placed it in Beto's hands. "Look," she said. "This is where Wash keeps his treasures."

Beto spoke then. A single word. Not even. A terrible sound. "Wash," he said. "Wash. Wash. Wash."

Naomi shivered. Her mind flooded with images of hurt. Wash in a car accident. Wash fallen into a grave, his ankle twisted. Wash delirious with fever in a strange bed.

"What is it?" she asked, gripping Beto's hand tight in hers.

"Wash," he said.

She gave Beto a shake. "It's going to be okay." She wrapped Beto in the blanket they kept there. She shook him again. "Wait here. Do not leave, *entiendes*?"

"Wash," he said again. "Wash."

She could still hear the hollow rustle of his words as she squeezed back out through the opening and rushed up the path toward Egypt Town.

NAOMI She thought she understood when she saw the flames. Wash's house. The car. The shed. A terrible loss. But then in the light from the burning house she saw something nailed to the trunk of the huge magnolia tree. Crude black letters on a white board. LIKE FATHER LIKE SON.

So many shadows. But she knew what she saw when she looked up into the branches and among the waxy dark leaves and the enormous buds like closed white fists.

Even through her tears, she knew what she saw. Two dark forms, swaying. Hung.

Father like son.

She ran back through the woods. She did not care if she ripped her good dress or tripped or fell. She wanted to fall. Not just to the ground but deeper. Into a darkness that would go on and on and never end. Make a shovel of her grief. So many losses.

But she kept running. Because there was still Beto.

He lay curled in a small heap of blanket inside the tree. She folded her body around him. Rocked and rocked. Mumbled, "*Yo te tengo a ti, yo te tengo.*" She held him, but she could not put anything right. There would be no comfort for them, not now.

There was only sleep.

They slept the sleep of those who wish never to wake up. They slept the sleep of brokenness and heartache. Pain sucking so hard at their spirits that they could not imagine a tomorrow. Did not want to imagine it.

◊ ◊ ◊

Naomi opened her eyes. It was still dark out and even darker inside the tree. Her skin was damp with sweat at all the places where Beto lay curled against her, roasting her with the heat of his small body. And there was the weight of her heart.

She felt the knowledge of what she'd seen settle back over her.

But she had dreamed Wash's footsteps on the path, Wash's hand on her cheek. Then she felt it again, the hand from her dream. She heard his voice. She did not answer because you do not answer voices in your head. Or ghosts.

"Naomi? Wake up."

It was his voice again.

She tried on the knowledge. Just in case.

Wash. Still alive.

Her heart refused to remember the body swaying under the magnolia.

She pulled free of Beto. He stirred but did not wake up. And then she exploded out of the tree and into Wash's arms.

He winced and took her hands in his. "Easy," he said. She trembled. She had hurt him. Ghosts did not feel pain.

"You're alive," she whispered. "I thought ... I saw ..." She touched him gently now. "You're alive," she said again. His flinches told her where he hurt, which was all over.

"I was going to leave you a note. But you're here so . . ." He drew in a sharp breath. "We've got big trouble."

"I know," she said. "I saw the house, the car. And . . . I thought it was you, I thought I saw ..." She swallowed the words. "But in the tree ... who did they get?"

Her hands were on his face, and she felt something like a smile. "Nobody, thanks to your preacher friend. He shook them up just enough.

They strung up our scarecrows. We got a bad beating, that's all. But we have to go."

She thought back to her moments in the Fullers' yard. In her shock, she had not seen what was missing from the garden. She only saw the flames, the horrible sign.

She gave herself over to this new knowledge: no one had died tonight. She did not owe his life to somebody else's death. She pulled his mouth down to hers, wanting only to taste him but mostly tasting the blood on his lips.

He kissed her quickly and then pulled back. "Pa's getting a car from Mr. Mason. I had thought . . . well . . ." he hesitated. "Come with me. But it's got to be now. Right now. We'll send for Beto somehow."

"He's here," Naomi said. "He came running here. He must have been there tonight."

Wash's face tightened. "Henry made Beto throw a stone through our window. There's something wrong with that man."

Naomi understood then. Poor Beto.

"I'll carry him if he doesn't wake up. We have to hurry," Wash said.

"And your parents?" she asked.

"I'll make them see," he said.

WASH Wash stood at the edge of the Masons' backyard on the opposite end of the street from the burned house. Beto and Naomi hesitated a few steps behind.

"What?" Wash said.

"Maybe you should talk to them first," Naomi said.

Wash studied them for a second and then shook his head. "We go in together." He reached for Naomi's hand, and the three of them walked to the back door of the house.

The relief on his parents' faces turned almost instantly to confusion. Wash didn't wait for them to ask. "Ma, Pa. We have some extra passengers."

"Who are they?" Jim asked, bristling. "Isn't that the boy who—"

"This is Naomi and her brother Beto. He didn't want to throw that stone. His father made him."

Beto took a small step forward. "I'm sorry, Mrs. Fuller." His eyelashes were wet and clumped from crying, and now the tears started again.

"Oh, honey, that's all right." In a flash, Rhoda was out of her chair, kneeling by Beto and thumbing away his tears. "I know you didn't want to," she murmured. "I saw your daddy make you."

"He's not my daddy anymore," Beto said in a whisper. "I don't want him."

"You know this boy?" Jim said to Rhoda, his voice accusing. "Did you know about . . . about this?" He jabbed a finger in Naomi's direction.

Rhoda pulled back from Beto, but she kept her hands on his shoulders. "I know the boy. About her . . . I had no more idea than you. But it's done."

Jim glowered. "What are you talking about, woman?" His eyes flicked down to Naomi's stomach. "Is there something I'm missing here?"

"I guess you've forgotten what it's like," Rhoda said.

"She's white," his father spluttered.

"No," Naomi said. "Mexican."

"That doesn't fix a thing. What about this boy? I saw his daddy, and he was white and mad. White daddies don't like their daughters running off with black boys."

"He's not my father."

Jim rolled his eyes. "Everybody's keen on denying that man—"

"No, truly. My mother remarried. My father died."

"She's my girl," Wash said. He couldn't help smiling; it felt so good to say it, even if it set his father off.

"All of this is beside the point!" Jim shouted. He lowered his voice to an angry whisper. "You can never, never give them another cause to hunt you, James. What you two want—it's impossible. In this world, at least. Tell them, Rhoda."

Wash's mother didn't answer him. "We can work this out on the road," she said. "They need to get away from here, too."

"Naomi has people in San Antonio," Wash said.

"You think putting on a sombrero would be enough to make us blend in?" Jim's voice dripped with sarcasm. He lowered himself back into the kitchen chair. "This is a mess, this is all a mess."

"Let's go, Jim," Rhoda said.

◇ ◇ ◇

Wash was leading the way to Mr. Mason's old Chevy when Beto began to cry.

"Now what?" Jim said.

"Edgar," Beto whispered. He grabbed Naomi's arm. "Edgar."

"It's his cat," Wash explained.

"Beto," Naomi knelt beside him. "We can't go back for Edgar. There's no time, *mi amor.*"

"She's a living thing," Beto said. "I can't leave her."

"She'll be all right," Wash said.

"He'll kill her, I know it. He's said as much before." Beto ran to Jim and tugged on his sleeve, pleading eyes turned up.

Naomi bit her lip and looked at Rhoda. "He's lost so much."

"There's money, too," Naomi offered. "Nearly fourteen dollars."

Rhoda laid a hand on Jim's arm. He shook her off. "We have to be practical," he said. "Think about what matters."

"If we take the path through the woods," Wash said, "we can get the money and the cat and be out where 37 crosses the county road by the time y'all drive by there," Wash said.

"You're in no shape to run," Naomi said. "I know the way. I'll go."

"Naomi—" Wash started. His skin prickled at the thought of her going too near Henry.

"He's madder at Beto," she said. "If anybody should go, it should be me. And anyhow, by now we can pretty much count on him being passed out drunk."

Wash's father swallowed hard, then threw his hands up. "Get the money. Twenty minutes. We'll be waiting just off the road past the Spender oil lease."

HENRY Henry sat in his empty house, hunched over the table and a tumbler of whiskey. He tossed the glass back. The night had not gone like he'd expected, not with Tom's meddling, and now he wanted comfort from the drink, from his home. But he could see only what was missing.

Henry went to his bedroom to refill his glass. He'd hidden his new bottle out of habit. At the nightstand, his hands wandered to the Bible. He had tried to read it so many times. Always the words lay dead on the page, refusing to come into his heart the way Pastor Tom had promised they would. But then the preacher had said a lot of things, most of which had proven untrue.

Still, there ought to be some answers in that book. For once, there ought to be something for him. Henry lit a cigarette and smoked it. He studied the fake leather binding and gold lettering. Finally, he flipped the Bible open and laid a finger down at random. He wiped his mouth with the back of his hand and leaned closer to see what it said.

Above the grimed crescent of his fingernail was the verse, "They that wait upon the Lord shall renew their strength."

He slammed the Bible shut and knocked it off the nightstand. It skidded across the floor and thudded against the dresser.

Henry was done waiting on the Lord. He was done sitting by while he was robbed of what was rightfully his and those responsible went unpunished. He was done with disobedience from his son, done with the wanderings and false boundaries of the girl who was his by rights. He was done trying to rise above himself. He stubbed the cigarette out on the nightstand and went back into the kitchen with his whiskey.

WASH "We have it all worked out—" Wash began. He started to explain to his father about the train tickets, the first step of his plan.

Beside him, Peggy was muttering frightened pleas. "Let's go now, let's go now."

Wash gave her an elbow to the side. She whimpered and then quieted.

Jim turned in his seat to face Wash. "It can't be. Face it, son. We can take the girl and her brother back to their family in San Antonio, but that's the end of it."

"At least hear his plan," Rhoda said.

"There's no north that's north enough for a mixed couple," Jim said, his voice gritty with exasperation. "You know that."

"The girl could pass for black," Rhoda insisted.

Jim shook his head. "Think, Rhoda. There's the boy, too."

Wash felt Beto stiffen. He slid his arm around Beto and whispered in his ear, "It's going to be fine, buddy, don't worry about them." He turned his voice toward his parents. "Beto's coming with us. And we're going south."

"Oh, sure," his father gave a bitter laugh. "Try Alabama. No, how about Florida? I hear just last year they cut off a man's parts, fed 'em to

367

him, then killed him for being with a white woman he'd never even met. How's that sound to you, Wash?"

"Pa—" Wash's voice cracked. He pushed down the memory of Cal's story about Blue and sucked in a deep breath. "Did you ever read about some folks trying to start a black colony in Mexico? In a place called Baja California?"

"It didn't work, son," his father interrupted. "The Mexican government denied their immigration papers and reversed their land grant. It was just another dream that went nowhere."

"I'm not saying we would go there," Wash said, rushing to explain. "But Mexico. We could slip in, no papers. Lay low. I've got a plan to get there, too. I'll sign on as a porter. And I'm learning Spanish."

His parents began arguing then, but Wash stopped listening. The idea of Mexico took hold of him again. Warmth. Everyone shades of brown. No Jim Crow shadowing them. He reached for Beto's hand and squeezed it. For the moment, it still seemed possible that there was some place with room for the three of them.

NAOMI Naomi walked as lightly as she could across the muddy yard of Henry's house. His truck was parked at a wild angle on the gravel patch, but all the lights were off. Naomi peered under the truck in case Edgar had crawled under it, as she sometimes did, for the warmth of the engine. She wasn't there. Naomi crept around to the front porch of the house where the window into their bedroom was. She eased up the front steps, avoiding the squeaky middle one, and crouched on the porch, listening. Nothing. The house remained dark and still.

Naomi slid the bedroom window open and dropped from the windowsill onto the bed she had shared with Cari. She waited for a long moment without moving. There was no reaction. She exhaled. Henry was asleep, then. Or better: passed out.

She stepped down from the bed and pulled the guitar case and bag out from under it. She placed them on the bed and turned, praying Beto's cat would be there, curled up on his pillow. It was so dark, she couldn't tell. She tiptoed across the room and held out a hand. Warm fur rubbed against her.

Naomi took Edgar into her arms and walked gingerly across the floor.

She climbed back onto the bed by the open window. She reminded herself to breathe. She set the cat down and lifted the guitar case and sack out the window and onto the front porch. Then she scooped Edgar back out and slid over the windowsill. She didn't bother to close it, just grabbed their things and hurried down the steps.

On the way back, though, she didn't think to skip the middle step. When it creaked, she ran. Every step in the dark night brought her closer to Wash.

HENRY Henry jolted awake. He steadied himself with a hand on the kitchen table and listened. He heard a sound at the front of the house, and for a moment his spirits lifted. He wasn't alone after all. Someone was back. Naomi. Beto. Both of them. But then silence swallowed the sound. He went down the hall to the living room and pulled the curtains back from the side window. The night was dark as pitch, but there was one streetlamp at the intersection of the road to town and the first road that led into the Humble camp.

He was about to drop the curtain when he saw her come into the circle of light. Naomi. She was carrying a bag and the guitar case. She was running. No, he realized, she was leaving. Leaving him.

Knowledge turned into anger, and anger turned into action. Henry ran for his shotgun, and while he was in the bedroom, he pulled the revolver out of his drawer and shoved it in his hunting bag. Then he set out to track down what was his.

◇ ◇ ◇

Naomi was far down the road when Henry came out of the house, but he could hear her footfalls. He ran after her, keeping to the softer dirt on the side of the road. He thought about calling out to her, but if she was meeting someone, he didn't want to alert him. The element of surprise was on his side. Just when he'd narrowed the gap between them, Naomi darted off the road and into a clearing. Through the dark trees, Henry saw taillights and heard the sound of a trunk slamming closed. He pulled the revolver from his bag as he ran.

Naomi was climbing into the backseat of an old Chevrolet, but Henry got there before she closed the door. He elbowed it back open and grabbed her by the sleeve.

"Get out," he said.

She gave a small cry but didn't move. He leaned in farther to get a better grip. The air smelled of iodine and hair oil and filth. Blackness. Some kind of knowledge lurched inside him even before his eyes adjusted to the dark interior. He tightened his hold and dragged her out of the car.

"Let her go!"

Henry knew the voice.

There was movement in the car, and then he was face to face with the nigger boy who should have been swinging from a tree.

"Shut up!" Henry spat at him and shoved him aside. "Listen up, in the car, kill the engine and then get your hands where I can see 'em." Henry trained the revolver on Wash and glanced back inside the Chevrolet. Now he could see that the rest of the nigger family was there, black hands lifted into blackness. And Beto. It was too much betrayal to take in at once.

He motioned Beto out of the car. "You don't run from your father, not ever. Did you think I wouldn't find you?" He saw that the boy was holding his cat. "I'm going to strangle that damn cat."

Beto stared up at him, eyes brimming. He didn't move.

"Please, Henry, leave him alone," Naomi whispered as she pulled against him and tried to put herself in front of Beto. Her yellow dress looked white in the moonless night.

"Hold still," he growled. "Stay put."

When she didn't listen, he wrenched her to the side hard, knocking her against the side of the car. He kept the gun pointed at Wash.

Henry glared at him. "I've had enough of you meddling in my affairs," he said. He dug his fingers deep into the soft flesh of her arm. He liked the feel of her trembling under his hand. "This is my family."

"We're not your family," Naomi whispered.

"Like hell you're not!" He pointed the gun briefly at Beto. "Who's your father, Robbie?"

"I don't have a father," the boy said.

"Damn it, Robbie!" Henry let go of Naomi and dragged Beto out of the car and slapped him hard. Naomi cried out, and when Henry turned to give her a dose, he saw that she had grabbed the nigger boy's hand. She released it, but he knew what he'd seen.

And then he recognized the shirt on the boy. Pale blue. The shirt he'd thought she was making for him. Now he understood the depths of her deceit. Like a goddamn fool, he'd listened to the preacher and let her into his house. He'd tried to win her over, and she had made him think she wanted to make things right.

"You nigger-loving cunt," he said.

Naomi stared at her hands.

Henry wavered for an instant. Her hands looked so much like Estella's. She looked so much like Estella. Then he looked up and saw the whites of the black boy's eyes, and purpose took hold of him again. He twisted his hand around her braid until her head was tipped back and she was close to him.

"Get over there," Henry said to Wash, pointing out a spot with his gun. "Stand right there where I can see you." He motioned for the driver to roll down the window. "Listen carefully, Mr. Blackie. You and Mrs. Blackie and Girl Blackie are going to drive away. And you keep driving until you're about ready to run out of gas. And when you stop to get gas, you say your yessirs and smile big, and then you go on your way. And you don't say nothing about these three, you hear?" He jerked his head at Naomi and Wash and Beto.

Henry could see the fear in the man's eyes. The wife just stared ahead. In the back, the girl was sobbing. Snot streamed out of her nose.

"I can't do that, Mr. Smith," Jim said.

"You can and you will."

"Pa?" Wash said. "You all go on. We'll be all right."

After a long moment, the engine started. "You know where to meet us. Don't be a fool, son."

"Bye, bye," Henry said, waving with the pistol. "Let's go, kids."

◊ ◊ ◊

Henry had them walk single file in front of him. Beto in the front, then Wash, then Naomi. As they moved slowly down the path the wrongness of it all swelled inside Henry. All the disaster, all the pain the colored boy had caused already, and now the thought of him sniffing around Naomi. And worse.

"A nigger, Naomi?" He didn't bother keeping his voice down. "You take up with this nigger all the while you was being cold to me? Me loving you and you acting like that was nothing?"

"Stop it, Henry," she said. She held her chin up.

"This looks all right," Henry said when they came to a small clearing deeper in the woods. He dropped his hunting pack to the ground but kept his shotgun slung across his back. "Now, nigger, you walk real slow over to that big oak. That's right, walk on over."

Naomi and Beto followed after Wash.

"Did I say for you two to move? I did not. Come here, son," Henry nodded at Beto. "Come stand by your pa."

Beto shook his head.

"Do what he says, Beto," Wash whispered.

"You, shut up!" Henry glared at Wash as Beto shuffled over, eyes down. Henry grabbed the boy's arm. "Listen to me, Robbie. You think you can make a fool of me and nothin' will happen? And you," he said to Naomi. "You."

Wash took a step toward them, but Henry cocked the revolver and aimed it at his head.

"Don't think you're the only one I'll shoot," Henry warned Wash. "Now listen, you dumb buck, move back with your hands up until you're up against the tree."

Wash raised his hands and took a step back, then another.

"Back against the tree. Now, arms by your side," Henry said. He glanced over at Naomi and Beto. "Y'all make a single move other than what I tell you, and I shoot him right between the eyes."

Wash stood stiffly against the tree. He lifted his palms up slightly. "Sir, please. It doesn't need to be like this. There's nothing we can't work out."

"Shut up," Henry said. "Robbie, I want you to reach into my pack and find the rope. There's a good length of it in there."

Beto shook his head no, but when Henry walked to the tree and shoved the gun under Wash's chin, Beto put his head down and ran to get the rope. He brought it to where Henry stood with Wash.

"Good. That's more like it. Now tie him up."

"Please, Daddy. Don't make me." The boy was crying.

"So now I'm your pa? Now that you want something from me?" Henry's eyes narrowed. "Do it, and do it right. I know you know how to tie those knots because I seen you reading up on it in your books. You tie him up tight. You do otherwise, and I'll shoot him dead."

"It's okay," Wash said. "I don't mind, buddy. It won't hurt me."

"Don't talk to him!" Henry pressed the revolver farther up under Wash's chin until his breathing turned to a shallow wheeze. "He's my boy, goddamn it."

BETO Beto tied Wash to the tree with shaking fingers. He was sobbing now.

"That wasn't so hard, was it?" Henry said when Beto finished. He crossed to the tree and tested the knots one by one before turning his back to Wash. "Look at me, son," he said to Beto. "Now I'm going to show you another side of what it means to be a man. What do you do with a field you own? You plow it." He walked over to Naomi. "Lie down," he told her.

"Don't do this, Henry." Naomi's lip trembled as she spoke.

"Down," Henry ordered.

She dropped to her knees. The clouds cleared then, and tears shone on her face. Beto wanted to run to her, but he couldn't move.

"Lie back. Open your legs. Stop crying. Don't try to tell me this is the first time you've done this," Henry said.

"Henry," she protested, "I haven't—I've never—"

"You've lied enough already," he said. Then he pushed her back until her head was on the ground. "Beto, you come here. Watch. But don't try anything. I've got the gun right here." Beto looked long enough to see the revolver his father held near his sister's face. The shotgun lay on the far side of Naomi, out of reach.

Beto did not watch. But he heard.

Naomi's pleas. Wash's shouts. The sound of him pulling at the ropes. Henry's fist slamming into his sister's face once, twice, three times. Henry shouting, "You like that? Keep it up, boy! Every time you holler, I'm gonna punch her again."

Wash's silence. The rustle of dry leaves. His father's rapid breathing. An agony of waiting. His sister crying out in pain. And then the end of it. Henry's shudder, grunt, and gasp. Naomi's sobbing.

When Beto could look, Henry was standing up and zipping his pants with one hand. "I'll be damned, girl," he said, pushing his hair back off his brow. "You were telling the truth—"

"Stop this!" Wash shouted, still straining at the ropes.

"You haven't had enough yet, huh?" Henry said. "I'll be getting back to you in a minute." He scooped up the shotgun and jammed the revolver into his waistband. He turned in a slow circle.

Henry paused when he was facing Naomi again. Blood oozed from her lips. Her left eye was swollen closed. The front of her dress was damp and smeared with blood. There were swaths of red on her arms where he had held her down. She tried to cover herself with the torn fabric of her dress.

Beto watched Henry's face, but he could not understand what he saw there.

Then Henry crossed to where Wash was. He hit Wash again and again. He kicked him. He pummeled and jabbed and slapped. If Naomi cried out, he hit Wash harder. He used the end of the shotgun like a baseball bat. He did not stop until the only thing holding Wash up was the rope that tied him to the tree.

"I think that's enough for now," Henry said. "Robbie, go untie him. I want to see him on his knees."

BETO Beto loosened the knots. He felt numb and dizzy now. Shocked at his own weakness. He would betray and betray and betray again. Betray the ones he really loved. He did not know how to make it stop.

When Beto undid the last knot, Wash tumbled to the ground and fell on his face.

"Here's your chance to redeem yourself," Henry said to Beto. "I'm going to give you this," he stretched out the hand that was holding the shotgun, "and I'm going to hold on to this." He pulled the revolver out of the waistband of his pants.

Wash pushed himself up on all fours. He coughed up blood and something white.

Teeth, Beto realized.

Wash crawled slowly toward Naomi.

"You remember what I showed you when we went out to the woods?" Henry pressed the butt of the gun into Beto's shoulder. "If you need more shots, remember to pump it. Go on now. Aim at him. He ain't moving fast."

Numbly, Beto did as Henry said.

His fingers remembered.

"Good boy," Henry said. "Now shoot him, or I'll shoot your sister."

Beto let the gun drop from his shoulder.

"I ain't playing, boy," Henry lifted the revolver and pointed it at Naomi.

Beto swallowed, lifted the shotgun again, and stared down the barrel at Wash. Wash who had taught him to fish. Wash who had taught him to handle a hammer. Wash who made the woods magic. Wash who had saved him. Wash who loved his sister.

When he still did not shoot, Henry's face hardened. "He's a murderer. He killed Cari. And all them other kids."

"No, he didn't," Naomi called hoarsely, pushing herself up on her elbows.

"Stay down," Henry warned.

Beto swallowed hard. "I can't, I can't." He could barely speak the words.

Henry took a step toward Naomi, the gun pointed at her. "One . . . two . . . three . . . I ain't counting past seven, son."

"Please," Naomi gurgled. "Please don't—"

"Four . . . five . . . six . . ."

A shot rang out. Wash moaned. Naomi's eyes widened in disbelief. Beto gasped at what he'd made happen.

HENRY Henry stared down at the gun in his hand. He hadn't known until the moment he fired that he was capable of shooting a woman. Red seeped from Naomi's thigh. Her eyes were glassy in the starlight.

"Tell Robbie to kill the nigger," he said to her.

She shook her head.

"Tell him!"

"*No lo hagas, mi amor. Sabes . . .*"

"Tell him, damn it!"

"*Nunca, nunca . . . ,*" Naomi murmured. Her voice sounded choked. Weak and weakening.

"I taught you to shoot, boy," Henry shouted, "now shoot!"

Beto held the shotgun in his trembling arms.

NAOMI Naomi did not hear Henry anymore. Pain knifed through her leg. Her body shuddered. She wanted to scream but could not. And then she felt very cold. She might have passed out from the hurt, from shame upon shame, but Wash was there, beside her, and her only wish was not to miss that moment.

He had dragged himself the whole way. It was only yards, but she could imagine the cost. He was shattered, too. Bleeding outside and in.

They lay together for a moment in their brokenness.

His hand found hers.

She looked up at him with her good eye. He smiled crookedly. Teeth were missing, and his mouth was full of blood. He spat to the side. "Strawberries," he said. "Just eating strawberries." Then he collapsed beside her, almost on top of her.

Naomi could not move. She watched the sky over Wash's shoulder with the eye that was not swollen shut.

It was the same view she'd seen when Henry held her down. She had wanted it to stop. The pain. She had thought, Henry is putting himself inside me. She had vomited a little, and bile had dribbled down the side of her mouth. But even in the midst of it, buried inside the desire to feel nothing and be nothing, was an even stronger desire. To live as long as Wash was alive.

Because the sky she'd seen as Henry raped her held the same stars that shone over Mexico. She had forced herself to imagine life going on. An after to this. She willed that after to wait for her. For them.

We are going to Mexico, she had told herself.

To Mexico.

**NAOMI & WASH**

"Just a dream, wasn't it?" Naomi whispered.

"That's right, baby," Wash said. "What you thought happened now, it was just a bad dream. When we wake up, we'll be there. We'll wake up . . . *en México, mi amor.*"

"*México,*" she repeated.

There was the ferocious pain in both of them but also the promise beyond it. A moment of warmth that they could stand up and walk around in. A world bigger than their tree. A sunny plaza. Bobbing hibiscus flowers the size of dinner plates. Golden-fleshed mangoes. Tiny oranges they could peel with their teeth. The clang of cracked cathedral bells.

They walked through that promise together, the Mexico they imagined. They would meet there. And it would be heaven.

They were far enough into their dream that neither of them heard the next shot.

BETO "Damn it, boy," Henry glared at Beto. "Look what you made me do. You were supposed to put him down and when you didn't—when you didn't—"

There was a patch of red spreading across Wash's back. Henry nudged the body with his foot and rolled him over. Now Wash and Naomi were side by side, mouths open like they wanted to sing. The patch of red on Naomi's chest matched the one on Wash's back.

Beto felt the life go out of them. He felt it as he had in the explosion, the sense of being left behind.

He swallowed.

He turned to Henry. "This is what you wanted," he whispered. "This was what you wanted to happen."

"No, son. I just . . ." Henry wavered for a moment, staring at the revolver as if he didn't recognize it. "You helped with this, Robbie. You were here. You're a part of this. Now, you fill that bastard with buckshot. Just in case."

"No! He was better than you!" Beto shouted. "Not just a little. Twenty times better! A hundred!"

"Do it!"

"I won't!" Beto screamed. But he felt his finger sliding onto the

384

trigger, felt the gun lifting to his shoulder.

"See? It's easy," Henry said. His Adam's apple bobbed against the skin of his neck. "I taught you this, son. Just fire."

And it was easy.

◊ ◊ ◊

Henry fell backward. A good part of his head was on the trunk of the tree behind where he had been standing.

Beto had been aiming for Henry's heart, but he missed.

He looked around at what had been his family.

◊ ◊ ◊

Beto did not notice Jim Fuller's arrival. Did not register his presence until he pulled the shotgun away and tossed it in the direction of Henry's body.

Jim crouched down beside Wash and Naomi and checked for a pulse.

Beto vomited, took a step toward the bodies, then vomited again. He was still dry-heaving into the leaves, choking on his own sobs, when Jim turned around.

Wash's father was dry-eyed and calm.

"Come with me, son," he said, taking Beto by the shoulders.

 Jim stopped Beto before they got back to the car. "You don't have to say anything," he whispered into his ear.

Beto nodded.

On the way to San Antonio, Beto rode on the back floorboards with a blanket over him.

It probably wasn't necessary, Wash's father told him. It was just in case. Jim didn't tell his wife and daughter about the horror, not right away. He simply said, "I only found the boy. Now we have to go."

It was too late for Wash and the girl. But he could save this child.

So Beto lay there under the blanket like something smuggled, and smuggled with him were the following:

(1) Edgar, curled tightly against his belly
(2) several fleas on Edgar's fur
(3) a knowledge that was as impenetrable as a stone
(4) a lifetime's supply of guilt and what ifs
(5) a memory

Edgar was only a cat. The fleas were of no practical use. The guilt, the what ifs, and the knowledge were for later. So Beto clung to the memory.

It was a warm day, just a month or two after they came to East Texas. And while Cari and Wash talked and Naomi walked alongside them, Beto noticed, really noticed, the path for the first time. Until then, he had only thought of where they were going. But suddenly he was freed to see. And hear. And smell.

He didn't have the words for it, the feeling that the high, straight pines gave him now that he really saw them. While he hadn't been watching, the leaves on the maples had turned the color of sweet potatoes. Above the trees, the enormous sky was the clear blue of robins' eggs. The dirt of the path was spongy and pungent with yesterday's rain. Wood smoke tickled Beto's nose. He heard the underbrush shiver with the passage of a squirrel. Then there was the heavier rooting around of an armadillo, stupid and awkward in its heavy armor.

"There's proof God has a sense of humor," Wash said.

"I think it's handsome," Cari said, contrary as ever.

"You would," Beto teased.

"We all are," Naomi said.

"Are what?" The question came from Wash.

"Proof." Then Naomi took off running, calling over her shoulder, "Race you!"

They were running, all four of them, Cari shrieking foul play even though she'd pulled the same trick herself a hundred times. They rushed over the path to the bank of the river and skidded down the last yards of incline, muddying their shoes.

A black-brown-white group on a sandy patch by the Sabine River. A human noisemaker flooding the woods with laughter and scaring away all fish within a quarter of a mile. A family with a short shelf life. Four souls perched on a wide, flat rock. A passing proof of God's sense of humor.

If only He liked laughing more, they might have won more time. Or maybe Wash and Naomi were wrong, and their borrowed time had nothing to do with God.

As he remembered, Beto made a mental note: the dead are not always right. The dead are not saints. But the dead are ours. We carry them with us like it's our job. And maybe it is.

Beto left his younger, happier self by the river and walked back up the path, searching the memory for the tree Naomi had taken him to. There it was. Mostly hidden from view by brambles. But now Beto knew where to look.

And so inside his memory, which was not a memory at all but a story he was telling himself, Beto ran for the hiding place. He made himself a beetle high in the rotten wood of the hollow tree and determined to stay there until he understood.

◇ ◇ ◇

In the stillness of the tree, wrapped in the faint smell of rot, Naomi and Wash held each other. Her fingers found his neck, worked their way into his dark hair. She marveled at its softness, like tightly coiled silk.

He took her hand in his, slid his thumb along the soft flesh between each of her fingers.

He stroked the smooth skin of her wrists. He kissed the stretch of her right forearm, which had healed from the burn at last. He continued, showing her the perfection of wrist, ankle, neck, collarbone—all the thresholds he could reach.

She bit her lip and thought she could not bear the delicious agony of his touch, and then a slow-boiling sob rose up into her throat. When it came out of her, it turned to laughter.

That was it, then. His first gift to her. The shuddering joy of her own laughter.

When the rain began to fall, they didn't notice, but they did notice the sudden shift in sound when it stopped. They climbed out, squinting a little. The sky was the color of wet slate, and the wind ripped through the crowns of the trees.

"Look," Naomi said.

A wedge of light had forced itself through the dense clouds. The cottonwoods along the river stood out like pillars against the gray backdrop of the sky, their white bark shining in the sudden sun.

"Look," Naomi said again, more insistently this time.

"I told you," Wash said, reaching for her face, "that there was beauty here."

Smuggled in the back of the Chevrolet, smuggled into a memory, smuggled into a tree inside that memory, Beto was starting the work that would save him.

EPILOGUE

When they got to San Antonio, Jim Fuller gripped Beto tightly by the arms. "The woods?" he said. "You were never there. You were here, in San Antonio."

Beto nodded.

San Antonio took him back, but it was not the same.

Instead of beginning the day by reading *La Prensa* or rearranging the canned goods in the store, Abuelito sat in a chair in the sun. He could not speak, but he was there. Beto kissed his bushy eyebrows each morning.

Beto slept on a pallet because the new family Abuelita had taken in was using the other bed. He wanted to go to work, but Abuelita would not hear of him missing school. "*No, señor,*" she said, shaking her head emphatically and pointing to the dictionary, the sole book to survive the pawning of items after Abuelito fell ill.

Every day, the fact of his breathing surprised Beto. He did not want to be alive and whispered as much into Edgar's fur each morning. But still he rose and folded his blankets. He washed his face and ate the eggs and beans his grandmother prepared. He went to school. He spent afternoons working in the store or reading aloud to Abuelito.

He moved around the enormous empty spaces in the world where

Naomi and Cari and Wash should have been. He did not forget.

Beto passed silently but brilliantly through his classes, blending in with white classmates at the junior high where a savvy elementary school teacher enrolled him by calling him "son" during registration. With his teachers' recommendations, he went on to the new Crockett High School, and he was the first Mexican American to be permitted to follow the distinguished scholar path to graduation rather than the vocational track. He was also the first Mexican American from San Antonio to attend the University of Texas at Austin. There, he annoyed his advisors by majoring in English despite his obvious brilliance in math and science.

He rarely spoke to his roommate, a lean, cheerful boy with sandy hair and an endless parade of girlfriends. When Beto wasn't reading for classes or working at the pharmacy where he'd gotten a job as a clerk, he wrote.

He bought a package of typing paper and wrote straight through the stack, then he turned it over and wrote on the backsides of the pages.

Only Beto knew the reason for his writing.

For years, he had saved his Christmas present from Naomi, that red notebook he'd found in the bag Jim Fuller had lifted from the car's trunk and pressed into his arms along with the guitar case. For years, he had waited to be ready for it.

He knew the story would not be easy to tell. By the time he began, it had been buried under the lime of falsehood for a decade. The March 23, 1937, newspaper article from the *San Antonio Express*, which he carried in the inside pocket of his wallet, was proof of that.

The piece was entitled "Backwoods Bloodbath Shocks East Texas Town Already Shattered by School Blast." It informed the reader of the following facts:

> Just days after the tragic New London school explosion that claimed nearly 300 lives, a survivor of the blast, Naomi Smith, was abducted, beaten, and raped by a Negro youth by the name James Washington Fuller. When the girl's stepfather, Henry Smith, noticed her disappearance, he suspected foul play and set out to search for her in the woods near the Negro community of

Egypt Town just outside of New London. He found her in the midst of the most terrible indignity a woman could suffer, and he struggled to rescue his stepdaughter from the clutches of the assailant. At some point, a gun was drawn, and an accidental discharge of the weapon killed both Naomi and Fuller. While there were no witnesses, police determined from evidence at the scene that Smith, crazed with grief and rage, then turned the gun on himself. Police have indicated that no further investigation will be conducted.

Beto knew each word of the article by heart. He knew the article because it was the ugly obverse of the real story, the one that lived inside him. It was the distorted black space around what had really been. Some nights, when he couldn't sleep, Beto went over in his mind the many details that must have been ignored to come to the conclusions reported in the article. Among them were the presence of two different guns, the bloody rope discarded by the tree, and the near physical impossibility of shooting oneself in the head with a shotgun.

Yet no one had asked any questions. The case was closed, another burden Beto had survived to carry.

It wasn't that Beto wanted to tell the story. It was that he had to. He hoped that, after, he could begin to dream of the fragile joy of the months before the explosion and of the family that they had made for themselves in the woods. They had been happy, for a time, before the rules found them. Before the terrible price was exacted for their transgressions. For the crossing of lines. For friendship, for love.

And so he worked. Piecing together memories. Imagining what he could not have known. Writing out the ruins of his former life. He wrote until the story was there, outside him, terrible in its truth.

He needs you, reader. All he asks is that you take the story up and carry it for a while.

This strange song, gathered out of darkness.

AUTHOR'S NOTE

The 1937 New London school explosion ravaged a community about ten miles from my hometown; it is still on record as the deadliest school disaster in the United States. With the exception of the explosion, the tragedies that unfold in the novel are products of my imagination. Still, they are generally consistent with documented occurrences in other parts of Texas and the South during the 1930s. There is considerable historical precedent for the racism, sexual abuse, violence against minorities, and other distressing facets of life portrayed in the novel.

An understandable protective impulse sometimes inspires efforts to conceal, diminish, or disavow such painful histories. The work of this book, however, was to bring to light experiences and narratives that might otherwise go unacknowledged. I have tried to balance the heartbreak, cruelty, and ignorance of my characters' world with a profound attention to the forms of kindness and connection that are also possible in it.

All characters in *Out of Darkness* are fictional; any resemblance to actual persons is coincidental. Despite my interest in the history of the New London school explosion, I've also taken many liberties with details, circumstances, dates, and local geography. For example, I placed Beto and Cari's classroom in the building that exploded when in fact this part of the school did not house the lower elementary grades. The scene at Wash's home and the tragic outcome of Wash and Naomi's romance are not based on any events in the New London area, although comparably gruesome events did occur elsewhere in the South. Lynchings and vigilante acts were especially likely in periods of economic difficulty or following a major community disruption like the explosion.

Factual details catalyzed some of my imaginings. For example, I learned that mounted Texas Rangers were sent to the homes of school board members, where they succeeded at diffusing threats of violence. This information caused me to consider what might have happened to a potential scapegoat not afforded this kind of protection.

The relative absence of historical information about the African American community in East Texas during the oil boom left me wondering: how might the school explosion have been felt by families whose children were spared precisely because they had been denied access to the state-of-the-art New London school? Similarly, when I discovered that at least one of the children killed in the New London explosion was likely Hispanic (although her family may well have downplayed this background, as the twins and Naomi are encouraged to), I began to consider what might have brought a Latino family to the primarily black and white community of 1930s East Texas. The educational experiences of Naomi, Wash, and the twins allowed me to incorporate glimpses of the tripartite segregation system present in Texas before the Civil Rights Movement, a system that separated children into "white," "colored," and "Mexican" schools.

In researching this novel, I was struck by the many ways in which whole swaths of lived experience have been largely excluded from historical accounts, in part because certain communities were not deemed worthy of note in newspapers and other sources considered authoritative and reliable. These silences need to be amended; I hope my fiction gives readers an appetite for stories lived in the margins of spotlit scenes.

ACKNOWLEDGMENTS

Much gratitude to my editor, Andrew Karre, for sharing my vision for this novel and deepening it. Thanks also to my agent, Steven Chudney, and to the excellent professionals at Carolrhoda Lab and Lerner. Special thanks to Alisa Alering, who read the manuscript multiple times and offered many insights and suggestions. Thanks to Tanita Davis for encouragement at a crucial juncture and to Terry Ray and Wayne Ray for insights on historical detail and oil field experience. Passages from *Out of Darkness* were initially published in the October 2013 issue of the *Texas Observer* under the title "3:17"; thanks to the magazine for permission to reprint the material here.

The curators and volunteers at the London Museum in New London, Texas, shared personal stories and provided me with generous access to the museum's archival materials. Two recent historical accounts of the explosion, David Brown and Michael Wereschagin's *Gone at 3:17: The Untold Story of the Worst School Disaster in American History* (Potomac Books, 2012) and Ron Rozelle's *My Boys and Girls Are in There: The 1937 New London School Explosion* (Texas A&M University Press, 2012), were also indispensable to me in the writing of this book. *Gone at 3:17* makes for especially fascinating reading in its own right. In addition to many histories of African American experience in the 1910s through the 1930s, Koritha Mitchell's *Living with Lynching* (Illinois University Press, 2012) helped me reckon with the ethical stakes of portraying lynching in fiction. The interviews, studies, and books I consulted regarding Mexican American life in San Antonio, school segregation in Texas, and the particulars of the East Texas oil field are too numerous to name here; for this important body of research, I am grateful. Any remaining errors or anachronisms in the novel are my doing.

Great thanks to my family and friends in Kilgore, El Paso, Pittsburgh, Columbus, Bloomington, Denver, Des Moines, and beyond. I owe a special debt of gratitude to my parents who, among their many other virtues, never stopped showing me the beauty of East Texas. And to my brave and bold boys, Liam Miguel and Ethan Andrés: You are my reason to fashion beauty out of darkness. I love you so.

ABOUT THE AUTHOR

Ashley Hope Pérez grew up in East Texas and taught high school in Houston before pursuing a PhD in comparative literature. She now spends most of her time reading, writing, and teaching on topics from global youth narratives to Latin American and Latinx fiction as an assistant professor at The Ohio State University. Her novel *Out of Darkness* received a Printz Honor Award for Excellence in Young Adult Literature and won the Tomás Rivera Book Award and the Américas Award. It was also named a Best Book of the Year by *Kirkus Reviews* and *School Library Journal*, and was selected by *Booklist* as one of their 50 Best YA Books of All Time. Ashley's other novels include *What Can't Wait* (Carolrhoda Lab, 2011) and *The Knife and the Butterfly* (Carolrhoda Lab, 2012). She lives in Columbus, Ohio, where she enjoys all four seasons and tries to keep up with her two sons, Liam Miguel and Ethan Andrés. Visit her online at http://www.ashleyperez.com.